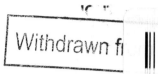

THE GOOD PRIEST

THE
GOOD
PRIEST

TINA BEATTIE

Matador
9 Priory Business Park,
Wistow Road, Kibworth Beauchamp,
Leicestershire. LE8 0RX
Tel: 0116 279 2299
Email: books@troubador.co.uk
Web: www.troubador.co.uk/matador
Twitter: @matadorbooks

ISBN 978 1789016 925

British Library Cataloguing in Publication Data.
A catalogue record for this book is available from the British Library.

Printed on FSC accredited paper
Printed and bound in Great Britain by 4edge Limited

Typeset in 11pt Minion Pro by Troubador Publishing Ltd, Leicester, UK

Matador is an imprint of Troubador Publishing Ltd

For my family.

PREFACE

The city of Westonville is fringed to the north by the muddy stretches of the Severn Estuary and the distant contours of the Welsh hills. The Church of Our Lady of Sorrows stands amidst neat rows of terrace houses. Yew trees shelter the graves of the nuns who rest in the cemetery behind the presbytery, which used to be a convent when there were nuns enough to fill it. Spring flowers bloom on a small child's grave watched over by a marble angel. The angel glows eerily in the early morning mist, conspicuous among the modest wooden crosses that mark the other graves.

In the presbytery garden, a blackbird clicks a snail on the concrete path, while his mate sings her prayers to the dawn. The priest's cat paws a dewy trail across the lawn, black as night, tail twitching, green eyes fixed on the distracted bird. The snail's shell click click clicks. The blackbird sings. The cat pounces. The bird escapes. On the hard path, the mollusc writhes, soft and alive in its shattered shell.

ONE

ASH WEDNESDAY

John awakes and licks the sourness from his lips. The sense of a dream lingers, but its memory eludes him. Only a fading anxiety remains on the edges of wakefulness. He lies in bed and listens to the singing bird, then he crosses himself to start the day.

Morning dribbles through the curtains, smudging the room in grey. He rasps his hand against the stubble of his chin, pushes aside the polyester duvet, and settles his feet on the bedside rug. It's Ash Wednesday.

He pulls back the curtains and looks down at the garden smeared in mist. He sees the cat lurking in the shrubbery, watching a blackbird that has alighted on the path. The cat is called Shulamite, Shula for short, after the beautiful black Beloved in the Song of Songs. The trees are greening with the buds of spring. The cherry tree spreads a blush of petals against the sky.

He goes downstairs to make coffee, then he takes his mug back to the bedroom and sits in the armchair next to the window. He crosses himself, and picks up his Missal from the table beside him.

Every Lent, he resolves to pray the daily Office as it should be prayed, though never yet has he managed to keep that resolution. This year he knows it will be no different, but he starts as he hopes to continue.

He tries to concentrate, but his gaze wanders to the window. Shula, bored with hunting, has jumped up onto the wooden bench beneath the cherry tree and is grooming herself.

The ghost of a child skips past. She's nine years old, dressed in jeans and wearing a pink sweatshirt with matching ribbons in her hair. She moves with pent-up energy unleashed, her small body a coiled spring set free from the constraints of sitting through the Sunday Mass.

John wipes his hand over his eyes. When he looks again, she has disappeared.

There's already a small queue of parishioners on the benches outside the confessional, when he makes his way through the presbytery door that leads into the church. A smell of incense and candlewax mingles with the remnants of last night's pancake party, wafting in under the door from the presbytery kitchen. He goes into the sacristy and drapes a purple stole over his black shirt, then he makes his way to the confessional.

Sister Gertrude, ninety two and losing her mind, is first in. She kneels on the other side of the grille. He knows it's her because Sister Martha is there to help her and he recognises the older woman's croaked complaint before Sister Martha leaves, closing the door behind her. He sees the shadowy outline of Sister Gertrude's veiled head through the lattice pattern of the grille.

A white lace curtain hangs across the grille, adding to the blur so that the body on the other side melts into the background. It was put there by Edith, who has appointed herself unofficial parish manager and minder to the priest. 'It's important for people to know they're anonymous Father,' she said.

He didn't tell her that he recognizes their shapes and voices if they're regular parishioners. Besides, very few of them kneel behind the grille. Most of them prefer to sit on the chair beside him, knees almost touching, speaking face to face. He doesn't know what Edith prefers, because she goes to confession in another parish.

'I prefer it that way Father. I don't like you knowing my secrets, when I have to see you every day.' It amuses him to think that Edith has a secret life that he knows nothing about – or at least, she wants him to think that she does.

Sister Gertrude is the only one of the parish sisters who still wears a veil. Her head wobbles with the onset of Parkinson's disease. He uses the formal rite, because he knows she prefers it.

'May God, who has enlightened every heart, help you to know your sins and trust in his mercy.' He reads a short extract from the day's Mass readings.

She wants him to know that Sister Martha has been spying on her again. He murmurs sympathetically and invites her to confess her sins.

'It's not me that needs to confess, Father,' she says. 'It's Sister Martha who needs to confess.'

'Even so, Sister Gertrude, you're the one in the confessional.' He speaks mildly, seeking to reassure rather than to chide.

He waits, listening to the wheeze and huff of her breath. When he first came to this parish as a young curate ten years ago, she was a youthful octogenarian. She ran the parish outreach project, taking meals to the homeless and collecting coats and blankets to distribute on winter nights. She visited the sick and gave singing lessons in the parish primary school.

He waits for a moment of lucidity to arrive. Eventually it comes.

'I'm jealous of her, Father. Sister Martha. She's been married, you know. She has a grown-up daughter. She joined the community when her husband died. Her daughter comes to visit her. Her name is Patricia. She has a little girl. A beautiful little girl called Lily. Martha's granddaughter. So pretty, Father. Six years old, she is.' She falls silent. He waits. 'The thing is, I'm jealous Father. I'm jealous of Martha. She's had it all, you see. And I regret not having all that. Marriage. Children. Grandchildren.' Another pause. 'My vocation. It was a mistake, Father. God forgive me.'

3

A mistake? No, Gertrude. That's not possible. His heart is beating too fast. If Sister Gertrude repents of her vocation, what then?

'Your vocation was your response to God's call, Gertrude, and maybe it was for the good of others more than yourself.' He can hear the chomping of her jaw on the other side of the grille. Her head wobbles uncontrollably. He seeks refuge in well-worn consolations. 'God is with us in our weakness, Gertrude. Of course God forgives you. Do you want to make an act of contrition?'

'I know why she's spying on me, Father.'

'Why, Gertrude?'

'She wants to steal my jewellery. She has a lover. They're going to run away together, and she's planning to sell my jewellery to pay for it. She thinks I don't know, but I do. When I went to bed last night, I caught her hiding in my wardrobe. She was wearing my tiara. You know, the one Princess Diana gave me. I wore it once to the parish dance.' She wheezes. Is she laughing? 'With my red ball gown,' she adds. She chomps and wobbles, then she says, 'I told Sister Dorothy to phone the police, but she wouldn't. She's sly, that Sister Martha. They all believe her. If they had seen what I've seen …' She stops abruptly.

He takes advantage of the silence to pronounce absolution. He wishes she would sit in the chair beside him so that he could rest his hand on her head. He makes do with speaking as gently as he can.

'For your penance, Sister Gertrude, you should say one Hail Mary. You can say it now if you like.' He doesn't want her to leave the confessional with even that small burden of duty on her conscience. But she says nothing, and he sees her struggling to her feet. He opens the door and goes round to help her. Sister Martha is there, waiting on the front bench. She gets up and comes over to take the old woman's arm. She's wearing a dark blue skirt and cardigan with a white blouse. She thanks John and shuffles slowly across the aisle with Sister Gertrude, to await the beginning of Mass.

A vision of Sister Gertrude in a diamond tiara and a red ball gown swims into his mind. He tries to imagine what she looked like when she was young. She still has warm chocolate eyes. Perhaps she was a great beauty. He pushes aside the thought of a laughing young woman at a dance. As he goes back into the confessional he sees Jane Sanderson heaving herself off the bench.

She parks her sleeping toddler in his pushchair outside the door and sits down heavily in the chair next to John's. She is pregnant again – mother of five and a sixth unplanned on the way. She says it's God's will – an uninvited gift perhaps, but who is she to turn it down? Again, and again, and again. She looks exhausted. Pale face, brown hair lank and unbrushed, as if time is too short for vanities. She crosses herself.

'Bless me Father, I have sinned. It's been a month since my last confession.' Jane is devout. She comes to Mass every Sunday and often on weekdays too, after she has dropped the older children off at school. She confesses regularly, once a month.

He invites her to confess her sins before Almighty God, who hears and forgives our darkest faults. She begins to cry. Jane's confessions often begin with tears, as if she carries them inside her from one month to the next, saving them all for Jesus.

'I'm just so tired,' she says. 'I long to be serene and calm and patient, but I lose my temper. I keep shouting at the children. Yesterday I slapped Susy because she wouldn't do her homework. My fingers left a red mark on her arm. She told me she hates me – and the baby. I'm so ashamed Father. She's right to hate me. She's only eight. I ought to understand. I ought to be there for her. I hate myself. I can't cope. I'm tired all the time.' She sniffs and rubs the back of her hand across her nose. He holds out the box of tissues he keeps beside him for such occasions. She takes one and blows her nose noisily. 'And when Pete comes home from work – he works so hard, I know that – and after he was made redundant, having to take that job in a supermarket, it destroys him inside – and all I can do is complain. And – then we go to bed – and we haven't made love for weeks, and sometimes I think that's the only real pleasure he has left in life, but – I can't bear him to touch me, Father. Because – because it's all his fault. All these children. I want us to stop. But he can't.' John waits as she blows her nose and cries into the tissue. 'Sorry,' she says.

'Take your time, Jane, he says. 'It's alright.'

Head down, she half-whispers to her bulging belly. 'So Father, I hate myself, I hate my husband, and – and most of all I hate God.' She twists the soggy tissue between her fingers. Eventually she shakes her head and offers him a wobbly smile. 'Well,' she says, 'I suppose there's nothing more to say after that, is there?'

'For your penance, Jane, I want you to kneel in front of the statue of the *Pietà* and say three Hail Marys.' Then he's astonished to hear himself saying, 'And I want you to say after each Hail Mary, "I am beautiful and God loves me."' Where did that come from? He thinks of the beautiful young woman in a red ball gown and a tiara. He wonders if by some miracle it came from Sister Gertrude.

Jane looks surprised. 'Do you really think that's true, Father?'

'Of course I do Jane.'

Her face is transformed. Jane has dimples when she smiles. He remembers those dimples, framed in a froth of white on her wedding day. She stands up, and he notices that the hem of her dress is coming undone. The dress might once have been bright yellow with white flowers – a springtime dress – but like its wearer it has been wearied by too many pregnancies, and its colours have faded.

He watches her go with a heavy heart.

The door opens and Deacon Jack Logan comes in and settles himself on the chair with a sigh of resignation. Jack's wife Penny died of a heart attack eight months ago, at the age of seventy three. She and Jack lived in the parish all their lives. They were childhood sweethearts. They have eight children and seventeen grandchildren. Now he is inconsolable. His face is red with shame as he confesses that he is masturbating to relieve the loneliness. John aches, and he recognises it as the ache of envy.

Next in the queue is Luke. John feels a tightening in his chest as Luke sits down and rests his hands on his knees. His skin is smooth and pale against his faded jeans.

Luke has a soft Irish accent. He says he hasn't been to Mass since Christmas. He's had a short-term relationship and lots of hasty fucks. That's what he calls them, 'hasty fucks'. He goes cruising sometimes. He's not confessing to being gay – he has made his peace with God about that – but he knows that this is not the way to live.

'I'd like to meet somebody and get married, but that's not possible, is it Father?' There's something sardonic in the way he says 'Father'.

'With God all things are possible, Luke.'

'With God maybe, Father John, but not with the Church.'

'It's God's Church, Luke.'

'I'm not sure I believe that John.'

John allows a flicker of recognition to pass between them, then he fixes his gaze to the right of Luke's face, where his dark hair curls over the top of his ear.

'We must pray for a spirit of discernment,' he says. 'We're only human. God is with us in our humanity.'

'You don't really believe it either, do you John?'

'Believe what, Luke?'

'That it's God's Church.'

'This isn't about my beliefs. This is the confessional. You need to think of yourself as being alone with Christ.'

'That's another problem. You know one of the reasons I haven't been coming to Mass?' He pauses, eyeing John up and down, calculating. 'You've surely noticed, John, the crucifix above the altar. Have you ever really looked at it?'

'Yes, of course I have.'

'So you'll know what I mean?' Yes, John knows what he means. 'It's a man up there dying in agony, and I lust after that body. It's beautiful. He's beautiful. The muscles in his arms and legs. The shape of his head. Jesus John, he's practically naked. And I feel so bad about the thoughts I'm having, when I'm meant to be concentrating on the Mass. I want to be alone with Christ, but not in the way you're suggesting.'

'Pray for God's help, Luke. Some of the great mystics used the language of erotic desire in their prayers. Think of Saint John of the Cross. Our human desires are complicated, but what matters most is our desire for God. Maybe it's better to desire him in that confused way, than not to desire him at all.'

He pronounces absolution, and as Luke leaves he keeps his eyes lowered and prays for mercy. He allows himself one quick glance at Luke's buttocks in the firm clutch of his jeans. He wonders if he should have answered Luke's question. Of course I believe this is God's Church, Luke. Otherwise, how could I bear it?

Last in is Holly in a blaze of colour and a waft of perfume mingled with stale cigarette smoke. Holly has orange hair and she's wearing a green scarf around her head. Her neck and wrists and hands are festooned with heavy silver jewellery. His heart lifts.

He remembers the little ghost of his morning prayers. It was some time after Sarah died that Holly emerged from the drab world of despair with dyed hair and brightly coloured clothes and silver jewellery, as if she had decided to make her whole personality a statement of anarchic defiance in the face of death. She dedicated herself with renewed zeal to her academic career, even as she regularly berates herself for not having given more time to Sarah and the rest of her family. She has risen through the academic ranks to become Professor of Medieval Studies at Westonville University.

'Hello John,' she says, sitting down next to him.

'Good morning, Holly.'

'Here I am again, with my burden of guilt and sin,' she says. Holly's appearances in the confessional are intermittent and brash. She does it, she says, out of fidelity to a tradition if not to a god.

'It's the same old things,' she says. 'I drink too much, I smoke too much and I can be bitchy as hell to my colleagues at work. And I still fight with Steve, and my bloody lazy sons get on my tits, but I think they need to take some share of the blame for that. I love them all – adore them really – even Steve though he can be a totally miserable sod, and I pray for them every day in spite of the fact that I'm not sure there's anyone there to pray to, but I don't need to drag all that angst in here. It's not sin. It's just life.'

She fixes him for a moment with those green eyes that always seem to hover between laughter and grief, as if she hasn't quite decided how to react to the absurdity of life. John thinks this is grace. Holly makes him feel the way he would like to feel – but rarely does – when he prays.

'If there's a god, I don't blame him,' she says. 'You know that. I don't hate God either. I don't think why me, because why not me?' She swallows, and wraps a corner of her scarf around her finger. 'I just wish it didn't hurt so much. I'm tired of the grief of being alive. I'm tired of Steve hating a god he no longer believes in, and resenting me because I refuse to become an angry atheist like him.' She gives a wry smile. 'Do you remember John, when you first came here, Steve was the stalwart of the parish? The best of buddies with God. Huh.' Her voice thickens. She looks away, then she sighs and looks him full in the face.

'I wonder if what I'm feeling is despair, and I know that despair is a terrible sin. So John, I really do repent of my despair, and if there's a god anywhere out there, I beg him to give me the grace to forgive myself and to learn to live again. What happened to Sarah – I'm not going to let it destroy my marriage and my family, but sometimes I think it really has destroyed me John.' She emphasises the word 'me', as if that's the one thing she has been unable to salvage from the wreckage. Her voice has slipped down the registers of grief.

He wonders if Holly's intermittent confessions are linked to these moods. She never speaks like this when they have dinner or go walking together. But then, people don't, do they? They don't say in public what they say in the confessional. They don't even say in the intimacy of friendship what they say in the confessional, and he regards Holly as his best friend.

He wants to reassure her. Surely, despair is drab and cold and lifeless? Despair doesn't swirl in the colourful excess of a person like Holly, does it? Or is all the gaiety of the world a gaudy veil thrown over the void?

He watches her as she whirls out, then he takes off his stole and bows his head to say a final prayer before leaving the confessional. He is surprised when he looks up to see a figure kneeling on the other side of the grille. He must have come in very quietly. At the same time, John becomes aware of how cold it is. He hadn't noticed before. He wonders if the church heating has been turned off, and makes a mental note to check. He puts the stole back on and waits for the figure to speak.

'Bless me Father. I have sinned.' The voice is smooth, with a slight lisp. Ssinned. A faint smell of aftershave or cologne drifts through the grille. John remembers the feeling of anxiety upon waking that morning – the forgotten dream that left its mood upon him. It's a feeling of *déjà vu*, but it skitters away before he can make sense of it.

He pronounces the opening words of the rite and invites the man to make his confession.

'My sin is a sin of intention. I intend to do evil, pure evil,' says the voice from the other side.

'What?'

'I'm sure you know what Augustine said about Lucretia, Father. According to Augustine, Lucretia should not have committed suicide because she was raped. Being raped isn't a sin, even if a woman gets some pleasure from the experience, because she had no intention of sinning. So a raped virgin is still a virgin. On the other hand, if a virgin dies on her way to an assignation, even though she never actually commits the sin, she's no longer a virgin when she dies. So even if I die now and never get to do what I plan to do, I shall go to hell because I intend to do evil, and only some accident or act of God can stop me. Perhaps you should pray for that, Father John. Pray for God to stop me, so that you'll never know the horror of what I intend to do.'

'Do I know you?' Something is stirring, a distant association trying to become a conscious thought.

'What matters is that I know you, Father John. You are to be put to the test.'

'I don't know what you mean.' The man can surely hear the dread in his voice. What is this? What's going on?

'You'll find out soon enough. But now, what are you going to do, Father John? This is the confessional. I've come to confess to you that I intend to do evil. You can't absolve me, because I don't repent of that evil intention. If I repented of it, the intention would no longer exist, and therefore my sin would have vanished even before I confessed it.' He laughs softly. It's a terrible sound. 'It's the perfect sin, the impossible confession – to intend to do pure evil. The perfect act of contrition – to repent of the intention. A firm purpose of amendment – I shall never have such an intention again. The perfect confession – forgiven and cleansed even before the words are out of my mouth.' He pauses. John's mind is reeling. His hands are clammy. The man continues. 'But the intention remains Father, and I don't intend to change my mind – or rather, my will. It's the will, isn't it, that's involved in sin? The devil can't change a person's will. He can only exploit an existing weakness, a desire we haven't conquered. So I take full responsibility for willing what I intend to do. It's my heart's desire.'

'So why are you here?' John forces the words up past the constriction in his throat.

'Because I want you to pray for me, Father John. Pray that I'll see the evil of my ways and repent. Pray for me to be delivered from evil. Oh, and pray for yourself while you're at it. Let's see who wins, eh?'

'This is insane. You need help.'

'On the contrary. I'm probably the most rational and sane person you'll ever meet.' He waits for that to sink in, then he says, 'Think of Job, Father John. An innocent man. A good man. But he just happened to be the one God and Satan picked on to play dice with the universe. And now, they're at it again, and this time they've chosen you. Oh, happy man, to be chosen by God. God must love you very much. God must trust your faith to put you through this, to invite me to torment you as Satan tormented Job.'

'This isn't a confession. You're not repenting of anything.'

The man laughs that awful quiet laugh again. 'I'm confessing an evil intention. I'm asking you to pray for me to repent. What more do you want, Father John? And remember, you're bound by the seal of the confessional, so I know that I can absolutely trust you never to tell anybody about this. Pray for me, and let's see if God can redeem us both. But in the meantime, my intention is pure I can assure you, untainted by any doubt. I intend to commit acts of pure evil.'

It's so cold. John sits in silence, unable to pray or to speak. The stranger waits, and eventually a voice speaks. It's John's voice, but it feels as if it's coming from somewhere outside of himself.

'It isn't possible to do pure evil,' says the voice, 'because evil is lack, and pure evil would be pure lack. Every act of evil is possessed of some good, because it exists in the act, and the act is an act of being, and being is good. You can't do pure evil, for evil has no existence. It could be pure only in nothingness and non-being. Pure evil would actually be pure good, for evil wouldn't exist.' He must have heard that somewhere. It must be some memory of a lecture he once sat through, dredged up through his frozen mind.

There's a long silence. He feels the stranger peering at him through the curtained grille.

'I knew you'd be a good priest,' says the man eventually. 'Let me go away and reflect on those words. Save the absolution for another time. As I say, I'm not sorry, so there's no point in absolving me, is there? But you can pray for me. Ask God to show me the error of my ways, before it's too late. As we both agree, with God all things are possible. And I'm sure I don't need to remind you again about the seal of the confessional. This is just between us. Well, us and God, of course, and Satan. I must congratulate you on your recall of Aquinas, Father John. As you know from your own argument, Aquinas argues that even the devil is not pure evil because he exists, and existence is a good. Well, well, well, that means there are four of us all in on the secret. How crowded these confessionals can become. Goodbye Father. I'll be back.' The man slithers soundlessly out of the confessional.

John's limbs are still stiff with cold. He dreads going out there. He has a sudden horror of finding them all dead or disappeared. The silence is so absolute.

But they are there, waiting for Mass to begin. Bob Carpenter is playing the organ, with the tune of *Ave Maria* in there somewhere struggling to get out. He has been the church organist for thirty years but his playing never did improve with practice, and now his arthritic joints mangle whatever vestiges of tunefulness there once were in his playing.

John forces his body between the pews and smiles a greeting to the people gathering for Mass. The church is relatively full.

Ash Wednesday still draws people with some atavistic sense of obligation. In the front row, the prayer group is praying the rosary, and a few rows back Jane is sitting with her toddler on her lap. Sister Gertrude is complaining about something to Sister Martha, and in the background are the familiar watery gurgles coming from the ancient central heating system. He nods to Bob as he passes the organ and Bob nods back, his brow furrowed with concentration and the tip of his tongue protruding from the side of his mouth.

John's knees feel weak as he goes into the sacristy and prepares to say Mass. Deacon Jack is there, alone with his guilt and his grief. John struggles to focus. His hands shake as he ties the girdle around his waist, praying for continence and chastity as he was taught to do.

The liturgy unfolds and the people come up to have the sign of the cross smeared on their foreheads with ash.

'Remember you are dust, and to dust you will return,' he says in rhythmic repetition, lingering over the touch of each forehead beneath the cushion of his thumb. Some priests don't say that any more. It's too morbid, they say. They substitute something more benign, like 'The peace of Christ be in your heart'. But he doesn't find it morbid. It astounds him anew every year to be reminded that, in the vast mystery of the cosmos, each mortal being is a speck of dust pulsating with the being of God.

'Remember you are dust, and to dust you will return.'

'Remember you are dust, and to dust you will return.'

'Remember you are dust …'

'Remember ….'

TWO

FRIDAY AFTER ASH WEDNESDAY

The rain patters against the window. John rolls over onto his back and gazes up into the mottled darkness. It's ten to four, too early to get up. That feeling is there – the anxiety of some bad dream that he can't remember. The feeling coagulates and becomes the memory of the stranger in the confessional on Ash Wednesday.

Was he real? John thinks of the others who came to confession, and they all seem equally unreal in the pre-dawn swirling of thoughts. Perhaps none of it is real. We're the insubstantial dreams of God – or the nightmares.

Shula is curled up on the bed against his thigh. He reaches down and buries his fingers in the cat's thick, soft fur. With his other hand, he takes his rosary from the bedside table and twines his fingers through it. He closes his eyes and tries to pray.

John doesn't think of himself as a good man. He lacks the courage to be a saint, the concentration to be a mystic, the intellect to be a theologian. Yet he hopes and prays that he is a good parish priest, and he thinks that his ordinariness equips him well for his vocation.

He can't imagine leaving the priesthood. He knows other gay priests who have left because they have fallen in love, or because the celibate life has been too gruelling and lonely, or because the

15

double life of pretending to be celibate has sapped their energy and their faith.

He can't remember when he first knew he wanted to be a priest. It was that that made him feel different from other boys, not being gay. The vocation had been more powerful and more compelling than the awakening of sexual desire. Sometimes he is tempted, of course he is, but God has forgiven him for his early lapses, and he resists the lure of self-punishment and guilt.

A memory presses in on him. Swirling steam. Glistening bodies. The pungent reek of sex. He pushes it away. He refuses to brood on what has been forgiven and should therefore also be forgotten. That's what he tells people in the confessional, over and over again, reciting the words of the psalm: 'As far as the east is from the west, so far has He removed our transgressions from us.' They must put down their burden of guilt and accept Christ's forgiveness with joy and thanksgiving. If he asks that of others, then he must also claim it for himself.

An image of Luke floats into his mind. He allows himself a moment's indulgence – the hands, the shape of his body as he left the confessional, the curl of hair over the top of his ear. His body stirs and his imagination tries to go further, but suddenly it's the stranger who crowds into his thoughts, and the stranger is mocking him, judging him, finding him guilty of unclean thoughts.

Again he has that feeling of *déjà vu*, but it fails to form into anything recognisable. It's just there, an amorphous dread lurking, refusing to come out of hiding.

He rolls over and tries to lose himself in the velvety darkness, as soft and warm as Shula's fur, which is the closest he ever comes to feeling immersed in the presence of God. His mind is racing, his heart is pounding, but he breathes deeply and waits. Gradually he feels the darkness enfolding him, until there's nothing but the encompassing silence and stillness. He rests in that space until the blackbird sings to the dawn and the central heating clicks into action. Shula yawns and stretches and comes to rub her nose against his face.

'Hello Shula,' he says, and strokes her as she purrs and pummels his chest. He crosses himself, as the radio alarm emits the time signal for the six o'clock news.

He goes downstairs, and his bare feet stick to the polished wooden floor as he pads down the wide corridor to the kitchen. The corridor was designed to give the impression of cloisters, but cloisters are communal spaces and he feels dwarfed and isolated by the high ceilings and echoing walls. A statue of Our Lady stands on a pedestal in a corner near the lounge. Somebody has put a vase of flowers at her feet. He kisses his fingers and lays them on her bare foot as he passes.

He prays as he waits for the kettle to boil. Shula slinks past him and rattles out through the cat flap. John takes his coffee upstairs and opens the curtains. Low clouds billow up from the edges of the day, mingling with smoke from fashionable Victorian chimney pots. The church is at the end of a narrow road lined by terraced houses carefully restored with glossy front doors and walls painted in pastel shades of cream and blue and yellow and pink. The parish school has a good reputation and the area is popular with young families. He likes standing there looking out as windows light up and people awaken to the day. It comforts him to be in their midst.

He sits down and picks up his Missal to say the Office.

> Lord, guard me from the hands of the wicked;
> From the violent keep me safe;
> They plan to make me stumble ...

He thinks of the stranger. He feels as if something has been dislodged inside him, a pebble tumbling down into a deep dark well. The sound of its falling startles something brooding within him, and the thing rises up on black wings.

Too distracted to concentrate on the readings, he goes to check the diary in his study next to the bedroom. There's the school Mass at nine o'clock, and at eleven there's a Requiem Mass for Dorothy Baker. The Mass will be a celebration of a long and loving life. Dorothy was 97. Four generations of family will be there, as will most of the parishioners.

The children are sitting lined up in the pews when he goes in to say Mass, wearing their red and navy winter uniforms – navy skirts and red sweatshirts for the girls, navy trousers and red sweatshirts for the boys. Every year there's a debate about whether or not to have school uniforms, and whether or not the girls should be allowed to wear trousers rather than skirts if they want to. Every year the traditionalists win by a narrow majority over the liberals and feminists. The debate is played out with an intensity out of all proportion to the issue, but that's what schools and parishes are like. People sometimes overreact, because deep down these places are the essence of their lives. He read recently about the row that broke out when a six year old boy wanted to wear a skirt to school. His heart sinks at the thought of further quarrels to come.

Dorothy's coffin is in a side aisle, draped in a white baptismal shawl with a spray of yellow roses on top. It was welcomed into the church yesterday evening. A non-Catholic visitor to the children's Mass once expressed shock to him that there was a coffin in the church, awaiting a Requiem Mass later that morning. 'What if it upsets the children?', she asked, mouth pursed in disapproval.

John stands in front of the altar and looks at the young faces turned towards him, sees the restless fidgeting of small bodies that are already bored with sitting. He likes the juxtaposition of Dorothy in her coffin and these young lives just beginning. Why should it upset them? Every day they are exposed to a diet of violence and death on television. Surely, this is showing them a different perspective – an old woman many of them knew, who lived a good life and died a peaceful death with her family gathered around her bed? He decides to say something about it in his homily.

When the time comes, he steps down off the altar to stand in the aisle on the same level as them. He enjoys their smiles, and the eyes turned towards him.

'People talk about miracles,' he says, 'and they always mean something out of the ordinary. We know that Jesus performed miracles. Who knows about Jesus's miracles?' he asks. A few eager hands shoot up.

'Yes, Rachel?' he says.

'Jesus fed five thousand people with loaves and fishes,' says the bright-eyed girl.

'That's right Rachel. Good. And Mark, what miracle are you thinking of?'

'Jesus helped blind people to see again.'

'Very good.' There is a forest of hands now. 'Elizabeth, what miracle are you thinking of?'

'Jesus raised Lazarus from the dead.'

'Excellent. Now, I'll just take one more. Simon, what's your miracle?

'Jesus made a road through the sea and then he drowned Pharaoh and all his horses.'

'Ah Simon, you're thinking of the story of Moses and the Red Sea. Maybe I'll talk about that next time.' He makes a mental note to find some way to account for the drowning of the Egyptian army. He remembers a rabbinic story that somebody told him, about God weeping as all the angels rejoiced over the deliverance of the children of Israel from slavery in Egypt. 'Why are you weeping?', the angels asked God. 'Because my children are drowning,' God replied. Yes, he would use that for next week's homily. But today, he wants to talk about Dorothy, and death and resurrection.

'You know, children, miracles are not so much about changes that happen out there in the world, but about changes that happen in the way we see the world. They're about changes in our own hearts, which help us to see that everything is a miracle. So when Jesus fed the people, he was showing us what happens when we share what we have, even if it's only very little. When everybody shares their food, there's enough for everybody. Nobody needs to be hungry in God's world. And Jesus raised Lazarus from the dead, to show us that love is stronger than death. We're in the season of Lent now, when we prepare ourselves to remember Jesus dying and rising again. Maybe some of you have given something up for Lent.' Their hands go up, so he asks a few of them.

Chocolate. Fighting with my brother. Complaining when I have to help with the washing up.

'Sometimes we find it hard to believe that the dead can rise again,' he says. 'Do you find that hard to believe? I know I do.' There's a murmur of assent, and a small girl in the front row puts her hand up. He is conscious of the time, but he can't ignore her. 'Amy, what do you want to tell us?'

'We raised my hamster when he died. We put him in a plastic box and buried him in the garden, and then me and Jenny dug him up the next week. He was all dead and smelly.'

John feels uncomfortable. Amy is a thin, hollow-eyed child. Her parents separated when she was four and her sister was two. It saddens him to see the intensity of her gaze. It reminds him of the way Holly sometimes looks, in unguarded moments.

'That's sad Amy, but Jesus tells us that what looks like death to us is really the beginning of a wonderful new life in heaven.' Her hand goes up again. 'Yes Amy?' He dreads what's coming next.

'Is my hamster in heaven?'

Thomas Aquinas would have said definitely not, only humans are in heaven, and even then, only the chosen few, but imagine a heaven without hamsters and butterflies and cats and blackbirds. Imagine heaven without Shula.

'Of course your hamster is in heaven, Amy, with a beautiful new hamster body.'

She nods seriously. 'I hope Jesus remembers to feed him,' she says.

'I think the angels make sure that all the creatures in heaven are fed,' he says, and then he tries to pick up the thread of his homily.

'Think of what the world looked like a couple of months ago, at Christmas. Everything seemed dead. The trees looked dead. There were no flowers. The world seemed dark, with only a few hours of sunshine every day. And look now, how everything is coming back to life around us. Did anybody see the primroses as they came past the presbytery this morning, and the buds on the trees? The cherry tree – did you see how beautiful it is, with its pink flowers? That's a miracle, isn't it? That's the whole of nature rising again from the dead.

'You see, it's a miracle, but we need to know how to look to recognise it. Miracles happen all the time, to people who know how to look at the world.' He looks at their faces, and he feels warmed by the affection and eagerness he sees. Children know when they are loved, they are hard-wired to respond to love, and these children know how much he loves them. 'Have any of you ever helped your mum and dad to plant bulbs in the garden?' A smattering of hands goes up. 'Well then, you'll know how amazing that is. We plant those dry old bulbs in the ground, and in spring – what happens to those bulbs in spring? Yes, Mary?'

'Flowers grow.'

'Flowers grow. What kind of flowers? Paul?'

'Daffodils.'

'Daffodils, and tulips, all sorts of lovely, colourful flowers.' More hands go up, but he is aware of the watchful eye of Dorcas, the headmistress, in the front row, sending him signals that he has gone on long enough.

21

Dorcas arrived in Britain as a traumatised refugee from the Congo fifteen years ago, before he came to the parish. She was twenty. Gradually she built a new life, going to university and training as a teacher, marrying a Nigerian Catholic called Ignatius and now mother to three children. Her grandparents were converted to Christianity by Methodist missionaries, and she is being received into the Catholic Church at the Easter Vigil. She's a tall, dignified woman with high cheekbones and a rare glowing smile. Firm, gentle and loyal, she is widely respected by the parents and loved by the children.

He gives her a small nod to acknowledge that he's keeping an eye on the time, and moves on to what he really wants to say.

'Some of you will have noticed that we have a coffin in the church this morning, and some of you will remember a lady called Mrs Baker who lived in the parish. Do you remember Mrs Baker used to come to the school Mass, and she used to sit just over there where Bethany is sitting?' He points, and they twist round to look. 'Mrs Baker died a few days ago, and this morning we'll have her funeral which will be a happy celebration of her life. Her family are sad because they miss her, but they know they will be with her again in heaven. We're just like the flowers and the trees. When it seems as if we're dead, we're really waiting for a wonderful new life. Like the daffodils and the tulips that will soon grow as beautiful flowers from the bulbs we planted last year.' He smiles as he draws to a close. 'So children, remember, God loves us, and God's love is stronger than anything that can happen to us in this life. That's what Jesus came to show us. That's what we think about during Lent. That even though Jesus suffered and died and his mother was very sad and his disciples were frightened, he did that to show us not to be afraid. He did it to show us how much God loves us, and he rose again to prove that God's love is life, and God calls us to be happy with him forever.'

Suddenly, he becomes aware of a smell. It's the smell of death – sweet, sickly, underlined with the tang of formaldehyde. Dear

God. Is it coming from the coffin? It's cold too. Why so cold, all of a sudden? He looks at the children, but they don't seem to have noticed. An image flashes through his mind of two small children holding the decaying body of a hamster. He feels dizzy and breathless. The smell is a thick fog, obliterating everything.

Then his gaze wanders to the back of the church, and he is there, standing in the shadows half inside the door. He knows it's him – the man from the confessional.

John forces himself to make the sign of the cross and smile at the children. He turns and navigates the steps back up to the altar. As he does so the smell fades and the warmth comes back. When he turns to face the children from behind the altar, he is not surprised to discover that the stranger has disappeared.

THREE

SATURDAY AFTER
ASH WEDNESDAY

Morning comes at last, oozing through mist and rain. John huddles beneath the duvet, glad of the warmth that seeps through from Shula's sleeping body. The central heating hums into life and he waits for the room to warm up before he gets out of bed. He reaches out to switch off the alarm before the radio can deliver its daily diet of fear and misery in the morning news. His chest feels tight and his heart is fluttering.

Every Saturday he hears confessions before the morning Mass. Lent is always busier than normal, but all night there has only been one thought, blotting out everything else, startling him awake every time he fell into a restless sleep. He dreads the arrival of the stranger in the confessional.

He sits in the chair by the window and tries to focus on the words of the Office, but they float meaninglessly off the page.

> *God said to Moses, 'I AM WHO I AM.' Say this to*
> *the people of Israel, I AM has sent me to you.*

The rain dribbles miserably down the window pane. He can just make out the shape of a jogger in the alley that runs behind the shrubbery. He imagines the stranger lurking there in the mist.

I am who I am. He looks out at the sodden world and wonders, but can give no name to the wondering.

The stranger doesn't appear in the confessional. Instead, it's the usual Lenten outpouring of sins that hardly seem like sins at all, of actions named as sins because beneath them there lurks some primordial guilt that cannot be named. John has always sensed this, but never before has he felt it so acutely. It's as if the threat of the stranger overshadows all those innocent confessions with some monstrous and unthinkable reality.

Eight year old James Berkeley confesses that he stole a Mars bar from a classmate's lunch box, then denied that he had. 'Danny says his daddy's a policeman. He says the police are going to come and get me from my house.' The child pauses. His face is pale beneath a smattering of freckles. 'I'm frightened,' he says, half-whispering.

John would like to ruffle the child's hair or to hold his hand, but he knows better than to do that. No priest would touch a child in the confessional these days. He tries to put all his affection and reassurance into his voice. 'James, that's not what the police do. You shouldn't have taken the chocolate bar, but it's not a crime. The police are there to protect children, not to punish them.'

'I saw it on the telly. The police went to somebody's house early in the morning. I saw the children crying. Mummy says they were being exported back to Africa. I don't want to be exported.' His lip quivers.

'James, I think you're really sorry that you took Danny's chocolate, aren't you?' The child nods and rubs away a tear from the corner of his eye, leaving a smear of grime down the side of his face. 'So why don't you buy him another Mars bar with your pocket money, and tell him you're sorry?'

'But he'll know I lied.'

'Tell him you're sorry about that too.' The child sniffs and rubs his fist over his nose, spreading the grime around. John hands him a tissue. 'Here you are, give your face a little wipe. That's it. And down the side, there, by your eye. No. Other side.' John touches his own face to show him where. 'Good. That's better.'

'I wish I had chocolate in my lunch box,' James says. 'Danny always brings chocolate.'

'I'm sure you have good things in your lunch box too.'

'I have fruit. Mummy says chocolate is bad for you. She says it'll rot my teeth and make me fat.'

'She's probably right,' says John mildly, though he thinks James could do with putting on a bit of weight. He pronounces absolution in words that he hopes are simple and consoling enough for the child to believe in and trust. 'For your penance James, I want you to tell God you're sorry about taking the Mars bar and not telling the truth. You only need to do it once. God will hear. Maybe one day you'll decide that you'd like to tell Danny what happened, but for now just tell God you're sorry. Will you do that?' James nods tearfully, giving his nose one final rub. John goes through the tissue routine again.

James's mother Susan is next in. Was she sitting outside, listening? John half hopes that she was. She confesses that she gossiped about a friend and broke a promise not to tell anyone that her friend was having an affair. She is tormented by the thought of what will happen if her friend's husband finds out about the affair because of the gossip. John wonders whether she feels ashamed and sorry about the gossip or afraid of getting caught. In some ideal world, maybe that would be the difference between a good confession and a bad one, but these things are rarely so tidy. John thinks of Luke, and of the unspoken desire between them. Does he resist out of respect for his vows, or because he's afraid of getting caught?

Susan is waiting for her penance. Some people sit with eyes downcast as they wait, praying or struggling not to cry. Susan is watching him, looking impatient. Come on, her face seems to say. Don't you know I have better things to do? She is a sleek, fine-boned woman. He sometimes sees her jogging past the presbytery. He wonders why he finds it so hard to like her.

He tries to think of a penance. He remembers something Holly told him – that in the Middle Ages, the penance for gossip was to shake out a feather pillow and gather up all the feathers again. The point was, you never could. Or what about, Susan, for your penance I want you to put a Mars bar in James's lunch box every day for the rest of the term? In the end, he settles for an Our Father and three Hail Marys.

Next in is Lucy Pierce, nineteen years old with wide blue eyes and long, silky blonde hair. Lucy's parents Carol and Jim are in the parish, and she has a younger sister called Karen. John knows Lucy from when she was a schoolgirl. She stopped attending Mass when she was twelve, soon after her confirmation, but she still comes to confession sometimes.

'Hi Father John,' she says.

'Hello Lucy. Lovely to see you,' he says as she sits down. She never uses the formal rite, so he waits for her to set the tone.

She shrugs and smiles self-consciously. 'It's that time of year again,' she says, flicking her hair back with a nervous toss of her head. 'I've come home from uni for the weekend, and mum reminded me it's Lent, so I thought I should – you know …'

He nods. 'So, Lucy, remembering that the Lord hears and forgives all our sins, you tell him in your own words whatever it is that burdens your conscience, and remember that he loves you and listens with mercy and compassion.'

'I went to a party and took Ketamine. I feel bad about that. I don't do drugs. Not that kind of drug anyway. I smoke the odd joint, but that's different.' She glances up as if waiting for confirmation, but he says nothing. She lowers her eyes again. 'And I'm still having sex with my boyfriend, but I don't feel guilty about that, so would it be wrong to confess it?' This time, she looks him straight in the eye, as if challenging him. She wouldn't have done that before. It must be going to university that's done that to her. He wonders how to reply.

'We all struggle in different ways, Lucy. It's not easy, to know the will of God and follow the teachings of the Church. God is merciful and supports us in our struggles. We must listen to our consciences, but we must also pray for wisdom and understanding so that we know what's best for us in the eyes of God.'

She chews her lip and eyes him warily, but she doesn't say anything. He invites her to make her confession. She closes her eyes and mumbles so that he can barely hear what she's saying. She promises Jesus that she will never do Ketamine again, and she also promises to give up dope for Lent. She doesn't mention sex.

He makes himself a cheese sandwich for lunch. He forgot to buy fresh bread, and the sliced white loaf is dry in his mouth. The cheese tastes of soap.

The presbytery echoes around him. He tries to pray, but the words refuse to join up. Jesus – holy Mary – help – be with us – what's going on?

He never dwells on what happens in the confessional. He thinks of it as a discipline of forgetfulness. Of course he doesn't really forget, but he has become adept at pushing things out of his mind before they get a grip on his imagination. He doesn't want to be saying one thing and thinking another when he's with all those people whose private worlds are hidden behind the masks they wear. He doesn't want those unmasked souls to sit on the surface of things, the festering wounds and bruises and scars of living that they speak of in confession.

He tells himself that the stranger belongs there too, out of sight and out of mind, but he can't help the sense of dread that has begun leaking out of that secret space and into all his conscious thoughts.

The familiar figure of Deacon Jack passes the kitchen window, wearing his gardening overalls and pushing a wheelbarrow. His solid presence chases away the hauntings.

Ever since his wife died, Jack has taken to looking after the presbytery garden. He has always been a keen gardener, but Penny and he moved into a flat a few months before she died, because she thought their family home with its long, lush garden would be too hard to maintain as they grew older. The heart attack came suddenly. It would, with hindsight, have been far better for Jack if they had never moved and he could have consoled himself with his beloved garden. But hindsight's a fine thing.

John decides to join him. When he moved here, he discovered a love of gardening. The presbytery garden is a sheltered oasis nestling between the lane and the presbytery, extending out beyond the building to the carpark and the graveyard fence. It used to be part of the convent grounds, where the sisters grew flowers and vegetables and created a place of retreat and refuge.

In its heyday, the convent was home to thirty sisters from all over the world. As their numbers dwindled, the few remaining members of the community bought two semi-detached houses next door and converted them into a smaller convent more suited to their needs. The former convent chapel was extended to become a parish church, and the old convent was converted into the church office and the presbytery. The church was called 'Our Lady of Sorrows', in recognition of the sisters' religious order – The Sisters of the Consolation of Our Lady of Sorrows. Later, a hall and club house were built on the land behind the presbytery which used to be the vegetable garden. A private girls' school run by the nuns on land adjacent to the convent was converted into a thriving state primary school which serves the children of the parish.

The school was established by the order in the nineteenth century for the education of poor girls, including Irish migrants fleeing from the famine. The intention had never been to provide elite private education for those who could afford it. The sisters used the money that was left from the sale of the property to buy a disused church in Saint Peter's. They turned it into a drop in centre, soup kitchen and clinic, and they run it with a team of volunteers. The parish has adopted it as a project, funding it with cake sales and raffles and weekly donations. The project is called 'Women at the Well', after the Samaritan woman in John's Gospel.

Saint Peter's is a mile away from Our Lady of Sorrows, near the city centre. Its streets are populated by prostitutes, homeless people, drug addicts and alcoholics, and a growing numbers of refugees – first from Somalia, then from Iraq, now from Syria. It also attracts a young community of artists and anarchists, who have transformed it into a place of vibrant graffiti art and political protest. Cafés and bars and fashionable boutiques have opened up, so that the poorest people in the city now live side by side with a flamboyant bohemian population.

John changes into his gardening clothes and goes out to join Jack. There's a ripple of warmth in the air, and the garden smells of rain and springtime flowers. He thanks God for Jack. He's a conscientious and trustworthy deacon, a little plodding in his ways and not the most engaging of preachers, but he knows the parish better than anybody else and the parishioners trust him.

'Pruning and composting today,' says Jack, pointing to the mound of compost in the wheelbarrow. 'We need to cut back the wisteria and the clematis, and those shrubs over there could do with a bit of pruning. Should be safe to do it now, providing we don't get any hard frosts.'

He shows John how to prune the wisteria that climbs up the presbytery wall. John enjoys the delicacy of his movements – stubby fingers gently parting the branches and snipping away the wood to the fresh young buds.

Jack hands the secateurs to John and ambles over to spread compost on the flowerbeds. John tries to emulate the delicacy of his movements, choosing buds that are angled outwards to encourage the plant to spread, trying to envisage the shape of the vine as it puts out new growth and spreads its lilac fragrance over the garden in late spring.

'John, come and look at this.' He turns at the sound of Jack's voice. Jack is peering into the branches of the flowering cherry tree. John goes over and looks.

'It's a robin's nest,' says Jack. 'Isn't it lovely?'

It is indeed lovely. Four perfectly formed blue gems in a bowl of straw, nestling in a fork of the tree trunk. 'I frightened the mother away, but she'll be back.'

'I hope Shula doesn't find it and get the chicks or the mother,' says John, thinking of the tiny mangled corpses that regularly appear on the presbytery floor.

Jack nods. 'That's life,' he says, as he goes back to his digging.

'Do you ever wonder why?' asks John.

'Why what?' Jack doesn't look up.

'Why life's like that?'

'Why not?' says Jack, still digging. John waits. Why not? He wants to ask again, like a little child. But why? Jack thrusts the spade into the soil and straightens up. He pushes back his cap and wipes his forehead, leaving a smear of dirt that reminds John of little James in the confessional.

'How's that wisteria going, lad?' he says. Jack is usually deferential to John and calls him 'Father', but here in the garden their roles are reversed. Jack is the wise teacher, and John is the bumbling disciple.

They spend the afternoon digging and pruning and occasionally stopping for a cup of tea or a brief exchange about the weather. When they finish, Jack gathers up all the woody offcuts in his wheelbarrow and makes a neat pile of them next to the compost bins. The bins are in the corner of the garden nearest the cemetery. There's a small grave in the row nearest the presbytery garden, with a marble angel watching over it and crocuses and lily of the valley blooming around it. It's Sarah's grave. The nuns gave special permission for her to be buried there.

Holly planted the flowers. She explained their significance to John – crocuses to symbolise resurrection because they're among the first flowers to bloom in early spring, and lily of the valley to symbolise a mother's sorrow, because when Our Lady wept at the foot of the cross her tears fell on the ground and these tiny white flowers sprung up at her feet. That's why they're called Our Lady's Tears.

Thinking of Holly makes him feel lonely. Jack and he must get ready for Mass, but after that the evening is empty. He would like to suggest that they go to the pub for a drink, but there's not much point when he has given up drinking for Lent. Going to the pub for a lemonade hardly seems worth the effort, and he's not sure he could sustain a conversation with Jack without a pint to loosen his tongue. Besides, he has to write his homily for tomorrow.

The stranger doesn't appear at the evening Mass, but the threat is all-pervasive. Afterwards, John eats a humble, hearty supper of fish pie made by a parishioner. There are always cooked meals in the fridge and homemade cakes in the tin. It makes him uncomfortable the way some of the women in the parish fuss over him, but he tells himself to be thankful for their care, and sometimes, like tonight, he's glad that he doesn't have to cook. He resists the temptation to open a bottle of wine.

He finishes his meal and goes upstairs to the study to write his homily. He looks out of the window before closing the curtains. The houses are lit up and a group of young people are walking through the lane, their laughter drifting up through the window. He's glad they are there, because he is suddenly afraid of some brooding presence looking up at him, hidden in shadows. The lane is often deserted at night – a perfect hiding place for anybody who wanted to observe him. But why would anybody bother? Get a grip, he tells himself.

He puts on music – Brahms' violin sonata – and sits at the desk. He gave a brief homily at the evening Mass because that's all people want and they get impatient if he goes on too long, but those who come to Mass tomorrow morning will be expecting something more substantial.

He goes through the Gospel reading several times. Christ's hunger after forty days. The temptation to turn stones into bread. 'Man shall not live by bread alone.' The temptation to accept the devil's promise of power over all the kingdoms of the world if Jesus will bow down and worship him. 'Away from me, Satan. Worship the Lord your God, and serve him only.' The temptation to throw himself down from the temple and trust the angels to catch him. 'Do not put the Lord your God to the test.'

He looks up at the print of a Madonna and child hanging above his desk. It's an icon of Our Lady of Perpetual Help. Mary gazes sorrowfully out of the image while the baby in her arms looks over his shoulder at an angel holding a cross. Another angel holds the instruments of his torture. The child's face is calm, but he is clutching his mother's slender hand in his fists, as if a spasm of terror has gripped him. There is something reproachful about her gaze, as if she's wondering if the world out there is worth this anguish.

'This I will give you,' said the devil, 'if you worship me.' The power and the glory of all the kingdoms of the world 'for it has been committed to me and I give it to anyone I choose'.

The satanic gift of earthly power. Can he preach about that?

He picks up his pen and begins to write. He has a laptop, but he prefers to write his homilies by hand. There's something about the feel of the pen and the paper, the lamplight and the shape of his words appearing on the page, trailing behind the shadow of his hand. Every Monday, he gives the handwritten homily to Edith and she types it up and puts it on the parish website. However much she irritates him, John is grateful to her for doing this. It means the sick and the housebound, and those who can't or won't attend Mass, can still read the homily if they want to.

Sometimes he wonders if his homilies merit such publicity, but he sees his reluctance as a subtle form of pride. He fears that his lack of eloquence, his intellectual limitations and theological shortcomings will be there on display for all the world to see at the click of a mouse, and he knows that it's vanity of vanities to think like that. He is who he is, and he must trust God to use him as He will.

> *Ours is a world in which people fight violence with violence, seek power to conquer power, grow rich and powerful by living off the labour of the powerless. Today's reading tells us that such earthly power is the work of the devil.*

He writes for an hour, pausing to check the reading from time to time, letting the words tumble onto the page.

It's not always like this. Sometimes he struggles and has only a meagre offering at the end, bereft of insight or wisdom. But just occasionally, he feels as if a homily is being given to him. It becomes something that happens to him rather than something that he himself produces.

> *Imagine it. Jesus up on the highest point of the temple. Those of you who came on last year's parish pilgrimage to Jerusalem will remember what the temple is like, how it rises above the city. If you've ever been in a high building, you'll know how terrifying it is to imagine jumping off.*

An image flashes into his mind. A burning tower and tiny bodies falling into oblivion. Did they hope the angels would catch them? Why didn't God send angels to catch them?

> *Did Jesus have doubts? Did he wonder if God really would send angels to catch him?*

He pauses. Can he say that? Was it possible for Jesus to have doubts? He imagines Edith chastising him afterwards, as she sometimes does. Edith is rock solid in her faith, scornful of those who waver, vigilant in attending to and correcting his homilies.

Yet how could Jesus have been tempted if he hadn't doubted? Jump, Jesus, jump. The angels will catch you.

He puts down his pen. Just one glass of wine. It has been a bad week. He hasn't been sleeping well. Surely, there would be no harm in it? How is his abstinence from wine going to help people in Syria and Iraq and Palestine? How is it going to rescue refugee children drowning in the Mediterranean? How is it going to relieve Holly's anguish or help pregnant Jane with her exhaustion and misery or console Jack in his loneliness? How is it going to do anything significant in making God's love real in the world?

There's a wooden crucifix on his desk. It was given to him by Holly when she came back from a visit to the Holy Land. It's made of olive wood. He picks it up and runs his fingers over the silky smooth surface of the wood. The body of Christ is carved in close detail, gaunt and hollowed out by suffering. He thinks of Luke in the confessional, and he lets his fingertips linger on Christ's naked torso. He forces himself to go back to his homily.

He knows intuitively when it's finished, and he puts down his pen. Exhaustion overwhelms him, as it always does after these rare, intense experiences of inspiration.

He sits in one of the armchairs and clicks on the remote control to watch the television news. Shula curls up on his lap. He strokes her and the weary contentment of having written a good homily eases the bleakness of the news.

A Syrian child wails amidst the ruins of a village. The prime minister is involved in yet more negotiations about Brexit. An earnest young woman economist gives a weighty analysis of what the fall in the value of the pound will mean for the cost of living, and an American politician whines a threat that may or may not be empty against a new Islamist group in Pakistan.

John dozes off.

He wakes with his heart pounding and his mouth dry.

Shula is standing rigid on his knee, bushy-tailed and growling, digging her claws into his thigh. She is staring at something behind him.

It's cold. The heating must have gone off. How long has he been asleep for?

He waits, and his limbs turn to stone. Who or what is behind him? The hairs on the back of his neck prickle. He dare not turn around. Shula gives another low growl. He wants to say something to her, but his voice won't come.

Will it be a knife? A rope round his neck? A battering with a hammer or a rock? He holds his breath and listens. Is it the stranger? How did he get in? The cold. The terrible cold.

'Who are you?' he manages to croak. The newsreader is telling him that the body of a young woman has been found in the Saint Peter's area of Westonville. She has not yet been identified, but police are treating her death as suspicious.

Whatever is behind him doesn't move, doesn't breathe, doesn't announce its presence in any way, but it's there. He knows it's there. Shula is looking at it. He gazes into the cat's eyes. Her pupils have almost obliterated the green of her irises. Is there a shadow moving across those large black pupils?

There's no point in screaming. Nobody would hear. Nobody would come. He should pray, if he's about to die, but no prayers come. So he waits, and he can't tell if he waits for a minute or an hour, but eventually the room is warm again, and his limbs melt back into life.

He looks at his watch. It's only twenty past ten. The heating doesn't go off until eleven. Shula's fur is gradually settling back into place. And then he hears the faint rattle of the letter box downstairs.

'Hello? Who's there?' His voice is ragged with fear. He listens attentively, but there are no footsteps, no signs of any other presence in the house. He breathes deeply, trying to calm himself.

Eventually he says, 'Hey Shula, what's the matter?' His voice sounds normal now, reassuring himself as well as the cat. He strokes her and she blinks and begins licking her fur as if to clean away the panic. She settles down on his lap, and he closes his eyes and wonders what just happened. Was he dreaming? Has somebody broken into the house? A few weeks ago, a priest was beaten up and robbed one Saturday night by a homeless drug addict he had invited in for a meal.

He presses the mute button on the remote control and sits very still, listening for noises. The silence of the presbytery hums at him. From somewhere far away, he hears the wail of an ambulance and the persistent barking of a dog. He waits. There's only absence and aloneness. Whatever it was, it has dissolved back into the nothingness it came from.

'Sorry girl,' he says, easing the sleeping cat off his lap and standing up. He puts her on the chair, trying not to disturb her. She squirms and goes back to sleep, her tail still twitching with the aftershock.

He looks around the empty room to the corridor beyond, leading to his bedroom and the staircase. He switches the television sound back on to chase away the silence. The weather forecast is for a bright sunny day, frosty to start with but getting warmer so that it will feel like a lovely springtime day for much of the country.

Maybe it was just a homeless person looking for shelter. The rattle of the letterbox. Shula's sudden fright. It was probably that. There's probably some poor drunk sprawling on the doorstep, or a homeless person huddled under a stinking blanket.

People still come to presbyteries as places of refuge and shelter. He remembers the priest who was robbed, and confronts again the dilemma that never goes away.

What do you do when Christ comes to your door in the guise of a drunk or a vagrant or an addict? Sometimes, John lets them in, lets them use the bathroom and sleep in the spare room. Sometimes he turns them away. Tonight, he thinks he will let him in, whoever it is. Or her? No. Only twice has it been a woman on the doorstep, and he hasn't dared to let her in for fear of causing scandal.

John thinks of the woman whose body was found in Saint Peter's. That's the red light district. Was she a prostitute? Is there somebody out there now, prowling the streets, looking for another victim? If it's a woman on the doorstep tonight he will let her in to keep her safe, just in case.

He goes downstairs, humming tunelessly to himself to keep the silence at bay. He looks up and down the empty cloisters. The door to the kitchen is open, and the door to the lounge is closed. Everything is just as he left it. He goes into the entrance hall.

There's a folded piece of paper on the doormat. He stares at it. Shula has followed him downstairs. She nudges against his ankles. He picks her up and buries his nose in her neck, breathing in her familiar smell. Then he settles her down on the floor and picks up the paper. The handwriting is bold and scripted, like calligraphy.

> *Jesus said to his disciples, 'Causes of falling are sure to come, but alas for the one through whom they occur! It would be better for such a person to be thrown into the sea with a millstone round the neck than to be the downfall of a single one of these little ones. Keep watch on yourselves! If your brother does something wrong, rebuke him and, if he is sorry, forgive him. And if he wrongs you seven times a day and seven times comes back to you and says, "I am sorry," you must forgive him.'*

He looks up. The locked door gazes blankly back at him. He unlocks it and pulls it open abruptly. He steps out onto the porch and looks around.

There's no one there. Only the night, and the frost, a sliver of moon hanging over the rooftops, and the vast indifferent canopy of stars.

His breath turns to mist in the frosty air. The chimneys send up their fragrant woody drift, smoke signals telling of families and friends gathered together in warm rooms. He looks over at the tree with the robin's nest, and as he gazes a small shape forms, as faint and indistinct as the smoke from the chimneys. Sarah has come wisping out of her small grave to guard the robin's nest.

As he climbs into bed, he hears the distant rattle of the cat flap. Shula is going out. He wonders if the mother bird is sitting on her nest. He's glad that Sarah is there to protect her. Perhaps Sarah is there to protect him too, an angel sent by God to stand guard through the night. That thought consoles him and he falls into an uneasy sleep.

FOUR

FIRST SUNDAY OF LENT

Time and again through the night, he reaches for the consolation of that velvety darkness, but it keeps dissolving into lurid dreams that startle him awake with a racing pulse and a jumble of incoherent images swirling through his mind. When morning comes at last, he pulls Shula up to the pillow and rests his cheek against her fur, glad that she has returned from her nightly wanderings. He wishes he could simply stay there, huddled beneath the duvet with Shula for company. He forces himself to get out of bed with a deep sense of foreboding. Will the stranger come to Mass? Will he come up for communion? What will John do?

He goes downstairs into the kitchen and fills Shula's bowl. She pushes herself between his legs to guzzle down her food.

He tries to remember the exchange in the confessional, about whether or not pure evil exists. It seems abstract and esoteric, remote from this thing now clawing at his gut.

His brother in law Chris would say that these are the kind of nonsensical riddles in which theology dabbles. The purity of evil. The nature of existence. A God who plays dice with the universe. Chris is married to his sister Kate, and he is a determined atheist.

Unlike many other priests, John does not come from a large Irish family. His English parents had three children. John is the youngest, two years younger than Paul who lives in America with his girlfriend, Charlotte. Kate is two years older than John

– forty on her next birthday. She's a GP, and she and Chris have two children, Phoebe aged nine and Stephen aged seven. Chris writes scripts for television, though John has the impression he is not in high demand. Kate no longer practises her faith. She is mildly exasperated by her beloved little brother's stubborn clinging to a childhood fantasy, but Chris is caustic in his sarcasm and mockery.

John has always looked up to Kate. He feels a close bond with her, despite her rejection of the Church and her bemusement at his vocation. He hopes her patients know how lucky they are.

She and Chris live in the family home where John grew up. They were living there so that she could nurse their parents when their father was dying of cancer and their mother was suffering from dementia, and they stayed on in the house after their mother died ten months ago. They offered to buy it, but John has no need of the money and Paul said he would rather keep the house as an investment. John suspects that Chris and Kate pay him rent, but he has never asked.

He loves going to see them. The house gives him a sense of connection and belonging. It comforts him when the solitude of his priesthood feels like a burden too heavy to bear.

When he first came to the parish, there were two priests living in the presbytery, and between them they said four Masses every Sunday as well as the Saturday evening Mass. When the other priest moved to a different parish and there was nobody to replace him, the bishop told John that he had to drop one of the Sunday Masses. This created an outcry among the parishioners, and it took six months of wrangling in the parish council meetings to come to some agreement.

It was out of the question to drop the family Mass, and the eight am Mass was important for people who had other arrangements and needed to get their Sunday obligation over with. That meant the choice was between the midday High Mass with its incense, Latin chants and traditional hymns sung to the unreliable accompaniment of Bob Carpenter, or the evening folk Mass with its guitars and bongo drums.

Eventually and painfully, it was decided to keep the folk Mass and drop the High Mass. Some people left the parish and started going to the cathedral instead. He struggled not to take that personally. It felt like a failure on his part.

The eight o'clock Mass is just as it always is. The relief at the stranger's non-appearance is short-lived, because there are still two Masses to go. He makes his way up the aisle for the ten o'clock Mass with a mounting sense of sickness and dread.

Taking his place on the altar, he scans the congregation. Would he recognise the stranger? Maybe not, but the faces looking up at him are familiar and he sees nothing out of the ordinary.

As the time for the homily draws near, he feels nervous. It's not his usual style of preaching. The children file out for their own liturgy. Deacon Jack reads the Gospel and steps down from the lectern. John crosses himself and takes Jack's place. He draws a deep breath and begins.

> *Today we reflect on the temptation of Christ in the wilderness. We reflect on the loneliness of Jesus, the struggle through hunger and thirst and self-doubt. We take him as our model and companion for our own Lenten journey.*

He continues to the bottom of the page then he pauses. With an involuntary spasm, he glances at the back of the church but he knows the stranger is not there. The church is warm and the air is fragrant with incense and candle wax. There's no menace in this place today. It feels holy, a holy place filled with the people of God, in their bright springtime clothes. The morning sun filters through the stained glass windows and casts rainbow patterns on the walls. He glances down at his notes and continues.

Jesus could have abused his divine powers. He could have become a magician, a conjurer. And we must believe that he was really tempted. He wanted to take power into his own hands, to take control, and in resisting he showed us that there is no interventionist God, for to believe in such a God is to believe in magic, and that's not faith.

Edith, sitting in her usual place in the front row, scuffles in her bag and closes it with an audible click. It's part of the repertory of signs that she uses to communicate when she has to refrain from voicing her thoughts. Clearly, she is not enjoying the homily this morning.

In the temptations in the wilderness, Jesus had to discover what kind of God he was to reveal to the world. A God of satanic power over the earth, a God who could be conjured up by magic to meet every human demand, or a God who would surrender to the world's power in order to redeem it by love, in order to redeem it from within the heart of darkness by subjecting himself to the full force of its failure and anguish?

God's power is not worldly power. In this season of Lent, we prepare ourselves to celebrate the greatest manifestation of God's power, but the world sees only weakness, failure and shame.

The homily goes on for longer than usual, and people are beginning to fidget. He skips to the end and goes to stand behind the altar as the children file back into the church.

He raises his hands to begin the Eucharistic prayer.

'The Lord be with you,' he says.

'And with your spirit.'

FIVE

FIRST MONDAY OF LENT

Monday is his day off. It doesn't always happen that way, if a parishioner has a crisis or the hospital or prison asks him to visit somebody who is dying or in urgent need of support. But he tries to keep the diary free after the morning Mass, to go walking or sightseeing, to read and relax, or to spend the day in a mini-retreat with his spiritual director.

Other priests play golf on Mondays, but it has never appealed to him. There's a kind of camaraderie for which he has never acquired the knack, a way of talking about everything and nothing that leaves him feeling gauche and taciturn. He prefers his own company.

He decides to spend the day mapping out next week's parish walk. Once a month, after the family Mass, he goes walking with a group of parishioners. The size of the group varies with the weather and the route. Father's 'short walks' have become a joke among those in the know. 'Five miles we did on Sunday, through brambles and mud.' 'A short walk, that's what he called it. If that's a short walk, remind me never to go on a trek with Father. I hate to think where he'd take us.' 'The views were lovely, mind, when we got to the top of the hill, even if the climb nearly killed me. We could see right out over the Severn Estuary and into Wales.' 'It were a hard climb, sure enough, but worth it all the same.'

He hums to himself as he makes his morning coffee, keeping the darkness at bay, thinking about where to go next week.

Maybe if the weather's nice they'll go over the bridge and walk in the hills around Tintern Abbey. They can take packed lunches and stop for a drink in a pub on the way back. The morning has dawned bright and fresh and clear. It's a good day for planning a walk. He switches on the radio to listen to the weather forecast after the six o'clock news.

> ... *murdered in Westonville on Friday night has been identified as eighteen year old Nan McDonald. McDonald had been estranged from her Scottish family since developing a heroin addiction when she was fourteen, and had spent several years living on the streets. Nan's mother says she is devastated by the news. 'I want her back. My baby. My little girl. I want them to find this monster before he does this to some other girl, to somebody else's child.'*

The mother's voice is a searing interruption to the smooth tones of the woman presenter. John regrets turning the radio on. He prays for the grieving mother and her murdered daughter. 'Eternal rest grant unto her O Lord, and through the mercy of God may she rest in peace.' He adds a prayer for the murderer, that he will be found before he kills again, that he will come to see the wrong he has done, and will repent and know that nobody is ever beyond the love and mercy of God. Amen.

> ... *the spring sunshine will continue over much of the country, with chances of rain in the South West towards evening.*

He will plan the walk around Tintern, then on the way back he will call in on Kate and her family.

After the Mass, Edith comes in to the presbytery to collect his Sunday homily so that she can put it on the web. Her mouth is set in that little shrivel of disapproval that he knows so well. Like an anus, he thinks.

'I must say, it was a very strange homily you gave yesterday, Father. I didn't like it at all.'

'You can't please all of the people all of the time, Edith,' he says.

'I'm not sure you pleased anybody yesterday Father. Maybe one or two, but people don't come to church wanting a theology lecture, you know. Most people don't anyway. Holly might, but that's what universities are for. She shouldn't expect you to turn all uppity on the rest of us with your clever ideas. That's not what people want when they come to Mass.'

'What do you think they want, Edith?'

She shrugs and a furrow of concentration gathers between her eyebrows. 'Well, if we're living the faith and doing our best, we want to be comforted and encouraged. You know, we want something that will help us to get through the week. Of course, you have to say something about sin and all that. I mean, not everybody who comes to Mass is a good Catholic, obviously.' She looks down at the notes in her hand and waves them disdainfully towards him. 'But this was hard to follow, I must say. I much preferred that homily when you spoke about feeding the five thousand, and how giving to Cafod on family fast day was a bit like that. You know, each of us gives what we have, and everybody gets fed. I liked that. Lots of people liked it. It got lots of "likes" on the website, and lots of nice comments.'

Edith has taken it upon herself to manage the blog where she posts his homilies. She goes through the comments that get posted there, rejects the ones she doesn't like, and publishes the rest. He thinks it's an improbable task for somebody like Edith, and it never ceases to surprise him that she wants to do it. He wonders if it's a vicarious substitute for managing his life, to manage his online presence. He suspects it should bother him more than it does. She delights in refusing to post the comments

46

that come from vehemently anti-Catholic anonymous sources – 'trolls', she says they're called. It seems to feed her pleasurable conviction that they are living in godless times and Catholics are being persecuted for their faith. He is not convinced about that, but he leaves her to it and tries not to get involved. John hates the intrusion of the internet into his life. It's enough keeping up with the constant flow of emails, without getting caught up in Edith's blogs.

He takes a sliced loaf out of the freezer and makes a cheese and pickle sandwich, then he makes a flask of tea and takes an apple from the fruit bowl. He phones Kate and asks if he can call round later when she finishes work. She invites him to stay for supper, as he had hoped she would. It might mean breaking his Lenten resolve to give up meat, though he can safely avoid drinking because he has to drive home afterwards. He hesitates to remind Kate about Lent, because he knows she will scoff at him. It's good-natured and affectionate, but even so it wearies him.

He parks near Tintern Abbey and has breakfast in a café nearby. He wanders through the ancient ruin and feels a familiar sadness welling up in him. He is ecumenical, of course he is – who isn't, these days? – but even so, he regrets the destruction of the habitual Catholicism of medieval life. He would like to inhabit a culture where going to Mass was as normal as Sunday shopping, and where monastery bells marked out the hours within earshot of everybody living in the land.

Yet the ruin is beautiful too. Perhaps it speaks more of God in its openness and brokenness than it would in its former glory of stained glass and statues and singing choirs. He stands in the grassy avenue where the nave would once have been, and looks up at the infinite space framed within empty arches.

Clouds drift across the high blue sky. A hawk swirls and swoops in the thermals. The sun kisses his face with the first tinges of summer warmth. He closes his eyes, and imagines it's the kiss of God on his skin.

He remembers volunteering with a project for drug addicts when he was a seminarian. There was a file on a shelf called 'Kissing God'. It was the reflections and jottings of recovering addicts. One of them had written that taking heroin was like kissing God. He wonders if he would ever have had the strength to give up, if that's what heroin made you feel like.

He used to admire those recovering and failing addicts for their courage and their struggle in the face of such enslaving powers. He thinks of the young woman who was murdered, and her mother's voice on the radio. He pushes the thought away.

He feels the stranger lurking, trying to gain entry. 'Go away,' he says, and his voice sounds like a rude interruption in the stillness and silence. He opens his eyes and gazes up at the soaring bird, focusing on nothing but the warmth of sunlight on his skin.

He wanders away from the abbey and up through wooded hills to the devil's pulpit, where Wordsworth wrote his famous poem. He climbs up the side of the rock and perches on top of it to look out at the view. Legend has it that the devil stood on this rock to preach to the monks in the monastery below, tempting them to abandon their vows. He remembers the reading and his homily. 'Throw yourself down'. Here, there is no city to command, no worldly power to be had. There is just the ruined abbey, and the village with its early straggle of tourists, and the river far below, shimmering through the gleaming foliage of early spring.

He clambers down the rock and continues walking uphill, stopping to speak to some sheep balefully watching him over a fence. He consults his map from time to time, plotting the walk, trying to remember that there will be children and elderly people so the climb mustn't be too steep and the path mustn't be too rocky.

He stops to eat his sandwiches and drink his tea beside a stream. A kingfisher flashes past, a blue flame sparking across his vision. He sees the flickering shadows of a shoal of tiny fish in the stream. A robin alights nearby, trilling its joy to the world. A snatch of poetry crosses his mind. 'A robin redbreast in a cage, puts all heaven in a rage.' Who wrote that? Blake? Yes. Blake. He feels contented and at peace. The robin whirs away to continue its singing on another branch.

He continues walking until the sun blushes down towards the horizon. He has charted a loop from the car park up through forested footpaths and across the fields at the top of the hill, then back down a different path ending with a walk through the village where they can stop for a drink in a child-friendly pub. He thinks it's a reasonable walk – not too hilly or arduous, but long enough to make a day of it. Some of them will be driving, but the passengers can have a beer or a glass of wine. He drives back over the Severn Bridge, heading to the village where his sister lives.

Kate is sitting at the dining table writing up her notes when he arrives. The children are slumped in the lounge in front of the television. Phoebe rushes to welcome him when he walks in the door, throwing her arms around his waist and hugging him. He picks her up and holds her close.

'Hey Phoebe, good to see you,' he says, kissing her cheek and setting her down again. He cherishes these moments of intimacy, knowing that soon the inhibitions will set in and his sister's children will no longer give him that precious gift of physical affection, a rare experience in his priestly life where bodily contact with young people is to be avoided at all costs lest it be misinterpreted.

Phoebe has her mother's dark hair and brown eyes, but where Kate's face is soft and made for smiles, Phoebe has inherited her father's square jaw and high forehead so that she already has a determined, adult look about her. She is a bright, enquiring child, persistent in her questions, sometimes challenging in her candour. She will be a formidable woman one day.

'Hello Stevie, how are things?' Stephen has inherited the genes in reverse. He has Kate's elfin-shaped chin and sweet smile, and his father's fair hair and blue eyes. He is quieter than Phoebe, shy and hesitant with adults, but doting on his uncle in a way that makes John feel a deep, sad sense of unworthiness that he cannot explain. He wants to be worthy of these children's love, and that seems an awesome challenge as well as a gift.

People say that Kate and he look alike. There's a photo of them together on the mantelpiece, taken on her wedding day. She refused to wear white satin and lace. 'For heaven's sake, we've been living together for two years. I'm hardly a vestal virgin.' It's taken close up. She has a spray of cream silk flowers pinned behind her ear, matching the simple neckline of her dress, and her brown eyes are glowing with some deep inner happiness. He is an inch shorter than her. He's wearing black clerical garb with a dog collar. He was a seminarian then. Why on earth did he dress like that for his sister's wedding? He is smiling into the camera with the same soft smile as hers, but his eyes look different. Not sad exactly, but wistful.

He has never liked that photograph, but he is not sure why. Glancing at it now as he kneels down and feels Stephen's arms around his neck, he thinks perhaps it's because it reminds him of all that he can never have or be. Was priesthood a way of avoiding all that – avoiding the confrontation with himself, the choice between a life of secrecy or a life of scandal and rejection? Maybe it was some unacknowledged impulse of mourning that made him dress in clerical black to his sister's wedding.

But it's not like that now, is it? Men like Luke are accepted by the other parishioners, if not by all priests and bishops. Gay men can get married. Even the Church has grudgingly accepted civil partnerships. He suddenly imagines himself married to Luke, a wedding photo on the mantelpiece, adopting children, living a life like Kate's. He wraps his arms around Stephen's small, thin body and picks him up. He must be thankful for what he has. He mustn't dwell on what he doesn't have, because he has so much.

Kate pushes her papers aside and stands up. She wraps her arms around him and kisses him, squeezing him tightly to herself.

'Come into the kitchen while I get us something to eat,' she says. She takes a bottle of white wine out of the fridge and opens it. She holds it out to him. 'Want a glass?'

'No thanks. I'm driving.' He doesn't add, 'and it's Lent,' but she does.

She gives him a teasing smile. 'It's alright, John. I'm doing macaroni cheese for supper. I didn't forget.' He feels a surge of love for his sister. She has always been there for him. She knows he's gay, but she shrugs it off. 'You're a priest. It doesn't make much difference one way or the other, since you're celibate.'

She tells him that Chris is working late so it's just the four of them for supper. 'At least you won't have to deal with him doing his Richard Dawkins impersonation for your benefit,' she says, sounding irritable. He is not sure whether her irritation is directed towards him or Chris. Both perhaps.

He sits at the table with Kate and the children and they chatter about gentle, lovely, trivial things. Afterwards, he drives home through the starry countryside, listening to the radio.

When he gets home, he has a cup of tea and then he takes his Missal into bed to say his evening prayers, opening it with the fraying blue ribbon that marks his place.

In the Lord I have taken my refuge.
How can you say to my soul:
'Fly like a bird to its mountain.

See the wicked …

His eyes are closing. He tries to stay awake and concentrate.

See the wicked bracing their bow;
They are fixing their arrows …

He snoozes and forces himself to wake up.

> *… fixing their arrows on the string*
> *To shoot upright men …*

> *… to shoot …*

> *…upright men*

> *… upright men in the dark.*
> *Foundations once destroyed, what can …*

> *… what can the just …*

> *… what can the just do?'*

His head slumps to one side, and the Missal slides off his knees onto the floor.

SIX

FIRST FRIDAY OF LENT

Time has settled into its Lenten rhythm. He would find it hard to describe to an outsider exactly what that is, but he feels it as a shadow cast across his days. Some people say Lent should be a time of celebration and hope, but he doesn't experience it that way. He wonders if it's because he is weak and misses the ordinary consolations of wine in the evenings and the occasional breakfast of bacon and eggs or dinner of steak and chips. Some might think it strange that he finds the commitment to celibacy less of a burden than these Lenten sacrifices, but there's a difference between making a once-for-all vow about one's way of life, and resisting the daily temptations of food and drink drip drip dripping through the hours.

There's something else too. The nature of people's confessions changes during Lent. Those who hardly ever go to confession tend to do so at least once, usually on Ash Wednesday or Good Friday, but at other times as well. Those who confess regularly become more soul-searching and anguished in their penitence. Sometimes he hears the same thing week after week, month after month. Lonely Jack's masturbation. Pregnant Jane's guilt about her exhaustion and moodiness and anger with God. Jonathan Mellors who runs the parish pro-life group confessing to unclean thoughts about his neighbours' teenage daughter.

The stranger has not reappeared since his brief appearance at the school Mass a week ago. John is trying to convince himself that it was a hallucination. The stranger doesn't exist. He was a bizarre figment of John's imagination. That's what he tells himself, even as something acidic burns in his stomach and sends palpitations through his body in the darkest hours of the night.

He goes to confession after the morning Mass. He always goes once a month, but he tries to go more often in Lent. He goes to an elderly Jesuit priest, Father Martin, in the Jesuit retreat centre in Westonville. The centre is set in terraced gardens on a hillside overlooking the city, with a fine view of the river and the wooded hills beyond.

He goes into the meditation room with its Ikea armchairs, soft music, scented candles and pot plants, and waits for the old priest to arrive. In a corner, a candle flickers in a red glass holder beside the simple wooden tabernacle mounted on the wall.

Father Martin shuffles in and mutters about the music. He switches it off with a gesture that shows what he thinks of these New Age flourishes introduced by the nuns who run meditation groups and retreats in the centre.

He drapes a stole over his shoulders and eases himself into one of the chairs. They both cross themselves.

John's mouth is dry and his heart is beating too fast. He always finds confession difficult. Father Martin is his role model as a priest and confessor. Often irascible about little things, the old priest has a deep serenity about the vast, insoluble dilemmas of life, and seemingly infinite charity when it comes to human folly and vulnerability.

Today though, John brings an extra burden to the confessional, a theological dilemma that nobody addressed in the seminary or the university when they were studying the seal of the confessional. Can a priest break that seal in his own confession with another priest? Can he tell Father Martin about the stranger in the confessional – real or imagined – and the dread he has felt ever since? That question has burrowed into his brain and gone round and round without an answer.

He clears his throat. 'I've been tired recently Father. I've been under quite a lot of stress.' Father Martin nods and listens attentively, eyes discreetly lowered, hands folded in his lap.

'I've been tempted in the old way. I still desire another man. I still give in to that desire in my own thoughts and – and in my – my behaviour – with myself, I mean ... ' He swallows. 'I've betrayed my vow of chastity.'

The old priest nods again. 'We're only human John. You must hand these desires over to God and ask him to use them for good. Even what we think of as sins can help us to understand other people's weaknesses. As priests, that might be a painful gift, but it is a gift nonetheless.'

John thinks of Jack in the confessional, ashamed because of his masturbation. Yes, he understands Jack.

He confesses to the failings and temptations of everyday life – his irritation with Edith, his impatience with the unending tasks of parish administration, the sense of bleakness that sometimes makes him question his faith during this season of Lent, when the readings seem so relentlessly dark and he struggles to praise a God who sends plagues upon people and tests them beyond breaking.

Father Martin smiles again, knowingly, as if he has been through it all. 'Your faith is being tested John. Dostoyevsky once wrote that "My hosanna has passed through a great crucible of doubt." Doubt is part of a mature faith. Don't be afraid to question.'

John feels tearful. He licks his lips in a futile attempt to take away the dryness. 'I've had an experience, a troubling experience,' he says. 'I think it was a hallucination, but I'm afraid, Father. I'm very afraid.'

There's a shift in the old priest's attention. 'Go on John. Don't be afraid to say whatever it is.'

'It was something I thought I heard in the confessional, and then – the same person – I thought I saw him in church one day, but I can't be sure. I think I might have imagined it.'

There's a stillness in Father Martin now. Is he praying for guidance? 'John, you know that we must use wisdom about what happens in the confessional. Under no circumstances can we break the seal of the confessional. I can't tell you what to do, if you hear things that might cause harm to others. You can only persuade the person confessing to go to the authorities, or to give you permission to seek advice.'

John knows he is talking about confessions of child abuse. That's something they all have to deal with now. 'It's not – I don't think it's about that kind of thing. That's why I think I imagined it. It was cold, and – and when I saw him in church there was a terrible smell – like rotten flesh. I don't think he was real, Father.'

Father Martin nods and raises his eyes, looking at John with such compassion that he feels the lump rising in his throat again. He lowers his eyes, reluctant to meet the old priest's gaze.

'Maybe God is allowing some trick of your imagination for reasons you might not understand. Or maybe you should talk to a counsellor or a therapist if you really think these are hallucinations. Whatever you do, ask God to guide you John. Our Lord will not abandon you. And remember this isn't a sin, what you're telling me now. We're not responsible for the phantasms that haunt us and tempt us. We must learn to accept that they're part of the strangeness of our minds. Aquinas said that, but so did Freud.' He smiles. 'Our Lord was tempted by Satan, John. Whatever's going on, you must see it as a call to follow our Lord more closely, to share more fully in his time of temptation and testing, to understand what it means to walk with him on the road to Calvary.'

'I'm afraid Father. I pray for that. I say I want it. But I don't want it. I'm being dishonest when I say I do.' The words are coming freely now. 'I have a good life. I love my life Father. I think of all those people who are suffering, people being tortured and raped, refugees, people drowning to escape from God knows what, my own parishioners and the crosses they carry, and I don't want any of it. I don't want to walk with Jesus on the road to Calvary. I just want him to leave me alone, to let me get on with being an ordinary parish priest and doing my best to be there for the people I feel called to serve.' He stops. Had he intended to say all that? Had he even thought it before he said it?

Father Martin smiles again. 'That too is something our Lord understands, John. Didn't he pray in Gethsemane for the Father to take away the cup of suffering? And we're not Christ. We're not even Mary Magdalene and the other women. They stayed faithful. It was the men who betrayed Jesus – Peter and Judas above all. We have their spirits in us too John. That's the burden of our priesthood – the weakness of Peter comes with the job. Don't despair. Learn to live with the vulnerability of being human.'

The confession draws to a close, and John feels that cathartic sense of relief and consolation which he longs for his parishioners to feel too.

'For your penance John, I want you to pray the psalm from today's Mass readings. "Out of the depths I cry to you, O Lord …" Pray it slowly and reflect on it. Let yourself rest in the presence of the Lord.'

John spends the afternoon visiting sick and housebound parishioners. One of those is Patrick Donnelly, in his early sixties and recently diagnosed with terminal cancer. Patrick's wife, Mary, is a small, anxious woman who seems unable to cope with the devastation that is sweeping through her well-ordered life. They have five adult children – four daughters and a son. Their son Eamon lives in Australia, Ailish lives in South Africa, Colleen lives in Ireland, and Breda and Siobhan both live in Westonville where they grew up. Siobhan, the youngest, is engaged to Anthony and they have been to see John to plan their wedding later in the year.

Patrick is sitting in an armchair in the living room. His face is grey, his cheeks are sunken and his clothes are baggy on his gaunt body. He looks like an alien presence amidst the china ornaments, lace doilies and polished coffee tables. Siobhan and Anthony are there, sitting side by side on the settee. Mary makes tea and perches fretfully on the edge of her chair, her thin body zinging with tension. Siobhan also seems nervous. John drinks his tea while Mary talks about the grandchildren in Australia, smiling too often and too brightly at her husband, who seems exhausted by the effort to stay awake.

Siobhan clears her throat and grasps Anthony's hand. 'Father, we wanted to speak to you about something.' She glances at her father, and John is moved to see the tenderness in her gaze. Siobhan is beautiful, with classic Irish colouring of auburn hair and green eyes, her fair skin lightly dusted with freckles.

Patrick gives her a weak smile of encouragement. 'Go on,' he says. 'You can tell Father.'

'You see, Father, the doctors have told us that we ought to think of bringing our wedding forward. It's just – Pappy, we really want him to be there, and autumn – well, we don't know what might happen …' Her voice seizes up and she drops her chin. Mary begins to cry.

'It's alright,' says Patrick. 'Don't cry, Mary. I've told you, I'm not afraid. But I'd like to see Siobhan and Anthony married before the Lord takes me to himself.'

John has been with many families facing imminent death, and they all handle it in different ways. He respects the courage and honesty of those who can talk about it, as this family does.

There used to be a rule against getting married in Lent, but that no longer applies. Even so, he still has a lingering scruple about it. 'What about if we do it just after Easter?' he says.

'We'd like to do it sooner than that, Father,' Siobhan says. She's calmer now that she has said what she had to say, with an edge of determination in her voice.

He agrees to check the parish diary and get back to them that evening. They pray together and he gives them communion before he leaves. Anthony is Anglican but John gives him communion too. He thinks nobody should be excluded from receiving the Lord if they desire him. He never says so – it's not his way to rebel or to openly question church teachings – but he has never turned anybody away.

By the time he gets back to the presbytery, the sun is low in the sky and the garden is gilded in gold and green. He is relieved to see the mother robin sitting on the eggs, watching him with bright button eyes. He doesn't go too close in case he frightens her. He wonders if Sarah is there too, slipping invisibly between the beams of light, ready to keep watch through the night.

He remembers that he hasn't done his penance yet. The garden is so beautiful, he decides to sit on the bench and reflect on the psalm.

> *If you, O Lord, should mark our guilt, Lord, who would survive?*
>
> *Out of the depths I cry to you, O Lord,*
> *Lord, hear my voice!*
> *O let your ears be attentive to the voice of my pleading.*

He listens to the sounds of the garden emerging as his ears grow used to the silence. The blackbird high in the cherry tree, whistling its hymn to the oncoming night. The distant rumble of the traffic, as people head home from work. The drift of music from an open window. Shula emerges from behind the presbytery and saunters over the grass. He glances anxiously at the robin's nest, but the cat shows no interest. She sits at John's feet and begins grooming herself. He bends down and scratches the soft tufts of fur at the side of her neck. She purrs and rubs her head against his arm. He envies her the simplicity of her way of being in the world.

There's a chill in the air and the damp of evening settles around him. The yew trees in the cemetery stretch fingers of darkness across the lawn. He stands up and strolls over to the wooden fence to gaze at the humble graves beyond. Sarah's grave is a bright patch of colour amidst the shadows. He pushes open the wooden gate and goes into the graveyard. He breathes in the loamy smell of the earth, spongy and damp beneath his feet. The evening light filters through the yew trees and lights up the wings of the angel, so that it looks as if it's about to take flight. He reads the words on the tombstone:

Sarah Jane Foster
Beloved daughter of Holly and Steve,
sister of Jason and Tom

When you awaken in the morning's hush
I am the swift uplifting rush
Of quiet birds in circled flight.
I am the soft stars that shine at night.
Do not stand at my grave and cry;
I am not there. I did not die.

He reads the date and it reminds him that it will soon be the anniversary of Sarah's death. It happened six weeks after he arrived in the parish, bonding him to Holly with an unbreakable bond of love and grief.

The shadows trickle across the ground, flooding the puddles of light with darkness and night. Then she is there beside him, nothing more than a slight congealing of the air and a breath of life in this place of birdsong and sleeping souls. He doesn't turn to look. There would be nothing to see. But he senses her, and he feels the lightest brush of her hand upon his, before she vanishes. Has she gone to stand beneath the robin's nest, to take up her night watch? He hopes so.

He turns and makes his way up the presbytery path, and he tries to take with him the peace of the dead.

SEVEN

FIRST SATURDAY OF LENT

He is hearing confessions before Mass. He puts on his stole and goes into the church. The day is overcast and the church is gloomy, with a few candles flickering on the stand at the Virgin's feet. He looks around, his heart fluttering with fear. There's nobody there, and the heating is on. He switches on the lights, and goes into the confessional.

He hears the squeak of rubber-soled shoes approaching down the aisle, and tries to guess who it is. The door opens on his side of the confessional. Maureen Franklin comes in and sits in the empty seat beside him. She looks tired, bundled into her brown woollen coat with her sensible shoes planted on the floor in front of her. Maureen works in the post office.

She talks of her guilt and her fears, blinking away tears behind her glasses. She has worked in the post office in the high street for twenty years. She thinks of it as her vocation, to be kind, to listen to the people who come in with stories to tell and burdens to share. But now the post office is closing because it's not profitable, and she doesn't know what will happen to all those people. Her voice wobbles and she fumbles up her sleeve for a hanky and dabs away a tear.

'People tell me things, Father. It's almost like – I'm not being presumptuous or irreverent or anything – but sometimes I think it must be a bit like that for you, when you're hearing confessions. Last week, there was a lovely young mum came in with a pile of birth announcement cards, all bright and happy and wanting to show me her baby, and the next person was a young lad who'd lost his job and was posting off application letters. He began to cry, Father. He told me his dad had called him a waste of space, and – I don't know – who will listen to people like that now, if the post office closes? It won't be the same, will it? They'll have nobody to talk to.' She swallows and sniffs. 'The thing is Father, I'm grumpy too. I don't always have the patience to listen, and I feel terrible. I'm worried about money. I don't earn a fortune, but it helps to pay the bills. When they close the post office, I'm not sure I'll be able to find another job.'

John wants to tell her that she is good, she's one of the ordinary saints whose acts of love keep the earth spinning on its axis and ensure that the galaxies keep moving in their orbits of grace. Yet a scruple prevents him. In the confessional, people must be the authorities of their own consciences before God. So he pronounces an act of absolution, and for her penance he tells he to say three Our Fathers.

Jennifer Simpson from the Justice and Peace Group is in next. She has fair hair so fine that it barely frames her face, and she rarely smiles. She fixes John with a glare as she begins her confession.

Jennifer's confessions are always the same. She feels angry with the Church. It's so misogynistic. She can't bear to call God Father, and she hates being referred to as a brother in the Mass. The parishioners don't support the Justice and Peace Group. Sometimes she wonders if she belongs here. His attention wanders. He has heard it all before.

When she pauses, he tries to placate her. 'You're doing God's work, Jennifer. Sometimes it's frustrating and challenging, but he will give you strength to do what he asks of you.'

'How often do I have to remind you, John, that I can't call God "he"? Don't you realise how impossible it is, when even our prayers are patriarchal?'

'God is also a mother,' he says mildly. 'Pray to her, if that feels more truthful. And the Church is a mother too. Maybe Our Lady could help you in your prayers.'

She makes an exasperated huffing sound and rolls her eyes. 'I don't pray to Mary. All that virginal submission and obedience. I prefer to think of her as a mother in Gaza, somebody who needs courage and passion and conviction, not just virginal submission.'

'That's a lovely image, Jennifer. Maybe that's the image God has given you to pray with, and surely our prayers are needed for the people of Gaza.' He senses that she has a great deal more to say on the subject of Gaza, but he's conscious of others waiting outside. 'If you would like to pray for God's forgiveness Jennifer, remembering that He – sorry, She – or – umm – God hears and understands and is with us in our weakness.'

A few more people come in and he listens to their sins and struggles, though Jennifer has rattled him and he feels edgy and ill at ease. He is glad when the last one leaves, and he can prepare to celebrate Mass.

But as he reaches up to remove his stole, he feels it. The sudden cold, raising the hairs on the back of his neck. The door on the other side opens, and a vast shadow slithers across the wall. He resists the urge to flee, as the shadow settles itself on the kneeler. John replaces the stole around his neck and sits down, staring transfixed at the silhouette on the other side of the grille.

'Bless me Father. I have sinned.' The lengthened hiss of the 's's awakens again that elusive sense of *déjà vu*. There's something that John has forgotten. Something important. Something he ought to remember.

He makes the sign of the cross and uses the formulaic opening. 'May God, who has enlightened every heart, help you to know your sins and trust in his mercy.' He hopes his voice sounds normal.

'I know my sins John, but I don't ask for God's mercy. I shall pay the price of my sins, but first I'll bring many to God.'

'Why do you come to confession then, if you've nothing to repent of?' John abandons any hope of a pastoral response. All he wants now is clarity, an explanation, maybe a prompt that might help him to remember.

'Because I want to boast of my sins before God, John. I'm proud of my sin. I shall bring so many miserable sinners to God, and I shall endure the punishment which by rights should be theirs. I damn myself, John, in order to save them. I'm the greatest of saints, greater even than Judas. He despaired, but I don't despair. He had to do what he did. It was written in the stars the day he was born. Poor Judas. Somebody had to betray Jesus. Somebody had to make all those prophecies come true. He just had the bad luck to be the one. But me. I'm free. Nobody prophesied what I do. Nobody preordained it. I just saw the flaw in the logic of redemption, and I've decided to put it right.'

There's a pause. John wonders if he is supposed to respond, but what can he say?

Eventually, the shadow shifts and the voice speaks again. 'They used to teach us that God is rational, God is the perfectly rational being, but I spotted the flaw in the reasoning. If you're going to take the sins of the world upon yourself, you must also take on the punishment of the damned. Do you remember the argument that hell is uninhabited? Hell exists, but it's empty. I suppose God likes to keep it burning, just in case. Some might call that environmental vandalism – all that sulphur churning eternally into the atmosphere, and for what?' He sniggers. The sound is terrible. 'Greater than Judas? Dear God, I'm greater than Christ, my sacrifice is absolute, my commitment is total.' Again, that long drawn out pause. This creature has all the time in the world. It comes from beyond time, and John is trapped in the wordless panic of its presence.

The voice comes again, at last. 'If hell exists, then it exists for some purpose. As you reminded me, evil is lack. Evil doesn't exist, and its non-existence is what makes it evil. But if hell exists, then it has some purpose, it serves some good end. And I am that good end. I'm the Messiah who saves humankind from hell, because hell was made for me alone.'

When language returns to John, the words tumble out. 'You're mad. This is the talk of the insane.' But John knows this is not madness. It is sane and calculated and terrifying. 'How do I know you exist?' he says. 'How do I know you're not just some trick of my mind, some – some phantasm or hallucination?'

'You don't know. Maybe I don't exist. Maybe none of us exists, John. Existence itself is after all the great riddle, isn't it? Why is there something rather than nothing? Maybe there's nothing.'

'Do I know you? Where did I meet you?'

'Oh, you know me John. You're just very good at forgetting what you wish you didn't know.'

'What's your name?'

'I have no name. None that you would know, anyway. Mine is the name of a dead man. A man who died on 9/11. You remember 9/11, don't you John?' A pause, as if John needs time to remember. 'By the way, I liked your homily. I read it on the website. "Throw yourself down." It was quite eloquent, compared to your usual standards. But it's a bit hard to swallow, isn't it? Satan promises that angels will catch Jesus, but where were the angels to catch those falling bodies on 9/11 or when Grenfell Tower was burning?'

John feels sick. Surely, this horror is coming from inside his own head? He will wake up soon, and he will realize it was all a nightmare.

The voice continues. 'It's a trick, John. A great big conjuring trick. After all, Jesus resisted the temptations in the wilderness but he got it all in the end. Power, glory, wealth, domination. King of the Universe. Everything that Satan had to offer, and so much more besides. Poor old Jesus. Just like Job, he was a pawn, that's all. A plaything in the great machismo battle between God and Satan.' He makes a sound too mirthless to be called a laugh, too sardonic to be called a sob. 'I'm the true Messiah. When I die, there will be no memory and no glory. No power and no domination. People will long to forget. I shall become the anonymous face of God, sacrificing my eternal life so that others might live. I shall be the dead God forever. I renounce for ever and ever what Jesus only bargained away for a couple of years.'

'I want you to go. Either make your confession, or go.' John doesn't care that this thing from the other side can hear the fear in his voice.

'John, that's not like you. Don't you see, this is your chance to save me? This is your chance to save God. Are you really sending me away unforgiven? Can you live with that on your conscience?' He makes a sound, a slow, lascivious murmur that once again stirs something in John. He has heard that sound before. 'I wonder if you'll also be damned because you failed to save me? Maybe hell was made for both of us John. Mmmm. We can be together for all eternity. You and your doppelganger. You and your alter ego. You and the dark twin you carry inside you. Your phantasm. Your hallucination.'

John feels panic rising and rising. He must get away. He has to say Mass, he has to endure a whole long day before he can open himself to what is knocking at his consciousness, wanting to get in. He rushes to speak before the demons take hold of him.

'I pronounce absolution. Your sins are forgiven in the name of the Father, and of the Son, and of the Holy Spirit. Amen.' He hears the terror in his voice as he makes the sign of the cross in front of the grille, tracing its contours above the man's head. He imagines the sign lingering there, like smoke or jet trails, in the emptiness between them.

He has no homily to write that evening. He has asked Deacon Jack to preach. The Gospel reading is Luke's account of the transfiguration, when Jesus was transformed to radiant light before the eyes of his exhausted disciples. The Feast of the Transfiguration comes later in the year, in August, on the day that America decided to drop an atom bomb on Hiroshima. John finds it almost impossible to speak meaningfully about a human body irradiated by divine light in the face of such horror. He is happy to let Jack do it, and Jack loves preaching.

He spends the evening slumped in front of the television, dozing off repeatedly and waking with a jump as the images and sounds blur around him. Eventually he undresses and decides that he can't be bothered showering. He wriggles into his pyjamas and climbs into bed. The sheets feel cold. He pulls the duvet up under his chin and huddles without moving, trying to create a pool of warmth around himself. Where's Shula?

It's hot. The air is clogged with steam that reeks of sweat and semen. It's dark. He can feel them but he can't see them. Hands reaching for him. A tangle of legs and genitals. He fumbles blindly. A hand takes his and wraps it around an erect penis. Voices murmur obscenities around him. He gasps. No. Yes. Yes. Yes. No. He cries out. He panics. A small red bulb that casts no light marks the door. He rushes for it and plunges out into a space of eerie blue light and Grecian pillars. Men with glistening torsos sit in a jacuzzi. Others saunter beside a swimming pool, small towels elegantly knotted around their loins. He is lost, helpless. A tall man approaches him. He has a sweep of silvery hair that glows blue in the light, and his body shimmers as if rubbed with oil. He looks like a god. This is an epiphany, a transfiguration. He is coming closer. His body begins to glow. There's no escape from this rapture, this shock of recognition.

The man smiles. 'Hello John,' he says. 'What an unexssspected pleasure. Come. Come on, don't be shy.' He guides John by the hand to a lounger. He removes his towel and reclines elegantly on the lounger. 'Sssuck my cock,' he says. His words hiss beguilingly in the semen-scented air.

John awakens to the smell of his own sweat and semen. The memories fly at him through the night, angels of death with their wings pounding the darkness. No. No. No.

He sits up. Shula is asleep on the bottom of the bed. He gropes for the cat and lifts her to his face, burying his nose in her deep, warm fur. It's quarter past four – too early to get up, but he won't sleep again tonight.

He climbs out of bed and feels the cold air on his skin. He takes his dressing gown from the hook on the back of the door and wraps it around himself. He pushes his feet into his slippers and pads through to his study. He sits down at the desk and lifts the lid of his laptop.

There's a bold black list of unread emails. He clicks on one from Holly, because he wants the comfort that only she can give him.

> *Dearest John,*
>
> *How quickly this time of year comes round. It's nearly ten years since we lost our beloved Sarah. She would be nineteen in May. The anniversary of her death is the week after next, on Thursday. I'd like to have our usual little ceremony by her grave. Can we arrange to do it before the morning Mass? It will probably just be the two of us. I'm not sure if I can persuade Steve to join us. I think deep down he'd like to, but you know how stubborn he is.*
>
> *Love and hugs, my dearest darling friend,*
> *Holly.*

He ignores the other emails and clicks into Google. He types in a name. Cardinal Michael Bradley. The Wikipedia entry is first. He clicks on it and begins to read.

> *Michael James Bradley, 9 June 1952 – 11 September 2001, was an English priest and a cardinal of the*

Roman Catholic Church. He lectured in theology in England and then in Rome, and was elevated to the cardinalate in 1990. He disappeared in 1999 amidst unconfirmed rumours of a sex scandal. He was later reported to have joined a global finance corporation based in the North Tower of the World Trade Centre in New York. He died in the attack on the Twin Towers on 11 September, 2001.

John vomits, with just enough warning to turn his head away from the desk. He heaves and retches until his ribs ache and his throat burns and his stomach is empty. He stares at the foetid mess on the carpet, and it is like staring at the shame he has tried to avoid for all these years.

Shula comes in and begins licking at the mess. He pushes her away with his foot more roughly than he intends. He remembers the story of Saint Catherine of Siena drinking pus from the wounds of the dying people she cared for. He picks up the cat and murmurs meaningless sounds into her fur, knowing she won't mind his sour breath and the traces of vomit on his lips, wanting only her warmth and her forgiveness.

He feels it on his shoulder, lighter than air. A small hand, forever nine years old, innocent of all that comes with adult life. Holly is wrong about Sarah's age. She wouldn't be nineteen. She will never be nineteen. Sarah's life isn't about 'would'. It's about 'is'. She hasn't gone anywhere. She has just slipped between the molecules and the moments to become a different kind of body inhabiting a different kind of space or a different kind of time, or maybe a different realm altogether beyond time and space.

What would Holly say if she knew? He ponders the question, because it lets him escape all the other unbearable questions. He wonders if he should ask Sarah, but he has never spoken to this elusive visitor. He fears that the sound of his voice would be too heavy. The reverberations might shatter that translucent membrane between now and forever, which lets her pass backwards and forwards between worlds.

He sits in silence for a long time, the cat in his arms and the hand on his shoulder. Then when the hand evaporates like morning mist, he pushes down the lid of his laptop and goes to fetch a cloth and bucket from the kitchen.

EIGHT

SECOND SUNDAY OF LENT

The darkness dissolves into grey morning light. The windows are smeared with rain. It's the parish walk today. He goes downstairs to make coffee and switches on the radio to listen to the weather forecast – a rainy start but brightening up later so that much of the country will enjoy a warm, sunny day. The forecast gives him a moment of pleasure before the news begins with its litany of sorrow and violence. He switches it off. He tries to pray, but his throat feels scorched and the words won't come.

He scans the faces of the congregation as he says the Entrance Antiphon at Mass, even though he intuitively knows that the stranger will not reappear. Not yet. This is a game of cat and mouse. His tormenter will enjoy the gradual act of clawing away his life, bit by bit, and will watch him shiver and squirm and bleed in the gaps between the torture. And he is no stranger. He is the cardinal.

Carol Pierce, Lucy's mother, is doing the first reading, from the Book of Genesis. She reads slowly and clearly. As he sits in the high backed chair to the side of the altar, his fears come swarming back. He tries to concentrate. '*Abram put his faith in the Lord, who counted this as making him justified.*' The strangeness of the reading intensifies his anxiety. '*Get me a three-year-old goat, a three-year-old ram, a turtledove and a young pigeon.*' Raw fear is mingled with something that he feels but cannot think, knows but cannot speak of. '*He brought him*

71

all these, cut them in half and put half on one side and half facing it on the other; but the birds he did not cut in half.' The words fall apart and lose whatever meaning they might have had. 'Sssuck my cock.' *Birds of prey came down on the carcases but Abram drove them off.* He feels a wave of nausea and he panics in case he vomits there in the middle of Mass. He swallows, and begs Jesus not to abandon him.

He tries to draw comfort from the familiar faces in the congregation. He sees various expressions of distractedness that tell him they're not making much sense of the reading either. '*When the sun had set and darkness had fallen, there appeared a smoking furnace and a firebrand that went between the halves.*' He sees Holly, bright and extravagant as always, sitting alone at the end of a pew because her husband and sons refuse to come with her to Mass. There in the front row is the Mellors family – Jonathan, Mary and their eight children. They always sit in the front row – 'flaunting the fruits of their fucks,' says Holly. Jonathan is a deacon, and John dreads the times when it's Jonathan rather than Jack who helps at Mass. Mary and he run the parish pro-life group, and they help with the marriage preparation courses. Holly thinks he's crazy letting them do that – 'Jesus John, they're bloody fundamentalists! Those young couples don't stand a chance' – but he isn't sure how to stop them. They are a model Catholic family. He tells himself they're a blessing in the life of the parish, but in his heart of hearts, he agrees with Holly. '*That day the Lord made a Covenant with Abram*'. 'Ssuck my cock.'

Dark images swoop down on him, but he makes himself think of Lucy. She looks like her mother, with her fair hair and blue eyes. There are people in the parish for whom he feels a special affection and concern, and Lucy is one of them. He remembers her as an inquisitive child when he used to visit the school in his early days in the parish. She was in the same class as Sarah. They were best friends. She witnessed the whole thing. He has often wondered what scars that left on her soul.

Deacon Jack reads the Gospel about the transfiguration, and John listens as he meanders his way through a homily, trying to link up Abram's sacrifice in Genesis with the transfiguration and losing his point somewhere along the way. He mentions the atomic bomb, but the reference sits there awkwardly in the midst of the homily, and becomes part of the general confusion.

After Mass, they set out in convoy for the village of Tintern to begin the parish walk. There are twenty six of them altogether, with people sharing cars and offering lifts to those who don't drive.

They walk up a grassy slope and through a wood carpeted with bluebells, their dusty fragrance mingling with the smell of wild garlic. Knobbly kneed lambs frolic in a field, to the delight of the children. Amy, the little girl with the haunted eyes who dug up her dead hamster, comes to stand beside him. She slips her hand shyly into his.

'Hello Father,' she says.

'Hello Amy. How are you?'

'I'm alright,' she says solemnly.

'Aren't these lambs lovely?' he says. She nods, but doesn't respond. There's something about Amy that is beyond the reach of words. He would like to hug her, but he satisfies himself with squeezing her hand gently and then lets go, feeling as he so often does the resentment against the priests who took away the innocence of touching a child.

In the afternoon, as they amble back across the fields to the car park in the setting sun, he finds himself walking with Siobhan and Anthony. He has agreed to bring their wedding forward to three weeks today – the fifth Sunday of Lent.

'How are the wedding plans going?' he asks Siobhan.

'It's a bit rushed Father, to be honest,' she says, 'but you know, it's a learning experience too. It's made us stop and think, hasn't it Anthony?' Her young man nods. 'I was getting so caught up in it all – the dress, the catering, the guest list, the bridesmaids

– it goes on and on, sure it does. Then, when we discovered how sick Pappy is, and, you know, watching him dying slowly like this, and – and seeing how brave he is, and coping with Mammy being so anxious and all – well, and here's me worrying about what the bridesmaids are going to wear. It puts it all in perspective. I think – don't take this the wrong way – but I think I'm appreciating the meaning of getting married more, because the wedding day has suddenly become less important. That's what I told Anthony, didn't I, Anthony?' Anthony nods again.

John is familiar with these dynamics between young couples as their wedding day approaches. The brides are eager, talkative and increasingly anxious, while their fiancés go along with the whole thing in a bemused spirit of detachment tinged with irritation, as if wondering how they got into all this.

Marriage is like a foreign country he has studied closely and learned its language, but has never visited. Sometimes he asks himself if he would like to be married. He would enjoy the companionship and the sense of intimacy with another human being. But then thoughts of Luke always come creeping into his imagination and he seeks refuge in prayer, asking God to help him to live his vocation well and to accept the impossibility of those other fantasies and desires.

'… and maybe with a posy of yellow flowers which will look lovely against their lilac dresses, won't it Anthony?'

'Yes,' says the bridegroom without enthusiasm.

'And Anthony and the best man will have yellow buttonholes and lilac bow ties, and we'll pick up those colours in the church flowers too.' She pauses for breath. 'Anthony, did you remember to order the buttonholes like I asked you to?' she says.

'I'm going to do it on Monday,' he says.

'You haven't done it yet?' Her voice is irritated now.

'There's plenty of time,' he says mildly.

'No there's not darling. I keep telling you, everything is really urgent now because of bringing the date forward.' She forces a little laugh. 'Honestly Father, what would you do with him?' she says.

'Well, as you were saying Siobhan, the important thing is not the wedding day and the button holes but the beginning of your life together, and it's wonderful that your dad will be there to celebrate with you.'

'I hope so Father. Oh, I'm so afraid that he'll die or be in hospital and won't be able to be there. I don't know how Mammy would cope with that and then the wedding too.' She chokes up. Anthony puts his arm around her and she leans her head on his shoulder.

John deliberately slows his pace so that they walk on ahead of him. He watches their silhouettes wobble and blur in the jelly light of evening as they cut a swathe across the meadow, holding hands. It's easy to imagine angels ascending and descending on such beams of light. The demons cease their relentless clawing at his gut, and he lets the peace seep through him. 'Dear Jesus, please let Patrick live until after the wedding, and keep him well enough to be there. And please bless Siobhan and Anthony as they begin their life together.' Somewhere, the cardinal is laughing at the naivety of his prayers.

NINE

SECOND MONDAY OF LENT

He sits in the window and pulls the fraying blue ribbon to open his Missal and say the Office. The good weather has persisted, and the first flush of dawn is spreading over the garden.

He tries to focus, but his thoughts whisper back to the silken-tongued prelate with the hissing lisp who lectured on moral theology at the college in Rome. He was an austere conservative, condemning of all who advocated a more pastorally sensitive and forgiving approach to matters of sexuality and sin. Contraception, abortion, homosexuality, feminism, divorce, promiscuity – these were the molten core of sin and depravity around which the cardinal's brilliant mind prowled. He was so convincing in his arguments that many of the seminarians came to think like he did.

Cardinal Bradley was an aesthete, as were the young seminarians who hero-worshipped him. They liked to walk the streets of Rome in their white dog collars and black soutanes, slim and alluring. The cardinal was known for his elaborate vestments of red silk and white lace, his handmade red leather pumps, the *cappa magna* he wore at every opportunity, his retinue of beautiful young altar boys and his love of the Latin Mass. Those were the early years of the last papacy. It was a good time to be a gay seminarian in Rome.

Yet John remembers only the loneliness. There were gay groups aplenty, but the risk of being discovered made many of the new seminarians avoid disclosure. John was one of those who maintained his vows of celibacy. For his first year in Rome, he spoke to nobody about his sexuality, though he never doubted the recognition that he saw in the eyes of some other seminarians and priests. Sometimes it was a look of warmth and understanding, sometimes it was lascivious, occasionally it was predatory. At first he had been taken aback by the gay subculture beneath the surface of that ancient city. The looks in the streets, the whispered propositions, the seethe of male desire beneath the oblivion of the camera-toting tourists and pilgrims.

He was shy, a sheltered youth in an alien culture, struggling with the language and the people. Was he also disillusioned? He overheard things that disturbed him. References to cruising the parks and ruins of the city after dark. A conversation about male prostitutes between two newly ordained priests who hadn't realized that he was in the room next door. Rumours about senior members of the hierarchy and their sexual peccadillos. He can't remember how he coped with these discoveries. He suspects he just bracketed them out of his daily world, learning to accept them as another aspect of the strange environment that he had to adjust to and learn to accept.

He always wanted to be a priest. Growing up, he never brooded on his half-formed, barely acknowledged desire for other boys. His parents were liberal Catholics, part of a fashionable young group who met because they both attended the university chaplaincy during the heady days of Vatican II. When he was seventeen, his mother first brought up the subject of his being gay. He can remember almost every word of the conversation.

It was late at night. They were sitting in the living room of the house that Kate and her family now live in. His father was out and his mother had opened a bottle of wine. She had that flushed, bright-eyed look that wine gave her. He had never seen her drunk, but she became more vivacious and talkative after a few glasses of wine. The television was on, with a late night chat show burbling in the background.

'John darling, don't you think it's time you found a boyfriend?' she said, out of the blue.

His heart leapt against his ribcage. 'What do you mean?'

'Pour yourself a glass of wine. Let's talk about it.' He fetched a glass from the kitchen and poured himself some wine. She tucked her legs up beneath her skirt and turned to face him. They were sitting at either end of the plump and faded sofa that is still in the same place in Kate's living room.

His mother's dark hair had a few silvery streaks, and the skin around her eyes was becoming webbed with fine lines. She was a tall, handsome woman, more authoritative and in command of the family than her shorter, quieter husband. John had been blessed with good parents and a happy home.

He sat in silence, lost for words, torn between wanting to have that conversation with his mother and wanting to run away.

'Are you shocked that I know?' she said. He wanted to answer truthfully. He thought about her question. She waited.

'Know what?' he said. He wasn't being evasive. He wanted to know what she thought she knew, because maybe it would help him to come to some certainty about himself.

'That you're gay.' There. His mother had given it to him. The naming. The acceptance. And that was when he fully acknowledged for the first time that yes, he was gay. And almost simultaneously, he knew that there was something more important and more difficult to tell her. He said nothing.

'Have you ever, you know, tried things out, experimented?' she asked. Really, that was going too far. He felt himself blushing and shook his head. 'It's nothing to be ashamed of, you know that, don't you?' He nodded. 'What about girls? Do you ever feel any desire for a girlfriend?'

He liked girls. He had always preferred being with girls to being with boys of his own age. Had he ever desired any of them in that way? Sometimes there was a feeling, when the sun lit up a girl's hair in a particular way, or when a girl looked at him with that strange light in her eyes which told him she liked him, or when a soft touch awakened some quiet longing in his body. But no, he had never gone on to imagine what might happen beyond the moment, whereas sometimes, when it was a boy, he did.

He swallowed a mouthful of wine and met his mother's eyes. 'Yes, I'm gay, but I don't want a boyfriend.'

'Why not? You don't need to worry about us, you know. Your dad might take some time to get used to the idea, but we'd accept him just the way we accept Paul and Charlotte.' By that time, his brother Paul had been living with Charlotte for nearly a year. Kate was away at university, doing her degree in medicine. She wouldn't meet Chris until she was in her mid twenties.

'I want to be a priest.' There. He had said it for the first time, and he could see from his mother's face that she was shocked.

'A priest?'

'Yes.'

'You want to be ordained, to be celibate?'

'Yes.'

'Why?'

'I don't know, mum, but I know that I've always wanted that. It's more important to me than sex, than being gay. It's much more part of who I am.'

'Sweet Jesus Christ and Holy Mary Mother of God,' she said, lapsing into the kind of language her Irish grandmother might have used. She glugged at her wine. 'I don't think it's an easy life, you know John. Particularly not these days. They seem a bit lonely, the priests around here, and some of them seem quite disillusioned. The young ones are a bunch of misogynistic repressed gay homophobes, as far as I can work out. Is that what you're doing, John? Running away from yourself? Be careful John. It's no sin, you know, to be gay. It's the way God made you.

Don't you want to explore what that means – to be in love, to find somebody to spend the rest of your life with?'

He wanted to tell her, 'I'm in love with Jesus. I want to spend my life with him,' but his mother didn't use that kind of language, and he was afraid she might laugh at him.

A year later he joined a seminary with the grudging acceptance of his parents – though deep down, he suspects his father was relieved. His mother might think an openly gay son was preferable to her son becoming a priest, but there had been a glimmer of thankfulness in his father's eyes which suggested he did not share that opinion. In fact, though he was too reserved ever to say so, John thought that his father was proud of him, and that was a source of quiet, fierce joy to him. A few months later, after his preliminary assessments, the bishop sent him to study theology in Rome.

These are the memories that he revisits as the sun lifts over the city. His Missal sits neglected on his lap, open at the day's readings. He sees Shula going through her morning routine, stalking some invisible creature in the grass and then, bored with the chase, jumping up onto the bench to clean herself. He looks over to where the robin's nest is hidden in the branches of the tree, and wonders if Sarah is there. His world has become populated with ghostly visitors from other worlds – Sarah from an eternal paradise, the cardinal from the deepest realm of Dante's hell – not a sulphurous fire but a frozen lake of lovelessness and treachery.

His stomach cramps with fear. The steam. The heat. The smell. 'Ssssuck my cock.' 'Jesus, help me.' Who is he, this dead cardinal who is nothing like Sarah in his monstrous appearances and the solidity of his presence? This is no ghost. So who or what is it? John knows without doubt that he will reappear, that this is the beginning, not the end, of some malevolent plan unfolding with the precision of a genius mind at work.

He gives up on the Office and goes downstairs to make coffee. He switches on the radio. Another woman has been murdered in Westonville. Her body was found in woodlands near the river by a woman walking her dog.

'Earlier this morning, Detective Chief Superintendent Frank Lambert of Westonville's major criminal investigation unit spoke to reporters,' says the presenter.

'"Do you think this is the work of a serial killer?' a woman journalist asks.

'It's too early to say,' says the detective. Frank is Danny's father. John tries to hold on to the image of James Berkeley in the confessional, worried about stealing Danny's chocolate, but the horror unfolding on the radio claims all his attention.

'Are you saying you're going to wait until more women die?' the journalist asks aggressively.

'No. I'm saying that we can't be sure that both women were killed by the same person.'

'There are reports of similarities between the killings. Can you comment on that?' asks a different journalist, a man this time.

'We're waiting for the results of forensic tests,' says Frank.

'What advice would you give to women in Westonville?' asks another woman's voice.

'We're doing everything we can to catch the person or persons who did this,' says Frank. 'Until we do, we would urge all women to take extra care. Avoid being in dark places alone at night. Always make sure people know where you are and who you're with. We can't emphasise enough the danger of being alone with strange men.'

'Why are you assuming it's a man?' asks a male journalist, his voice betraying a hint of petulance.

'We're not assuming anything at this stage, but the reality is that, in murders like this, men are usually the perpetrators,' says Frank.

John switches off the radio with a deep sense of foreboding. The week stretches ahead of him. He feels like Sisyphus standing at the bottom of the mountain, with the boulder of dread, shame and responsibility threatening to crush him as he begins the weary task of pushing it up and up, up through the hours and the days and the weeks of Lent, towards – towards what? Crucifixion? Resurrection? Or simply a pile of bones in a stinking tomb, buried beneath the greatest deception in the history of the world?

TEN

SECOND WEDNESDAY
OF LENT

It's the monthly meeting of the parish pastoral council after the evening Mass. The plastic chairs are arranged in rows in the church hall, beneath the harsh glow of the fluorescent lights. Edith wants to replace the lights with something more attractive. The issue has come up at several pastoral councils, but no decision has been reached yet.

The metal chair legs scrape against the floor as parishioners shuffle in and take their seats. Jennifer Simpson is there, of course. Jennifer is always there, campaigning for the Justice and Peace Group. Jane's husband Pete is there, pregnant Jane of the fading frock and the tears for Jesus. Her husband is a thin, hollow-cheeked man with wire-rimmed glasses and a receding hairline. He walks with a slight stoop, as if defeated by the burden of living. He is a quiet man, supportive of the parish but reticent about whatever faith he may or may not have. He never comes to confession and rarely engages in conversation. John knows about him mainly through Jane's confessions, which arouse a sense of pity but also respect for the man's wounded dignity.

John is surprised when Frank Lambert walks in and finds himself a seat near the back. He doesn't usually come to these meetings, and surely he has more important things to do right now? He is a man whose affable demeanour doesn't quite conceal the steely determination of his character. He is lean and energetic with a smile intended to reassure and a bright, attentive gaze. Tonight, he looks tired and stressed, with grooves running down either side of his face from his nose to the corners of his mouth. John feels a deep sense of unease. Why is Frank here?

James Berkeley's mother Susan is there in her tight jeans and t-shirt, along with some of the other parents from the school. John wonders if Susan knows about her son's misdemeanour and his fear of being 'exported' by Frank. He suspects not.

Dorcas the headmistress has come with her husband Ignatius. She looks regal, towering head and shoulders over most of the other parishioners and greeting them with that dignified solemnity which commands such respect and trust. He suspects she is something of a mascot for the liberal-minded parents of the children in the school. Having a black headmistress is a badge of honour. For some, her Protestantism added to her credentials, but the fact that she is being received into the Church at the Easter vigil has reassured the bishop, who has been criticised by conservative Catholics in the diocese for allowing a Catholic school to have a Protestant head.

Edith is also there, of course, and Bonnie who runs the children's liturgy. Deacon Jack sits next to John at a table facing the people. He takes notes and chairs the meeting.

There's a desultory discussion about the recent repairs to the church roof. The leak in the Lady Chapel has been fixed and the ceiling has been repainted.

Dorcas announces that the school has once again received an outstanding report from its recent inspection. She delivers the news with her usual serious expression, but she finishes with a smile that briefly lights up the room. John thinks he has never seen anything quite so transformative as Dorcas's smile. There is a round of applause and murmurs of congratulations and thanks.

Jennifer stands up to report back from the Justice and Peace Group. She gives a list of statistics about the cost of bombing Syria, about the number of casualties, about the rising profits of the arms industry. She sounds accusing, as if her fellow parishioners were personally dropping the bombs and growing rich on the proceeds. She says the Justice and Peace Group is organising an online petition to stop the bombing and to allow more refugees into the country. 'I believe every parishioner has a moral duty to sign that petition and to help us to gather more signatures,' she says.

A hand goes up. It's Martin Blake, a retired solicitor. John knows what will happen next. Deacon Jack invites Martin to speak. He stands up portentously.

'I would ask Jennifer what she would do about Islamic State. Does she know what they're doing to people – torturing, murdering, raping? Should we really stand back and do nothing?'

Jennifer flushes. She is still standing, and they confront one another over the heads of the people. 'Dropping bombs on them isn't going to make things any better. You don't end violence by killing people. As followers of Jesus Christ, I don't believe we can ever justify war.'

'So you would have let Hitler conquer the world and totally annihilate the Jews, would you?' retorts Martin.

'We didn't go to war to protect the Jews. We would never have gone to war if Hitler hadn't invaded Poland. Anyway, we can't keep fighting wars just because we once defeated Hitler.'

Deacon Jack clears his throat. 'Um, these are very important issues, but I don't think we're going to solve them tonight, and we ought to get on.'

'Just one more thing,' says Jennifer, her voice shaking with emotion. 'Can I remind you all that we're hosting the annual interfaith service here next Wednesday evening? That will be instead of the Wednesday evening Mass. Father John has agreed.' John notes that she makes a small concession to her audience by calling him 'Father'. 'And we've invited our guests to stay for refreshments afterwards. Please make sure you support this important event. At times like these we need to show that we all worship one God and we are people of peace. And if you could bring along a plate of food, that would be helpful – sandwiches, cakes, that kind of thing. But please remember no pork products, no shellfish and no alcohol.'

Deacon Jonathan Mellors of the pro-life group puts up his hand. He is here on his own. Mary is presumably at home looking after all the children. Jonathan is a tall, sallow-faced man with a wispy beard. He wears a white badge with the red outline of a foetus attached to the lapel of his jacket.

John's heart is leaden. These meetings are a monthly endurance test, with all the same people saying all the same things, playing out the same squabbles over and over and over again.

'Yes Jonathan?' says Deacon Jack.

The man stands up. 'I want to register my concern about the cancellation of the Wednesday evening Mass. As Catholics we worship Jesus Christ. I don't think we should be praying to some interfaith God when we ought to be having the Holy Mass.' He has a high, reedy voice.

Jennifer stands up again. Her face is mottled now, and her eyes burn with indignation. 'People in this parish seem to think it's fine to bomb Muslims, but not to pray with them.' She swallows and takes a deep breath. 'And besides, I'd remind you that there's more to being pro-life than being anti-abortion. There's no point in caring about embryos if you care nothing for the people we kill and maim with our bombs, if you care nothing for the refugees starving on our borders.'

John senses Jack's helplessness. He decides it's time to intervene. 'Jennifer, thank you for your feedback from the Justice and Peace Group. I'm sure we're all very thankful for the work you do. Of course I understand that not all parishioners are entirely comfortable with us having an interfaith service, but there will be Mass as usual on Wednesday morning, and there's Mass up the road at Saints Felicity and Perpetua every evening. You know you'll be welcome there if you want to go to the evening Mass. I hope though that we'll have a good turnout for the interfaith service.'

Jennifer throws a furious glance at Jonathan and sits down. He remains standing. 'Perhaps while I'm on my feet I can give feedback from the pro-life group.'

'That's a good idea, Jonathan. Carry on.' Jack's voice is placid and friendly. John marvels at his composure. He has a sudden overwhelming sense of Jack's humble goodness, and he feels shoddy and tainted by comparison.

Jonathan clears his throat and gazes at his audience with a look of sombre intensity. 'A new abortion clinic is opening in Saint Peter's a week on Friday. It's no coincidence that it's in the red light district. It's intended to tempt prostitutes to have abortions if they get pregnant, rather than keeping their babies. Of course, the opening has been kept secret but we have sources who keep us informed. It's on Rowan Lane, just along from the Queen's Arms pub. Anybody who has driven down there at night will know that there are always prostitutes hanging around in that area. We're organising a protest outside on the day it opens. I hope some of you will come along and join the protest.'

Edith nods enthusiastically. 'Count me in Jonathan. You know I'll be there.'

Carol Pierce, mother of Lucy and Karen, stands up. She is a robust, no-nonsense woman. John likes her, though he wishes she hadn't decided to prolong this particular discussion.

'As a midwife I think I'm qualified to say something on this topic,' she says, her voice tight with indignation. 'If you care so much, you'd be better organising support for those sex workers and their children, born and unborn, rather than picketing the abortion clinic. I'm not sure you understand the reality of these women's lives. Have you ever seen what happens to newborn babies born to addicted mothers? Have you ever wondered what kind of lives those children will have, what kind of world they're born into? I agree with Jennifer on this. If you want to be pro-life, maybe you should care more about those who are already born and the kind of world they're born into. And if you must go hounding people with your anti-abortion placards, why not find the men responsible for the pregnancies and hold them accountable?'

'We can't just murder babies because we find them inconvenient,' says Jonathan sanctimoniously, and it strikes John how similar he is to Jennifer. They occupy opposite ends of the Catholic spectrum of moral principles, but they're alike in their unrelenting zeal for the causes they embrace. John is exhausted. He wishes the meeting would end.

It's Carol's turn to look furious. 'Jonathan, I've delivered babies and I've seen the products of early abortions and miscarriages. If you can't tell the difference between a blood clot and a human child, then actually you have no sense of moral responsibility whatsoever.'

'The Holy Father says that all life is sacred from the moment of conception to natural death. Just because it looks different from us doesn't mean it's not a sacred human life,' says Jonathan.

'When the Holy Father gets pregnant, he'll have some authority to speak on the subject. Until then, I respectfully suggest he shuts the fuck up.' There's an uncomfortable shuffling and even Carol looks taken aback. She knows she has gone too far. John feels a thrill of something that could be shock, or could be delight. He's not sure which. He wishes Holly were here. She would love this moment. He must remember to tell her.

'I'm shocked,' says Jonathan. 'I'm really shocked to hear you speak about the Holy Father in that way.'

'Well, okay, I'm sorry,' Carol concedes. 'But even so, there is no moment of conception. Conception is a process. It's bad science as well as bad ethics to go on about the moment of conception.' She glances over at the table. 'Sorry to get on my soap box,' she says to John and Deacon Jack, and sits down. She looks embarrassed. Unlike Jennifer and Jonathan, Carol doesn't usually air her views at parish meetings.

'No need to apologise,' says Jack. 'These are important issues. Bonnie, I think it's your turn to report back from the Children's Liturgy group.'

Bonnie is a sweet-faced young mother with a soft plump body and a gentle smile. But tonight, even Bonnie gives cause for dissent, by mentioning the First Communion group. Some questions have been raised about clothing. Some of the parents want to forbid the girls from wearing white dresses and veils. They think it's extravagant and inappropriate.

An interminable argument follows, with one side arguing passionately for ordinary clothes, and the other side – mainly made up of the Italian, Irish and Polish mothers and grandmothers – arguing just as passionately for bridal attire.

Jack allows it to go on until all the issues have been thoroughly aired, then he clears his throat and says benignly, 'Well, this is clearly an issue that people feel strongly about, but I've just noticed the time and I see that Edith and Sheila have gone off to make the tea, so unless there's any other business I think we should draw our meeting to a close. I'm sure you mums will all come to some agreement with Dorcas about the First Communion.'

John glances at Dorcas. She is sitting with her eyes lowered and her hands folded in her lap. At the sound of her name she glances up, but she looks distracted. 'Yes, we'll sort it out,' she says, but she seems far, far away. He wonders what's on her mind.

Thank God, no other hands go up. Edith and Sheila have set out tea and biscuits in the serving hatch to the kitchen. John has a cup of tea and does his best to engage with the people around him. He declines an invitation to join some of them in the parish club for a drink.

As he is leaving, Frank detaches himself from a group and comes to join him. 'I'm just leaving too,' he says, and John suspects he was deliberately waiting to have a moment alone together. He wonders why.

'I dread these parish council meetings,' says John, suddenly wanting an ally but also not wanting to ask about the murders. He is afraid to analyse the reasons for his reticence.

'Yes, as you know, I don't usually come to them,' says Frank. 'Tonight reminded me why not.'

As they make their way down the stairs towards the entrance, John decides he must mention the murders. Not to do so seems perverse, given that they're uppermost in so many people's minds. In fact, he is surprised that nobody brought them up this evening, as something that should in some way concern the parish.

'You must be busy,' he says, 'with these two murders.'

'Yes, I'm going back to the office on my way home,' says Frank. 'I need to see if there are any new developments. We've identified the second victim. She was also a sex worker. Her name was Sissy Jackson.'

'Poor women.' The words seem too feeble for such horror. He pushes open the doors that lead to the car park. 'Do you have any clues as to who might have done it?'

Frank seems cautious. 'We think it's the same person. There are certain features – I can't say too much, but we're trying to do a profile of the murderer. I'd rather you kept this to yourself for the time being, Father, but we think whoever he is, he knows quite a lot about Catholicism.'

John's world does a somersault. 'What makes you think that?' he says.

'There are certain features about the way he killed them that I can't disclose at the moment. Serial killers often have a signature theme. They do certain things, leave certain objects by the victims. It's the tension between needing to be completely unidentifiable if they're going to get away with it, and the desire for their handiwork to be seen and admired.'

John swallows. He realizes it doesn't matter if he sounds shaken and shocked. In fact, it would be suspicious if he didn't. 'Dear God Frank, is that what you're dealing with – a serial killer?'

'It looks like it, I'm afraid. If you ever have any clues or suspicions, Father, would you let me know? We're not placing too much emphasis on the Catholic angle at the moment – it's easy to become so obsessed with details which might just be coincidences that you lose sight of the bigger picture – but I thought I'd mention it to you just in case you come across anything that might be significant.'

'Such as? I mean, you know that priests can't break the seal of the confessional under any circumstances, so I can't make a promise that I couldn't keep, in the unthinkably remote possibility that this killer would come to confession.' Does he sound plausible? He hopes so.

'Yes, well, don't get me started on that, Father. I'll never understand a church that says it's better to let a person get away with abusing a child than to break some stupid religious rule. Anyway, aside from the confessional, you might hear gossip among priests. Maybe one of them is behaving strangely. Sometimes, we have to rely on nothing more than intuition, and you strike me as somebody who has an intuitive nature, Father.'

John feels as if the colour has drained from his face, and his knees feel weak. But that's a natural response, isn't it? 'I don't know what to say,' he says. 'I'm finding it hard to take it in.'

'I'm concerned that if we don't catch him soon, there will be more murders. Anyway, I'd better get back to work. Thanks for your time, Father.' He shakes John's hand and walks away to his car parked at the far end of the car park.

John turns and heads towards the gate that leads into the cemetery. There's a path that's a shortcut to the presbytery garden, and saves having to walk around the building to the front gate. He hears voices and music seeping out from the parish club. If it were not Lent he would be tempted to go in for a nightcap, but he would struggle to socialise in the mood he's in without a couple of drinks.

A full moon casts shadows across the car park. Frank drives away, and his brake lights blink ominously at John as he stops at the entrance to the main road. John's eyes are drawn as they always are to the innocent looking parking space on the left, near the white picket fence. He hears again that terrible howling, Holly tearing at her hair and her clothes and sending up such a lament that it will surely echo eternally through the skies. He closes his eyes and wishes he could switch off his thoughts, purge himself of all his memories and fears.

He pushes open the cemetery gate. The wooden crosses on the nuns' graves are stark in the moonlight, and the yew trees cast rippling shadows across the ground. A dark shape slinks across the path ahead of him, startling him until he realizes it's only Shula. They say it's bad luck for a black cat to cross your path – an omen of death or disaster. If so, Shula's constant presence must be a portent of terrible things to come. Normally that thought would amuse him. Tonight it terrifies him. He makes the small clicking sound that calls her to him, and she comes hurrying out of the shadows. He lifts her up and takes comfort from her warm, familiar shape in his arms. The path curves and he sees the angel on Sarah's grave glowing like a celestial visitor keeping watch over the sleeping child.

But Sarah isn't asleep. As he makes his way across the lawn to the presbytery, he senses her beneath the cherry tree, with its pale blossoms as ethereal as the angel on her grave. He wishes she would speak to him, that she would step forward from that moonlit horizon between now and forever, and become a body that could be touched and held.

There's a huddled shape on the porch. His heart lurches, but it's a familiar visitor – a cause for irritation perhaps but not for fear. He puts down the cat and gently shakes the shoulder of the man sleeping beneath a stinking grey blanket. 'Ben, wake up Ben.'

The man opens his eyes and peers at John. He has a woollen hat pulled low over his brow. He struggles to his elbows and the blanket slips down to reveal a shaggy grey beard and a torn pullover with the wool unravelling around his wrists. 'Hello Father,' he says.

'Hello Ben. What's the problem?' John notices a bottle of white cider beside him.

'They kicked me out of the shelter. They said I was being drunk and disorderly, but I'd only had a couple of drinks.' His voice slurs and he dribbles into his beard.

'Come on now Ben, tell me the truth.'

'Well, alright Father, more than a couple. But the fact that I'm drunk doesn't mean I don't need a bed. I don't stop being human just because I'm drunk, do I? I still need somewhere to sleep and a roof over my head, no matter how drunk I am. It's a human right. It's about my human dignity, Father. I'm still a man made in the image of God. I'm still a child of the living God. Does Jesus not love me, Father? Does Jesus not love the prostitute and the tax collector and the sinner?' The words slur and blur and collide into each other. Ben sometimes comes to Mass and sits at the back of the church. He does a good line in soliloquies stitched together from snatches of homilies he has heard over the years. He struggles to sit up, and the reek of his unwashed body blasts John's senses.

'You need a bath Ben,' John says.

'That's what I told them. I need a bath and a bed, but they wouldn't listen.'

'Okay, come on then, but just for tonight. Tomorrow I'll ring them and ask them if you can come back, but you have to promise you'll stay off the booze, alright?' These promises have been made and broken more often than John can remember.

'Of course Father. You know I don't drink much. I just like the odd drink to take my mind off things. I have a hard life. I get depressed sometimes. My life is a vale of tears Father. I'm a man of sorrows, Father, like our Lord. A man of sorrows, that's me. I walk with Jesus every day. Who would begrudge a man like me the solace of the occasional drink?'

John takes his arm and helps him to his feet. Ben sways beside him as he opens the door. 'I think we'll leave the blanket and the bottle outside,' John says.

'Can't I bring my drink in with me?'

'No, Ben, you've had more than enough already.'

'You're a hard man Father.'

There's a small bedroom with an adjoining bathroom downstairs. It used to be the housekeeper's office, but John insisted they turn it into a guest room and the storage cupboard next door into a bathroom. Edith was appalled when she discovered the real reason he wanted a second guest room. There was already a large room upstairs, with an en suite bathroom, for visitors.

'Father, this place stinks to high heaven,' she said, the first time he let a homeless person stay over. 'You can't let vagrants and tramps sleep in the presbytery. Every drunk in town will get to hear of it, and you'll have queues of them on the doorstep every night.'

In fact, he has learned to say no often enough to discourage most of them. There are just a few regulars, like Ben, who sometimes appear and hope to be let in for the night. If he doesn't open the door, they sleep on the porch and leave in the morning.

He runs a deep, hot bath and helps the old man out of his clothes and into the bath. His heart aches for the mottled flesh, the bloated belly and thin arms and legs, the genitals hanging forlornly between emaciated thighs, the buttocks sagging over the pelvic bones. Ben is drinking himself to death.

He washes him as he would wash a baby, carefully sponging the grime from the folds of his skin, shampooing his hair and soaping his tangled beard. When he's finished, he wraps him in a large clean towel and dries him, then he gives him a clean pair of pyjamas and tucks him into the single bed with its freshly laundered sheets.

Ben is still grumbling about his bottle of cider and the sorrows of life. John sits in the small chair in a corner of the room and waits until he's snoring loudly. Once he's sure Ben is asleep, he bundles up the clothes in the bathroom and puts them in a bin bag, then he goes out to the porch and puts the stinking blanket and the bottle of cider into the bag as well and throws everything into the dustbin. He will give Ben a clean set of clothes and a freshly washed blanket in the morning. The parishioners know he collects clothes and blankets to give to the homeless. Even the ones who disapprove tend to be generous in their giving. They have their differences and disagreements, and these parish meetings can be an endurance test, but at heart they're good people and he loves living among them.

He pauses on the step to look once more at the high full moon shining down on the shadowed graves, its light congealing around the figure beneath the cherry tree, then he goes inside and locks the door behind him. He is glad to have somebody else in the presbytery tonight, even if it is just a dying old tramp – or perhaps especially because it's a dying old tramp. To reach out to a vulnerable human being, to care for a suffering body, helps to purge some of the guilt that's creeping in from the banished and negated hinterland of memory, dragged out of oblivion by the cardinal.

ELEVEN

SECOND THURSDAY OF LENT

John has taken his missal downstairs to the kitchen, because he wants to be there when Ben wakes up in case he's disorientated and needs to be reminded of where he is. He has laid out clean clothes in the bedroom. The underpants and socks are new, but the trousers, shirt and pullover belonged to Deacon Jack, who donated a wardrobe full of clothes he had hardly ever worn to John's supply.

'Penny made me buy all these things,' he said, laughing in a way that wasn't as easy as he pretended. 'She always wanted me to look smart. She said I was her beau. You remember, Father, never a day went by when she didn't put on lipstick and make herself look nice. Even when she was just doing the garden, she always wore her lipstick.' There was a long, sad pause. 'Not much point in me looking like a beau these days, is there Father?'

John teased him, because humour was their stock in trade and made it possible to carry the weight of love and sorrow that each in his different way shared and understood. 'I keep telling you Jack, Edith would marry you tomorrow. I think she's head over heels in love with you.'

'Get away, John. You and your parish romances!'

It's a conversation that plays out time and again, with variations on the words but always with the same theme. John knows that he only risks such jokes because Edith never comes to confession. If she had ever once confessed her love for Jack, he would never mention it in any context, however light-hearted.

He opens the kitchen door to look out at the garden as he waits for the kettle to boil. The dawn chorus is starting up, and in the half-light he sees the robin returning to her nest with something in her beak. Her chicks must have hatched. There's no sign of Sarah. Perhaps the light has already bleached away her elusive presence.

Ben appears in the kitchen, transformed in his clean clothes and bearing himself with an aura of dignity that makes John's heart ache.

'Good morning Father,' he says.

'Good morning Ben. Tea and toast?'

'Yes please Father.'

'How did you sleep?'

'Like a baby. I slept the sleep of the just, Father. I always do.'

John makes the tea strong, the way Ben likes it, and spreads a thick layer of butter and jam on the toast. He sits at the table opposite Ben and drinks his coffee.

'So what are you doing today, Father?' asks Ben.

'Saying Mass, visiting parishioners, going to a meeting, then having a quiet evening I hope. How about you Ben?' He watches Ben's face, knowing it's an impossible question to answer. How does Ben fill his days? What goes through his mind as he sits there contemplating the emptiness ahead? John feels helpless. He wishes he could offer something more substantial than tea and toast and a brief conversation.

'I'll keep myself occupied,' says Ben. 'I might go to the nuns' drop-in place for lunch – you know the one, down in Saint Peter's.'

'Will you try to stay off the booze Ben?'

'Of course Father. You know me. I'm not a drinker. I just have the odd little tipple now and again.' He avoids meeting John's eyes. 'Father, would you mind putting the wireless on? I'd like to listen to the news.'

John switches on the radio. The recession is deepening. A senior cabinet minister has resigned after being accused of inappropriately touching a young parliamentary intern. The item that John dreads is third.

> *Police in Westonville are continuing their investigation into the murders of two women. The second victim has been identified as seventeen year old Sissy Jackson. Jackson grew up in Manchester and moved to Westonville last year. She had a troubled background and was in the care of the local authorities, who say they lost track of her whereabouts when she ran away from her foster home in March last year. She was believed to be working in the sex trade.*

Ben shakes his head and sighs. 'She was a sweet girl, Sissy,' he says. 'She was just a kid. Who would do that to a homeless teenager?'

'You knew her?' John can't keep the surprise from his voice.

'Of course I knew her. I know all the girls down in Saint Peter's. We're the people of the streets, Father. We're the invisible people of the city. Nobody notices us, until something like this happens. But we stick together, Father. We look out for each other.'

John feels ashamed. He has never really noticed the prostitutes down in Saint Peter's. He has never thought about the lives of the women standing on street corners and sashaying down the side roads, occasionally making eye contact as he drives past. He thinks of Sister Gertrude and the sisters who run the outreach project for the people of the streets. He admires their work from afar, but it strikes him that he has never asked about the people they work among, the stories they hear and the lives they're involved with.

Somebody from social services in Manchester is being interviewed. The interviewer is asking her how it's possible for a sixteen year old girl simply to disappear when she is supposed to be in their care. The interviewee is defensive. She talks about cuts to public spending and staff shortages, about the rise in the number of young people in care with fewer and fewer resources.

Ben shakes his head. 'They're scared, I'll tell you that Father. Those girls out there, they know they're vulnerable. Already there's talk about a serial killer.'

John wants to escape. He looks at his watch. 'I need to go and get ready to say Mass Ben. Do you want to come?'

'I'll think about it Father. I might see you in there.'

John is glad he's had a bath and a change of clothes. Sometimes Ben appears off the streets to sit in the back of the church during Mass, and the parishioners complain about the way he smells. Today he looks and smells just like the rest of them. That's how easy it is for a person to cross the threshold between the human and the inhuman, between the wilderness and society. A bath, a good night's sleep and a change of clothes. That's all it takes.

But Ben has his own society. He said it himself. The society of the invisible people of the streets, where prostitutes and homeless alcoholics and drug addicts look out for each other, far from this comfortable middle class parish with its self-proclaimed Christians salving their souls.

Dear God. What cynicism. Where did that thought come from? He crosses himself as he goes upstairs to his bedroom, and asks for God's forgiveness. He vows that he will begin to take note, to see what he hasn't seen before, to make visible – at least to himself – those he has been too blind to see and too indifferent to care about.

TWELVE

SECOND FRIDAY OF LENT

His mobile phone wakes him at half past five on Friday morning. It's Sister Martha. Sister Gertrude has had a stroke and has been taken to hospital by ambulance. Sister Martha is sitting with her. Will Father John go and see her?

He drives through the streets of the city, deserted except for a few shopkeepers opening up for the early morning trade. He has to drive through Saint Peter's to get to the hospital. He notices a few women hovering in doorways or standing on street corners. Why are they out so early in the morning? Maybe men stop by for sex on their way to work.

He tries to imagine these women's lives. What must it be like to sell your body to passers by? These are the people Ben was talking about. Saint Augustine compared prostitutes in a city to sewers in a palace. Take them away, and the place would be overrun by filth.

He has an urge to stop and engage one of them in conversation. He wonders if they are afraid. What desperation would drive them onto the streets when there's a serial killer about? He pushes the thought away and heads for one of the side roads near the hospital to look for a parking space.

He parks on a steep hill overlooking the city, its contours softened by an early morning mist tinged pink and lilac by the dawn. It looks like a place of dreams and spirits, with all the human dramas of the night submerged beneath the rising tide of morning light. It doesn't look like a place where people loved and battled through darkness, where babies were born and old people died, where lovers whispered and mothers sang lullabies and embittered couples cursed and fought, where people lay alone clutching for consolation and hope as their waking nightmares invaded their sleep, where a killer prowled the streets looking for his next victim. If God looks down from heaven it must be so easy to remain indifferent to the sorrows of life, to see only what the camouflage of distance offers up to the divine gaze.

He makes his way up in the lift to the fifth floor and through the familiar corridors of the hospital until a nurse directs him to a small private side ward. Sister Gertrude is lying on a bed covered with a white blanket, with tubes coming out of her body and an oxygen mask over her mouth and nose. Sister Martha is sitting on a chair beside her. The old nun's breathing is harsh and ragged. Her white hair straggles around her face, with her pink scalp showing through. He has never seen her without her veil before. Her chin sags and her eyes have sunk into their sockets, as if her skeleton is already pushing through its fragile covering of flesh.

'Gertrude, Father John is here,' says Sister Martha. 'He's come to visit you. He's going to anoint you and pray for you.' Her voice is tender. John understands. He too has often sat with the dying, and he knows that even when someone appears deeply unconscious, their sense of hearing can still function.

He speaks gently, trying to put all the affection and respect he feels for the old nun into his voice. 'Good morning Gertrude. It's a beautiful morning out there.' He rests his hand on the gnarled old hand on top of the blanket, carefully avoiding the needle and tube coming out of a bulging blue vein. A nurse comes in and pulls up a chair for him. Her name is Anne. He recognises her from previous visits to the hospital.

'Hello Father John,' she says. 'It's early for you to be out and about.' She shifts her attention to the old woman on the bed.

'How are we doing, Sister Gertrude? We'll take good care of you here. Father John will tell you. You'll get five star treatment with us, won't she Father John?'

'Absolutely. It's the best care in town,' he says. He means it. During his many visits to see sick and dying patients in this hospital, he has been overwhelmed by the dedication and compassion of the nursing staff. However stressed and over-worked they are, he has rarely seen them treating a sick patient or a grieving relative with anything other than patience and kindness.

The nurse leaves and John takes out his stole and his anointing oils. He lays his hand on Gertrude's forehead. Her skin feels papery beneath his palm. He anoints her forehead and hands and prays for the Lord to bless her and heal her in body and soul, to make her firm in faith and serene in hope. He pauses to speak to the nurse on his way out. She tells him that Sister Gertrude's heartbeat is irregular and her pulse is weak. It's always hard to predict what will happen when a person has a stroke, but the consultant thinks that Gertrude might not regain consciousness. John hopes the end will come quickly, that she won't linger in a twilight zone between the living and the dead, or recover just enough to continue her half-life of frailty and dementia.

He drives back through the waking city to the presbytery, choosing a different route this time to avoid the red light district.

There are a few people waiting when he goes to hear confessions before Mass. Already in the second week of Lent people's resolve is waning – weekly confessions, daily Mass attendance, giving up alcohol or chocolate, going to the gym – all the good intentions dissolving in the apathy of everyday life.

He hears the last confession and resists the urge to leave at once in case the cardinal arrives. It's half an hour until Mass begins, and it's not just the cardinal who sometimes comes late. Often, people arrive at the last minute to make a hurried confession before Mass, bringing with them a burden that they have carried for years and have struggled to confess. It's those who arrive late and leave too little time for a good confession who are often most in need of the sacrament, and who have had to battle hardest with themselves to go to confession at all.

The minutes crawl past. He tries to distract himself, letting his mind drift over random images and thoughts. Sister Gertrude in her hospital bed. The interfaith service next week. Kate and the children. Thinking of them holds his attention for a short time, giving him a brief sense of security and warmth, but his mind strains against the leash and he can't stop it from returning to the brooding fear that has become a perpetual undertow in his soul.

As the days have gone by, the cardinal's silence has become a daily torment. Every day, John wakes up thinking that this is the day that he will reappear, and every day his absence screams inside John's head with an unrelenting persistence that feels like a physical ache.

He tries to focus on his daily prayers and to immerse himself in the routines of the parish. He says Mass with a dedicated intensity, seeking refuge in its mystery and telling himself that the emptiness he feels is a manifestation of the divine abyss. He holds the warm body of Shula to his face in the long hours of the night and tries to lose himself in that velvety darkness. He resists searching online for the cardinal's name, and he refuses to dwell on the horror of the murdered prostitutes sending ripples of alarm through the city and haunting John with some terrible intuition.

There are no latecomers to the confessional, and the cardinal does not appear. John says the school Mass and deals with some parish admin work before setting out to visit parishioners and to chair a meeting of the school governors. Bonnie has invited him to join them for supper after the governors' meeting, and he is glad of the distracting normality of her home. People are wrong when they think the ordinary is common and dull, for in fact it is rare and beautiful. Few people have the physical and emotional well-being to live ordinary lives, and the grace to know that they are blessed in their ordinariness.

After supper, John leaves to walk the short distance to the presbytery. Bonnie and her husband Michael stand waving at the door, Bonnie holding their three month old baby and Michael with three year old Susie perched on his hip.

John walks up the garden path, avoiding the tangle of brambles and dandelions spilling over from neglected flower beds. He knows so many families with tidy houses and neatly tended gardens who live stressed and restless lives. He wishes they could learn from Bonnie about what really matters.

It's not even eight o'clock yet. The evening stretches ahead. There are emails he ought to answer, and he has to look at the parish accounts. He ought to go through the readings for Sunday's Mass, and begin thinking about his homily. He sits down at his desk and opens his laptop. He skims through the unread emails in his Inbox.

There's one from Fiona, mother of Amy and Beth, explaining why she does not want Amy to dress up like a bride for her first communion. It runs to several paragraphs, a rambling mix of self-justification and complaint that he can't bring himself to read properly. There's another from Jennifer, about the order of service for next week's interfaith service. She hopes the parish will support it. Please would he make sure he announces it at all the Masses on Sunday? He makes a note to remind himself, fearing Jennifer's wrath if he forgets. He hopes it's in the parish bulletin. He scrolls down to Edith's regular Friday evening email attaching the weekly bulletin and clicks to open the file. Yes, it's there, along with news of a cake sale to raise funds for SPUC, a fund-raising appeal for the HCPT pilgrimage to Lourdes the week after Easter, an announcement about the diocesan pilgrimage to Walsingham, and a reminder that donations for the food bank can be left in the box at the back of the church.

He closes his laptop and goes to sit in the chair by the window in the bedroom, opening his Missal at Sunday's readings. The Old Testament reading is the story of Moses and the burning bush. 'And God said to Moses, "I Am who I Am."' He has a vague recollection of having read this before during Lent, so that it feels like a reverberation arcing across the days. Aquinas come to mind again. He tries to remember some of the lectures, but that brings thoughts of the cardinal too close, so he pushes aside the memories and focuses on the Gospel reading. It's from Luke's Gospel. Jesus tells his disciples, 'unless you repent, you will all perish'. John quails at the harshness of the words. He reads the parable of the fig tree that bore no fruit. 'Sir, leave it one more year and give me time to dig round it and manure it: if may bear fruit next year; if not, then you can cut it down.'

He closes the Missal and stands to look out at the garden. The cherry tree is shedding its blossoms and putting out fresh green leaves. There is no sign of Sarah. The garden seems forsaken without her. He hopes the robin and her chicks are alright, and wonders where Shula is. He has never told Holly about Sarah's appearances. Would it comfort her, or would it only intensify her distress?

He turns away and goes back to his desk in the study, but he feels restless and unable to concentrate. There's no point in trying to work on his homily tonight. He is defeated by the readings, unable to rescue Jesus from the mire of punishment and destruction to offer his parishioners a message of tenderness and mercy.

He wonders how Sister Gertrude is, and decides he will go and visit her. He won't take the car. It's a half hour walk to the hospital, and he needs some fresh air.

He puts on his waterproof anorak and walks through a light drizzle to the hospital. Sister Gertrude's breathing is laboured, but she seems at peace. Sister Margaret is with her. Margaret is the most senior of the sisters – in the old, hierarchical days, she would have been the Mother Superior. She was the headmistress of a Catholic sixth form college in London before she retired and moved to the house in Westonville. Now she volunteers at the drop-in in Saint Peter's and exercises a benign regime of order, discipline and hospitality in the house which is not nearly institutionalised enough to be called a convent.

He sits with Sister Margaret at Gertrude's bedside and the nurse on duty brings them tea and cake. They say Compline because Margaret says that it will comfort Sister Gertrude if she can hear them:

> *Lord my God, I call for help by day.*
> *I cry at night before you.*

It's a dark psalm, full of anguish and foreboding.

> *For my soul is filled with evils;*
> *My life is on the brink of the grave.*

The words melt and flow to the rhythmic whuffle and gasp of the old nun's breath. He hopes that death is coming towards Gertrude more gently than the fearful darkness confronting the psalmist. As they say the *Nunc Dimittis*, he prays that God will be gentle with her, and that she will indeed go in peace, according to His promise.

He hadn't intended to turn off into the side streets of Saint Peter's, but that's where he finds himself as he walks back to the presbytery. The weather has cleared, and the air feels clean and cold on his face. A starry sky spangles above the city. The narrow cobbled roads and the wet pavements glisten with the reflected orange glow of the streetlights. A woman walks towards him, head down, hands thrust in the pockets of her quilted jacket. As she becomes aware of him, she raises her head and meets his eyes. She shows her teeth in what is perhaps intended to be a seductive smile, but it makes her face look like a skull. Her teeth are yellow. She has sunken cheeks and bruises of exhaustion beneath her eyes. Her dark hair hangs long and greasy about her face.

'Nice man. Want good blow job? Me got deep throat. Want fuck? Me got good tight cunt. Thirty pounds with condom. For fifty pounds, no condom.'

Holy Mary Mother of God. 'No. No, I don't want sex.'

'Okay. For you, thirty pounds no condom. You nice man. Handsome man.' She sounds eastern European.

'No. No sex.' He waves his hands and shakes his head to try to make her understand. 'But it's dangerous. You shouldn't be out here. Go home.'

'Sorry? No speak English. Nice cunt. Deep throat. You want fuck? Suck? Up the bum? I do up the bum if you like. Tight arse.'

Sssuck my cock. No. No. Don't think about it. Forget it. He feels helpless as he hurries away from the woman, wondering what her story is, wondering who taught her those few terrible words so that she could sell her body to men whose language she does not speak.

Another woman calls to him from a doorway on the other side of the street. 'Thirty quid for a blow job.' He glances over at her. She's wearing a short skirt and high heeled platform shoes that emphasise the thinness of her legs. She has on a black jacket which is unbuttoned to show her low-cut top. Isn't she cold?

His instinct is to look away and hurry on, but something draws him to her. He crosses the road. She smiles as he approaches, and there's a dark gap where one of her front teeth should be, framed in the scarlet gash of her lips. Her hair is dyed jet black, which emphasises the sallowness of her face. He thinks she must be in her forties or maybe even her fifties – or is she just a ravaged thirty year old worn down by life? She drags on the cigarette she's holding and looks him up and down, blowing smoke in his face before she speaks. He resists the urge to turn away.

'Blow job thirty quid. Hand job twenty. Full sex forty and you must wear a condom,' she says. 'Funny business by negotiation.'

'Don't you know it's dangerous to be out here on your own?' he says.

Fear flickers across her face. 'What's it to you?' she says. 'I know how to look after myself, so don't try anything.'

'I'm not going to hurt you,' he says. 'I'm a priest.' What on earth made him say that?

'Jesus Christ,' she says. 'You think that makes it better? Some of the girls think it's a priest that's doing it.'

'Doing what?' Stupid question.

'Murdering those girls.'

The pavement tilts beneath him. 'Why do they think that?'

'Because of what he does to their bodies. Weird things. Pervy Catholic things. Lots of us girls out here were brought up Catholic. We know all about that stuff. All those fucking virgin martyrs dying for Jesus. Christ. It fucks you up, I'll tell you that.'

'Have you spoken to the police about this?'

'We don't encourage the pigs to hang around us,' she says. 'They scare the punters away.' She drags on her cigarette again. 'What's your name?' she says.

'John.' Why did he tell her his real name? What's wrong with him? 'And yours?'

'Barbara. Call me Babbs.'

'You should tell the police everything you know, Babbs. For your own good. They've got to find whoever's doing this.' He hardly dares to ask, but he has to know. 'These – these things he does – how do you know?'

'One of the girls has a pig as one of her regulars. He says the police aren't telling people the details, but they think it's some Catholic nutter because of what he does to them. Jesus, the fucking church is full of fucking paedos and pervs. Us girls could've told them that years ago.'

His forehead is clammy and his hands are shaking. He thinks he might faint.

'Are you alright?' she says. 'You don't look well.'

'I'm fine,' he says, though he knows he's not.

She nods. 'It's an occupational hazard, Father. Murder. Rape. We ought to be insured.' She laughs. There's a stale, unwashed smell seeping off her body. She grinds her cigarette out beneath her heel. 'Anyway my lover, thanks for the concern, but I've got to earn some money. If you want sex, say so. I don't mind that you're a priest. I've done priests before, though I hope not that perverted bastard. If you don't want sex, fuck off. No punter's gonna stop while you're standing there. I'll give you a discount if you hurry up about it.' There's no animosity in her voice, just weary resignation tinged with kindness.

'I don't want anything from you. It's not about that. I just – I saw you and I wanted to warn you.'

'Thanks my lover, but I'm a big girl, and anyway, like I said, I need the money. Now, nice speaking to you, Father John, but goodnight.' She turns and walks away. She pauses and calls back over her shoulder. 'Thanks for the chat. You're a kind man.' She waves and continues on her way.

He stands beneath the streetlight, watching her go. She totters on her spindly legs and ungainly shoes. As he watches, a blue car draws up alongside the kerb. She bends down and speaks to the driver through his open window, then she totters around and climbs into the passenger seat.

'Dear Jesus, look after her. Keep her safe,' he says. As the car disappears around a bend, he thinks he should have taken the registration number.

He walks on, and an awful foreboding bears down upon him – something monstrous beyond conscious thought. He doesn't want to follow where it might lead, so he tries desperately to empty his mind of mutilated bodies and murderous acts.

He turns a corner into Rowan Lane, a narrow cobbled road with fashionable shops, restaurants and pubs, which draws a certain kind of bohemian glamour from its shabby surroundings. He walks past the Queen's Arms, a well-known gay bar. It has pink walls and a rainbow flag hanging outside. Light spills warmly through the windows, and inside he sees men clustered around the bar and sitting at tables, talking, laughing, luring him in. There are a few women too. It looks welcoming, a haven away from the horrors of the streets. He walks past. He remembers what Jonathan Mellors said about the new abortion clinic being near the Queen's Arms, and wonders where it is. All the doors look equally anonymous. It could be any one of them.

In a restaurant a little further along the lane, he sees couples and groups sitting at tables, eating and drinking, not knowing or not caring that it's Lent. He wonders what it would feel like to be so indifferent, so free from the incessant and impossible demands of God.

He is lonely and afraid. The isolation presses in on him from all sides, surging towards him from the closed and shuttered shops and the empty road with its parked cars and puddled pavements. He turns back. Ignoring the warnings screeching in his brain, he pushes open the pub door and steps inside.

The warm air enfolds him, thick with conversation and laughter. He refuses to let his anxiety crowd out the sudden longing to be part of whatever this is.

He makes his way to the bar. The barman has an elaborate Mohican streaked scarlet and blonde, and a tight green vest that shows off his tattooed arms.

He licks his lips and gives John a look that would be lecherous, were it not so good humoured. 'What's your preference?' he says.

John hesitates. 'Umm, a lemonade please.'

'Takes all sorts,' says the man.

As he pays and picks up his drink, John wonders what to do next. Should he go and sit at a table? Should he stand alone at the bar? What on earth is he doing in here? He begins to panic. Is he out of his mind? What if somebody sees him? He puts his lemonade down on the counter and is about to turn and walk out, when he feels a hand on his shoulder.

'Hello John. This is a surprise, I must say.' It's Luke. He doesn't need to look round. He knows that voice so well. He turns, and Luke is smiling at him. He smiles back.

'I'm not sure what I'm doing here,' he says.

'Are you on your own?'

'Yes, I am.'

'I'll join you.' Luke summons the barman and orders a glass of wine.

They sit side by side on bar stools, drinking and chatting. Their conversation is careful, feeling for boundaries and possibilities. It's as if they're dancing clumsily together, trying to keep to the rhythm of the music while not standing on one another's toes.

'I've never seen you in here before,' says Luke.

'I've never been in here before.'

'So why tonight?'

'I was walking past. I've been visiting at the hospital and decided to walk instead of taking the car. I took a detour.'

Luke nods but doesn't say anything. He is gazing at John. John looks away.

'I've been troubled by the murders. I felt – I know it sounds stupid – but I felt I wanted to warn the women to stay indoors,' John says.

'I think we're all a bit worked up and nervous about that,' says Luke. 'Some of them come in here occasionally. Queers and whores – we're all on the wrong side of the fence, no matter what they tell you to the contrary,' he says.

It's John's turn to nod without saying anything. He drains his glass.

'Let me buy you another drink,' says Luke. 'What are you drinking?'

'Lemonade please.'

'Lemonade?!'

John feels embarrassed. 'It's Lent,' he says.

Luke laughs. It's an affectionate laugh, loving and warm. 'Jesus John, you really are a wonderful priest. You are the holiest man I know. Have a glass of wine, for Christ's sake. One glass will hardly send you to hell. You can always go to confession.'

He's smiling. His gaze is tender on John's face, and candid in its desire. It would be so easy. A glass of wine, and then what? Another. And another. Until? Until what? What next?

'Sorry Luke,' he says. 'I've changed my mind. I have to go.'

'Don't go, John.'

'I must. I have to hear confessions and say Mass in the morning. I have to prepare my homily for Sunday.' He dreads Luke trying to persuade him. His willpower hangs by a thread.

But Luke nods and smiles knowingly. 'Okay. I come in here often John. Most nights in fact. I hope it's not the last time we do this.'

'Thanks Luke. We'll see. I shouldn't be in here, but it was good to see you.'

THIRTEEN

THIRD WEDNESDAY OF LENT

Saturday blends into Sunday and Monday and Tuesday. At first the city seems to be holding its breath, but as the days pass with no news of another murder, it seems to relax. John senses a mood of relief tinged with disappointment. Deep down, people were enjoying the drama, with an atavistic appetite for violence and death so long as it happens to somebody else. Otherwise, how would Hollywood survive? How would they ever sell newspapers?

John's days are stitched together along the ragged edges of restless nights. His sleep is punctuated with unsettling dreams that make no sense when he wakes up. He is trying to run away from some dark force, but his legs won't move. He looks in a mirror, and sees only an infinitely receding tunnel of half-formed images. He wanders through a cavernous and desolate car park, trying to remember where he left his car. Each time, he awakes and reaches for Shula, holding her close to blot out the fear.

Sister Gertrude lingers on. He drives when he does his hospital visits, to avoid the temptation of making a detour through Saint Peter's.

On Wednesday evening, the parish stalwarts gather dutifully for the interfaith service. It's a good turnout. Maybe they are all a little afraid of Jennifer.

There are a few parishioners from the nearby Anglican and Methodist churches, and the local Quakers are there in force, consisting mainly of elderly grey-haired women with short fringes and sensible shoes. Three women from the local Bahai community bring musical instruments and do some chanting during the service. A Muslim girl in a hijab does a reading from the Qur'an. She seems to be the only Muslim there. Jennifer reads a reflection about peace and love and everybody believing in the same God. She tags on a Native American prayer at the end. There are some inspirational songs and more prayers that carefully avoid any reference to Jesus as Lord or to the Holy Trinity, and that avoid using any masculine pronouns for the Almighty. John thinks the service is bland and characterless, but he's glad that it seems to be going well. Jennifer might be a bit difficult, but she works hard for what she believes in, and he wants her to feel supported by the parish.

Afterwards, they serve tea, soft drinks and sandwiches in the parish hall. There are some cream cakes and a bowl of trifle at the end of the table, with a pile of dishes and spoons. John has a brief conversation with Jacob Latimer, a member of the liberal synagogue who has been involved in interfaith work for many years. He goes to talk to the Muslim girl and discovers that she's a student at Saint Catherine's, the nearby Catholic sixth form college. Her name is Salima. The head asked her to come and do a reading.

As the last stragglers depart he thinks he ought to help with the clearing up. He carries a pile of cups into the kitchen to discover Edith and Jennifer confronting each other by the sink. Jennifer's mouth is tight with disapproval. Edith looks indignant.

'There's no need to be like that,' she says, 'It was just a drop of sherry.'

'A drop of sherry? It's alcohol Edith!' Jennifer emphasises each syllable of the word 'alcohol'. AL-CO-HOL! Her voice is quavering with suppressed rage. She pushes her hand angrily through her hair. 'I was so careful to explain that we mustn't have any pork or alcohol! I give up. Honestly, I give up on this parish. I do my best but I just don't think things will ever change.'

John knows it's too late to escape. He goes over and tries to mediate. 'Oh dear ladies, this doesn't sound too good. What's the problem?'

'Edith brought a sherry trifle as her contribution to the food. Honestly, can you believe it? I'm so upset,' says Jennifer, which seems to be stating the obvious. 'And I'm not a "lady",' she says, scowling at him.

'I was only trying to help Father,' says Edith. 'I don't think a sherry trifle counts as alcohol anyway. It's a pudding, not a drink.'

'These mistakes happen, and I'm sure you meant well Edith. I had some of the trifle. It was delicious. And there was lots of other food,' he says.

'That's not the point, John,' says Jennifer. 'The point is that we offended our Muslim guests by serving alcohol. Devout Muslims aren't even meant to be in the same room as alcohol.'

'As far as I could see, there was only one Moslem there and that was Salima from Saint Catherine's College,' says Edith. 'She doesn't usually dress up like that. I've seen her in here on a Friday night in jeans and a t-shirt drinking beer with some of the other young people.'

'That's not the point,' says Jennifer again, 'It's the principle.' She shakes her head and glares at Edith. 'Anyway, I have better things to do than to stand here and argue about a stupid trifle,' she says, and flounces away.

'That woman is impossible Father,' says Edith. 'I don't know how you put up with her. Besides, if these Moslems want to live in our country, they ought to do things our way. Otherwise, they should go back home.'

John thinks he ought to object – from her accent, he suspects Salima was born and raised in Birmingham – but it's easier to placate Edith than to argue with her. He wishes the stragglers good night and returns to the lonely hauntings of the presbytery.

FOURTEEN

THIRD THURSDAY OF LENT

The charred and mutilated remains of a woman's body are found late afternoon on Thursday, in a rubbish skip on a building site. It's the main item on the six o'clock news. The images on the television screen show a desolate wasteland of half-demolished buildings, cranes and piles of rubble, cordoned off by police tape.

'Detective Frank Lambert of Westonville constabulary's serious crimes unit issued a statement to the press at the murder scene.' The screen switches to Frank's familiar face, looking strained and ill at ease, but with a glint of excitement in his gaze. Horror brings with it a rush of adrenalin. It awakens some desire for death and destruction that slumbers in the human soul. It's what makes people stop and stare at road accidents, and hungrily devour stories of rape, abduction, torture and murder. Surely, for a detective like Frank, it's no different? However noble his motives, however zealous the struggle for justice, there is still the thrill of the chase.

Frank is confident and articulate. He stares straight at the television camera and manages to look both accusing and reassuring. 'The victim of this latest killing has yet to be identified, and it's too early to know if this is the work of the same person who has killed two other women in the last month. However, we are urging women to avoid being on their own on the streets after dark, and to take extra precautions with their personal safety. We would also ask the media to exercise restraint in their reporting of these tragic events. Misleading speculation and rumour hinder the police in our enquiries, and make it more difficult for us to identify witnesses and possible leads. We urge any member of the public with information to come forward. Somebody out there knows who did this. If this is the work of a single person, then it's vital that we identify him before he kills again. Thank you.' He is looking directly at John, and there is no reassurance in his gaze. He is accusing John. Of that, John is sure.

Dear God Almighty. He switches off the television, unable to bear any more. He imagines walking down the road to the police station half a mile away, or better still, phoning Frank at home. 'I know who the murderer is. It's a cardinal, a man who might have been Pope were it not for rumours of a sex abuse scandal. The only problem is, he's dead. The murderer is a ghost.'

Would they laugh at him? Or would they arrest him on suspicion of murder? Sweet Jesus. His mouth is dry and his stomach cramps with fear. The doorbell rings. No! He imagines the cardinal standing there, translucent in the evening light, waiting, waiting. Sssuck my cock. Or the police, blue lights flashing, curtains twitching, rumours breeding.

He goes downstairs and pulls open the heavy wooden door. It creaks on its hinges. Lillian DuPlessis is standing on the doorstep. She's a South African woman who moved to Westonville with her husband Piet and two children, Marius and Janine, five years ago. They spent all their meagre savings on the deposit on a small house. Piet found a job as a car mechanic, and Lillian works in the local supermarket. The children go to the parish school. Lillian's round, homely face peers out from a patterned scarf tied around her head. He knows why she has come. Usually these visits from Lillian plunge him into misery, but tonight he is glad to see her, thankful for the distraction of the mundane violence of everyday life.

'Hello Lillian, come in,' he says.

117

'Thanks Father.' She steps inside and removes her scarf. He is not surprised to see a swelling and a small cut on her left cheek. 'He's hit me again,' she says, needlessly.

'Come and sit down.' He guides her to the bleak living room with its array of unmatched chairs and its long bulging sofa. He settles her in a chair. Her hair straggles about her face, blonde with dark streaks showing through.

'I don't know what to do,' she says.

He sits in the chair next to hers, so that they're on the same level. 'You need to leave him, Lillian, for your sake and for the children's sake. You can't go on like this.'

'You know I can't leave him Father. Where would I go? I have no money. How would I support the kids? His pay isn't enough for us to survive on as it is.' She swallows and looks away, her mouth turning down in disgust or despair. 'He got home drunk. I knew I shouldn't say anything, but I was tired and I'd had a bad day. My till was short at the end of the day, and they made me pay twenty pounds. I must've given someone too much change. What's twenty pounds to them, Father? It was our Sunday lunch. I was going to do a roast. I thought things might be better – you know, between Piet and me – if I tried a bit harder to make things good at home.' She clenches her fist and drums it on the arm of her chair. 'Twenty pounds. He must've spent more than that in the pub on his way home from work, the state he was in.' She shakes her head. 'I knew I shouldn't shout at him, but I was so angry, Father. It was my fault. I know what he's like when he's drunk. I know I should just leave him alone. He hit me. He hit me in front of the children. Again. I had to get out. I knew you'd understand. I won't stay long. I just had to get out of the house to calm down.'

It's a familiar story. How often has it happened before? Four times, maybe five. The first time he wanted to call the police. He was shocked and distressed. Gradually, he has come to realise that Lillian will never leave Piet. She comes to him because she trusts him not to tell anybody.

'Lillian, it's not your fault. Piet must take responsibility. You did nothing wrong. He has no right to hit you ever. Shall I make us a cup of tea?'

She nods and bites her lip. Her eyes brim. 'Thanks Father.'

He goes into the kitchen, sets a tray with a clean cloth and takes the bone china tea set down from a cupboard. Lillian's battered stoicism makes him want to treat her as an honoured guest. He remembers that one of the parishioners brought him a cake, so he cuts a slice and puts it on a plate. He carries the tray through to the living room and puts the cake and a cup of tea on the table next to her.

'Thanks Father. I won't stay long,' she says again.

'That's alright Lillian, take your time.' He knows it's futile to go through the same old rigmarole, but he tries all the same. 'You might be able to get a place in a refuge,' he says. 'I'm sure you'd be eligible for social housing, Lillian. We have people in the parish who could help you, if only you'd tell them what's happening.'

She shakes her head vehemently. 'No. I don't want anybody to know. Promise me, Father, promise me you'll never tell anyone.'

'I promise you Lillian. I've told you that. But think of what this is doing to the children.'

'It's better than being out on the streets.' She drinks her tea and nibbles on the cake. 'So pretty, these cups,' she says, tracing the gold-edged rim with her finger. Her finger nails are bitten to the quick.

'Do you want to bring the children here for the night?' he says. 'I could make up the spare beds.' It's a foolish offer, and one he hasn't made before. He can't possibly start having female parishioners staying in the presbytery. He is relieved when she shakes her head.

'No, Father. Definitely not. But thanks all the same.' She sips her tea and eats the cake in silence. Eventually, she gets up to go. 'Thank you Father. I'm grateful. You know that, don't you? I'm so grateful that I can turn to you. I don't know what I'd do without you.'

'It's alright, Lillian, that's what I'm here for. Where will you go now?'

'I'll go home, of course. He'll have calmed down by now. He'll be feeling terrible. You know what he's like. We both have tempers, but we love each other really.'

It's always the same. As her distress abates, she begins telling herself the same old story again and again. And she's not entirely wrong. In the confessional, Piet has an anguished conscience. Regularly every month, he tells the Lord he's sorry, he's going to stop drinking and stop hitting Lillian. Every month.

John sees her to the door and waits as she ties the scarf around her head again, tugging at the edges to hide her battered face. He watches her go out into the darkening night, her stout body tightly buttoned into a brown coat that he suspects came from a charity shop.

He calls after her. 'Lillian, be careful. Hurry home, won't you? Don't stop for anybody.' It's only a short walk, but the murderer could be lurking anywhere – behind a wall, in an alley, in somebody's garden. A tall, hissing ghost of a man, out to avenge himself on the world. Why? How? What for?

John goes back upstairs to his study and sits down at the desk. He scans the list of unanswered emails, and he feels nauseous. He doesn't want to spend the evening up here on his own, wading through emails, trying not to think, not to be afraid. 'Do not be afraid'. He read somewhere that that phrase occurs more often than any other in the Bible.

His mobile phone rings, startling him. He looks at the screen. It's James Forrester, parish priest at Saints Felicity and Perpetua. 'Hello James.'

'Hello John. How are you?'

'I'm fine, and you?'

'I have a tummy bug, unfortunately. That's what I'm ringing about. I'm supposed to say Mass for the students at Saint Catherine's tomorrow morning, and I'm looking for somebody to take my place.'

'I have the school Mass tomorrow morning at nine. What time is Mass at Saint Catherine's?'

'Eleven, so you could get there in time.'

John quails at the thought of rushing through two morning Masses, but he can't say no. 'Yes, alright then. I hope you feel better soon. It's nothing serious, is it?'

'No, but the doctor says I should avoid contact with people for twenty four hours.'

'Oh. Alright then.' John wonders if he should chat. He has never been free of the awkwardness he feels with most other priests. James is an affable, gregarious man, popular with his parishioners, pragmatic in his theology, but more interested in playing golf with his fellow priests and dining out with his friends than debating the finer points of faith.

'Terrible thing about these murders, isn't it?' James says.

'Yes, it's horrific,' says John, wishing he had ended the conversation sooner.

'Rumours are that there's some Catholic connection. Weird, if you ask me,' says James.

'That's just gossip, isn't it?' says John, though he remembers the conversation with Babbs and his stomach churns.

'No smoke without fire,' says James cheerily, 'though that's probably an unfortunate metaphor given that this latest body was burned.' Is he laughing? John swallows. He doesn't know what to say. 'Anyway, it's all we need. Some mad psycho priest running around killing whores. As if we weren't hated enough already.'

'Why do you think it's a priest?' John asks. Does he sound frightened? So what? It's a natural reaction, isn't it?

'I listen to the rumours. Anyway, thanks for agreeing to help out. Let's have a game of golf some time.'

'I don't play golf.' All the priests know he doesn't play golf.

'Oh, I forgot. You should, you know. It's a good way to relax, get to know the other priests. Come and join us some time.'

'Thanks. I'll think about it. Hope you feel better soon.'

John ends the call and gazes at his computer screen. His hands are shaking. He pushes his chair back and goes to look out of the window. The days are slowly lengthening. The clocks will go forward soon. An aeroplane makes a distant growl as it comes in to land at Westonville airport. He watches its landing lights gleaming a path through the low clouds. What is he afraid of?

He is afraid of what prowls the city streets tonight. He is afraid of the cardinal. He is afraid of his memories. He is afraid of his desires. He is afraid of himself. He is afraid of God.

He falls to his knees and closes his eyes. 'Dear God, please help me. Jesus, Son of the Living God, have mercy on me, a sinner. *Salve Regina, Mater misericordiae, vita, dulcedo, et spes nostra, salve.*' The hologram of a body appears against the darkness of his eyelids. Tall. Beautiful. Monstrous. Ssssuck my cock. He tries to push it away, and it morphs into another body, a more slight and delicate body, a body imagined and desired and caressed over and over again in the long, dark stretches of the night, before he seeks refuge in the all-encompassing darkness of Shula's fur.

He reaches out and traces his finger down the side of Luke's face, lingering to entwine his fingers in the strand of hair that curls around his ear. He lets his hand drift down the line of his neck and across to the hollow at the base of his throat, and then down, and down.

'*Ad te clamamus exsules filii Hevae, Ad te suspiramus –*

He whispers his name, and it drifts and curls like the smoke of incense around his head. 'Luke. Luke.'

'*Gementes et flentes* – Luke! My love. My love.'

In hac lacrimarum valle.

FIFTEEN

FOURTH MONDAY OF LENT

The city of Westonville is tense today, dreading the discovery of another body following the murder of three women over the last three weeks. Police say that the woman whose body was found on Thursday has not yet been identified and they have not established an exact time of death, but they are treating her death as murder.

John thinks he should switch the radio off and take his coffee upstairs to say the Office and reflect on the readings for the morning Mass, but he sits spellbound at the kitchen table.

'Our crime reporter Caroline Smith spoke to Detective Chief Superintendent Frank Lambert of Westonville's major crimes unit in his office a short time ago.'

'Detective Lambert, would you say that you are now looking for a serial killer?' says the woman.

'Good morning,' says Frank. 'We're keeping an open mind at this stage, but yes, that's a strong possibility.'

'There have been suggestions in the press that these killings have a ritualistic element – that they might be linked to a satanic cult or even to the Catholic Church. Can you give us any information about that?' She sounds eager.

'There are always wild speculations in cases like this,' responds Frank.

'But surely you can say whether they're true or not?'

'I've just said they are wild speculations.'

'So they're not true?' persists the interviewer.

'Our first priority is to find the person or persons doing these terrible things, and we would appeal to the public that if anybody has any information, please contact the police. Whoever did this would have had blood on his clothes. He would have been behaving in ways which would arouse suspicion. Somebody out there knows who this is. Somebody has the information that will help us to prevent any more murders. That's our main priority right now. Until we find the killer or killers, we strongly advise women to avoid being out on their own after dark.'

The interviewer keeps pushing. 'The first two murders were carried out on Friday nights. Do you think this latest victim was also killed on a Friday – that would be last Friday of course, and how likely is it that there will have been another killing this Friday just past?'

'I can't answer those questions right now. We haven't established a time of death for the woman whose body was found on Thursday, and so far we have no reason to believe there was another murder this Friday.' He sounds impatient. 'We have to stick to what we know. Now if you'll excuse me, I'm sure you understand that this is a very busy time for me.'

The newsreader takes up the story. 'With us in the studio to discuss that interview is Patsy Atkins of the Union of Prostitutes, and Betty Robinson who works for a church-sponsored charity called Support for Women on the Streets. Good morning to you both. Patsy, the Union of Prostitutes campaigns for the legalisation of prostitution. You argue that it would help to protect women from this kind of attack. Can you tell us more about that?'

'The law in this country is frankly a mess.' The woman is well-spoken and confident. 'It's not illegal to be paid for sex, but you can't run a brothel or solicit in a public place. So sex workers have no alternative but to hide in dark corners and to work in secret. We're arguing that prostitution is a profession like any other, and should be treated as such. Women own their own bodies and should be entitled to sell sex to customers if they want to, in a safe and legal environment. We're not criminals. We're professional women and we demand to be treated as such. In exchange, we would agree to pay taxes, to have regular health check-ups, and to cooperate with the police in identifying violent and dangerous men.'

'Betty, your organisation opposes the legalisation of prostitution. How would you respond to Patsy?' asks the newsreader.

Like Patsy, Betty sounds articulate and sure of herself. 'I think we have to be realistic about what life is like for women on the streets. Patsy is a rare example of a highly educated woman who treats prostitution as a lifestyle choice ...'

'Actually, it's my job Betty. I have to earn a living like anybody else.'

'Yes, but you chose prostitution as a career. You have a PhD in sexuality and the capitalist economy. You're a professional woman.' The two women are clearly old sparring partners. They sound good natured about their differences and disagreements. 'That's not true of the women we see on the streets,' says Betty. 'Nearly all of them grew up in abusive homes. They've been groomed, sometimes by the men in their own families. Part of that grooming is to get them addicted to drugs, so that they have to go out onto the streets to earn money to buy drugs, and then they're caught in a vicious circle. They need drugs to bear the torment of their lives, and they need to work as sex workers to pay for their drugs. We try to give them real choices, to help them to break out of that spiral of addiction, abuse and prostitution.'

'That's a very negative picture Betty. Of course you only see the desperate cases, if you spend your time with women forced onto the streets. You don't see the women working from the safety of their own homes, perfectly respectable wives and mothers who need a bit of extra cash, professional escorts working discreetly in hotels. We want every woman to have that kind of respectability and choice, then there wouldn't be this whole terrible industry of grooming and abuse.' Patsy sounds cheerful and upbeat.

'I think that's far too rosy a picture Patsy,' chides Betty, with a hint of patronisation in her voice. Besides, we're seeing more and more women who are asylum seekers and victims of trafficking. How are they going to register legally as professional sex workers, when they're not even meant to be in the country at all?'

'This is a fascinating discussion, but we'll have to leave it there,' says the newsreader. 'Now for the rest of today's news.' She switches from the solemn tones appropriate for discussing murder and prostitution, to a brighter and breezier tone.

John goes upstairs. The day stretches ahead, empty apart from the morning Mass. Sometimes Mondays bring with them a deep sense of contentment, but now his day off has become an endurance test. Solitude yields to the ache of loneliness, and leisure becomes an acute form of boredom as he tries to avoid brooding on his fears and rekindling all the guilt and shame that he refuses to let back into his life.

He contemplates going for a long walk, but it's a grey, damp day with a forecast of rain. He sits at his desk to check his emails but he can't concentrate. He picks up his missal and goes to sit in the chair by the bedroom window.

It's the Feast Day of Saints Felicity and Perpetua. The Missal gives a potted hagiography, pointing out that their suffering and martyrdom in the early third century were unusually well documented by Perpetua herself. Perpetua, a well-educated Roman woman, was still breastfeeding her baby when she was imprisoned and separated from the child because of her Christian faith. Felicity was a slave woman, eight months pregnant, arrested with Perpetua. The Romans waited until Felicity gave birth before they stripped them and threw them into the arena among the wild beasts, because they were afraid of killing a pregnant woman and having the innocent blood of the child on their hands. The crowd were so appalled by the nakedness of these two women, one of whom had clearly just given birth, that the Romans had to take them away and clothe them before throwing them back into the arena and slitting their throats, along with three other martyrs.

John thinks of Babbs with her contempt for all those virgin martyrs. Felicity and Perpetua were not virgins, but their deaths were as gruesome as any, and the Church takes them as exemplars of holiness. Something twists inside him. What's holy about women being humiliated and tortured? How does that bring glory to God? Why has he never thought about such questions before?

His phone rings shortly after he finishes saying Mass. It's Siobhan. Her father has been taken into hospital. They say it's just to monitor him and adjust his medication, but it would be lovely if Father John would visit him if he has time. He agrees readily, glad of the focus and purpose this gives to the day. He will visit Sister Gertrude and ask if there are any other people in hospital who might like him to visit and take them communion. Maybe he will phone Kate and ask if he can have supper at her place. The day suddenly seems less burdensome.

Sister Martha is sitting with Sister Gertrude. There are shadows under her eyes and her body droops with exhaustion.

'You look tired Martha,' he says.

'I am tired John. I decided to sit with her through the night because they thought she might be deteriorating and I don't want her to be alone when she dies. She seems just the same though. This could go on for days. They're still giving her fluids through a drip. The nurse says that's all that's keeping her alive now. I suppose eventually they'll ask us about disconnecting the drip.'

'What will you say?'

She looks at him and something resolute appears in her gaze and in the shape of her jaw. 'We'll say yes. We've discussed it – the other sisters and I – and we agree that there's no point in keeping her alive just to linger in some kind of twilight zone. Where's the dignity or life in that, Father?'

He holds her gaze, though he finds it awkward to do so. 'I think there's a difference between prolonging life and prolonging the process of dying. She ought to be allowed to go in peace.'

Sister Martha's face softens. She looks relieved. 'Thank you,' she says. She reaches out and strokes the dying nun's hand. 'Can you hear us Gertrude? You can let go, my darling. You don't need to struggle. We're with you. Father John is here. Abandon yourself to God's mercy and love, my darling friend. Jesus is waiting for you with open arms.'

John chokes up. He feels like a clumsy intruder in the delicacy of the moment. They look like an Old Dutch painting, framed in the bleached colours of the hospital room with the morning light filtering through the window and resting on their heads. A tear pools in the sunken socket of Gertrude's eye. Is she crying, or is it just that her eyes are watering? Who knows? How could anyone tell what she hears and knows in that shrivelled, gasping body?

'Martha, I need to do a few other visits, but I'm happy to take over from you after that,' he says. 'You should go home and get some sleep. It's my day off and I'm not doing anything, so I'll sit with Gertrude until one of the other sisters can come and take over.'

'They're all out, Father. They won't be back until late afternoon.'

'That's alright. I'll buy myself a novel and a sandwich in the hospital shop and I'll just sit and read.'

She looks relieved. 'If you're sure …'

'Of course I'm sure.'

'Can I trust you not to steal her jewels and tiara?' she says. John glimpses the wit and worldliness of Martha's personality, forged in the crucible of marriage, motherhood, bereavement and religious conversion. It feels good to laugh, and they laugh longer and louder than the joke deserves. A young nurse pads in to check on Gertrude, and John registers the confusion on her face. Should a priest and nun be laughing like this beside an old nun's death bed?

He makes his way to the Oncology Ward to visit Patrick. He is sitting up in bed with tubes coming out of his body. John pulls up a chair and sits by the bed. They talk about the football and the weather and the wedding until John senses that shift in mood which always heralds a time of revealing and confessing. People need time to gather their courage, to find words for their gut-wrenching questions and fears.

'You know Father, I've loved our Lord all my life. I've not been a good Catholic, but I've been a faithful one. I'm not one of these intellectuals. Siobhan, now she's one to question and challenge, but me, I've just accepted what I don't understand, and it's never bothered me.' He shifts against the pillow and shakes his head. 'But now, I'm thinking, what if it's not true? What if there's nothing there at the end of it? This is all there is. And then – nothing. Nothing ever again.'

John waits. This is the kind of conversation that needs to unfold slowly, without the silences being immediately filled with platitudes. 'Does that frighten you, Patrick?' he asks eventually.

'It terrifies me,' says Patrick. 'Don't you ever have such thoughts, Father?'

John wants to answer truthfully. It's a debt we have to the dying – a debt of courage and candour. He chooses his words carefully. 'I don't have those thoughts exactly. I don't think I ever really doubt that God exists. I suppose my fears are more to do with finding that I'm on the other side of some great chasm. That God exists, but there's some lack in me that makes me resist what God is offering me. That I'm too cold-hearted maybe, too indifferent, to accept the love of God.'

Patrick gives a feeble laugh. 'Father John, if you think that, there's no hope at all for the rest of us.'

'What makes you say that?' asks John.

'You're the love of God among us John. We all say that. You're the best priest any parish could want.'

'Oh no. Don't say that. You'll add the sin of pride to all my other sins.' But there's a consoling warmth deep in John's heart.

'You know Father, when our Ailish came home and told us she was – well, you know – a lesbian, Mary and I, we didn't take it well. She's our daughter and we love her come what may, but church teaching and us being Irish Catholics and all, we didn't know what to say. And now, with same-sex marriage and all, and us having changed like, Mary and I go down on our knees and beg God to forgive us. If the truth be known, Ailish and Julia have a much happier marriage than Eamon and Linda. If I wish anything for Siobhan and Anthony, it's that their marriage will be as happy as Ailish and Julia's.' He sags back against the pillows and closes his eyes, his face ashen with the effort of talking.

John's heart aches. 'Don't overdo it Patrick. You need to rest,' he says, laying his hand on Patrick's cool translucent skin, once again avoiding the needles and tubes as he did with Sister Gertrude.

Patrick gives a feeble nod. 'I understand son, I understand,' he says, and he cups his other hand over John's. 'You're a good priest. None of us condemns you for who God made you. We all love you. Remember that.'

John swallows. 'Thank you,' he croaks. He watches as Patrick drifts into sleep, then he closes his eyes and fat, reluctant tears roll down his face.

He stays with Patrick a little longer, then he goes down to the hospital shop and looks at the newspapers. SERIAL MURDERER IN WESTONVILLE, screams the headline in the

Daily Mail. It has three pictures on the front page – close ups of the faces of the two murdered girls, and the shadowy outline of a third face with a question mark. SATANIST ON THE LOOSE IN WESTONVILLE? screeches *The Sun*, also with photos of two of the three murder victims on the cover. The broadsheets have the murders as their main story, with the same photos but less sensationalist headlines. He picks up *The Guardian* and goes to browse through the blockbuster novels with their garish covers. It's a choice between slushy romances and detective thrillers. He chooses a thriller.

Back in Sister Gertrude's room, he says goodbye to Sister Martha and settles himself in the armchair. He tries to concentrate on the newspaper, but there's something about the figure on the bed that holds his attention. The ward is small, with a rain-spattered window looking out over the city to the hills beyond. Through the half-closed door, he can hear the clatter of hospital trolleys and the chatter of the nursing staff, but the rhythmic, laboured breathing coming from the bed reduces everything else to so much white noise. After a while, it becomes hypnotic. He has sat with the dying many times and he has witnessed gentle and traumatic deaths. He was there when Sarah died in Holly's arms and he has given the last rites to people dying of horrific injuries, but Sister Gertrude's dying fills him with peace.

Did he fall asleep? He must have done. The nurse is asking him if he wants anything – a cup of tea, a sandwich?

'I'd love a cup of tea – thank you. I have a sandwich here. I bought one in the shop downstairs.'

To his relief, Sister Gertrude is still breathing just as she was before. He had a moment of panic in case she had died while he was asleep.

He unwraps his sandwich and picks up the novel. It opens with a vivid description of a woman being murdered. He wonders what on earth inspired him to buy it, but he keeps reading. The story draws him in, with its badly written stereotypes and clichéd plot. He tells himself that it's bizarre to seek escape from the reality of violence and murder by reading a book about violence and murder, but it offers him such an escape nonetheless.

Chris opens the door when he arrives at his sister's house for dinner. Kate has phoned to say she'll be late. There has been an emergency at work. John's heart sinks at the prospect of having to make conversation with Chris until Kate gets home. He follows him into the lounge.

Stephen lunges towards him and throws his arms around John's waist. 'Uncle John!'

John picks him up and surrenders to the bony awkwardness of the child's embrace, enjoying the easy weight of his body in his arms. He swings him through the air and puts him down.

Phoebe looks up from the table where she's writing in a notebook and smiles her solemn, knowing smile, as if discreetly distancing herself from her little brother's exuberance. 'Hello Uncle John,' she says.

'Hello Phoebe. Are you doing your homework?'

She shakes her head. 'No. I'm writing a book.'

'A book? Really? That's wonderful. What's it about?'

'It's a novel. I don't want to show anybody until it's finished.'

'Good idea. I hope you'll let us read it when you've finished it.'

She looks thoughtful and then nods. 'I will if I think it's good enough.'

John feels a pang of curiosity. What goes on inside his niece's wise young head? He only knows the inner thoughts of children from the confessional, and that's rarely about creativity and imagination. Out of nowhere, he feels a wave of revulsion. Why would anybody inflict confession on a child? In the name of what god must a child be made to sit in a cubicle and dredge up a sense of sin in order to be acceptable to the Almighty?

'Want a beer or a glass of wine, John?' asks Chris.

'Do you have a lemonade, or fruit juice?'

'Oh yes. I forgot. It's Lent.' There's a sneer in Chris's voice. John ignores it and focuses his attention on the children.

He is glad when he hears Kate's car in the driveway. She comes in looking tired and stressed. He can read his sister's face like the map of a familiar landscape. When she's happy, the corners of her mouth are permanently upturned in the hint of a smile, so that the dimple in her left cheek deepens. When she's anxious or sad, a furrowed cushion sits between her eyebrows, and her left eyelid droops. That's what she looks like now. Her hair is tousled as though she has been running her hands through it.

'Sorry, sorry, sorry,' she says, kissing each of the children and Chris absent-mindedly. She hugs her brother and kisses him on the cheek. 'Lovely to see you,' she says. 'Jesus, I've had one hell of a day. Chris, pour me a large glass of wine darling. Please. John, come and chat to me in the kitchen while I get supper ready.'

He feels irritated with his brother-in-law. Couldn't he have done supper? Chris never helps in the house, even though his job is less demanding than hers.

They gather round the table – John on one side next to Phoebe, Stephen on the other side, and Kate and Chris at either end. Kate begins spooning lasagne from a large oven dish onto plates then she stops, spoon in mid-air.

'Oh God John, I've done lasagne. I forgot. It's Lent. You don't eat meat.'

He laughs. 'It looks fantastic Kate. Pile it on.'

'Sorry,' she says.

'No apologies. I'm just glad to be here.' He means it.

'You might as well wash that down with a glass of red wine,' says Chris. 'Might as well be hung for a sheep as a lamb.'

'I'm driving,' John reminds him.

'One glass won't do any harm.'

'I'd rather not,' says John, though in fact there's nothing he would like more.

'Suit yourself,' says Chris. 'Cheers.' He lifts his glass and the light gleams enticingly through the wine.

'What a day,' says Kate, leaning her elbow on the table and pushing her fork into her meal.

'Did somebody die?' asks Phoebe. John loves the way these children are included in their parents' conversations, yet they're never precocious. Looking around the table, he feels a sense of belonging that he feels nowhere else. This family is his special circle of love.

Kate puts down her fork and looks at her daughter, as if weighing up how much to say. 'Somebody died, sweetheart. I've been looking after her for six months.' She is addressing them all now. 'She was thirty two. She has three children, all under five. The youngest is only a year old. The cancer was diagnosed a few weeks after the baby was born.' Her voice chokes up. 'Sorry,' she says, and takes a swig of wine.

'That's so sad,' says Phoebe. 'What will happen to her children?'

'Her husband is lovely, and she was close to her mother and two sisters. Her children will be fine. It just seems so awful. She had so much to live for,' says Kate, her voice thick with sorrow.

Phoebe turns her watchful gaze on John. 'Uncle John, do you think God really loves us – I mean, really, really loves us?' His heart sinks. The question is asked with the utmost seriousness. Has her father been getting at her? He glances at Chris, who gestures with his fork.

'Well?' Chris says.

'Yes, of course I think God loves us,' he says.

'I told my RE teacher you're a priest,' says Phoebe. 'She told me I should ask you how you can believe in a good and powerful God when there's so much suffering in the world.'

'Is your RE teacher a Catholic?' asks John.

'No. She's an atheist,' replies Phoebe.

'She's an atheist?' John can't keep the shock out of his voice.

'Yes. She says children should learn about religion like we learn about poetry and novels and other made-up things, but also because religion makes people do violent and terrible things to each other, and we've got to learn to be tolerant and loving so we should be careful of religion.'

'Religious people also do loving and good things,' he says to Phoebe. 'The newspapers only tell us about the bad things.'

'Such as? What good things?' she asks. There's curiosity, not confrontation, in her voice.

'Well, there are organizations like Cafod which work with poor communities all over the world. The Catholic Church runs hospitals and schools in lots of poor places. Even here, the people in my parish work with refugees, they work with homeless people and drug addicts. I wonder if your RE teacher knows about people like that.'

'That's got nothing to do with religion,' interjects his brother-in-law. 'You don't have to be religious to be good.'

'I didn't say that,' says John. 'But you don't have to be religious to be bad either.'

'You have to be religious to do terrible things to other people in the name of God,' answers Chris.

John thinks of the murdered prostitutes, and the Catholic connection Frank told him about. A swarm of terrors swoops in on his imagination.

'Anyway, Phoebe's first question was about God. How can your loving God stand by while a young mother dies of cancer?' Chris persists.

'This is a really boring conversation,' objects Stephen, but nobody listens.

'I don't know. Maybe – maybe God's not over and above the suffering but there in it. Isn't that what the cross means?' John wishes somebody would change the subject.

'Oh Jesus John, spare me your crucified God.' It's his sister now, welling up with frustration and fury. 'You mean I'm meant to take comfort from a God who delights in the torture of his own Son, when I've just watched a young mother howl and drown in blood while her husband held her hand and wept and I could do nothing to help her? Don't tell me that some conspiracy of suffering between God and Jesus takes away the horror of that, because I'm not that stupid or gullible, and I don't run for cover in the face of agony for which I'll never forgive God. I had a Catholic education too, remember! I know what I'm talking about. And I won't expose my children to that sado-masochistic romance with God.'

An awkward silence descends over the table. Chris looks smug.

'Our silk worms hatched today,' says Stephen.

His mother laughs, and the sound is a ripple of delight and relief. 'Did they darling? You've been watching them in the classroom for ages. So do you have lots of beautiful moths now?'

Stephen nods. 'They're all furry and yellow. My teacher cut open one of the cocoons so that we could see inside. It was just jelly. The caterpillar had disappeared, and then the moth growed out of the jelly.'

'Evolution is an amazing thing,' says Chris. 'It explains the whole mystery of life. Science takes away all the need for gods and miracles.'

John's lasagne feels dry in his mouth. He would like to wash it down with some wine. It's his sister who comes obliquely to the rescue. Perhaps she's feeling guilty about her outburst.

'Science didn't do much for that young mother who died today,' she says.

'Her death would have been worse without modern science,' Chris answers complacently. 'Surgery, painkillers, chemotherapy – huge strides are being made in the treatment of cancer. It won't be long before it's banished, just like polio and smallpox have been banished.'

'It will be too late for Carol,' replies Kate, cynicism mingled with irritation at her husband.

'Was that her name? Carol?' asks Phoebe.

'Yes my love. Her name was Carol,' says Kate.

'What are the names of her husband and children?' asks John.

'Her husband is Michael, and the three children are Jenny, Peter, and Heather. Heather is the baby, Peter is two, and Jenny is five. Why do you ask?'

'I want to pray for them,' he says, because it's true and he suddenly doesn't care whether they approve or not.

'I'm sure that will make all the difference,' says Chris. 'Maybe you should have started praying sooner, and God might have saved the mother's life.'

'Oh don't be ridiculous,' says Kate, her fury turning from God and her brother to science and her husband now. 'You don't have all the answers either. I don't see how your atheism does any more good than his religion at times like this.' She flicks her hand towards John. 'You're both just looking for answers when there are none. Science. God. Spare me your faith, both of you. And you know, I sometimes think that modern science causes as much suffering as it avoids. For every miracle cure scientists discover, they seem to invent yet more weapons to kill and to maim, so don't give me your scientific messianism, Chris. Carol had ten months of hell – two operations, chemotherapy, baldness, vomiting, excruciating pain, when she just wanted to be with her new baby and the rest of her family. In the end, there was nothing we could do to stop the pain and the internal bleeding. Nothing. Now I ask myself if we should just have allowed her to have a few months of peace to say farewell to her kids, and given her a hefty dose of morphine when the pain became too much. She'd have died sooner and she'd have died better. A plague on both your houses – science and God!'

'I don't like it when you fight,' says Stephen, gazing wide-eyed and solemn-faced from one parent's face to the other.

Kate gives him a forced smile. 'We're not fighting, darling. We're having a discussion.' Then she turns the same smile on her brother, and an extra twist in the corner of her mouth makes her smile darkly ironic. 'But they were evangelical Christians. She died clutching a Bible. I think they'd really appreciate your prayers John. So yes, please pray for them.'

He drives home through the countryside, brooding darkly beneath a cloudy sky. It has been a day of death and dying, and he feels drained by its demands upon him. He regrets the antagonism over dinner. There's often light-hearted banter and squabbling between Kate and Chris, but tonight seemed more serious than that. He hopes they're not having difficulties in their marriage. Maybe it's just because Kate had such a terrible day.

His sister and he have that in common – they walk through the valley of the shadow of death, because of what they do.

His head hurts in the glare of the headlights as oncoming cars swish past, their rear lights glowing red and fading into nothingness in the rear view mirror. He drives slowly because he doesn't trust himself to navigate the twists and turns in the road as it snakes towards Westonville. He is glad he resisted the temptation to have a glass of wine, because whatever else has caused this sudden tiredness and disorientation, he can be sure it's not alcohol.

He falls prey to a childhood terror that has never entirely vanished from the wilder reaches of his imagination. He imagines somebody sitting in the back of the car, meeting his eyes in the rear view mirror. The thought panics him so much that he grips the steering wheel and doesn't dare to look in the mirror. It's the cardinal sitting there. He's sure of it. He can feel his presence. He is sitting there naked in the back seat, his erection standing proud of his body. Ssssuck my cock. Jesus, help me.

There are no streetlights and the darkness is like some great beast clawing at the windows, wanting to be let in. Images from the novel he was reading earlier leap out at him. A man cuts a woman's throat and drags her body into the middle of the road.

She stretches her arms out towards him and screams as he drives past. Another woman leaps onto the bonnet of the car. She has been strangled. Her eyes bulge and her tongue protrudes like a purple mollusc from the hollow of her mouth.

Jesus. Holy Mary. Sweet Jesus Christ, what's happening to me?

SIXTEEN

FOURTH TUESDAY OF LENT

Sister Gertrude dies in the early hours of Tuesday morning. John goes to the hospital and says prayers over her body. She looks peaceful, bathed in a silence so benign that it seems to contain within itself all the clamour and bustle of the hospital corridors outside. He gives thanks for her life, praying from a deep well of gratitude that Sister Gertrude walked the earth for more than ninety years, and left it more beautiful than she found it. Of that he is convinced.

He can believe that Sister Gertrude has been born into paradise. He imagines a laughing young woman wearing a red ball gown and a diamond tiara, slipping between the sunbeams and the atoms through the invisible cracks in the surface of time, where dead children morph into epiphanies of light shining through the loose weave of the material world.

Driving back to the presbytery as the sun rises over the city, he switches on the radio. It's the first item on the news. The female newsreader's voice is silky smooth and laced with darkness.

> *Police have identified the woman whose body was discovered in Westonville last Thursday as Ana Milkovic, an Armenian asylum seeker. The woman's burned and mutilated body was found in a skip on a building site. Forensic tests established that she was*

killed some time the previous Friday night, making
this the third killing on three successive Friday nights.
One woman who knew Ana agreed to be interviewed.
Her voice has been disguised to protect her identity.

John forces himself to listen.

'You knew the murder victim, Ana Milkovic,' says the interviewer.

'Yeah, I knew her. She was trafficked. They promised her a job as an au pair, but then they raped her and locked her up. She managed to escape, but she had no money and nowhere to live, so she had to go back to them. They didn't lock her up after that. They didn't need to. They just sent her out here to make money for them.' Even through the distortions of her voice, John can hear a strong west country accent. He wonders if it might be Babbs.

'Why didn't she go to the police when she escaped?' asks the interviewer.

The woman gives a derisory snort. 'What, so that they can deport her back to where she came from? A prostitute, addicted to heroin? That's what they did to her. How can she go back? It's sad that she's dead, but maybe it's better than all the alternatives.' She sounds resigned and pragmatic.

'Detective Frank Lambert who is in charge of this case will be speaking to the press later this morning,' says the newsreader. 'For now, it seems that residents of Westonville must accept that they have a serial killer in their midst, and the city dreads the discovery of another body. If there is a pattern – and it looks as if there is – then somewhere out there is the body of another murdered sex worker, murdered last Friday night.'

He calls in at the corner shop to buy milk on his way back to the presbytery. The front page of the *Westonville Post* blazes up at him from the newsstand. EVIL KILLER'S THIRD VICTIM IDENTIFIED. He looks at the photograph. The lank hair. The sallow face and sunken eyes. It's a ghastly photo, but that's what she looked like. The young woman with her vocabulary of degradation and abuse, offering to sell him her body with a price tag on every orifice. He picks up the newspaper and pays for it along with his milk.

'How are you today Father?' asks the young man behind the till.

'I'm alright thanks Adnan. I've just come from the hospital. Sister Gertrude died during the night.'

'Oh Father, that is sad news. My mother will be very sad. Sister Gertrude was a good woman. We all liked her.'

Adnan and his family came to the UK as refugees from Pakistan soon after John moved to the parish. They are Ahmadi Muslims, and therefore not true Muslims at all in the eyes of the Islamists who persecute them. Adnan was fifteen when the family opened the corner shop.

'These murders are terrible Father,' he says, as he takes the money from John.

'Yes, they are Adnan. These poor women.'

Adnan smiles shyly. 'Mrs Franklin, that lady who works in the post office, I think she comes to your church.'

'Yes, she does.'

'She is sad about them closing the post office. We're all sad.'

'I know Adnan. Local communities are being destroyed. Places like the local post offices and corner shops like yours keep us going.'

He smiles more confidently now. 'Don't worry Father, he says. 'We will not be closing our shop. And something else.' His face glows with delight now. 'My father has offered Mrs Franklin a job in our shop. We're very happy. She's a nice lady.'

As John walks back to the presbytery, he feels a lightening of his spirit. There is still goodness in the world.

SEVENTEEN

FOURTH THURSDAY OF LENT

It's the tenth anniversary of Sarah's death. Holly arrives just after eight in the morning, allowing them time to pray at the grave before the nine o'clock Mass. She is ablaze with bright, defiant joy. John has resisted listening to the news, concentrating all his energy and thoughts on Holly and Sarah. Now she stands on the doorstep, with a swirl of yellow silk around her head and a dress splashed with red and yellow and green and blue. She has a blue shawl around her shoulders, and her ears and neck and arms are festooned in silver jewellery. She is beautiful, a rare and precious jewel standing there in the morning light. In her arms she carries a bunch of scented flowers – freesias and lilies and roses that waft their fragrance over him as he opens the door. She is wearing orange lipstick, and her eyes glitter with that light which radiates from somewhere deep within.

'Holly! You look beautiful.'

'I've brought us fresh orange juice and croissants. I thought we could have breakfast together after Mass,' she says.

She follows him into the kitchen and lays the flowers carefully on the table. She rummages in the large bag slung over her shoulder and takes out the croissants and the bottle of juice.

'I'm on my own, as you can see,' she says. 'Steve told me it's morbid to do this every anniversary. It's time to move on. He said he wanted to take the boys camping, to celebrate his memories of Sarah somewhere beautiful and not in a graveyard. I think the boys were scared of hurting my feelings, but I told them to go. They hate all this religious stuff, and it's better for Steve if they have a couple of days being blokes together. I don't mind.' Her eyes tell him that she does mind, not in an angry, resentful way but because she would like to gather with her husband and her sons by Sarah's grave, to have them recognise the beauty and hope that she is trying to sustain with the flowers she brings and the prayers she says, to a god she no longer believes in.

He puts on an alb with a stole around his shoulders because Holly likes these signs of ritual and tradition. They go out into the garden. Tendrils of cloud wisp across the sky, and jet trails make celestial hieroglyphics in the sunlight. He looks across at the cherry tree with its blossoms yielding to fresh green growth. Sarah isn't there. Would Holly see her if she was?

'I want to show you something,' he says.

They pick their way across the dewy grass. Yesterday, when he looked, the baby birds had hatched and four hungry beaks were gaping out of the nest. There are only three fledglings this morning. He instinctively looks for Shula, but the cat is nowhere to be seen. He is on the point of telling Holly that one of the chicks is missing, but intuitively he knows that Holly's joy is woven out of emotions so fragile that even the death of a tiny robin might tear through that delicate veil and leave her grief raw and exposed.

'Aren't they lovely?' he says.

'Oh John, how glad I am you showed them to me.' She takes his arm and squeezes it. 'I wonder where the mother is.'

'Out looking for food, I expect,' he says, desperately hoping that she too hasn't fallen victim to Shula or some other cat.

'Life goes on,' she says. 'Look – it's everywhere.' She looks around, her expression one of sorrow and wonder. 'You know, I wish more than anything, with all my heart and every minute of my life, that Sarah had never died, but if it had to happen I'm glad she died in spring. It must be desperate to lose a child in the heart of winter, when there's nothing but darkness and death.'

They make their way across the lawn to the gate that leads into the cemetery. As they push open the gate, the mother bird flits past with a worm in her beak. John wants to weep with relief.

Sarah's small grave is nestling beneath the angel's wings, and the sun is angled so that it glistens on the dewy flowers blooming on the grave and the gold lettering on the tombstone. Holly arranges the flowers at the angel's feet, in a large glass vase she has brought with her. She kneels down on the wet grass and presses her lips to Sarah's name. She steps back and takes John's hand, raising it to her lips so that he imagines the imprint of Sarah's name upon his palm. They stand together in silence, and after a while she says, 'Will you read the poem now John?'

It's the same ritual every year. She doesn't want elaborate prayers or incantations – just the reading of the poem on the tombstone, and a quiet time of standing side by side.

> *When you awake in the morning hush*
> *I am the swift uplifting rush*
> *of quiet birds in circled flight.*

The rising sun catches the tips of the angel's wings, and the marble glows as if the angel has come to life. There, standing on the grass beside Holly's flowers, a small figure emerges. She has her hands raised in front of her, and she is cradling a tiny bird. It's the robin, missing from the nest, now transposed to Sarah's world of mist and light. There's something about the image that strikes a chord. He has seen that pose before but he can't remember where. He looks at Holly. Does she see her daughter standing there?

Holly is gazing at the tombstone, her eyes bright with tears. She is smiling, but it's not a smile of recognition. It's a smile of resignation, maybe of hope, too enigmatic to decipher. He wishes the child would come closer. He wishes she would touch her mother or say something. But as he watches and wills her into some more substantial and tangible form of being, she vanishes back into whatever dimension she inhabits, together with the fledgling bird.

They go back to the presbytery and he prepares to say Mass. Edith is there, bustling around the sacristy as usual. Jack is there too, and John is grateful for his solid, tranquil presence which seems to absorb some of Edith's energy.

The Mass is for Sarah. The church is more full than usual because so many parishioners know the family and because Sarah's death still binds together those who were there in a trauma that will not relinquish its grip on them. They must find ways to go around it, beyond it, through it, but it will never not be there.

Afterwards, Holly and he go down to the basement beneath the parish hall to get the garden furniture from its winter storage, so that they can have breakfast in the garden. The basement opens off the car park, with concrete steps leading down to a wooden door. It smells musty. It's a large, damp space with an uneven floor, peeling paintwork and cobwebs draped around the ceiling. It has been a general dumping space for years, with broken furniture, an old chest freezer and various bits of gardening equipment piled against the walls.

Holly stands in the gloom and looks around. 'I hate this place,' she says. 'It spooks me out.'

'Yes, I know what you mean,' he says. 'Edith is always on about it. She thinks we ought to clear it out and turn it into a prayer space.'

'She's bloody bonkers, that woman,' says Holly. 'Who would want to pray in a place like this?'

'She says it could be like a crypt in an old cathedral,' says John.

'Jesus. Well, it certainly feels like a place of death, but without any of the redeeming features of a medieval cathedral.'

John is suddenly filled with a sense of foreboding. The damp air squeezes the breath from his lungs and makes him want to escape. The smell of decay reminds him of the cardinal and the smell of death that signals his presence. He locates the garden furniture in a corner and tries to ignore the cobwebs brushing against his arms and head as he drags the table towards the door. Holly picks up two folding chairs. They carry it all up the concrete steps and into the sunshine.

They sit a little distance from the cherry tree, so as not to disturb the mother bird who comes and goes as she feeds her chicks. Once, John catches a glimpse of Sarah, not standing under the tree but skipping across the grass with pink ribbons in her hair, the way he remembers her. Again he watches Holly but she remains oblivious to her daughter's presence.

The morning light spangles on her jewellery and sets her henna hair ablaze. As she lifts her glass to her lips the orange juice is iridescent with sunshine. He has never been so intensely aware of Holly's vulnerability and strength. Maybe it's her maternal love that holds Sarah on the edges of the living, even if Holly herself is unaware of its power. Sarah is a drifting, whimsical play of light on the edges of his vision, as she dances across the garden and gradually fades from view.

'John, will you come and keep me company this evening?' Holly asks. 'I'll do us some supper. I don't want to be on my own.'

'Yes, of course I'll come.' He is relieved that the day now has some purpose and focus to steer him through the fearful hours. He's also irritated with Steve for going away and leaving Holly alone at such a time, but then he reminds himself that grief takes many forms, and Steve's grief too is deep and inconsolable. Steve, he realizes, has sunk into a deeper darkness than Holly, because he has lost even the meagre consolation of keeping alive the rites of an empty faith.

Somehow, the hours pass until it's time to go to Holly's house for dinner. She opens the door. She is wearing a long red and black kaftan, and she's holding a glass of wine. There are smudges of mascara under her eyes, and when she smiles there's a smear of lipstick on her front teeth.

'You're going to have to work hard to catch up with me,' she says. 'I've just about finished the first bottle of wine.'

John has already decided that Lenten abstinence takes second place to being with Holly. He hugs her and feels the soft nakedness of her breasts beneath the fabric of the kaftan. Holly knows he's gay. Hers is the only body he is ever permitted to cuddle and love without reservation, apart from Stephen and Phoebe.

He follows her into the living room with its Indian drapes and flickering candles. Holly's home is an Aladdin's den of rich colours and textures. Steve complains about the clutter, but there's something mysterious and sensuous about the atmosphere Holly has created. The lounge reminds John of a small Orthodox chapel with its glowing icons and incensed air.

Incense wafts from a wooden holder on the mantelpiece among the family photos, and a fire glows in the grate. There's music playing – something orchestral, smooth and undemanding. There's a framed photo of Sarah on the coffee table, with a candle burning in front of it. Sarah is grinning, and one of her front teeth is missing. Her hair is tied in ponytails with pink ribbons, the way he still sometimes sees her, the way he saw her this morning, the way she was that other, dreadful morning. It's a familiar photograph that normally stands on the mantelpiece along with the others. He has often looked at it.

It suddenly occurs to him that his visions of Sarah might be nothing more than images of this photo lingering in his memory. The mind can play strange tricks. But if Sarah's ghost isn't real, what about the cardinal? Is he also some trick of the mind, a repressed memory breaking through the surface because John is tired, he's been working too hard, he needs a break? Is it all a monstrous fantasy? Out there, somebody is murdering women, but it has nothing to do with the cardinal or John or anything John has heard or imagined he heard in the confessional, or anything John has done in the oblivion of a forgiven but not quite forgotten past.

They have pizza and salad for supper, washed down with a bottle of red wine. Afterwards, they go back to the living room and Holly opens another bottle of wine. She flops on the settee with its faded velvet colours and he sits near her, almost embraced by her arm along the back of the cushion.

She reaches for a pile of cards on the table beside her. 'I'm amazed how many people still remember the anniversary and write to us,' she says. 'There were lots of emails too, but I'm glad people still send cards. Emails aren't the same, are they?'

'No, they're not.'

'Some of the messages are beautiful,' she says. 'You can read through them if you like.'

He shuffles through the pile of cards, moved by the ways in which people struggle to articulate their feelings, trying to reach out through the clunking inadequacy of words. 'Thinking of you in your loss.' 'I found this poem and thought of you.' 'We're holding you in our prayers and we remember darling Sarah every day.' Some are less helpful. 'The Lord giveth, the Lord taketh away.' 'There's another angel in heaven.' 'Only the good die young.'

Suddenly, his heart does a somersault. The card in his hand has a picture of a child holding a dove on the front. It's by Picasso. He recognizes it, and he knows why that image of Sarah looked so familiar this morning. It reminded him of this painting.

'That's from Steve,' says Holly. 'He sent me flowers today too. He knows I love that painting. It always makes me think of Sarah.'

'I see her, you know,' he blurts out.

A stillness descends upon Holly. She sits with her arm extended, reaching for her wine glass, frozen, her eyes wide, fixed on his face. 'Who?' she whispers, though she knows.

'Sarah. In the garden. She was there this morning, standing by the grave while we were praying. She was holding a baby bird. There were four in the nest yesterday, and only three today.' He hears himself babbling but he can't stop. There's something about Holly's deep, deep silence, something about the way she is looking at him, that terrifies him. He blunders on because he doesn't know what else to do, conscious that the wine is blurring and slurring his speech. 'She's been there under the tree, keeping watch over the nest. Sometimes she skips across the garden, looking just like she does in that photograph.' Why doesn't she say something? Why doesn't she move or breathe or do something, anything, to end this torment? Why doesn't he shut up? 'Sorry. I'm sorry Holly. I shouldn't – I should never have told you.'

She lets out a garbled cry and falls to her knees on the floor. She buries her face in the rug and howls. Dear God, what has he done? Her body shakes and she pummels the floor with her fists, howling and howling like some tortured beast. He has no idea what to do, so he does nothing. He wants to go down there and join her. He too wants to howl and beat the floor. He closes his eyes. Help us Jesus. Help Holly.

It seems to go on forever, but gradually the noise subsides and she rolls over, curling onto her side with the firelight playing on her blotched face with its smudges of mascara and lipstick.

'Holly, I don't know what to say. I'm so sorry.'

'Shhhh. Don't apologise John. Please, don't say you're sorry. Just tell me, is she alright? Is she still hurt? What does she look like? Please don't lie to me John. I want to know.' Her voice is thick with booze and mucus.

'She looks like Sarah, Holly. She's just the way Sarah used to be. Perfect in every way. She is beautiful and so alive.' He pauses. He senses her holding her breath. 'And the peace, Holly, I can't begin to describe the peace to you. She exudes peace.'

She breathes out, a great slow exhalation of breath. 'How old is she?'

'She's the same age she was when she died. She's exactly the child she was then.'

Holly's face contorts in a spasm of grief. 'Does she speak to you? Can you touch her?'

'No, she doesn't speak. Occasionally, I think I feel her hand on my shoulder or my arm, but it's not a touch exactly. It's more like, when a light breeze brushes against your skin. I don't think I'd ever try to touch her. What I see – it's real, but it's not real the way you and I are real. It's different. It's like some different dimension, some different substance. I can't describe it Holly.'

There's a long, motionless silence, with only the crackle of the fire and the music playing quietly in the background.

'I wish I could see her,' she says eventually. 'Oh, I wish more than anything else that I had seen her this morning, but maybe she knows I would never let her go. I'd hold her and I'd keep her and I'd trap her forever. I'd never, ever give her back to God, John. When I died, I would keep her in my arms and lock her between my hands until my bones were frozen and we both turned to dust and she would melt back into me and she would never ever be free. I'd never ever let her go. I'd unwind myself and rewind my body around hers, and I'd be pregnant forever. That's what I'd do.' She lies there for a long time. Eventually she wriggles to her knees and stands up, keeping her back to him. 'Jesus, I must be such a fucking mess,' she says, and lurches unsteadily to the door.

He hears her footsteps on the stairs. His limbs feel heavy and his heart is a dead weight of regret and fear and loss. What now? How will Holly ever claw her way back from this? What will become of their friendship?

He feels alone and desolate. He wonders if he should leave, but he lacks the energy to stand up. It's only a short walk back to the presbytery. The fresh air would do him good. He sits there, willing his body to move. He's still there when he hears her coming downstairs. He sees her shadow flit past the door as she goes into the kitchen. She comes back carrying a bottle of champagne and two flutes. Her appearance is transformed. She has washed her face and redone her make-up. Her hair is brushed and shining, and she's smiling. He has never seen such a smile on Holly's face.

She puts the bottle and glasses on the coffee table next to the pile of condolence cards, and she holds her arms out to him. 'John, come here. Give me a hug.' He stands up unsteadily and goes over to her. She wraps her arms around him, and he rests his head on her shoulder. 'Oh John. Oh sweet Mother of God. Oh John. Dear God.' She's rocking backwards and forwards, as if he is the dead child in her arms.

'Sorry Holly. Sorry.'

'Shhhh. You've given me a gift John. You've given me the most precious gift you could have given me, other than giving me back my Sarah.' She squeezes him. 'It's all so sad and futile and so fuckingly irresistibly beautiful,' she says. 'Jesus, John, why do we struggle on? Why don't we just end it? I dream of dying, you know. I dream of just not waking up, and then the morning comes, and I'm glad I'm awake in spite of it all. How do you explain it?'

'I don't. I can't, but I feel it too Holly.'

Her body gives a shudder of laughter against his. 'Really John? You feel it too? I can't believe you ever wake up wishing you had slept forever. I sometimes wonder, what does it feel like to live as you do, totally immersed in the certainty of the love of God. I can't imagine that, John, but you're my anchor. You're my rock, my harbour in the storms. Jesus, talk about mixed metaphors. I don't believe in God but I do believe in you. Maybe that's what it means to be a priest.'

'No, no, don't say that Holly. You don't understand. My faith isn't like that. I probably have less faith than you do right now Holly.' He feels garrulous and incoherent, but he no longer cares. Holly loves him. Holly has forgiven him. Holly has faith in him. That's all that matters. 'I'm in love with somebody Holly. I don't know what it feels like for a mother to lose her daughter the way you lost Sarah. I don't know what the mothers of those murdered women feel like. But I know that sometimes, I would squander all the eternal love of God for just one night with the man I love. And I also know that I'm terrified, and I don't know what I'm terrified of, and oh – oh – oh – I could go on if I weren't so drunk. But I love you Holly, I love you. I shall stand here and be your harbour, your rock and your – your whatever. I can't remember what the other thing was. I won't tell you that we're both at sea. We're both drowning. Your anchor. That's the other thing. I'm your anchor, you say. I won't tell you that I have nothing to hold onto and we're both drifting together. We're all at sea, Holly, all, all at sea.' He tightens his grip around her, and he loves the soft acceptance of their bodies against one another.

She pulls her head back and looks at him. She is smiling, and her eyes are glowing with that strange inner light. 'John, do you know what I used to do, when the first numb shock was over and there was just an endless abyss tumbling towards me every moment of every day?'

'What did you used to do?' He can feel himself being irresistibly drawn into the magic of her mood.

'I used to dance. I used to put on loud music and I used to dance. That's what I want us to do now.'

She goes over and clicks her iPhone until Queen begins to play. She turns up the volume on the speaker until 'You're My Best Friend' blasts through the room. She fills the champagne flutes and hands one to him. 'Here's to us and to life,' she says.

'To us and to life.'

They swirl and leap and dance and sing at the tops of their voices, drinking as they dance. 'You're my best friend.' She drains her glass, puts it down and wraps her arms around him. They rock together. 'You are. Dearest John, you are truly my best, best friend.'

He feels happy and free for the first time since that dark Ash Wednesday morning when the cardinal oozed back into his life. 'And you are my best, best friend too Holly.'

No wonder mystics compare the love of God to the finest wine he thinks, as he lurches his way unsteadily home through the dark, deserted streets.

EIGHTEEN

FOURTH FRIDAY OF LENT

John awakes with a pounding headache and a dry, rank mouth. He sits on the edge of the bed and waits for the room to stop spinning. He gropes his way to the bathroom cabinet and drops two Alka Seltzer into a glass of water. As he waits for them to stop fizzing, he tries to keep at bay the clawing anxieties. It's Friday. It's Lent. He is hung over. He has to hear confessions, say Mass, prepare for Siobhan and Anthony's wedding on Sunday. He feels terrible. He thinks he might die. He wishes he would die.

He showers and cleans his teeth until his gums bleed then gargles with mouthwash. He hopes his breath doesn't stink. It's one of his enduring memories, going to confession with a priest who had halitosis.

He was twelve, and it was the first time he had ever masturbated. That was bad enough, but he had fantasised about Clive Peterson, a boy in his class, while doing it. He had been gripped by a profound terror that, if he died before he confessed, he would go to hell.

It was a Saturday morning. He had ridden his bike to another parish, not daring to go to his own parish priest, and waited in the queue for confession. He had fumbled his way through an admission of what he had done, and the priest had solemnly warned him that he was putting himself at risk of eternal damnation.

'You must never put yourself in such a situation again. Do you understand? If you feel like that, even if it's the middle of the night, you must get up and pray to be delivered from evil. Have a cold shower. Make your body suffer. Punish your body in order to save your soul.' And all the while, the smell wafting over him from the priest's sulphurous mouth was the stench of hell.

But now he remembers something else. The priest had his hand on his knee while he was speaking, pummelling it, squeezing it, and then squeezing up and up his thigh to his groin. 'This is the source of all evil,' he had said, kneading the erection that John had been impotent to control. 'You must discipline this in every way you can. Do you understand?' As his breathing became heavier, the smell became unbearable.

John falls to his knees. The room is still spinning, so he rests his elbows on the toilet seat and clasps his hands. 'Dear Jesus, you are my Lord and my saviour. You are full of compassion and love. You are light and truth and beauty. In you there is forgiveness, redemption and hope. Be with me, my sweet Lord. Be with me. Don't abandon me. Don't forsake me. Don't leave me alone. Don't leave me Jesus. Please don't leave me here.' He rests his forehead on the toilet seat and sobs.

He makes himself a cup of strong black coffee and eats a piece of dry toast to settle his stomach. He switches on the radio in time to hear the seven o'clock news.

This morning we report from Westonville, where a glorious spring morning cannot disguise the sense of dread that hangs over the city. Police confirm that the estimated time of death of the latest victim, Ana Milkovic, was between Friday evening and Saturday morning the week before last, making that the third in a series of murders that happened over three consecutive Fridays. So far, there is no evidence that a fourth murder was committed last Friday, but as another Friday arrives there is a terrible fear that somewhere, a body has yet to be found, and that tonight the killer will strike again.

Police have also confirmed that there may be a ritualistic element to the killings, though they have refused to give further details. Rumours that the killings might be the work of somebody with a knowledge of Catholicism, possibly even a priest, have not been confirmed. The police are appealing for anybody with information to come forward. Our reporter went to talk to one of the sex workers on the streets of Westonville yesterday evening. The woman's voice has been disguised to protect her identity.

The voice changes and the controlled silence of the studio yields the bustle of the city streets.

'Hello. My name is Juliet Barnes and I'm out here in the Saint Peter's district of Westonville. It's a cold, damp night here, but in spite of the dangers, there are still sex workers out on these streets tonight. I'm here with one of these women, who has agreed to be interviewed.' There's a pause when John can hear the muffled sounds of a siren and somebody shouting in the distance. 'So what brings you out onto the streets tonight, when you know there's a serial killer around?' asks the reporter.

'We still have to eat,' says the woman. Her voice sounds defiant and sassy. John is sure it's Babbs, but maybe that's because all of them sound the same when their voices are disguised.

'Is that why you're out here? To get money to buy food? But surely, you could just go to a food bank?'

'Nah. It's not just food, is it? We girls, we all do drugs. We drink. It's the only way we can cope. We do drugs so that we can do sex, and we sell sex so that we can buy drugs. That's life.'

'Aren't you afraid?' asks Juliet, who sounds prim and remote and startled.

There's a long pause. 'Course I'm afraid,' says the warped voice, 'but if we stay away because we're frightened, he wins, don't he? So yeah, I'm out here, and no [bleeb] murderer is going to scare me away.' John wants to believe that this brave, rebellious spirit is Babbs.

'What about the suggestion that these are ritual killings, that maybe they're even the work of a Catholic priest? Does that trouble you?'

'If you're dead, you're dead. Why would you care who did it? Anyway, I keep a rosary in my pocket and I have a miraculous medal pinned to my bra. If some Catholic perv tries anything with me, I'll ask Our Lady to look after me.'

The voice switches back to the news reader in the studio. 'Well, that was a sex worker who was out on the streets of Westonville last night, talking to our reporter Felicity Barnes. With us in the studio to discuss the killings we have Professor Peter McBride, Professor of Criminology, and Dr Linda Harris, theologian, both from Westonville University, and Father Ronald Barton of St Joseph's Seminary.'

John turns up the radio and sits down at the table with his coffee. He knows Ronald Barton vaguely. He is one of a new breed of ardent young conservative priests, the type John was surrounded by in the university in Rome. That thought sets something squirming inside him, but he pushes it away. Not now.

'So Professor McBride, do you think we've seen the last of the killings?' asks the newsreader.

'I very much doubt it. These killings have all the hallmarks of a serial killer. The murders will only stop when he's arrested, or if he comes to some harm that prevents him from continuing.'

'You say "he". Could it be a woman?' asks the interviewer.

'There's a very remote possibility, but it's extremely rare for women to engage in this kind of torture and serial killing,' he replies.

The interviewer turns her attention to the theologian. 'Dr Harris, you've recently published a book called *God and Gynocide*, making a link between killing women and the Catholic Church. Can you help us to understand the suggestion that this might be the work of a Catholic – though of course that report hasn't been confirmed yet?'

The woman clears her throat. 'Of course, we don't know all the details of the killings, but the Catholic Church has a long tradition of sanctifying female suffering. There's a fine dividing line, you know, between martyrdom and masochism, and the exaltation, the sanctification, of starvation, mutilation and death in the cult of the female saints is a symptom of widespread misogyny that still infects the Catholic priesthood.' She has a monotonous, slightly nasal voice that reminds John of Jennifer from the Justice and Peace Group.

'So you would give some credence to the suggestion that this looks like the work of a Catholic priest?' asks the interviewer.

'I'm not a detective so of course I can't say, but there are certainly some priests who hate women, and the fact that the women killed so far have all been sex workers suggests some kind of punitive aspect to the killings,' says the theologian, still in a monotone. John pities her students if this is her lecturing style.

'Father Barton, do you agree? This might be the work of a woman-hating priest?' asks the interviewer.

'I think that's an outrageous suggestion, if I may say so.' Ronald is almost spluttering with indignation. 'Dr Harris doesn't seem to recognise that the Catholic Church reveres women. Look at the honour we show to the Virgin Mary, and the protection we offer to women against the abortion industry. We hold motherhood in very high regard, and we celebrate Mary Magdalene – a former prostitute – as one of the greatest saints and one of the people closest to Our Lord.' He sounds patronising as well as outraged.

'Mary Magdalene was not a prostitute,' responds the theologian, her voice tight with anger now. 'It's evidence of the misogyny that I was speaking about, that the tradition has known her first and foremost as a prostitute when nothing in the Bible supports that belief. The denigration of women in the Catholic tradition goes all the way back to Eve. You might put Mary on a pedestal, but virginal motherhood is an impossible ideal and the result is that you despise ordinary female sexuality and ...'

'This is total nonsense,' interrupts the priest. 'Women play a key role in the Catholic Church. We know we wouldn't survive without all the work women do. Arranging flowers. Cleaning. Visiting the sick. Organising the children's liturgy. Organising cake sales and jumble sales to raise money for the poor. I could go on and on.'

'Emm, if I could bring us back to the Westonville murders,' says the interviewer. 'Professor McBride, the Catholic Church hates women and the murderer might be a Catholic priest. Does that make sense to you?'

'I think it's a bit speculative, to be honest. The murderer might just as easily be an atheist or somebody who has a grudge against the Catholic Church and wants to implicate it in the killings.' The professor speaks with the assured confidence of a man who is used to being listened to.

'What the Professor says is highly plausible,' says Ronald, sounding deferential now. Clearly, the Professor knows how to solicit admiration. 'We know there are atheists out there who hate Catholics, and without God in their lives many of them lack a moral compass.'

'Oh please, this is outrageous,' interrupts the theologian. 'Are you suggesting that atheists are more prone to become serial killers because they don't believe in God? And where's the moral compass of all those priests who go around raping and abusing children?'

'Em, well, this has certainly been a lively interview, but I think we'll have to leave it there.' The presenter sounds flustered. 'That was Professor Peter McBride, Dr Linda Harris and Father Ronald Barton, discussing the recent spate of murders in Westonville. As another Friday night approaches, people in this vibrant west country city have good reason to be terrified of what the night might bring. Now, on to the rest of the morning's news.'

As he makes his way to the confessional before Mass, John sees that a small queue has already formed. Lucy Pierce is there and so are Siobhan and Anthony. He offered to let them say their confessions in the presbytery on Sunday morning before the Nuptial Mass, but they said they were happy just to come along to the Friday morning session.

Siobhan had giggled self-consciously. 'We've decided not to see each other from Friday morning until the wedding, so we won't be tempted, you know what I mean. We won't have done anything we need to confess, will we?' She had blushed, which had heightened the sparkle in her eyes and the spattering of freckles across her cheeks.

John had considered pointing out that sex was not the only nor indeed the most serious sin a person might commit in two days of ostensibly normal life, but instead he had smiled and said, 'See you on Friday.'

He is startled by the change in Lucy when she comes into the confessional. She sits down and avoids his eyes, twisting a strand of hair nervously around her finger. There are dark smudges under her eyes, and she looks pale.

'Hello Lucy,' he says, trying to communicate a sense of acceptance and welcome.

'Hello Father John,' she mutters.

He senses that she's waiting for him to say something. 'Maybe we should say a little prayer to begin,' he says, and bows his head and closes his eyes. 'Dear Lord, thank you for Lucy.

Thank you for the lovely person that she is. Be with us now and help her to feel your grace and your love as she seeks to deepen her friendship with you. Amen.'

She sniffs and mumbles 'Amen'. She keeps her eyes lowered, still twisting her hair.

'Remember that the confessional is a place of love and mercy, not of judgement and punishment, Lucy. Take your time. When you're ready, tell the Lord what's troubling you, and trust in His forgiveness and compassion.'

'I, umm, I've broken up with my boyfriend.'

'I'm sorry to hear that,' he says. 'This must be a difficult time for you.' She nods. He waits.

'I broke off with him.' Another pause. 'You see, umm, you remember I told you about the ketamine.' She swallows. He wonders if she's about to cry, but she takes a deep breath and carries on. 'We used to use condoms, but that night, that night he said he wanted to do it without, and I said okay, and I got pregnant.' She stops speaking, but he knows better than to break the silence. Finally she meets his eyes, challenging him. 'I had an abortion.'

He nods slowly. His mouth feels dry. 'It's alright Lucy, I'm not going to judge you.'

She stops twisting her hair and clasps her hands in her lap. 'I wouldn't have done it, but the ketamine. I told my mum. I didn't know what to do. I was scared. You know, being pregnant, and taking drugs. What if there was something really badly wrong with the baby?' Her voice wobbles. 'I didn't know what to do,' she says again. 'It would have been my fault if there had been something wrong.'

He would like to take her hand, but instead he simply looks at her. There was a time when he would have resorted to a set formula in a situation like this, pronouncing absolution and leaving the rest to God, but this is Lucy. He has known her since primary school. He wants to offer her more than a formulaic rite of absolution.

'Lucy, you're here because you're sorry, not just about the abortion but about the whole situation in which you find yourself.' She nods. 'We all make mistakes Lucy. It's part of the painful process of growing up and learning about life. God made us and God loves us. That's the most important lesson of all. That's the only lesson that really matters.'

'What about the baby?' she whispers.

'God made your baby too Lucy. Pray for yourself and pray for that small flicker of life which has returned to the source of all life.'

'Am I a murderer? Will I go to hell?'

'Ah Lucy, even murderers don't go to hell if they repent, but no, you're not a murderer. You're a good and loving young woman who did what you thought was best at the time. You're here to make your peace with God, and that's enough.' He feels inadequate. How can he possibly understand? What can he say? He is a man, a priest. Who is he to claim the power of God in this situation? Yet she seems to be waiting for more. Does she want him to keep talking? 'Your boyfriend refused to wear a condom. He has some responsibility for this too,' he says.

'He didn't want us to break up. He was glad I decided to have an abortion because he says he's not ready to have a baby, but he says he loves me. He would like us to have children together one day, but not yet.' John is angry with that faceless, nameless young man, but he holds back from saying anything. She swallows then continues. 'I just – I realized I didn't love him. I mean, I suddenly realized what a kid he was. I know that sounds stupid. He's twenty one, two years older than me, but even so, I just – I suppose I didn't respect him much after that. I mean, it wasn't being pregnant that was the worst thing. I'd have been okay with that. It was the ketamine, and what it might do to the baby. He didn't seem to care about that. He just seemed so obsessed with his own feelings, with what he wanted and didn't want.' She is crying now. 'He was so selfish. I couldn't bear it. He didn't care about me, or the baby, or anything or anyone but himself.'

'I think I understand Lucy. He behaved badly and you were right to leave him, though in time I hope you'll be able to let go of your hurt and anger. Those are heavy burdens to carry through life. They will hurt you far more than they'll hurt him.' He pauses, and then he permits himself to say what he knows he absolutely should not say. 'Maybe in future Lucy – I know that sometimes situations arise – when you get another boyfriend maybe – but – well, you must follow your conscience of course, but if you need to go on the pill, I mean, I know boys aren't always good at taking responsibility, and I do think it's best to save sex for when you're married, or at least for when you've really made a commitment to be together, but if things don't work out that way, I don't think it's always wrong for you to protect yourself from getting pregnant. You don't want to be in this situation again.'

She looks at him, narrowing her eyes and studying his face as if she has never really seen him before. 'Mum said I should go on the pill.' She giggles nervously. 'But she said I shouldn't tell you because what would you know about it.'

He laughs quietly. 'She's right of course.'

'Really?'

Something is welling up in him, some huge desire to reach out before this small space of trust closes up. 'Lucy, I'm a man. I have no idea what you're going through, but I've also made mistakes. I've done things I wish I hadn't done. I've also been afraid of hell. I know what that feels like.'

She looks at him, with that lovely blue gaze of hers. 'Really? But you're a priest.'

'I'm also a human being.' He smiles.

She hesitates, then she returns his smile. 'What have you done that's so bad?' she says, and he is glad to hear the feisty provocation in her voice. This is the Lucy he knows.

He laughs again. 'This is your confession, not mine.' She shrugs, but she's still smiling. There's something about her that makes him want to keep speaking, to confess. He hears himself saying, 'I'm gay Lucy.' My God, what am I doing? But it's okay. The trace of a smile lingers, but she's attentive and serious now. She wants him to say more. 'I'm not a woman. I'll never know what it's like to have an unwanted pregnancy, to stand in that place of condemnation where the Church seems so far from the love and mercy of God, but I do know what it's like to be condemned on other grounds, and I know that such condemnation is not of God.'

'How do you know?'

'Lucy, do your parents love you?' That's not a question he would ask of many teenagers in the confessional, but he knows he can ask it of Lucy.

'Yes.'

'How do you know?'

'I just do.' She smiles again. 'Okay. I think I get it. You just know God loves you?'

'Yes.' He hopes he sounds more confident than he feels.

He wonders if he should ask her not to tell anyone about this conversation. Should he tell her that the seal of the confessional works both ways? Does it work both ways? Then he decides that one way or the other, it's alright. He's gay. Surely people know that he's gay by now? Maybe they all talk about it. Maybe it's an open secret. But it doesn't matter, because this parish accepts him just as he is. Isn't that what Patrick was trying to tell him?

As she leaves he feels a sense of overwhelming gratitude for something that he cannot put a name to.

Siobhan is next in. She sits down in the chair next to him and her face is aglow with delight. 'I know this is confession Father, but I'm just bursting to tell you. Pappy's in remission. He phoned my mam this morning. Those tests they were doing – they changed his medication, and – and the tumour has shrunk.'

John remembers the wasted, frightened man he visited in hospital. Is this possible? He feels bewildered, but he says, 'Oh Siobhan, what wonderful news.'

'It's a miracle, isn't it Father?'

'Yes Siobhan, I do believe it's a miracle.'

'Thanks be to God! He's not better – we know that. The cancer is still there. But even so, he might even live for another year. And at the wedding on Sunday, he'll be able to walk up the aisle to give me away. He says he's feeling so much better with this new medication. Isn't that just great, Father? Isn't it just great? In just one day, he's become a different person, more like the daddy he used to be.'

'I'm so pleased Siobhan. It's God's gift to you, as you start your married life.'

She blushes and lowers her eyes, but she can't stop smiling. 'There's another gift too, Father. I suppose I should be confessing it, but it doesn't feel wrong. It feels – it does feel like another gift.' She glances up at him.

'Go on. What is it, Siobhan?'

'I'm pregnant, Father. A few months ago, when we knew Pappy was dying, we decided not to wait. We knew it would take a while to arrange the wedding – that was before we decided to bring it forward – and we just thought that if there was any way he could see his first grandchild before he – you know – before he died, we wanted that to happen. I'm only just pregnant, and I know he might not make it but now it looks as if he might, and I'm so glad, and so I'm confessing because we had sex before marriage and all that, but I'm not really sorry, so I don't know if I should confess or not.'

For her penance, he asks her to say the Lord's Prayer for her family, Anthony, their marriage and their baby.

'See you on Sunday,' she says as she leaves.

'See you on Sunday,' he says, and his heart lightens at the prospect of a wedding.

He looks at his watch. He should wait a bit longer in case anyone else arrives. He still feels queasy and his headache hasn't gone, but Lucy and Siobhan have left a lingering aura of sweetness and vulnerability that briefly consoles him.

As he waits, the dread trickles back. Will the cardinal come? His stomach twists and his head throbs. That silken sense of human warmth disappears. All he feels is the sludge of despair rising up around him, choking him.

The door opens. It's Pete Sanderson, Jane's husband. He looks terrible. His face is drawn with anxiety, and his shoulders seem even more stooped than usual. John can't remember Pete ever coming to confession before. Does he go somewhere else, or does he not go at all? He remembers Jane's last confession – her tears, her exhaustion, her faded maternity dress. He has a sudden image of Siobhan looking like that in ten years time, and he prays in a flash of quiet intensity that she will be spared such desolation.

Pete sits down and rests his hands on his knees. He is awkward and ill at ease. 'Morning Father.'

'Good morning Pete.' He makes the sign of the cross and waits to see if Pete will say something. Sensing his hesitation, John prays and recites a short passage from the day's psalm, then he says, 'So Pete, maybe you'd like to start by briefly saying how long it has been since your last confession, and how things have been for you recently.'

'Years. It's been years Father. I can't remember my last confession. And – umm – things haven't been good. The thing is –' He pauses, rubs his palms against his knees, and starts again. 'Things haven't been good between Jane and me. You know, with the pregnancy, and the kids, and she's always tired, and – since I lost my job, I suppose I've been struggling.' He dries up. He wipes his hand over his face and looks around, as if trying to pluck words from the air.

'It's alright Pete. Take your time.'

'It's these murders Father,' he says, blurting out the words.

John's stomach heaves. Dear God, not this. 'What about the murders Pete?'

'I've been – I'm so ashamed Father – I've been visiting prostitutes. You know, because of the way things are with Jane, and us not having sex.' His voice is shaking. 'I don't do it often, but I've been down Saint Peter's a few times. I've paid women to – you know – but, oh God, Father, I'm so scared. I'd never hurt them. I'd never do anything like that. Honestly. It's just sex. With a condom. I'm not taking any chances. You know, with disease or things. But I'm so scared Father. They're saying it's a Catholic doing those things. I'd never do things like that Father. I'd never hurt somebody. But what if the police find out? What if they come looking for me? Jane will find out. I'm so ashamed Father. What if she finds out? She'd leave me. I couldn't bear it. I couldn't bear it Father. Jane and my kids – they're my whole world. I've been such a fool Father. I've been such an idiot. God forgive me.'

John's head is spinning. His fears swarm and leap around him. Pete has crossed his arms about his body as if to fold himself up into the smallest possible space, and he is whimpering in distress. John tries to control his voice.

'Pete, maybe you should go to the police and tell them about this. They won't tell Jane.' He is less certain of that than he sounds. 'Frank Lambert in the parish is leading the investigation. You know Frank. If you like, I'll ask him to speak to you. I'll explain about your anxieties.'

'Would you Father? Would you tell him not to tell Jane? Will you do that for me?'

'I'll do my best Pete. I can't make any promises, but I'll do my best.'

Pete reflects for a moment, then he shakes his head. 'Maybe not Father. I mean, nobody needs to know, if I just keep quiet. I'll never do it again. I'll never visit another prostitute as long as I live. I swear to God.'

'Pete, you've nothing to hide. The police aren't interested in your marriage or your sex life. You just need to make sure they eliminate you from their enquiries. Of course it's up to you. This is the confessional. It's a place of absolute secrecy, you know that.' He has a sudden dreadful thought. What if the cardinal is outside, listening? What if the cardinal frames Pete?

But the cardinal is a priest. Once a priest, always a priest. Betraying the seal of the confessional – isn't that an even worse sin than murder? The thought appals him. How can it possibly be worse than killing somebody? His heart is pounding. He feels close to panic. 'Pete, let me speak to Frank for you, please. I won't tell him anything. I'll just say you want to speak to him.'

'Would you come with me Father? Will you come with me to speak to him?'

No God. Please not that. 'Of course I will Pete, if it would help.'

'Alright then.' A long pause. 'Yes, alright. When?'

'I think it's best to do it today Pete. You need to act quickly to make sure they don't come knocking at your door.'

Pete looks ashen-faced. 'They wouldn't do that, would they? What if Jane answers the door? I'm so scared Father. I'm so scared.' His whimpering turns to stifled sobs.

'Pete, Jane loves you. I'm not saying she wouldn't be shocked and angry if she knew about this, of course she would. But maybe she understands more than you realize. I think your marriage and her love for you are stronger than you think.' John wonders if that's true. How much can a husband or wife forgive, before the marriage falls apart? How much is it possible for love to bear?

'She says she hates me Father, because of all the babies. She says it's my fault, because I can't keep my hands off her. But I love her Father. I'm not good with words, but it's my way of being close, making love. I wish I had some other way. I bring her flowers sometimes, but – well –' He dries up again.

'Maybe you two should think about some counselling Pete. There are excellent marriage counsellors who could help you through this,' says John, glad that his voice betrays nothing of his inner turmoil.

'Do you think so Father?'

'Yes. Yes, I do think so Pete. I can help you to set that up as well. Why don't you speak to Jane and see what she thinks? I have a feeling she'd welcome the suggestion.'

Pete agrees to think about it. As he shuffles out of the confessional, John wonders which of them is more terrified, which of them feels more helpless and hopeless. Dear Jesus, I can't do this. I'm not strong enough. Please help me.

The silence of the universe roars back at him.

In the sacristy before Mass, he senses some tension, irritation maybe, in the way Edith bustles around him. Finally he breaks his own rule of silence.

'Edith, is something bothering you?'

'Oh. No. It's nothing Father. I just need to tell you that the plumber says he left the presbytery key under the mat this morning.'

'What plumber?'

'The plumber you rang about the heating in the church,' she says.

'I didn't ring a plumber.'

'That's very odd. I did wonder – I mean, you know I'm always here to help with things like that. You don't have to do it all yourself. I did wonder why you hadn't mentioned it.'

Something is crawling up John's spine. It slithers against his flesh. 'So who was this plumber Edith?'

'I don't know Father. He emailed the other day. Let me think. Today's Friday. It would have been Wednesday. No. Maybe Tuesday.'

He wants to shake her. 'It doesn't matter what day it was,' he says too abruptly so that she looks hurt. 'Sorry Edith. What I mean is, I just need to know what happened. What did he look like?'

'Oh, I never saw him Father. He emailed – you know, the email I use for the office and for keeping the newsletter and the blog up to date. It's ourladyofsorrows@gmail.com. That's the one I use for church business. You know that of course. It's the email address that's on the newsletter. I don't use my personal email address. I don't want these anti-Catholic trolls to know any personal details. You never know what people might do. There are some fanatics out there. I mean, this murderer, and all those violent Moslems and other people.' She looks woebegone – an innocent abroad in an evil world.

John wants to scream. 'What about the plumber, Edith?' he says, trying to keep the exasperation from his voice.

'Oh, him. Or I suppose it might be her. You never know these days, with women's lib and things, though I've always thought plumbing is a man's job, like the priesthood, you know.'

'So what happened?' He marvels at her inability to respond to the urgency in his voice.

Well, he – let's assume it was a he – he emailed to say he'd arranged to meet you at the presbytery but he'd been delayed, and you'd said to just leave the key under the mat and he would collect it. I can forward you the email if you like.'

'Yes. Yes, please do that Edith, if you don't mind. Do it straight after Mass.'

She eyes him suspiciously. 'Are you alright Father?'

'Yes, I'm fine Edith. Did he tell you why he thought I'd contacted him?'

'He said you were concerned that the heating in the church wasn't working properly. As I say, Father, I was a bit surprised because that was the first I'd heard of it. And I haven't noticed any problems with the heating myself. But then, you can be so independent about these things, I just thought you had taken it into your head to organise it yourself. But as I say, I haven't

171

noticed the heating not working, and nobody's complained. I think it would have been Tuesday, now that I think of it. It was the day before that interfaith service, though don't get me started on that again.'

Back in the presbytery after the regular Friday Mass for the school, he goes straight to his office and switches on his laptop. It takes an age to grind through the start up process. Edith tells him he should get a new one, but he doesn't normally mind that it's so slow. He sits at the desk and watches the screen, and his stomach cramps with the anxiety of waiting. Shula rubs herself against his legs. He forgot to feed her this morning.

'In a minute,' he tells her, and his voice booms in his ears. She jumps up onto his lap, expertly aiming her body through the gap between the desk and his legs. She sits watching the screen with him, as his emails slowly appear. He scans down the thick black list. There's the agenda for the deanery meeting next week. There are several about the First Communion and what the children should wear, squabbling mothers ping ponging back and forth and copying him in every time. There's a promotion for priestly vestments – hand-embroidered silk and satin, on special offer. He clicks 'mark as junk'. There's an offer of hot teenage sex, and he wonders how such emails get through the various defences Edith says she has installed. He marks that as junk too. There's an email from Holly.

'Darling John, thank you thank you thank you. I'm a new woman today. Words won't express what I feel. I have a stonking hangover of course, but oh John. Thank you. xxx

He leaves that on the screen and goes downstairs to feed Shula. She purrs and weaves around his legs as he fills her dish, bumping her nose against his forehead when he bends down to put the dish back on the floor. He decides to ring Frank, to allow more time for Edith to send the email. He goes to the phone in the living room. He still resists using his mobile when he can use a landline. His sister tells him he's a technophobe. He once tried to explain to her that he just prefers to live in a world of matter and substance. She said that was an odd thing to say for someone who believes his life is controlled by a supernatural being. He told her she sounded just like Chris when she spoke like that. She laughed and admitted that was more or less what Chris said.

Thinking of Kate, he craves her company. He wants the normality and love of her home. He decides he will ring her and ask if he can go round for supper on Monday evening. But first, he looks up Frank's direct line in the address book beside the phone, and calls him. It goes straight to the answer phone.

'Hello Frank. It's John here, Father John from the parish. I need to speak to you about something. It's quite urgent. Would you give me a ring? I'll be in the presbytery all morning. Thanks.' He hangs up and dials his sister's mobile.

Her voice is warm. 'Hi John, this is a nice surprise. You've caught me in my tea break luckily. Things are hectic here, as usual. How are you?'

'I'm hung over actually.'

'Really?' She gives a delighted laugh. 'But it's Lent.'

'I know. What a miserable sinner I am.'

'Thank God you show symptoms of the human condition.'

'I was wondering if I could come for supper on Monday.'

'Of course you can. It would be great to see you. The children will be delighted. Come for Sunday lunch if you'd rather. I'll do a roast.'

'No, there's a wedding on Sunday, but I thought I'd go for a walk on Monday and come and see you afterwards.'

'A wedding? In Lent? Jesus John, are you losing your faith or something?' She is clearly in a good mood.

'The bride's father is dying,' he says. 'Sometimes you have to break the rules.'

'Mmm. Some of us have torn the rule book up. We get on fine without it.'

'You always were an anarchist,' he says affectionately. 'See you on Monday.'

'See you on Monday,' she says, and there's a smile in her voice so that he feels flooded with love for her.

As he hangs up, the phone rings. 'John? It's Frank.'

'Frank. Thank you for calling.'

'You said you wanted to speak to me urgently.'

'Yes. It's about the murders.'

There's a long silence, then Frank says quietly, 'I can come round now. Stay where you are and I'll be there in twenty minutes.'

The dread starts with a prickle in his scalp and pierces like icicles all the way to the tips of his toes. Does Frank think he wants to make a confession? 'No, Frank, wait. You've misunderstood. It's a parishioner who wants to speak to you. He asked if I'd be there. He wants to know if you can come round this afternoon.'

Another pause. Frank lets out a long slow breath. 'John, it's Friday. We're all preparing for the prospect of another murder tonight. Is it really worth my precious time doing this, when there are so many other things I could be doing? I mean, is this likely to result in an arrest? Is it likely to prevent another murder? Can't it wait?'

'No, it can't wait.' He doesn't know what else to say.

Frank sighs again. 'Alright John, I'll come because it's you, and I trust you not to waste my time. I can be there at about three. See you later.'

John goes back upstairs to the study, and his body aches with the effort of moving. He would like to go back to bed and sleep for the rest of the day. He eases himself into the chair and looks at the computer screen. There are two new emails at the top of the list, forwarded from ourladyofsorrows@gmail.com. He reads the message from Edith:

Dear Father John,

Here is the first email from the plumber. As you can see, it was sent on Wednesday. I left the key under the mat as requested.

Blessings,

Edith.

He scrolls down and looks at the email address: robertmcd@ yahoo.com. He reads the message.

Good morning. I'm the plumber Father John asked to check the heating in the presbytery and the church. He said I could collect the key from you after Mass but I have been held up on another job. Please would you leave the key for the front door under the mat and I'll return it when I've finished? Father John said it's fine to leave it there for me. Thank you.

Robert McDonald

Plumber

The name leaps out at John. Robert? No. It's not possible. What monstrous trick is this? His hands are shaking as he clicks on the second email:

Dear Father John,

Here is the second email, which came early this morning.

Many blessings,

Edith.

He scrolls down again.

Good morning. I have checked the plumbing system and discovered a small fault which I have repaired.

I am happy to do this as an act of service to the Church. I have left the key under the mat.
      Robert McDonald
      Plumber

John stares at the screen, then he goes to the window and looks out. There's nobody there, not even Sarah under the cherry tree. A canopy of clouds has obliterated the day's blue and gold beginnings. It billows low over the rooftops, threatening rain. He goes downstairs and opens the front door. He looks around to be sure that there's nobody lurking in the shadows, then he lifts the doormat. The key is there. He goes back inside and closes the door. He leans against the wall and closes his eyes. Robert. No. It can't be. He is losing his mind. There can be no other explanation.

Pete arrives just before three, and Frank arrives a few minutes later. Pete tells Frank about his visits to prostitutes, and his dread that Jane will find out. Frank listens sympathetically. John wonders if he believes Pete, or if he is filing away information for further investigation. Frank is behaving almost as a priest might behave in the confessional. Pete and Frank have both been in the parish for years, though as far as John is aware they are only passing acquaintances.

By the time Pete finishes, he's sobbing and wringing his hands in his lap. 'I'm sorry Frank. I'd do anything not to have done it. I was such a fool. I'm just terrified that Jane will find out. If she left me, my life would be over. She's my world.'

Frank speaks briskly, but there's no accusation or blame in his voice. 'Just avoid the area, Pete. You're not under suspicion. You don't feature in any of our investigations. The women have given us some names, but nobody has named you. They know who the violent punters are. They have an instinct for these things. Go home to your wife and family. Masturbate if you must, but please, stay away from the hookers for the time being. Okay?' He reaches out and squeezes Pete's shoulder.

As they walk to the door, John feels a lump in his throat. The kindness of ordinary people fills him with wonder. Pete walks down the path to the lane, and John thinks that he looks less defeated, less bowed under the weight of his guilt and fear, than when he arrived.

'Do you mind if I come back in for a few minutes?' asks Frank.

Why does his heart lurch? He has nothing to hide. Yet guilt claws at his belly, filling him with dread. 'Yes, of course. Come in.' They go back into the cavernous lounge and sit down.

'John, I'm going to be blunt with you. We're beginning to suspect that this is the work of a Catholic priest, or at least somebody who is obsessed by Catholic ritual. I need help. Is there anybody among your fellow priests who might be capable of doing these things?'

John realizes that he has been so focused on the cardinal, so preoccupied with the conviction that the cardinal is the murderer, that it hasn't even entered his head to suspect anybody else. He feels a sudden lightening of his soul, so intense he almost wants to laugh out loud. Why hadn't he thought of that? Of course it's not the ghost of a dead cardinal. It's one of the other priests.

'Well?' Frank prompts him.

'I'm just trying to think. I don't know Frank. It's not the kind of question I've asked myself.'

Frank narrows his eyes. He no longer has that consoling demeanour he had with Pete. Something has hardened in him. This is the man who confronts suspects in interrogation rooms. 'You priests must look at each other with suspicion all the time,' he says.

'Why do you think that?' asks John, surprised.

'I'd have thought you're all wondering which of your fellow priests is going to be the next to get found out in the sex abuse scandal.'

John reflects on the question. He wants to answer as truthfully as possible. 'I don't know,' he says eventually. 'I don't think we do that. I can't speak for the others, but I couldn't live like that Frank. Yes, there have been scandals and there will no doubt be more scandals, but – I suppose there's something about having to survive and get on with life. I couldn't bear to live with that constant level of doubt and suspicion about the men I work with.'

Frank is still staring at him with that keen-eyed vigilance. 'John, this is a man who hates women. And – I can say this to you, though the others in the investigation team would laugh at me if I said it to them – even more than women, he hates Our Lord.'

'What do you mean?' asks John. How can his voice sound so normal?

'He mutilates them John. We think they're still alive while he carves them up.'

Cold. It's so cold. The breath of the tombs is wafting in from the cemetery outside, and skeletons are rattling and clamouring to be let in. 'What do you mean, "carves them up"?'

'He hammers nails into their hands and feet. He pushes barbed wire crowns onto their heads. He puts rosaries around their necks. And – and he rapes them with crucifixes which he leaves in their bodies.' Frank shrugs. 'Sorry John, I know it's gruesome. It offends me to tell you all this, but I have to. If you know the details you might be able to help me to work out what the hell is going on. Nan MacDonald also had her throat cut. Sissy Jackson was beheaded. Ana Milkovic was set on fire, which is why it took us so long to identify her.'

Tell him. Tell him about the cardinal. I must tell him. This is the work of the cardinal. As sure as my God lives and will one day be my judge, I know who is doing this.

But what do I know? I know a dead man has been visiting the confessional. I know I see ghosts. I see Sarah every day. The cardinal is a ghost. Ghosts can't murder people. And besides, it's the confessional. I'm sworn to secrecy. I'm a priest. I can't betray the seal of the confessional.

'John?'

'I – I don't know what to say Frank. I'm struggling to take it in. Who would do such things? I'm sorry. It's just – I've never heard – I don't know – dear God, Frank.'

Frank fixes him with a gaze so focused and intense that John feels trapped in its grip. 'I need your help, John. If you suspect anything, if you hear anything, if you have even the faintest intuition that you know who this is or why anybody might do this, you need to tell me.'

John nods. He remembers being caught in a rip tide once when he was swimming in the sea. He remembers the water pulling him out and out, the shore receding, and the sudden certainty that he was about to die.

Maybe this time too, the danger will pass and he will be delivered safely onto dry land. But now, he is being dragged out to sea and he can do nothing but allow this force to carry him where it will.

'I give you my word, Frank. If I think any living soul might be doing these things, I'll tell you.'

Frank narrows his eyes. John knows it was an odd thing to say. 'Do priests go to confession, John?'

'Of course we do.'

'Do you all confess to one another?'

'I suppose some do. I have a spiritual director, but yes, we go to confession, and that means to another priest.'

'And what happens if somebody confesses to something like this – to murder, for example?'

John has to be honest. He can't lie to this man. 'The secrecy of the confessional is absolute,' he says, and he knows there's conviction in his voice. This is non-negotiable. He stares down the detective and keeps his gaze unflinching before the probing eyes that are trying to defeat him.

'So you would rather a young woman is tortured, mutilated and murdered than betray the secrets of the confessional?' Frank doesn't try to disguise the contempt in his voice.

'I have no choice, Frank. I'm a priest. My duty to God comes before everything else.'

It's Frank who averts his gaze. 'That is the most chilling thing I've ever heard,' he says.

After Frank leaves, John prowls the presbytery, going from room to room as if in one of those rooms he will find the answer to a question for which he has no words. The presbytery echoes around him.

He sits at his desk and tries to answer emails, but he can't concentrate. He clicks into a local news site and reads the headlines. '**WHO WILL BE NEXT?**' the headline screams in bold black lettering. There's a picture of a woman in Saint Peter's at night, her pixelated features looking tiny and vulnerable in the darkness.

He pushes down the lid of the laptop before it seduces him into ever more complex searches through the labyrinth of the internet, looking for the cardinal and trying to find out who the man in the confessional is, and what he wants. He's afraid that the more he knows, the more intense the pressure will become to go to the police and tell them everything.

Beneath his priestly obligation to protect the seal of the confessional, there's another darker, unacknowledged fear. He knows that sooner or later he is going to have to follow that fear wherever it leads, but he has spent so many years – most of his priesthood – resisting that temptation. He does not dare to go there now.

Robert. Robert McDonald.

For the next two hours, he busies himself listlessly with tasks around the presbytery. He makes himself a bland meal of pasta and grated cheese, then he does some tidying and hoovering. He tries to read a book, but wild imaginings about what might happen on the city streets tonight claim his attention and prevent him from concentrating.

He feels lost and alone. Maybe he should go into the church and try to pray. He pushes open the door and a tremor of fear runs through him. The church is gloomy and deserted.

Facing down his fear, he takes a golden monstrance shaped like a sunburst out of the sacristy and carries it over to the side altar. The candle pulses in its red glass lantern, announcing the presence of consecrated hosts in the tabernacle. The bronze doors of the tabernacle are engraved with the figures of Mary Magdalene and Christ outside the tomb on Easter morning. Above the altar is an icon of Our Lady of Perpetual Succour, gleaming gold in the candlelight.

He goes up the steps to the altar and opens the tabernacle doors. He places a host in the monstrance and sets it carefully down on the altar. He goes down the steps to kneel in front of the altar, and lets the silence engulf him. The thick walls of the church shut out the distant rumble of traffic and the voices of people passing by. The blank white host with its glittering surround of jewels and sunbeams holds him in silent scrutiny.

Time slows and melts into emptiness. He allows himself to be drawn into some dense, soundless realm beyond all seeing and sensing.

The church door swishes open and gives a dull thud as it closes. His body is catapulted back into consciousness and all his senses are at once alert. He hears the footfall of somebody at the back of the church. Cold air washes over him and seeps into his bones, and at the same time he becomes aware of the nauseating stench of something rotting.

He waits. He doesn't need to turn around. He knows who it is. He listens for the footsteps coming closer, but there's nothing apart from a faint rustle far behind him. He begins to shiver. There's a constriction in his throat, and a terrible pounding in his ears.

Help me. The host gazes back at him across an infinite abyss, ruthless in its featureless white mystery, beyond all prayer and supplication. Help me. He raises his gaze to the figure in the icon above the altar, but she too is indifferent, lost to the world, consumed by her own agony and abandonment.

He turns around. At the back of the church, a tall figure is standing in front of the Pietà, shadowy and insubstantial in the shimmer of candlelight. It reaches out and places a tea light on the stand. It takes a taper and lights it from another candle, then holds it to the wick of the tea light until it catches.

John stands with his back to the tabernacle and wills himself to say something, but he is frozen with fear. The man looks up, and they watch each other across the empty pews and shadowed aisles.

Finally, John finds his voice. 'Wait. Don't go. I need to speak to you. I know who you are. I know what you've done.' His voice echoes in the high dark roof vaults.

'Another time, perhaps. It's a busy night for me.' There's the familiar lisp, the hissing menace of the voice.

'Wait! Cardinal Bradley. I'll go to the police.'

'I don't think so John. I know too much about you.'

The figure turns and leaves, swiftly and almost soundlessly, even as John forces his legs to carry him along the aisle to the back of the church. He pulls open the door and rushes out into the cold, damp night, but the cardinal has vanished into the mist and rain.

'I know too much about you.' What did he mean?

John knows what he meant. There's no more running away. The memories must be confronted. He must face the truth. All is forgiven, but the effort of forgetting has failed. It's all there, waiting. It has been there all along, waiting.

He makes his way wearily back to the presbytery. His limbs feel heavy and he is conscious of being hung over and needing to sleep. He contemplates listening to music, letting it all come back. Maybe it would be better to go for a walk, to let the cold night air revive him and sharpen his mind.

He puts on his anorak and pushes his way out through the presbytery door, locking it carefully behind him. Then he remembers the key under the mat, and he breaks into a cold sweat. Has the cardinal been in the presbytery? What was he doing? Has he had a key cut? In the demands of the day, John had forgotten about that disquieting incident, but now it looms large in his mind. He resolves to get the locks changed first thing on Monday morning.

He walks down the path to the lane, glancing over at the garden to see if Sarah is there. The garden is empty. He walks to the junction at the end of the road, trying to hold on to the normality of the terraced houses with their bright windows and the muffled sounds of family life seeping under the doors. The corner shop is aglow with light as it always is, from seven in the morning until eleven at night.

At the junction, he pauses. If he turns right, he will be heading towards Saint Peter's. The temptation is almost irresistible, terror and yearning inextricably linked in his imagination. It's a place of dread and horror tonight, but it's also the place where Luke goes, the place where a warm and welcoming pub opens its doors to those whom the Church rejects.

Behind him, Our Lady of Sorrows is steeped in darkness and absence. Out there, shining brightly in the night, is the Queen's Arms where human beings live and love without the constant fear of being found out, of being condemned. Surely, Jesus is there, waiting for him, waiting for him to accept the gift of love that is being offered? But he turns left, walking away from the centre with its people and lights and dramas of sex and death, going nowhere.

The road is busy with Friday night traffic. People scurry home with umbrellas thrust up against the sky, closed off from the world. The rain drifts around him, congealing on his face and running in rivulets down his forehead and the sides of his mouth. He pulls up his anorak hood and tugs it forward for protection. He walks fast but aimlessly, heading along the main road until he sees the red brick walls of the Church of Saints Felicity and Perpetua standing staunch against the night, with light spilling from its stained glass windows.

As he approaches, people begin to shuffle out from the evening Mass. Too late, he sees some of his parishioners coming out and heading in his direction. Edith, Mary Carpenter and Sadie Johnson. During Lent they go to evening Mass at Saints Felicity and Perpetua, grumbling that John doesn't say Mass every evening at Our Lady of Sorrows. He wishes he had thought of that and avoided walking this way, but it's too late.

'Oh my goodness, it's Father John!' says Mary. 'Look at you, scurrying along like some young hoodie looking for trouble!' She laughs, and the others laugh with her.

He pushes back the hood and tries to look relaxed. 'Hello you three. I forgot you come to Mass here.'

'Yes, well Father, we'd rather stay in our own church, quite frankly,' says Edith with that note of accusation in her voice. 'We're not too keen on Father Forrester. He's a bit too full of himself, if you ask me. Don't we all think so, girls?' The others nod in agreement.

'I'm sure he dyes his hair,' says Sadie. 'It's jet-black. It's unnatural.'

'I hear he's very popular with the girls at Saint Catherine's,' says Mary. 'I suppose objectively speaking he's a bit of a looker.'

Edith titters girlishly. 'Oh dear Father John, I hope you don't think we gossip about you like this.'

The comment startles John. It tells him that they do indeed gossip about him. Of course they do. What do they say, he wonders? He smiles warmly at Edith. 'I don't dye my hair, but I wouldn't mind being popular with the girls.' He feels uneasy, saying that. How much do they know?

Mary nudges him with her elbow and gives him a conspiratorial wink. 'If I were a bit younger, I'd certainly fancy you Father,' she says.

The three of them laugh good-naturedly, then they link arms, bid him goodnight, and head back in the direction of Our Lady of Sorrows.

He walks on. He turns down a side road to get away from the traffic. The houses are larger here, semi-detached with loft conversions and garages, primly lined up in their neatly tended gardens. He discovers it's a cul de sac, but there's a narrow lane leading off to the right, with a footpath sign pointing towards it. He heads along it, and then begins to feel nervous as it leads him away from people and traffic and houses. The intermittent lights cast grey shadows, emphasising the darkness and the solitude. He quickens his pace, hoping he soon comes to another road. It seems to go on forever.

He strains his ears, listening for following footsteps. He turns around, but the lane behind him is deserted. He pushes his hands into his pockets and hurries on.

Suddenly, he hears the slightest of sounds behind him and a dark shadow flits into the corner of his vision. His heart leaps and he spins around. There's nothing there. He continues on his way, and as he thrusts his hands deeper into his pockets he hears it again, that whispered hiss and the shadow of a hand or some other object reaching over his shoulder. He turns again but sees only the snarling emptiness.

He's half-running now, and his laboured breathing fills the night. Again, that shadow appears, and again he spins around. 'Please,' he whimpers. 'What do you want?' He wraps his arms around himself. 'Please Jesus, please. Holy Mary Mother of God.' His anorak hood tugs forward with the movement of his arms. The nylon hisses, and the hood appears more clearly now over his shoulder. Oh Jesus. Oh Mother Mary. His knees feel weak, and he's ashamed of his cowardice and his stupidity. He laughs, and his laughter sounds demented in the silence. Would you believe it, Jesus? I'm running away from my anorak hood.

At last, the lane joins a road. It seems to be some kind of industrial estate, with a couple of dark warehouses and a builders' yard. He turns right and walks on, to discover that he has come out on the far side of Ladywell station, where small suburban trains still run a few times a day. If he crosses the footbridge over the tracks, he can take a circular route back to the presbytery.

He climbs the steps and pauses on the bridge to look down at the deserted station. It seems bleak and desolate. He feels vulnerable, but now he is determined to get a grip on his fears. He will not let the cardinal frighten him like this. He will not cower indoors for fear of facing the darkness, for fear of facing himself, for fear of what tomorrow might bring. Whatever this test is, he will show God that he is strong enough to bear it. He will not be defeated. He will not be intimidated. He makes the sign of the cross and says an Our Father.

NINETEEN

FOURTH SATURDAY OF LENT

The bleep of the alarm clock startles him awake. The first thing he notices is the smell. It's the rotting stench that the cardinal sometimes trails in his wake, faint but unmistakable, and it's here in his bedroom. Dear God. Where is the cardinal hiding?

The room is small and sparsely furnished, with few hiding places. Is he in the wardrobe? Is he under the bed? A childhood horror of a skeletal hand reaching out from beneath the bed and grabbing his exposed arm makes him burrow deeper under the duvet, shuffling away from the edge of the bed towards the wall. Shula, curled up on the bottom of the bed, yawns and stretches and comes to pummel his chest. He imagines a human form pushing through the wall, the way they sometimes do in horror films.

He wraps his arm around the cat and rubs her neck. 'Hello girl,' he says. His voice is still hoarse with sleep. He waits and listens, but all he can hear is Shula purring. 'Is anybody there?' he croaks, and immediately feels foolish. What does he expect? An answer coming from inside the wardrobe or under the bed? 'Cooey. I'm here!' He sniffs the air and wonders if he's imagining it, but he can still smell it. He eases Shula off his chest.

He stretches his legs as far away from the edge of the bed as he can, and takes a small leap onto the floor. He pulls open the wardrobe and sees only his meagre supply of shirts and two jackets hanging there, with his three pairs of shoes beneath them

– a pair of trainers, black leather shoes for special occasions, and the battered old brown shoes that he wears every day. He keeps his walking boots in the car.

He turns and looks at the bed. Shula is sitting there watching him, still purring, anticipating breakfast. Surely, if the cardinal were anywhere in the house, Shula would be showing signs of fright?

Cautiously, he bends down and peers beneath the bed. His slippers are there, just as he left them, and he can't see anything else. He wriggles closer and the smell becomes stronger. Whatever it is, it's not the cardinal. Feeling slightly reassured, John pulls the bed away from the wall. There in the corner is the tiny body of a mouse, its rotting entrails spilling from its belly. He feels simultaneously sick and relieved.

He goes downstairs and Shula follows him, eager to be fed. The radio sits on the kitchen table, daring him to turn it on, heavy and expectant with its announcements of the horrors of the night. He ignores it. Instead, he speaks to Shula.

'I wish you wouldn't do that,' he says. 'That mouse was a living creature, just like you. It's one of God's creatures. I feed you so that you don't have to catch mice or birds or any other living things.' She rubs herself against his legs and pushes her moist nose against his face as he bends down to fill her bowl. He wonders how long she tortured the mouse, before it finally died and she lost interest. 'You don't even eat the things you catch, that's what really offends me,' he says. 'I understand your natural instinct might be to stalk your prey and eat it, but I really don't understand why you just torture things to death and then leave me to clean up the mess.'

He gathers up disinfectant, rubber gloves and an old newspaper to wrap the body in.

Eventually, he knows he must face the morning news. He remembers that moment of defiant courage on the bridge last night and tries to summon it back.

He looks at his watch. He will listen to the news, then he'll take a cup of coffee up to his bedroom and do the Office and pray the readings for the morning Mass. He has to reflect on what he will say at Siobhan and Anthony's wedding tomorrow. He must be calm and behave normally. Weddings are highlights in the parish, particularly when they involve generations of parishioners. Everybody will be there. He thinks of Siobhan's joy in the confessional, as she told him about Patrick's miraculous recovery. He wishes he didn't feel so sceptical. It seems churlish to doubt such a wonderful gift. He puts the kettle on and switches on the radio.

> *There is only one question on the minds of everyone living in Westonville this morning. Will a body be found today? Was another young woman murdered last night in the city's red light district? Or have the killings come to an end? After the murder of three young women, police wonder if a serial killer is at large and a pattern is emerging. But so far, there is nothing to suggest another murder last Friday night, and nothing has yet been reported about last night. So have the murders stopped?*

The presenter is called Susan Lindon. Her voice is easy on the ears, despite her sombreness appropriate to the topic. There's also a tinge of excitement in her words. After all, this is news that interests everybody in the country. Serial killers are so much more interesting than global finance or international diplomacy.

'With us in the studio to discuss the killings is criminologist and psychiatrist Dr Stuart Johnson, who specialises in the diagnosis and treatment of psychopaths. Welcome, Professor Johnson,' she says.

'Thank you Susan. Just one correction – there is no treatment for psychopathy. A psychopath can't be treated. We haven't yet discovered a treatment or a form of medication that can induce compassion, empathy and sociability in place of hatred, cruelty and isolation. We haven't discovered any threat of punishment or imprisonment that can make such a person change their ways, for they are beyond love and they are beyond fear. In our current state of knowledge, we would have to say that psychopaths are lost to the world.'

'That sounds extremely bleak.'

'It is bleak. It's the harshest reality that someone in my profession has to face, that sense of total failure in the face of one of humanity's worst ailments. We scientists shy away from the language of evil, but if there is such a thing as an evil person, then I think I'd have to say it comes in the form of the psychopath. And they are often extremely cunning and manipulative – evil geniuses, if you like. Charming, seductive, deceptive and narcissistic, but with a vast abyss at the core of their being where conscience and empathy are formed.'

The man's voice is smooth and soothing, almost like the cardinal's but where the cardinal's voice is cold and sardonic, this voice is kind and reassuring. It's a good voice for somebody who has to deal with people's mental anguish.

'It has been suggested that these murders might be the work of a Catholic or a Satanist. Do you believe those stories?' asks Susan.

'Like the rest of us, psychopaths operate in the worlds of language and meaning that are familiar to them. If this person has been influenced by Satanism or Catholicism, then there might well be signs of that in his methods.'

'Might it be a woman?'

'It might, though this kind of killing is rarely if ever associated with female perpetrators. Is psychopathy gendered? That's an interesting question that researchers are just beginning to investigate. It may be that psychopathy manifests itself differently in women, for all sorts of cultural and psychological reasons.'

'And do you think these killings definitely are the work of a psychopath?' Susan doesn't quite manage to hide the thrill of horror in her voice.

'It's hard to say at this stage. We must be careful not to label every murder, however cruel, as the work of a psychopath. The human soul is complex and easily wounded. People can be driven to do terrible things to one another for all sorts of reasons. Hatred is a powerful emotion, as powerful as love. In fact, I'd say hatred is love in its most disfigured and wounded form. The real psychopath is beyond both love and hate. I'm not a religious man, but I'd say the psychopath has no soul.'

'That sounds religious to me!'

'Actually, Freud always used the language of the soul. The English aren't comfortable with that kind of language, so it was translated as "mind" in English. But "mind" is a reductive word. Whatever you believe about the ultimate meaning of life, "soul" refers to the psychic life of a person in a way that encompasses all our feelings and reactions and emotions and intuitions. It's a much richer, more all-embracing term than "mind". Psychopaths most definitely have minds, but do they have souls? I'm not sure.'

'Dr Johnson, I wish we could continue this conversation because it's fascinating but we must leave it there. Thank you very much for being with us in the studio this morning. Let's just hope that whatever the reasons, those three murders were not the work of a psychopath, and I'm sure I speak for everyone in Westonville when I say that I hope no more bodies will be discovered today.

'Now, have you ever wondered what causes cellulite, that dimpling of the thighs which we women of a certain age know so well! Scientists have been looking into ...'

John turns the radio off. His brave resolve has been displaced by a profound unease. Is it possible for a human being to have no soul? Is that what it would mean to be human but not made in the image of God, a kind of rational animal as Aristotle and

Aquinas would call it, but more a robot than a person? What God would create such a creature?

They were taught in seminary that a human is not necessarily a person. Personhood is a grace that comes about with a transformation of the soul, from lonely individualism into relationship with God and with others. It was Professor Jones who taught them that, a soft-spoken American priest who did his best to keep alive the spirit of Vatican II but who eventually lost his post because of the conservatism creeping through the Church. Professor Jones dared to suggest in passing during a lecture that there was no good reason why women could not be priests. One of the students reported him to the rector, and when challenged he refused to recant. That was all it took to strip him of his teaching role. Meanwhile, Cardinal Bradley prowled among them with his razor sharp mind, his unflinching absolutism, and his insatiable appetite for beautiful young seminarians.

Shula pushes past him and goes out through the cat flap. He fears for the fledgling birds. He fears for himself. He is afraid for the women out there in the city streets. He is afraid. He is afraid of everything, even God. Especially God. Behind him, the kettle gurgles and clicks off.

He sits in the confessional full of dread, but the cardinal does not appear. Only a few people drift through the door with their burdens of blame and shame, blushing and struggling through the tender failings of their own humanity.

He is so weary of listening, and he laments this change within himself. Confession has always been the most intimate and pastoral side of his priesthood. He has cherished the grace that comes with the speaking and forgiving of sins. Now he feels only frustration and futility.

This is the lowest time of Lent. By now, most of the resolutions have been broken, the spiritual energy of Ash Wednesday and the start of Lent has drained away, and a sense of listlessness settles over the parish. Next Sunday is Palm Sunday, the start of Holy Week, his favourite week of the liturgical year. Holy Week still retains something of the awe and mystery of the faith, with its deep sense of penitence, reflection and hope.

This year, will it be different? In his heart of hearts he knows that the worst is yet to come, and for the first time he sees the days leading up to Calvary as a time of horror and desolation. Whatever the cardinal is doing, John has a deep intuition that these murders have something to do with him, and the timing is intentional and calculated.

The day grows warmer as the sun climbs in a clear, bright sky. John decides to go for a walk, to calm his thoughts and reflect on his homily for tomorrow's wedding. He packs a sandwich and a flask of tea. As he locks the door, he remembers again the strange incident of the plumber and wonders if the cardinal has a key. He thinks of getting the locks changed and having to tell Edith why. The thought of all those arrangements and explanations exhausts him. He feels unable to think clearly. In the car, he listens to a CD called *The Best of Bach*, avoiding the radio because he doesn't want to know if another woman was murdered last night.

He drives to the hills west of the city. He follows a winding footpath up through the woods, and the drift of sunlight among the fresh green leaves relaxes him. He likes walking through deciduous woodlands, which allow things to grow in the light and space beneath the trees. The overgrown path takes him along the side of a disused quarry, with its scarred and broken rock face veiled in ribbons of ivy. He pushes aside brambles that claw at his clothes, and the concentration needed to navigate the patches of mud and fallen branches stops him from brooding on more insurmountable problems.

Eventually, he comes to an open meadow with views across the trees and the rolling countryside to the sea beyond. There are standing stones up here, enigmatic symbols of an ancient people's faith. He takes off his anorak and sits on a log to look at the view. He thinks he should take out his missal and reflect on tomorrow's readings, but he'd rather enjoy the bird song and the ripples of warmth in the air. He relinquishes himself to the tender forbidden memories that rise up in his soul like morning mist, innocent of the horror to come.

The seminarians have just finished their exams in Rome, and they're celebrating. It's late June, and the air is aglow with evening light brushing up against the buildings and seeming to seep into the ancient ruins, casting a shimmer of gold over the city.

There are six of them in the group. They are all gay. By now, John has become less anxious about hiding his sexuality – he has realized that it's the heterosexual men, not the gay ones, who are out of place in the seminary – and he has also become more confident about asserting his celibacy. He is not alone in that either. Two of the other seminarians in the group are celibate, which is why he has agreed to join them.

Robert McDonald is from Glasgow and David Williamson is from Chicago. They have become close friends during their years in Rome. Although they have only acknowledged it briefly and in passing, the three of them find a common bond in their celibacy as well as in their homosexuality. They want to be good priests, and they sustain one another in quiet bonds of faith and friendship. He feels safe going out with this group so long as David and Robert are there, even though he hardly knows the other three men and at least two of them have reputations for cruising and frequenting gay clubs and saunas. Damian Thomas and Patrick Byrne have a swagger that comes from knowing their notoriety and revelling in the interest and adulation of seminarians who long to be like them. The other one, Peter Drake, minces rather than swaggers, in an elaborate display of camp piety that goes well with his porcelain features and full mouth.

They are all dressed casually in slacks and open-necked shirts, not wanting to attract the attention of the tourists in the cafés they drink at along the way. They share a vibrant sense of release and anticipation. They will all be returning home soon, to begin their work in parishes and chaplaincies. Only as John contemplates leaving Rome does he realize how much he has fallen in love with the city.

They make their way to the *Campo Dei Fiori*, where they stop for cocktails. Street artists perform and vendors peddle trinkets to tourists amidst the stallholders who are closing up for the day, leaving trails of crushed flowers and squashed vegetables for the pigeons to dine on. The flowers lend an exotic perfume to the air, and John feels a deep sense of contentment. Was there ever a better life than this?

They cross the *Ponte Sisto* and meander through the cobbled lanes of Trastevere, stopping in a café in the square outside *Santa Maria in Trastevere* for more cocktails. The golden mosaics on the façade of the basilica catch the evening light, setting the robed female figures aglow with some secret message that resists interpretation. A man plays an accordion, sitting on the steps of the fountain, and an old beggar woman dressed all in black hunches in the porch outside the basilica.

They leave the café and make their way up the steep, narrow roads to the Gianicolo Hill and look out over the city. They stand side by side, and Robert's arm brushes against his. He feels a frisson of desire and wonders if the touch is deliberate. The cocktails have made him reckless. He leans into the touch. Robert doesn't move. Then he feels Robert's hand stealthily enclosing his own, and he returns the pressure. The six of them stand there – perhaps others are touching and holding hands, he doesn't know – as a crescent moon rises behind the Esquiline Hill. He thinks that this is the most perfect moment of his life. He would like to stand here forever.

An evening chill creeps through the air, and they turn to continue down the hill to Saint Peter's. They walk through the encircling arms of Bernini's columns and along the *Via della Conciliazione*. They stop at the Hotel Columbus and sit on the terrace, drinking wine. He sits near Robert, conscious of every move and gesture of the other man's body – the delicacy of his hand as he reaches for his wine glass, the slight upturn of his nose in profile, the softness of his lips as he speaks. He vaguely wonders where this might lead, but there's neither urgency nor trepidation in the thought. The cocktails and the wine have smoothed the sharp edges of conscience. It's their last night together in Rome. They might never see each other again after tomorrow. What harm would it do?

As they stand to leave, his legs feel unsteady and his head spins. He is only vaguely aware of crossing the *Ponte Vittorio Emanuel* with its triumphal papal statues, and weaving through the narrow streets to *Piazza Navona*. They pause to leer at the muscular body of Neptune fighting with an octopus, and then they stop at another pavement café and order yet more bottles of wine. It's dark now, and the night life of the city floats beneath a sprinkling of stars.

Another group of seminarians sashays past, elegant in their black soutanes. 'See you later,' they say knowingly, and John wonders what they mean. He watches them weave a smooth path through the jostling sightseers, and he feels an ache of longing and sadness. How can he bear to leave this city with all its enigmatic promises and secrets that he hasn't even begun to explore?

At some stage, one of the group mentions going to *La Dolce Vita*. David Williamson raises his hands and stands up. 'Count me out, you guys. You know it's not my kinda thing. I better get going. See you at breakfast.'

John watches him go, and realizes that now, Robert and he are alone with these other three, and already boundaries are being breached and unthinkable possibilities are presenting themselves. He feels a flicker of excitement tinged with apprehension.

'What's *La Dolce Vita*?' he asks. Surely, they don't intend going to the cinema now? He couldn't possibly concentrate after drinking so much.

'Come and see,' says Damian, and there's something dangerous and exotic and seductive in his voice.

The memories curdle, and John's heart tightens with resistance and fear. The day is clouding over, and he's getting cold. He stands up and his legs feel stiff with sitting for so long on the log. He puts on his anorak and begins to make his way back down the hill. It starts to rain, and it takes all his concentration not to lose his balance on the muddy path.

On the drive back, he switches on the radio to listen to the four o'clock news. There is no news of another murder in Westonville, and that in itself is headline news. Back at the presbytery, he goes up to his sitting room to prepare his homilies for Mass tomorrow and for Siobhan and Anthony's wedding. He sits at his desk with his Missal open beside him, wilfully resisting the dark magnetic force of forbidden memories.

The Gospel reading is from John's Gospel, with the priests and Pharisees plotting the arrest of Jesus. Nicodemus pleads on Jesus' behalf: 'Surely the Law does not allow us to pass judgement on a man without giving him a hearing and discovering what he is about?'

Lent is drawing to a close, and the readings are building towards Holy Week. The penitential mood becomes tense as the high drama of Good Friday and Easter Sunday approaches, with the long blank Saturday in between.

He tries to focus his thoughts. The readings are about wrongful accusation and the persecution of the innocent. He gropes in his memory for some recent news story that he might link to the story of Jesus. Innocent people are wrongly accused all the time. Surely he can think of something to make his homily relevant and topical?

Unable to concentrate, he goes downstairs and wanders restlessly through the house. He pushes open the door to the spare room, clean and waiting for Ben or some other homeless person to arrive on the doorstep looking for a bed. He goes along the cloisters and into the lounge. The radiators are turned off, and the room feels damp and unwelcoming. A low sky pushes against the windows, smearing them in drizzle and mist. He looks out, and even the cherry tree looks despondent. He wishes Sarah were there and hopes that the fledglings are alright.

He thinks of the persecution of the innocent, and suddenly the story is there, waiting for him to drop his guard. It's about Robert McDonald, but to get to the story he has to go through the gates of hell. He has to confront what happened with the cardinal.

He can't. He skips forward to the time after Rome, like fast forwarding past the scene in a film that one cannot bear to watch.

He never saw Robert again after that night in Rome. He might never have thought of him again, so determined was he to move on, had Robert not committed suicide.

It was a year after they all left Rome, when yet another Catholic sex abuse scandal was in the news. Robert was working with young drug addicts and homeless people in a hostel in Edinburgh. One of the young men accused Robert of indecently assaulting him, and the story made the newspapers. Robert's photograph was there on the front page of the tabloid press. EVIL PAEDO PRIEST, screamed *The Sun*. PERVERT PRIEST, shouted *The Daily Mail*. John ached with regret and longing and confusion as he gazed at the soft features and the gentle smile in the grainy photograph, remembering that evening in Rome before their world collapsed. Surely not. Not Robert. But he knew that there were no longer any certainties. Possibly Robert. Possibly anybody at all.

After a lengthy investigation, Robert was found innocent of all wrongdoing. The young man who had accused him went into rehabilitation and admitted that he had made the story up, because Robert had evicted him from the hostel for dealing drugs. But it was too late. Robert had been found hanging from the banister in the presbytery three months earlier. 'Surely the law does not allow us to pass judgement on a man without giving him a hearing and discovering what he is about?'

The sky glowers through the windows, thick with storm clouds. Thunder rumbles in the distance, and the room sinks into gloom. John switches on the lights, but the dim grey light of the low energy bulbs only intensifies the bleakness. A rumble of thunder rattles the window panes. There's double glazing in the windows upstairs, but the money ran out before they did the downstairs rooms. Edith says they should set up a special collection to finish the job, but how in a world of such hunger and misery can he ask parishioners to give money for double glazing? He'd rather put up with the draughts and wear an extra pullover.

'That's all very well Father, but we all freeze when we come to meetings in there,' harrumphs Edith.

He can't use the example of Robert for tomorrow's homily. He can't use any example that would suggest that a priest accused of abuse might be innocent. Too many have been found guilty as charged. There's too much resentment and anger over the lies and the betrayals and the cover-ups. 'There's no smoke without fire, Father,' Edith had told him, when she read about Robert's innocence. Robert was dead, unable to defend himself. John didn't have the heart to try to defend him. He left Edith to think her poisoned thoughts and tried to wrap his memory of Robert in a soft, concealing veil.

The cardinal has a key. The thought leaps unbidden into his mind, and all the terrors congeal around that single certainty. Lightning cracks the sky and flashes through the windows, and the thunder growls and grows to a bone-rattling roar. He pulls the curtains, because there's something out there that frightens him more than everything else.

He must change the locks. Surely, there are emergency locksmiths who do such things? He hurries through the yellow-gloomed cloister to the front door. It's the same door that was there when the convent was built, heavy and forbidding with its iron lock, intended to guard the chastity of the women inside. He feels helpless as he stares at it, suspecting that changing such a lock would be a feat of carpentry and engineering that would take a master craftsman to achieve.

He has an idea. He goes back through to the cloister and pushes open the door into the church, making a mental note to himself to lock it afterwards. The church is empty and the nave is drenched in the dense gloom of the storm, but the lights around the altar have been left on and there are rows of candles burning in the lady chapel so that a soft glow melts the darkness. Siobhan and her mother and sisters have been in to prepare the church for the wedding. He likes that they've done it themselves. He hates it when the bride's parents – or sometimes these days the couples themselves – pay hundreds of pounds for florists to come with exotic flowers and transform the church into a floral extravaganza.

Bright yellow roses and lilac freesias are arranged in posies along the pews and in tumbling exuberance around the altar, with trailing ribbons in yellow and lilac and purple and white. The air smells sweet and fresh. For a moment he is transported back to the *Campo Dei Fiori* and the memories of Robert. No, not now.

He kneels on the altar step and offers God his silence and his fear, which are the only prayers he has to offer. Then, feeling foolish but determined, he goes to where the altar servers kneel and picks up the brass bell that they ring at the consecration. It peals loudly in the echoing silence. He holds the gong to stop it ringing and makes his way back to the presbytery, carefully locking and bolting the door behind him. He feels the host in its tabernacle watching him, boring into his back. 'Are you locking me out?' Maybe. I don't know what I'm locking out, or what I'm locking myself in with.

He goes into the parish office leading off the hall, where Edith sits every week to do the accounts and organise the hall bookings and update the website. He rummages in the drawer for a ball of string, and then he ties it around the smooth polished handle on the front door. He unwinds the string behind him as he goes through the door into the cloister and up the stairs to his bedroom. He thinks of Hansel and Gretel, leaving a trail of breadcrumbs which would be eaten by the birds, and thus abandoning them to the child-eating witch with her burning fires. Dear God, what a story to tell a child.

He puts the bell beside his bed and winds the string around the gong, making sure it's taut and secure. Then he goes downstairs and pulls down on the handle. Upstairs, the bell clangs in the silence, loud enough to wake the dead.

And if the cardinal is a ghost? If the cardinal, like the risen Christ, can walk through locked doors? No. The cardinal is not a ghost. The cardinal cannot walk through closed doors. The cardinal is a man who pretended to be a plumber in order to get a key to the presbytery.

The bell does not ring through the long dark night. John sleeps restlessly with Shula beside him. He buries his face in her fur and longs for that annihilating darkness to seize his senses and his thoughts, but it eludes him and leaves him tossing and turning with fragments of dreams that make no sense, running through him like sand in an hourglass counting the minutes until doomsday.

TWENTY

FIFTH SUNDAY OF LENT

When sleep comes, it comes as a thick obliteration so that he wakes disorientated and confused to the beeps of the alarm clock. He sits up and tries to remember where he is and what day it is. He swings his legs out of bed and the bell clatters to the floor, bringing him to his senses.

He feels ridiculous. Get a grip on yourself, he mutters, as he picks up the bell and begins winding the string around his fist. He winds his way downstairs to the front door and unties the string, then he ties it in a tight little ball and stuffs it into the pocket of his anorak hanging beside the door, where Edith won't find it. He unbolts the door to the church and puts the bell back beside the altar servers' bench.

The day has dawned bright and glorious after last night's storm. Morning sun slants through the stained glass windows above the altar, turning the church to a kaleidoscope of colour. The air is sweet with the scent of flowers, and somewhere just beyond the reach of mortal ears, choirs of angels sing hallelujah to the wedding day.

He makes his way back to the presbytery with a new sense of confidence and courage. Shula is waiting for him in the cloisters. He gathers her up in his arms and carries her into the kitchen to feed her and make coffee. Boldly, he switches on the radio to listen to the news.

The headline news is about Brexit and the next item is about a change in American foreign policy. The no news of the murders is third. No more bodies have been found. That's enough for him. He switches the radio off and gathers his thoughts for the day.

Siobhan and Anthony sit side by side in front of the altar on red velvet stools, as Bonnie does the first reading. The family are all gathered together – Colleen has come from Ireland with her boyfriend Seamus, Ailish and Julia have come from South Africa, and Eamon has come from Australia with his wife Linda and their toddler Thomas. John knows that they have come not only to celebrate their sister's wedding, but to say goodbye to their father.

Siobhan is dressed in flowing cream lace with her auburn hair tied up and loose curls framing her face. Breda, Ailish and Colleen are bridesmaids, dressed in lilac dresses and holding sprays of yellow freesias tied with purple ribbons. Eamon is the best man, and Anthony and he are wearing lilac bow ties with yellow buttonholes, as instructed. Bonnie's daughter Susie is a flower girl. Bonnie and Siobhan have been friends since childhood. Susie fidgets and plucks at her posy, and Ailish lays a restraining hand gently on her arm.

> *Love is patient, love is kind. It does not envy, it does not boast, it is not proud.*

Patrick and Mary sit in the front row. John has rarely seen a man look as noble as Patrick did when he made his way slowly down the aisle with his daughter on his arm. Or rather, on the arm of his daughter, for he is thin and frail and she was helping him and guiding him and holding him up. The miracle is not in this modest recovery. The miracle is elsewhere. The miracle is everywhere.

> *And now these three remain: faith, hope and love. But the greatest of these is love.*

For the Gospel reading they have chosen the wedding at Cana. John gives a short, simple homily, with a deep sense of thankfulness for the blessing of Siobhan and Anthony's love, and for the family gathered together in the parish where the children grew up.

The couple stand at the altar and make their vows. He has done this so many times, and he knows how often these bright and hopeful weddings disintegrate in the realities of daily life. Nonetheless, there's something audacious about this sublime act of commitment which fills him with awe and with that haunting refrain of desire. Why not me? Why not us? What could possibly be wrong about this?

The reception is in a marquee in the school playing field next to the church. The marquee has been decorated with ribbons and bunting and flowers. He is sitting at the top table, between Mary the bride's mother and Siobhan's sister Ailish. He looks at the groups of families and friends gathered around circular tables, and he feels a welling up of affection. This is where he belongs. This parish is the only home he has and the only home he ever wants. One day, the bishop will move him on and he will have little say in when that happens or where he will be sent next, but he will deal with that when it comes.

After the speeches and the dining, the dancing begins. There's a live band on a raised stage in front of the marquee. Lozenges of light play on the white drapery as a rotating mirrored ball streaks the dancers in swirling streams of colour. The bride and groom waltz together in a rainbow nebula, the crystals on her dress sparking around her as she moves.

Mary and Patrick take to the dance floor and everybody cheers and claps. They do a slow, halting shuffle around the floor, her stout body encased in blue lace holding him up like a little puppet, and he is smiling, smiling, as if they are Fonteyn and Nureyev.

Holly and Steve are dancing too. They move with the practised assurance of a couple who have been dancing together for years, and the grace of their bodies mesmerises him. She whispers something in his ear and he laughs. She pushes herself back from him and twirls, and he catches her. The tempo of the music has changed, and they glide from a waltz to a jive. Holly's red dress swirls around her. She's wearing high heels and she is light on her feet, moving with the assurance and trust of someone who knows that her partner will never let her fall.

He lets his gaze drift around the room. Jane and Pete are there with their five children, sitting at a table with Lucy's parents Carol and Jim, and with the organist Bob Carpenter and his wife Mary. At the table next to them are Jennifer from the Justice and Peace Group with her husband Julian and their two children. Lillian and Piet du Plessis are at the same table, with their three children. It occurs to John what a complex task it must be, organising the seating at a wedding.

Edith and Jack get up and move towards the dance floor. Edith is wearing a pink chiffon dress with sensible court shoes and a feathered decoration in her hair. Jack looks stout and distinguished in a suit and tie. Edith smiles coyly as she moves into Jack's arms, and some small shiver of delight passes through them as Jack wraps his arm around her.

Lucy and her sister Karen are at the next table, with the Berkeley family – Susan and Colin, with their son James who stole Danny's chocolate bar. John notes that Danny and Frank are at that table too.

Frank's marriage broke up a couple of years ago. He told John he was resigned to the fact that a detective's life is too demanding for a settled relationship and domestic life. It was an amicable parting, and Danny spends alternate weekends with Frank when work permits. This weekend, with no more murders, John is glad that Frank has been able to bring his little boy to the wedding.

Finally, like leaving the best bit of food on the plate until last, he looks over at the table where Luke is sitting with Dorcas the headmistress and her family, and with Bonnie and Steve and their children. Luke is wearing a dark suit with a white shirt and bright blue bow tie. Bonnie has just said something to him, and he is smiling at her – white teeth, hair curling over his collar, fingers curved around his wine glass.

John looks away, and the yearning he feels is sweet in its intensity and reconciled to its impossibility.

Siobhan comes waltzing over to the table, holding out her arms. 'Come on, Father. Your turn to dance with the bride. We're doing the Gay Gordons. Everybody up on the dance floor!'

It's a long time since he danced, apart from that night with Holly, but the rhythm is easy to follow and he soon falls into step. Siobhan skips and twirls lightly beneath his upheld arms, in a froth of lace and laughter. The bandleader calls instructions. 'Forward. That's it. Now turn, and walk backwards. Now gentlemen twirl your ladies. And now in each other's arms, skip in a circle. And off we go again.'

They follow the routine until they all know the steps, then the bandleader says they're going to vary the routine. 'You're all to change partners after the skipping. Gentlemen stand still, and ladies move forward to the next gentleman.' He's Irish, a friend from Siobhan's school days who started a band a few years ago. 'Sure now, you might get a bit muddled, and we might end up ladies with ladies and men with men, but it's not called the Gay Gordons for nothing.' A titter of laughter ripples through them, and off they go.

John finds himself with Jane, large-bellied in her pregnancy. She seems to be enjoying herself. He tries not to think of Pete's confession and all that Jane doesn't know. As he takes her in his arms and twirls her carefully around, he enjoys the ripe bulge of her belly and breasts.

Lucy is next, her body seeming fragile and almost ephemeral after Jane's bulky girth. There's a sadness emanating from her, as if she too carries a burden but it's all inside, hidden away. She looks pale, with shadows under her eyes. Her hair is long and glossy, and it brushes against his cheek as they dance.

'Are you alright?' he asks her quietly, as she slides into his arms to skip before moving on.

She shrugs, her shoulder lifting lightly beneath his hand. 'You know,' she whispers.

He wonders if he knows, but he nods. 'Yes, I think I know,' he whispers back, and he squeezes her shoulder as she moves on, leaving a floral-scented sadness in her wake.

Holly is next, and she tucks herself under his arms with a reassuring familiarity. 'We could show them a thing or two, couldn't we?' she says, laughing. 'They've seen nothing till they've seen us dancing.'

He laughs too. She moves with light-footed grace, despite being tipsy and wearing ridiculously high heels. 'Don't stand on my toes,' he says, 'I'll never walk again if one of those heels gets me.'

She laughs again. 'You're just jealous. Go on, admit it, you'd love to strut around in shoes like these.'

He squeezes her hands and they twirl and spin and she dances on and then the miracle happens, by serendipity or grace or design. It doesn't matter how, all that matters is that Luke is there, and John is holding Luke beneath his arms. The right piece of the jigsaw has been found at last, and it fits perfectly.

Luke's hands are cool and fine-boned. John enfolds them in his own, and he holds them with a caress that allows every pore to enjoy the skin on skin nearness. Luke's body flows down his side, nudging and swaying against him as they dance. He cups his arm around his back and feels the momentary thrust of Luke's body against his, the intense, forbidden moment of pressure that threatens to obliterate every sense and all common sense, and he wishes they could move against one another like that for ever and ever.

TWENTY ONE

FIFTH MONDAY OF LENT

Monday morning dawns with a light, bright promise of spring in the air. The pleasure of the wedding still enfolds him with a sense of hopefulness and freedom. The radio tells him that there have been no more murders, and it feels as if the city is letting out a vast sigh of relief that drifts over the rooftops and mingles with the promise of spring seeping up through the unfurling trees.

He looks forward to the day ahead. After Mass, he will drive out to the coast and go for a long walk, then this evening he is going to Kate's for dinner. It has been two weeks since he saw the children, and he looks forward to their bright, uplifting company.

Always now, there's a tremor of fear when he enters the church. What if the cardinal is there? What if he comes to Mass or appears in the doorway? He realizes that this fear will linger for a long time, even though it has begun to loosen its grip on him. He steadies his breathing and draws reassurance from the normality of his surroundings. There are no sinister presences in the church, no sudden chills in the air and no foul smell of death and decay. On the contrary, the air is drenched with the perfume of the wedding flowers – a rich, languid smell that almost overwhelms the lingering fragrance of incense and hints at erotic mysteries, like walking into a scented garden from Arabian Nights. He can hear murmured voices from the sacristy, and he pauses to listen. He remembers Edith and Jack at the wedding yesterday – that blushing sense of something between them at last being acknowledged. He smiles to himself and pushes open the door.

The air is charged with some new sensation. It rustles around him, caressing his senses. Jack's slow, ponderous movements of preparation, Edith's quick, bird-like gestures, seem choreographed to communicate secrets rippling between them, turning the air to silk. His heart lifts. He realizes how much he would like these two lonely people to find companionship and solace together. He wonders if they spent the night together. He hopes so.

After Mass, he drives out through the suburbs and along the motorway until he comes to the winding roads that lead to the coast. It takes him over an hour to get to the rolling hills and beaches of the Jurassic coast where he likes to walk, looking for fossils and soaking up the sense of a vast evolving story of life on earth. He enjoys the drive through sun-gilded countryside, with the lambs skipping in the fields. He listens to music and tries to keep his mind free of dark and fearful thoughts.

He parks his car and puts on his walking boots. He puts his phone in the glove compartment because he wants to be free of interruptions and distractions.

The tide is out. He decides to walk up over the hills behind the beach, and then to walk back along the beach. The sun sparkles on the distant line of the sea as he climbs the footpath and sets off through swathes of wild garlic, thrift and bluebells dotted with pink and yellow primroses. He walks up over the headland and continues into a small town in a bay on the other side, where he stops and has fish and chips for lunch. The café has red checked plastic table cloths and there's that pervasive smell of frying which seems to linger over every British seaside resort.

The landlady is a stout, large-breasted woman with a florid face framed in a peroxide frizz. The café is deserted, except for a mother and father with three children sitting a few tables away.

'Are you just here for the day?' she asks, depositing a plate of sliced white bread and a bottle of tomato sauce on the table.

'Yes. I've driven over from Westonville for the day,' he says, and immediately regrets it as her face darkens.

'Terrible business,' she says. 'Terrible business, the murder of those girls.' She shakes her head. 'They're saying it might be a Catholic priest.' His heart does a fillip of alarm. Please, no, not on his day off. She shrugs. 'Not sure I believe that. But you never know.'

'We're all hoping it has stopped,' he says mildly. 'There haven't been any more murders these last two weeks as far as they know.'

She frowns and is about to say something, but the doorbell tinkles as an elderly couple comes into the café. She greets them by name and bustles away to serve them. He feels a surge of relief and tries to set aside his anxiety, hoping she won't come back to resume the conversation. The café gradually fills up as he eats, and he manages to escape with no further encounters.

The tide is coming in and the afternoon sun silvers the sea. He walks along the water's edge, dodging the waves and looking for fossils to take back to Kate's children. He imagines their faces this evening, as he presents his treasures. He would love to find something really spectacular to take to them – a large fossil, a dinosaur tooth.

There's something hypnotic about the suckling murmur of the waves and the slow creep of the tide. He finds several smooth dark stones indented with the serrated patterns of ancient fossilized plants and puts them in his pockets.

He is so absorbed that he barely notices the clouds beginning to billow in across the horizon. The wind rises from a soft caressing breeze to a whistling force that claws at his anorak and lashes against his body. The sea begins to churn and heave. It's only when he reaches the headland with a tumble of black rocks cascading across the shore that he realizes he has miscalculated. He must either navigate his way across the rocks in the storm with the incoming tide or turn back and find somewhere he can climb up to the path on the hills above. Either way, he risks being cut off by the tide. Here, there are landslides and crumbling cliffs that would be impossible to climb.

He looks back along the shore. He has been walking for over an hour. If he keeps going, it shouldn't take him more than fifteen or twenty minutes to scramble over the rocks. The car is just a short walk from there. He decides that's his only feasible course of action.

He makes his way up the shore to the foot of the glowering cliffs with their crumbling, fissured faces. The boulders strewn across the beach and out into the sea are evidence of the instability of the landscape. Huge rock falls reveal fossilized worlds that bring fossil hunters crowding to the beach with hammers and spades. Occasionally, the remains of dinosaurs are discovered almost perfectly preserved amidst the ruins of nature. He sometimes brings Kate's children here in summer to look for fossils, and they tell one another wild fantastic stories about dinosaurs and ancient forests.

It starts to rain, and the wind drives icy needles into his face. He begins to make his way across the rocks, looking for footholds as he scrambles from boulder to boulder across gullies of water and treacherous surfaces with jagged edges. Too close to his right, the waves pound and seethe against the rocky outcrop. The cliffs loom to his left with their rocky burdens glowering over him.

He loses his footing and bangs his knee against a rock. In the effort to save himself, he grabs at another rock and cuts his hand. The blood wells up and oozes between his fingers. A huge wave crashes so close that its spray adds to the soaking of the rain on his skin. Ahead, the obstacle course seems to go on forever, but there's no turning back and no standing still. He must keep his wits about him. If he panics, he will never get there. The tide will keep rising until it washes him away and batters him to a sack of broken bones against the rocks.

For a brief, wild moment he allows that thought to seduce him. He imagines the terror and the panic, the jolts of pain, the seeping away of consciousness, and then the long, long nothingness as he drifts out and out into the ocean. There are no divine arms waiting to welcome him home. There is no beatific vision, no saviour in glowing white robes, no choirs of angels. Just a blessed and welcome freedom from all the guilt and shame and pain of living, from the memories and fears, the violence and dread, the love and responsibility. Nothing. Just the eternal music of the spheres, and the dissolution of himself into emptiness.

He stands still, gazing out across the churning sea towards the empty horizon. Somewhere out there, the cardinal is waiting for him.

A force of resistance surges up in him, stronger than death. He feels his heart pounding in his ears, his skin tingling with cold, the cut in his hand zinging with pain and the dull throb of his bruised knee laying claim to his thoughts. He feels the swirling of the elements around him – the roar of the waves and the keening lament of the wind and the high indifferent scrutiny of the cliffs. He sees how the sky meets the waves in the heaving restlessness of the storm, and ahead and behind he sees the blackened landscape of the rocks challenging him, defying him, daring him to conquer them. He puts back his head and he lets out a roar. He wants his voice to be part of this, he wants his body to find its place in this world of wonders and horrors, and to be fully present in the midst of it all.

He scrambles on as the waves break closer and closer, but now he knows that he will make it. Ahead he can see the last scattering of rocks and the golden invitation of the beach beyond. The rain is easing, as if beaten into submission by his defiance. The wind subsides, and as he stumbles across the last few rocks a watery sun trickles through the clouds and lights up a rainbow far out across the sea.

He is dripping and shivering with cold by the time he gets to the car. He keeps a tracksuit in the boot for such occasions, because he has been caught in the rain before on walks, though never as dramatically as this time. The car park is deserted so he discreetly changes his clothes standing in the shelter of the car doors. He switches on the engine to warm the car, and rummages in the glove compartment for some tissues to wrap around his hand and stop the blood from seeping over the steering wheel. He takes out his phone. There are six missed calls and four new messages. Three of the missed calls are from Kate.

His heart flutters with alarm as he presses the voicemail key. 'Welcome. You have three new messages. First new message received today at twelve thirteen pm.'

'Hello Father John. It's Frank Lambert here from CID. I wonder if I could come and see you later today. I need your advice. I'm frantically busy as you can imagine, but if you leave a message I'll get back to you as soon as I can.' The fluttering in his heart changes to an ominous thudding, and a fist closes around his abdomen.

Frank's deep, urgent voice gives way to the staccato brightness of the automatic voicemail message. 'To return the call, press hash, to listen to the message again, press one, to save the message, press two, to delete the message, press three.' He presses two. 'Next message received today at twelve fifty two pm.'

'John? It's Kate. Can you give me a ring? If you get this in the next ten minutes call me back, otherwise I'll try to get hold of you later.' Her voice sounds tense. His mouth feels dry and his head is throbbing. He presses two to save the message and looks at his watch. It's quarter to five. 'Next message received today at two thirteen pm.'

'Hello Father John, it's Fiona, Amy's mum. I'm withdrawing Amy from the First Communion class. I've had enough. I don't owe you any explanations.' Click.

'To return the call, press hash, to listen to the message again, press one, to …' He presses two to save the message. There's something about Fiona's tone that cranks up his anxiety so that it begins to screech inside his head. His knee hurts, his hand is stinging, and the pounding in his head is unrelenting. 'Next message received today at four twenty three pm.'

'Jesus John, where the fuck are you? Can you ring me? I – um – we have to cancel tonight. Ring me.' It's Kate again. He presses her name in the list of missed calls.

She answers at once. 'John. Where have you been?' Her voice sounds as if she is being strangled.

'I went for a walk. It's my day off. What's wrong Kate? It's not one of the children, is it?' The panic in her voice is infectious. He hears it echoing in his own.

'No. I just – something's come up. I – we – we can't do dinner tonight.'

'What is it Kate? You sound awful. What's wrong?'

She begins to cry. He can't remember when he last heard Kate cry. 'Sorry. Sorry John. Just – oh God – can I call you back?' The phone clicks and she vanishes.

Outside, the sun is setting in a vivid glow of colour and light, so that the sky and the ocean are illuminated in a dramatic display that he is too anxious to appreciate. He answers his phone on the first ring.

'Sorry John. I can't talk long, but – but …' Kate gulps. Her words come out in a rush. 'It's Chris. He doesn't want you in the house John. Sorry. Oh God, sorry John.' She chokes and sobs. 'It's these murders, and all this stuff about priests. He doesn't want you coming near the kids.'

'Kate ...'

'I have to go John. Don't call me back tonight. I'm too upset to talk. I'll ring you tomorrow. I'll come and see you. Please John, this is as hard for me as it is for you. Please John. I just need some time.'

'But Kate, this isn't possible – I don't understand ...'

'Not now John. Tomorrow. I have to go.' The phone clicks off. He tries calling her back, but the falsetto voice tells him that the caller is unavailable. He knows that there's no chance of getting hold of her tonight.

He sits watching as the sun swoops down in a turbulent blaze of orange and yellow and red, bleeding out its light into the ocean. The heater has warmed the car, and his wet clothes on the back seat are fogging the air.

He has become nothing but pain. The ache in his knee, the throbbing of his cut hand, the hammering in his head, the griping pains in his stomach, are one with the molten core of despair where his heart should be. He sits in the steamy heat and turns on the radio to listen to the five o'clock news, and the knowledge of what he might hear still doesn't prepare him for the horror.

'Police in Westonville are today investigating another murder, suggesting that there is indeed a serial killer at loose in the city. The body of a woman has been found in the grounds of the Catholic Church of Saints Felicity and Perpetua in the city's Ladywell suburb. Police have cordoned off the surrounding area, and forensic teams have been working to gather evidence. Chief Superintendent Frank Lambert gave a press statement earlier today.'

Frank's familiar voice comes on the radio, and he speaks with masterful urgency. It's a tone simultaneously intended to reassure the innocent and terrify the guilty by evoking the power of the law and the efficiency of the police.

'We can confirm that a woman's body was found earlier today in a shallow grave in the grounds of the Catholic Church of Saints Felicity and Perpetua. Forensic specialists are working to establish the woman's identity and time of death, but their task is complicated by the condition of the body. We are urging all women to take extra care and to avoid being out in the city alone at night. If anybody has any information, however trivial it might seem, please contact Westonville Police Department on the special hotline set up for the case. The number is one five five, I repeat one five five. If you know of any woman who has gone missing, or of any individual behaving suspiciously, please get in touch. Somebody out there knows who did this. Somebody has the information we need to prevent more murders. Thank you.'

There is a clamour of questions but Frank has gone. The radio switches back to the studio. John's phone pings with an incoming message. He grabs it, hoping that it might be Kate saying that he can come for dinner after all.

'Why don't you go to the police?' it says.

He doesn't recognise the number. Hands shaking, barely thinking, he switches off the radio and calls the number. He knows who it is. The chirpy voice tells him that the number is unavailable. He throws his phone onto the passenger seat and stares out of the windscreen at the last tongues of light licking up the day.

He drives back to the presbytery through the tunnel of night, and his thoughts churn with a mad disjointed frenzy of fury, fear and grief. The drive seems to take forever. Oncoming headlights dazzle him and shapes loom up out of the darkness and leap along the roadside. He drives in silence, unable to bear whatever news the radio might bring, and unable to cope with listening to music.

Why don't you go to the police? Why don't you go to the police? Why don't you go to the police? The words hammer inside his head, and he can find no answer. His phone rings. He glances down at the screen, wanting it to be Kate, dreading who it might be. It's Frank Lambert. He drives on until he comes to a lay-by, then he pulls in and phones Frank back.

'Frank? It's John. Father John.'

'John. Where have you been? I've been trying to get hold of you.' For the first time, John hears fear in Frank's voice.

'It's my day off,' he says. 'I went for a walk.'

'You've heard the news, presumably.'

'Yes. I just heard.'

'Where are you?' It comes out as a snarl. Frank is on the warpath, and nobody and nothing will stop him.

'I'm in a layby heading back to Westonville. I'll be there in about an hour.'

'Okay. I'll come to the presbytery at seven thirty unless I get called away.'

John tries to concentrate as he pulls back onto the road. He must decide what he's going to say to Frank. Why does Frank want to see him? Is he a suspect? He must be a suspect. Will they arrest him? He has to tell Frank the truth. What is the truth? The murderer is a cardinal who is supposed to be dead. And what is the evidence that he's the murderer? His confession. He threatened to do pure evil. This is pure evil. This is the work of the cardinal.

He imagines the disbelief on Frank's face. The interrogation. The impossibility of proving anything. The deepening of suspicion. The finger of accusation pointing at him, John, because his story is too far-fetched.

And there's more. He would be betraying the seal of the confessional, betraying everything his priesthood stands for. It was drummed into them in the seminary. The seal of the confessional is absolute. Excommunication and banishment are the penalties for breaking it. There is no crime and no sin, however grave, however much a danger it poses to others, that would justify a priest revealing what was said during confession. Unless he has the permission of the penitent, he must keep silent. In the most extreme and unthinkable situations, if he believes that there is no purpose of amendment, no repentance or contrition, no genuine desire for absolution, he can refuse to hear the confession. Even then, whatever has already been said is inviolate.

The cardinal knows all this. The cardinal knows, and that's why he has chosen the confessional as the place of torture.

It's impossible. John can't tell Frank about the cardinal. Deep in the darkness of memory and imagination, the cardinal laughs, because the cardinal knows there's another reason. How much could John tell, before the whole story became public? Is this really about the responsibilities of his priesthood and his vows to God and the Church, or is it about his own secret shame and the terror of being found out?

Sssuck my cock.

The blood from his hand is oozing down the steering wheel and dripping onto the knee of his tracksuit. An oncoming car flashes its headlights and blares its horn. Just in time he swerves back to his own side of the road.

Did he stray into the oncoming traffic deliberately, or was it a lack of concentration? He grips the steering wheel and focuses on the road ahead, and the weight of his guilt drags him down and down. He feels foolish, and ashamed. What if he had caused a collision? It could have been a family in that other car, a mother or father going home to their children, a young couple falling in love, a man or a woman looking forward to the evening after a long day at work. Dear God. Death can leap out of the darkness in the blink of an eye, in a second of inattentiveness, and it would have been his fault.

A blue sign glows in the headlights, telling him there's parking ahead. He indicates and pulls into a sheltered lay-by with views over the valleys and hills. He gets out of the car and his knee sends a stab of pain through his body. His limbs are stiff, and he struggles to stand up straight. He feels all the confusion and shame and pain gathering inside to a mighty force, a rage so uncontainable that it might burst his body and scatter him in burning shards across the countryside. He wants to roar and hammer his fists against his head and curse God for the futility and despair of the world.

The night is clear after the storm, and the moon is gathering its fullness towards Easter. It hangs in a pale indented orb above the horizon. In the distance, the lights of Westonville glitter in denial of the savagery playing out beneath them.

'I hate you God,' he says, and his voice sounds shockingly loud in the silence. He says it again, louder. 'I hate you.' The moon is a cold unblinking eye, watching him. 'Do you hear me? Are you listening? I hate you. I refuse to worship you in your cruelty and vindictiveness and indifference. You're a lie. You're a monstrous deception and I will not bow down before your disgusting power and might. I will not. I will not. Let the cardinal worship you. Let the murderers and rapists bow down before you. Take them to your heaven and send me to hell. I want none of it. I want none of this. I reject you God. I denounce you.' He turns and spreads himself across the bonnet of the car. 'Kate. Oh no Kate. Please don't. Oh God. Help me God. Help me, dear sweet Jesus, help me. Mary, Mother of God. Somebody. Somebody help me.'

The cardinal laughs. Ssssuck my cock.

Frank arrives as he's unlocking the presbytery door. John can't bear the bleakness of the downstairs living room, so he takes Frank upstairs to his study. He navigates the stairs with difficulty, following Frank and trying not to wince with the pain in his knee.

'Would you like a drink?' he asks.

'No, I'm fine thanks,' says Frank, sitting down in one of the armchairs. 'Dear God, John, what have you been doing?' There's a hard, accusatory edge to Frank's voice.

John looks down. There are smears of dried blood on his left hand, and down the leg of his tracksuit trousers. He begins babbling.

'I've been walking. By the sea. A storm came up. I was hurrying to get back and I slipped on the rocks. I cut my hand. It's been bleeding.' He holds his hand out to show Frank the gash on the soft cushion of flesh just beneath his thumb.

'Go and get cleaned up. I'll wait. You might need a couple of stitches. I can drop you off at the hospital on my way back to town if you like.'

'No, I'm sure that's not necessary. I'll go and wash it and put a plaster on it. I won't be long.'

'Take your time. I have my phone with me so they can get hold of me if they need me. I'm on my way home now and there's not much to go back to. And on second thoughts, about that drink. Do you have any scotch?' Frank's tone has softened.

John takes a bottle of whisky and a tumbler from the cupboard beside his desk. The smell spikes his nostrils and the amber warmth of the whisky entices him, but he mustn't succumb. He needs all his wits about him right now, and he already feels dazed and confused.

'Would you mind if I have a quick shower?' he says, thinking that perhaps if he felt clean and smartly dressed he would be more at ease.

Frank nods. 'Go ahead.'

John stands in the shower and watches as the water turns pink with the blood from his hand. His knee is swollen and bruised. He wonders if something is broken and tries wriggling his ankle and toes. Everything moves, even if it sends hot rods of pain shooting up his leg.

He finds a large plaster and puts it over the cut, then he puts on his grey trousers and a clean white shirt. He brushes his hair and looks at himself in the mirror.

The eyes staring back at him are dark and ringed with exhaustion, and his face is unnaturally pale. He knows he looks younger than his years, but tonight he sees the face of his own childhood self gazing back at him, alone and afraid and longing for the comfort of home and family. Kate. He mustn't think of that now. Later, there will be hours and hours and hours to mourn and rage, but not now. Now, he must be calm. He must be in control of himself.

Frank is standing at his desk when he goes back through to the study. He has a moment of panic. Should he have left Frank alone for so long, to poke and pry about his personal space? But what could Frank possibly find? There's nothing at all to incriminate him or to make him feel ashamed.

Frank gestures to a piece of A4 paper taped to the top of the desk. 'You keep all your passwords written out on top of your desk,' he says.

'Yes. I can never remember them when I need to log on,' says John.

'It's a bit of a security risk, you know. Your bank, your email account, your Amazon password, all there for anybody to see.'

'Nobody comes into this room,' says John.

'Your housekeeper?'

'I don't have a housekeeper. Edith insists on hoovering and cleaning downstairs, but I do upstairs myself.'

Frank smiles. The smile is warm and catches John off guard. 'If all priests were like you, John, the world would be a better place. Even so, I'd advise a little more privacy.' He goes over to settle back in the armchair.

John eases himself stiffly into the other chair, wincing with the pain in his knee. He feels reassured. Surely, Frank wouldn't have said that if he suspected John of the murders? Or is Frank just luring him into a trap? Be careful, he tells himself. Don't let your guard down.

'I bashed my knee when I fell,' he says. He laughs, but it sounds less casual than he intended. 'I'm a bit of a wreck, to be honest.'

Frank looks deceptively nonchalant. Beneath his calm face and his relaxed posture, John senses the adrenalin surging through him.

'John, I'm here because I don't know what the hell is going on, and I need your advice.' John nods cautiously. 'These murders have all the hallmarks of a Catholic nutter. The body we found today, forensics are still working on it, but she was three months pregnant. There was a charred crucifix – she'd been raped with it, like the others. There's something else. It's weird as hell, but here it is. All the bodies so far have had undigested hosts in their stomachs. They must have swallowed them almost at the moment of death. Today's body was charred, but the internal organs weren't destroyed. We're looking at some kind of cultic killing, and it can only be a Catholic, though of course it might be somebody who has left the Church and has some deep hatred of its rituals and symbols.'

John cannot, will not, envisage what Frank is telling him. 'Why do you think it has to be a Catholic?' he asks, and his voice is thick with revulsion.

'Because he has a feel for it. He knows how to use the symbols and rituals to their best effect. What he's doing is designed to create horror, but you'd have to be a Catholic to feel the horror in your gut, the way he intends. That's why we're wondering if it might be a priest. These murders are carefully crafted performances. As I said, they're cultic in their attention to detail.' Frank's eyes are on him, almost friendly, almost warm, but wary and watchful.

John runs his hands over his face, partly to shield himself from that unsettling gaze. 'I don't know what to say Frank,' he says. 'I – I just – I can't imagine it. I can't even bear to think about it, to be honest. I don't think there's a priest on earth who would use the host in that way. Not if it were consecrated.' The words sound bizarre, even to himself.

'Jesus Christ John. You mean it's okay to force feed a tortured and dying woman with a host so long as it's not consecrated?' John shakes his head and closes his eyes. He has no answer. He has no idea what he meant. Frank continues. 'Forensics think she's been dead for over a week. There have been no reports of missing persons, but if she was a sex worker, that's not surprising. They think she was probably sixteen or seventeen, no more than that, maybe younger. She was emaciated, and she had suffered fractures to one arm and her collarbone some time over the last couple of years. The fractures hadn't been treated, but the bones had knit together after a fashion. She was probably in constant pain. So we're looking at somebody with a history of being abused. Possibly a trafficked woman, in which case we might never identify her.'

'Why are you telling me all this Frank?' John asks, not even attempting to hide his horror and disgust.

'Because you're a priest, and maybe you know someone or something that can give us a clue. Anything at all, however small or insignificant. Any behaviour in your fellow priests that you find odd. Any rumours or gossip about Catholic pervs. Anything at all John. We're clutching at straws, and I'm determined to get this bastard before he does this to any other woman.'

'But Frank, what you're telling me, I mean, it's – it's monstrous beyond anything I can imagine. If you ask me to think of all the priests I know, all the people I know, I can't even conceive of any human being who could do that to another.'

'Oh come on, John, you must hear some gruesome things in the confessional. Sure, not everybody is a serial killer, but we police hear it all. There are thousands of guys out there turned on by this kind of story, thousands who wish they had the guts to do the same. Jesus, Hollywood grows fat on the pickings of rape and murder and serial killers. It's the fantasy life of your ordinary suburban Catholic bloke, for all we know. And according to your theology, these are whores, wicked women leading men astray, like Eve. They deserve to be punished. Don't tell me you haven't heard men fantasise about such things.'

John gathers all his powers of concentration. He exempts the cardinal – dead or alive – and therefore with one single exception he answers as honestly as he can.

'Never, Frank. You know I can't betray the seal of the confessional, and yes, I've heard some strange fantasies and desires in there, but never ever have I heard anybody fantasising about random murder or violence of the kind you're describing. Never. Whoever is doing this, I think it's somebody who belongs in a human underworld far beyond the reach of ordinary sinfulness, the kind of sinfulness that people bring to the confession, the kind of sinfulness that's really about grace and sorrow and shame. That's what I hear in the confessional. People who do pure evil don't repent. Only good people come to confession. Only people who believe in the power of mercy and grace and forgiveness come to confession.'

Frank is staring at him now, not even trying to hide the spike of interest that John's words have aroused. He sips his drink, watching John over the edge of the glass in a way that makes him want to blink and look away. But he does not blink and look away. He holds that gaze. Frank drains his glass.

'Do you want another one?' John asks.

'I will if you'll join me.'

John doesn't want to drink. He wonders if he should remind Frank that it's Lent, but instead he shrugs and says, 'Why not?' Some instinct tells him that he must go along with this, he must let Frank direct this conversation and be as compliant as possible. He takes down a glass for himself and pours them each a generous helping.

'Cheers,' Frank says.

'Cheers.'

'I'm a convert you know,' says Frank. 'That's why I'm at a bit of a loss with all this weird ritualistic stuff.'

'No, I didn't know that,' says John, genuinely interested. Frank doesn't seem the type to undergo a religious conversion, but as soon as he thinks that he wonders if there is a particular type. Here comes everybody. Who said that about the Catholic Church? Oscar Wilde? James Joyce? Somebody.

'I met Mary at university. She was very devout. There was something about her that was different from the other girls – a kind of composure and self-confidence. She was clever and studious. I fell in love with her. We didn't even sleep together until a few weeks before the wedding. She was a virgin. I converted during our engagement. I wanted whatever it was Mary had – that settled, inward sense of knowing who she was and where she stood in relation to the world.' He swigs his drink. 'Even when our marriage was breaking down, when my work was driving a wedge between us, she never lost that quality of being at peace with herself. She just knew she couldn't live with a man who was so dedicated to his job, and so she left me. I still love her. She's still my best friend. She says she believes that marriage is for life, whatever this new pope might say. We're divorced, but she says she won't ever marry again. I'm not sure I can say that, but if she'd have me I'd go back tomorrow.'

'So why not find a different job, something that would fit in better with married life?' asks John.

Frank gives him a rueful smile. 'I'm addicted to my work John. That's the truth. I suppose it might be like you leaving the priesthood. Would you ever do that? I mean, if you met somebody and fell in love? Would you leave?'

John sips his drink and enjoys the burn of it in his mouth and throat. He is trying to drink slowly, to make it last as long as Frank intends it to last, without drinking their way through a bottle of whisky together. He's afraid that Frank is trying to lull him into a false sense of security, to make him careless with drink and gossip. But he's also glad of the company, and beneath their mutual suspicion and watchfulness, he knows there is respect and maybe even friendship between them.

'No, I couldn't leave,' he says. 'The priesthood is my life.'

'Don't you ever wonder what you're missing out on – you know, sex and marriage and kids and all that?' The question sounds innocent. Frank is no longer watching him with that keenly focused attentiveness.

'I'm gay,' says John, wondering if the question was intended to test his honesty, and deciding to answer truthfully just in case it was.

Frank nods. 'Even so, what about sex?'

'I'm tempted. Of course I'm tempted. But if a vocation is real, it brings with it the grace to sustain it. Like you being a detective perhaps. You chose that over your marriage. That was a hard choice, and you live with the consequences.' G.K. Chesterton. That's who said it. Here comes everybody.

'I'm not celibate though. Right now, I'm having a liaison with one of the other detectives in the murder investigation team,' says Frank, his smile tinged with fond eroticism. 'She understands the job. Not like Mary. That's confidential of course. We'd both get thrown off the case if they knew we're sleeping together.'

John smiles. 'We're all only human,' he says, because he can't think of anything else to say. He wonders if Frank ever goes to confession, and where he goes.

'I never got that inner peace,' says Frank after a while. 'That thing Mary had, I didn't get it. I suspect my parents made sure that even God would never be able to give me peace.'

'Why? What was so terrible about your parents?' John asks.

'That's a long story. I'll tell you some other time.' Frank drains his glass. John wonders if he should offer him another drink, but Frank is speaking again. 'I've never really felt like a Catholic. I come along to Mass mainly because of Danny, because I promised Mary we'd bring him up as Catholic and I suppose I still want her to think well of me. So on weekends when Danny's with me, I try to bring him to Mass.' He frowns and gazes down at his empty glass. 'These murders, they bring back to me what I don't like about Catholicism. There's something a bit too visceral, just beneath the surface, something a bit sick if you ask me. All those

226

bleeding crucifixes and instruments of torture. All that body and blood stuff. It unnerves me. God having to torture his own son to forgive the rest of us. It doesn't make sense to me John. It seems to me there's a dark continuum between worshipping one crucified body and being willing to torture and kill other bodies. And these women undergo all that torment without the reassurance of being the Son of God, destined to rise again.'

John feels giddy. 'We don't worship a crucified body,' he says. 'We worship the God of love, who raised Christ from the dead.'

'Yeah, sure,' says Frank. 'Do you remember Father Ignatius Brandon, John?'

'Yes, of course I do,' says John, and something huge and dark with talons and feathers flits across the room. How could anybody forget Ignatius Brandon?

'I was the detective on that case, John. To be honest, I think that did more than anything else to wreck my marriage.' He holds out his glass. 'I'll have a top up,' he says, 'and pour yourself one while you're at it.' John does as he says, and Frank speaks to his back as he's pouring the drinks. 'You say you can't imagine what I'm telling you about the murders. You know, until the day I die I'll never be able to forget the images Ignatius Brandon had on his computer. Hundreds of them. Children John, little children. Suffer the little children. Sweet Jesus, did those children suffer!' John hands him his glass. Frank takes a large gulp of whisky and wipes his mouth on the back of his hand. 'And then we began hearing the stories of what he had done. Thirty years of rape and abuse, boys and girls, but mainly boys. The youngest was six. It started with that child's first confession. Patrick McNeil, his name was. He committed suicide during the trial. He couldn't bear to remember what it had been like for eight precious years of his childhood, while everybody looked the other way and pretended not to know – even his mother. Brandon's oldest victim was fifteen. He liked them young. He lost interest when they became adults. And the bishops moved the bastard from parish to parish.

They even sent him to a mission in Africa at some stage. God knows what happened to the children there.' He shakes his head. 'So you see John, I keep going to church because of Mary, but I've seen and heard too much to believe in it.'

John remembers it all. Ignatius Brandon had been a popular priest, with a fine intellect and a reputation for brilliant homilies. He had bright blue eyes and a silver goatee beard, with a lavish sweep of silver hair to match. In many ways, he was a bit like the cardinal. He is serving a long prison sentence.

'Remember, one of those bishops has been sacked for his role in that,' he says lamely, knowing how pathetic an excuse it is.

'John, if they held to account every bishop who has covered up the actions of a paedophile priest, I wonder how many would be left.'

John can feel the whisky smoothing away some of the edges of the day. The panic and pain are receding, so that all he feels is a dull sense of futility sludging around in his gut. Everything in the end is too much. Life is not worth the effort it takes. He wonders if this is how people feel when they're suicidal. Is he suicidal? The question would take too much energy to answer. Besides, this is not the time. Concentrate. He must concentrate. Frank is deliberately trying to catch him off-guard.

He holds Frank's gaze. He hears himself speaking with a forcefulness and an honesty that come from somewhere else.

'Frank, let me tell you, as God is my witness, if I had heard anyone in the confessional confessing to murder, I would not tell you. I'm a priest, and that's absolutely non-negotiable. But I'm also telling you, as God is my witness, nobody in the confessional has confessed to murder. I don't know the name of a single living being who might have done this.'

Frank nods. 'A single living being? I suppose a ghost might have done it.'

John feels sick with dread. Frank is too sharp for him. He can't outwit him. 'Ghosts can't commit material acts,' he says, because it's something he remembers from his theology lectures but he can't remember the rest of the explanation.

'Just as well, or my job would be even more complicated.' Frank smiles reassuringly. 'Tell me about the parish priest at Saints Felicity and Perpetua,' he says. 'Father James Forrester.'

'Is he a suspect?' John is astonished.

Frank narrows his eyes and that steely detective look is back. 'You're all suspects, John, until we find the man who is doing this.'

John nods. Of course they're all suspects. Why should he be exempt from this pall of suspicion hanging over the city?

'I don't know James that well,' he says, 'but he's a popular priest. He's respected by the other priests and by his parishioners. I suppose some think he's a bit vain and full of himself.' He remembers a comment about James dyeing his hair and tries to remember who said it and when.

'What about his sex life?' asks Frank.

'He's a priest.'

'Jesus John. He has a dick, doesn't he? He's a normal red-blooded man. Is he gay? Does he have a mistress? Does he visit prostitutes?'

John wants to protest. Priests don't do those things, he wants to say. But of course priests do. He remembers what Babbs told him, and he realizes there's a whole dimension of his life over the past few weeks that he hasn't told Frank about. The walk through Saint Peter's, the conversation with Babbs and with that poor murdered girl, the drink in the Queen's Arms with Luke.

But that's none of Frank's business. It's not a crime to walk down a street and talk to a prostitute. It's not a crime to have a drink in a gay bar with a friend. It's not even a crime for a priest to sleep with a prostitute. A sin yes, but not a crime – unless having sex with a prostitute is illegal. Is it illegal? He doesn't know. How ignorant he is. He tries and fails to remember the interview on the radio the other day about prostitution.

'I have no idea about James's sex life,' he says. 'We priests don't talk about that kind of thing. I think I'd hear rumours though, and I've never heard any about him. I don't think he's gay. For all I know he could have a couple of wives and a dozen children hidden away somewhere, but I doubt it. He could just be what it says on the tin. Celibate. Most of us are you know.' He warms to his theme, suddenly craving the consolation of ordinary muddled benevolence that he believes constitutes the lives of most of the people he knows, including priests. 'You see the dark side of things Frank. Maybe that blinds you to the common goodness of people. Most priests aren't paedophiles and sex maniacs. Most of us are just ordinary men struggling to do our best and sometimes getting it wrong, the same as everybody else.'

'Yeah, well right now I'm concerned about the ordinary goodness of a pregnant teenage girl who spent most of her short life being abused and ended up as a charred corpse in the grounds of a Catholic Church, with her foetus still inside her and a crucifix in her vagina and a host in her stomach. She was just an ordinary, good person John, and if I could find the bastard who did this to her I would gladly crucify him with my own hands.' Frank's voice is filled with loathing and disgust.

Bile rises in John's throat. He swallows. What can he say? He tries to picture James Forrester's face, with his film star good looks. He remembers that little group of women he met outside the church after Mass, and he feels himself beginning to tumble out of control into some unthinkable stream of coincidences. He was outside the Church of Saints Felicity and Perpetua, that night he met Edith, Sadie and Mary. It was a Friday. It was the Friday before last. He was there, outside the church, on a Friday night. And now a woman's body has been found in the grounds of that same church.

'What's the matter John?' Frank misses nothing.

There's a laser beam pinning John to the spot, and the thing with feathers and talons has multiplied. The room is swarming with creatures that only John can see.

'It's too much to take in Frank. I just – I don't know what to say. You deal in this stuff all the time, but – but I don't.'

'You're a priest John. Stop playing the ingénue. You also walk on the dark side of life.' Frank has abandoned any attempt at kindness.

'I've told you, the people I meet are ordinary people. Ordinary sinners. Sometimes – often – they're saints in the guise of the ordinary.' John wonders who or what he is defending, and why.

'Yes John, and the people I meet are also ordinary people. It's ordinary people who get murdered, and it's ordinary people who murder them. It's ordinary people who do extraordinary things.'

Isn't that what John has thought sometimes, visiting prisons and hearing confessions? Frank is right. They both walk on the dark side of life. They both see what breeds in the human soul under cover of darkness. They are both in the business of guilt and confession and shame.

'But what you're telling me – I don't watch murder films, I avoid violence, it's all too much to take in,' he says, and he knows he sounds pathetic.

'You have a cheap murder detective novel on your bedside table,' says Frank.

'You've been in my bedroom? You were prying about my things while I was in the shower?' John is shocked.

'I'm a detective John. I'm doing my job.'

'I bought that novel when I was sitting with Sister Gertrude in hospital. I wanted something to read that didn't need too much concentration,' he says.

'You weren't looking for ideas then?'

'No! No, of course not. Who do you think I am, Frank?' He can't hide his distress.

'Calm down John. If it's any consolation, I don't think you're our man – though my colleagues think every priest in the city is a likely suspect right now.' Frank's voice is softer now, with some of the warmth trickling back. 'I'll protect you if I can, for as long as I genuinely believe you're innocent. But I'm a detective. I can't let personal loyalties get in the way. What you told me about the confessional, I hear you. Even if you knew a serial killer was going to walk out of that dark little box to commit rape and murder, you wouldn't tell the police. It's a price worth paying to protect your God. I suppose I almost get that. We detectives also have to be ruthless sometimes. We have to accept that violence and betrayal and deceit go with the job. Sometimes sacrifices have to be made in the name of some greater good. I know all about that John. It would chill you to the marrow if you knew what I've sacrificed for the sake of the law.'

'What do you mean?' The trauma of the day combined with the effects of the whisky are taking their toll. John is struggling to concentrate, but he wonders what Frank could have done that would be so shocking.

Frank brushes away the question. 'I don't want to talk about it, but we have so much in common, you and I, John. I worship the law and you worship the lawmaker, and when necessary we both break quite a lot of rules that most ordinary good people think are obvious, because we obey some higher law.'

'No! It's not like that Frank. That makes it sound awful.' John has an almost irresistible urge to curl up on the floor and go to sleep, to sleep and sleep and wake up in a different time and a different place and a different world.

'John, most ordinary decent good people would think it's awful to cover up abuse and rape and murder just because the culprit was in the confessional. Most ordinary people would think it's wicked to choose to obey the rules of a corrupted and abusive church rather than tell the police about the confession of a murderer. All I'm saying is that you and I follow a different law from what counts as ordinary goodness in everyday life. Anyway, you look ghastly. You need to go and get some sleep.' Frank drains his glass and stands up. 'Are you sure you don't want me to drive you down to the hospital to get yourself checked over? That hand is still bleeding.'

John looks down and sees the blood seeping through the plaster. 'No, I'll take a couple of paracetamol and go to bed,' he says. 'If it's still like this in the morning I'll go to the doctor.' He pauses. 'Frank, about Pete – Jane's husband. Do you suspect him?'

Again the eyes narrow, and the lips set in a thin, harsh line. 'Do you suspect him John?'

'No. I'm convinced he had nothing to do with any of this. It's just – Jane. I worry about Jane. She's six months pregnant. They've had an awful time recently, and it might destroy their marriage if she found out about the prostitutes.'

'I'm not a marriage therapist John. Her husband has been visiting prostitutes and therefore he is part of our investigation. We're not ruling anybody out until we find the murdering sadistic fuckwit who's doing this. And if his wife finds out in the process, well, you know what they say, what doesn't kill you makes you stronger.'

John feels the stiffness in his legs and the ache in his knee as he hobbles downstairs. He stands on the porch and watches as Frank gets into his car. He wonders how a detective can drive after several whiskies. Perhaps that too comes with being above the laws of everyday life.

He watches Frank's tail lights receding down the road, then he goes inside and closes the door with a heavy thud. The key grates as he turns it in the lock. He turns it far enough to make sure that it can't be wriggled out by somebody on the other side.

A thunderous solitude envelops him. It seeps out of the thick walls of the cloisters, descends from the ceiling and rises up like fog from the floor, blanketing out the sounds of the night. He goes along the cloister and through the door into the dark and silent church. The smell of the flowers has gathered to a cloying intensity, so that it feels like stepping into the fleshy darkness of a body ripe with desires and appetites, a body with the pungency of sex exuding from its pores. The tabernacle light pulses in the darkness.

He flicks on the light switch and a dim glow casts shadows across the altar and along the aisles. The near-naked Christ hangs on his cross above the altar, taunting him. He looks fearfully around, but there's nobody there. He hurries up the steps to the altar and picks up the bell, then he leaves quickly before the shadows can seize him and hold him captive in that closed up space of sex and death.

Once more, he goes through the humiliating routine of tying the string to the door handle. Tonight there is terror all around. He needs that small security of knowing that nobody can come in through the front door without him hearing. He puts the bell on the bedroom floor and undresses. He pulls on his pyjamas, wincing with the pain of moving his leg. He climbs into bed and pulls the duvet over his head, trying to shut out the world with all its contradictions and agonies.

The noise clatters around him and startles him awake. Somebody is trying to open the front door. The bell clangs and falls over onto its side, and the string tugs urgently as if somebody is pulling on the door handle again and again. He lies in the darkness, paralysed by fear. He reaches for Shula, but she is not there.

Dear God. Dear God. The cardinal has a key. The cardinal is trying to get in. What if even now he has managed to wriggle the key out of the door and is inside the house?

'Father John, are you there? Can I come in?' The voice echoes faintly from outside the front door, through the open crack in the window. John feels weak and exhausted with relief. It's Eric, a young homeless addict who occasionally turns up at the presbytery when he gets evicted from yet another hostel for selling drugs to the residents.

John eases his stiff and aching body out of bed and puts on his dressing gown. He pushes his feet into his slippers and limps to the door.

'Father John! Father John! It's me, Eric.'

'I'm coming,' John calls, and he grips the handrail because his knee hurts and his joints feel creaky and sore.

He opens the door and tries to push the string aside discreetly with his foot, though from the look of him Eric is not in any condition to notice. He is bug-eyed and forlorn. A tattoo fingers its way up his neck from beneath his grimy sweatshirt, amidst a tangle of dreadlocks. There's a gold hoop in his ear, and his face is thin and sallow. His brown dog Hercules stands at his feet, hopefully wagging his tail.

'Come in Eric. What's the problem?'

'Father John, it's those bastards in the hostel again. They kicked me out. Where am I meant to go? I don't even have a sleeping bag or a cushion. Bastards.'

'You can stay here tonight,' says John, 'but you'll need to find somewhere else in the morning. I'll make a couple of phone calls and see if I can help. Were you selling drugs again?'

'No Father. Of course not.'

'Eric?'

He hesitates and chews his lip. 'Maybe a bit. Just a few pills, that's all. I mean, I'm only trying to earn a living and get some independence Father. That's all.'

'Have you eaten tonight?' John asks.

'Nah. Some woman bought me a sandwich when I was sitting outside Tesco earlier, but it was eggs and I hate eggs.' Eric sounds offended. 'They ought to ask first,' he says. 'Even homeless people are entitled to choose what they eat, aren't they Father?'

'Yes, they are Eric,' says John, telling himself that in future, he must always ask before buying sandwiches for people begging on the streets. How callous people can be, in their misguided acts of charity.

John takes Eric through to the kitchen and makes him a cup of tea. He rummages in the cupboard and finds a tin of baked beans. He warms the beans up and puts two slices of bread in the toaster. He knows Eric likes baked beans.

'Have you any bacon I could have with that, Father?' asks Eric.

'No, I haven't.'

'Oh. Okay. Just asking.'

He sits at the table while Eric eats. He feels too tired and apathetic to talk, and Eric seems happy enough to eat in silence. When he's finished, John puts the plate in the sink and takes Eric through to the spare room. He finds a pair of pyjamas in the drawer and a towel, and some clean clothes for the morning. He doesn't go through the bathing ritual with Eric. He has no idea why it feels so natural and right to do that with Ben but not with anybody else. Ben's frail old body arouses nothing but pity and tenderness in him. He is afraid of what might happen if he saw Eric naked and freshly bathed. He shuts the door behind him and leaves Eric to his ablutions and his dreams.

He goes to the front door and unties the string, winding it around his hand as he climbs the stairs. He wonders where Shula is. He crosses himself and mutters a Hail Mary, then he lies down and tries to sleep. He is glad when Shula appears and curls up on the pillow beside him. He rests his cheek against her fur. He lies awake and the darkness crawls with living things that burrow under his skin and into his gut. He comforts himself with the thought of Eric and Hercules sleeping downstairs. He is not alone in the house. Clinging to that thought, he falls into a restless sleep.

TWENTY TWO

FIFTH TUESDAY OF LENT

As he waits for Eric to wake up, he follows his morning routine of making coffee and sitting with his missal by the window to say the Office.

> *Lord, why do you stand afar off*
> *and hide yourself in times of distress?*
> *The poor man is devoured by the pride of the wicked:*
> *He is caught in the schemes that others have made.*

He gazes out of the window and tries to concentrate. The words begin to play in a loop through his mind. 'Lord why do you hide yourself?' 'Why do you hide yourself?' 'Lord, why do you stand afar off?'

The dawn is hidden behind a thick blanket of clouds. A blackbird plucks a snail from the grass and begins dropping it again and again on the concrete path until the shell shatters and it eats the squirming flesh inside. 'Lord, why do you hide yourself in times of distress?'

He forces his eyes back to the page, suddenly conscious of how tired he is. It will be a long, long day.

> *In his pride the wicked says: 'He will not punish.*
> *There is no God.' Such are his thoughts.*

'There is no God.' 'There is no God.'

He closes the Missal and abandons his attempts at prayer. He showers and dresses, and wishes his hand and his knee didn't hurt so much. He makes his way downstairs and pauses outside the door to the spare bedroom. Eric is snoring loudly.

On impulse, he unlocks the door to the church and steps inside. The gloomy perfumed air wraps itself around him. He goes to the tabernacle and tries to kneel, but his knee sends pain stabbing through him so he sits in the pew instead.

He tries to pray but the words won't come. Eventually he says an Our Father, a Hail Mary and a Glory Be. He makes the sign of the cross and eases himself up off the pew. He goes out into the damp morning air. He tries not to limp as he walks down the road past the terraced houses, imagining central heating systems clicking into life and husbands and wives waking in a tumble of arms and legs and rumpled sheets, children in warm pyjamas rubbing sleep from their eyes, and family pets yawning and stretching to start the day.

He goes into the corner shop and stops to talk to Adnan behind the counter. Adnan smiles his bright, welcoming smile, but there's something about him – a sense of awkwardness or embarrassment – that makes John uneasy.

'How are you Adnan? It's not a very nice day, is it?' he says.

'I'm alright Father John, but I am sorry about the newspapers. I would like not to have them in my shop, but they have been delivered.' Adnan lowers his eyes and shuffles his feet.

John's heart does that thing of swooping down to his feet and up to his throat, before bouncing back into his chest to thud against his ribs. He turns to look at the bundles of newspapers on the stands behind him, and he sees the faces of five men gazing up at him from *The Sun*. 'PRIESTS OF SATAN', screeches the headline. The men are all dressed in black clerical shirts with dog collars. He is one of them. 'GOD'S MURDERERS' proclaims *The Daily Mail*, with a whole page of pictures and one blank silhouetted head among them. He is there too. Even the more restrained broadsheets have succumbed to the lure of the sensationalist headline: 'Serial Killer Priest at Large in Westonville?' They too have photos of Westonville parish priests in various poses and combinations on their front pages, and he features in several of them. He turns back to Adnan, but his throat has seized up and he can't speak. He grips the edge of the counter to steady himself.

Adnan gives him a reassuring smile. 'Don't worry Father. We love you here. We all know you. We will protect you.'

John nods and tries to smile, then he turns away. He picks up a wire basket and limps up the aisle to the fridge, holding the basket carefully so that the handle doesn't dig into the cut on his hand. He puts a packet of bacon and some sausages and mushrooms into the basket. He goes to another aisle for a tin of baked beans and a sliced white loaf, because he knows that Eric likes his toast made with white bread. He picks up three tins of dog food and a packet of dog biscuits. He shuffles back and pays Adnan, and he tries to thank him as Adnan carefully packs his shopping into a blue plastic bag.

'What have you done to your hand Father?' asks Adnan.

'I had a fall yesterday,' says John. 'I cut my hand and hurt my knee, but it's not serious.'

Adnan nods. 'Don't worry Father. We'll look after you,' he says again.

John feels ridiculous as his eyes fill with tears and his voice catches in his throat. He manages to squeeze out another thank you, and wishes he could put his arms around the slight, gentle man behind the counter and weep on his shoulder. He makes his way slowly out of the shop and up the road, the plastic bag clenched too tightly in his right fist.

He goes through the church door and into the presbytery. Somewhere he dimly thinks that he shouldn't have left the presbytery door to the church open, but he lacks the energy to care. As he walks past the hallway he sees a newspaper jutting out of the letterbox. He takes it out and unfolds it. Scrawled across the front in what looks like red lipstick are the words PERV!!! PEIDO PRIEST!!! CUNT!!!!

He rolls the newspaper up and stuffs it into the shopping bag. He goes across to the spare room and knocks on the door. He opens the door and goes in. Eric is asleep on his back, duvet rumpled around him, snoring loudly with his mouth open. Hercules is curled up on the bedside rug. He looks up at John and thumps the floor with his tail. The room smells stale and rancid, the musky reek of Hercules mingling with Eric's breath and body odour.

John shakes Eric gently by the shoulder. 'Wake up Eric. Come on, wake up.'

Eric snorts and grunts and opens his eyes. He looks disorientated, then he comes to and realizes where he is. 'Hiya Father. Alright?'

'Yes. I'm fine Eric. How about you?'

'Okay. Thanks for the bed.'

'That's alright. I'm cooking you breakfast. Bacon and sausage and baked beans on toast. I've bought some mushrooms too, because I know you like them. Go and have a shower and get dressed. It'll be ready in twenty minutes. I've left some clean clothes on the chair. If you want to put your dirty clothes in the washing machine you can. You can wait while they're in the tumble drier, or you can come back for them later.'

'Aw Father John, you're a good man. I tell all my friends, you're a saint. A real saint. We all say that. Even the working girls say it now, because Babbs says she knows you and you're one of us.' Eric yawns and a blast of halitosis hits John in the face.

'Babbs? You know Babbs?' he asks.

'Yeah. And Ben,' says Eric. 'Ben says he often stays here. But we don't tell everybody about that, Father. We look after you. We know you can't be having every alchie and junkie rocking

240

up on your door looking for a bed. It's not as if you're a hotel or a hostel. We know we're your special friends and that's why you let us stay. We look out for you, see Father. We're on your side.' He scratches his chest and yawns again.

John looks at his matted hair and sallow face peering up from the pillow, and he is overawed. He nods and chokes up again and whispers a thank you. Then he goes into the kitchen to cook breakfast, resisting the mute, accusatory glare of the radio.

Eric declines the invitation to come to Mass. He says he has to get going, and don't worry about the clothes, he will go to a launderette later. John suspects he will put them back on unwashed tomorrow or the next day.

The atmosphere in the sacristy is swirling with unspoken fears and desires. Edith is wearing lipstick, and perfume that smells like a mix between vanilla essence and fly spray. She flutters around like a caged bird as she prepares the chalice and the missal for Mass. Jack's movements are careful and ponderous as ever, but John notices that his hands are shaking as he puts on his alb and drapes the stole over his shoulder. John tries to behave normally, maintaining his usual silence as he ties the cincture round his waist.

He glances up and Jack is looking at him. He looks away quickly as John catches his eye. John sighs. They have seen the papers. Of course they have. Everybody in Westonville will have seen the papers by now.

'We have nothing to be afraid of,' he tells them both. 'We have to keep faith and pray that they find the murderer soon, but we must also remember that God is with us and we have a duty to offer the sacraments to the people in the parish during Lent and Easter. That's all we have to do. And we must pray for those poor women and their families, and for the murderer too, whoever he is, even if he's a priest.'

Edith flaps her hands in the air. 'Oh Father, it won't be a priest. If you could see what those trolls say about us Catholics.

241

They're wicked Father, wicked. They hate us. I wouldn't be surprised if it's one of them that's doing it, some atheist or Moslem pretending to be a priest.'

Jack looks embarrassed. 'Actually Father, I know you don't like us talking in here, but Edith and I wondered if we could come and speak to you later. We have something to ask you.' He blushes.

Edith smiles and cups her hands around her cheeks. 'Oh Jack, we said we wouldn't mention it until after Mass,' she says, and she is blushing too.

John can't help himself. He has to smile. This is grace, the ordinary, humdrum everyday grace that holds the cosmos together.

'Come and have coffee with me in the presbytery after Mass,' he says.

He walks into the church and he sees a quiet miracle. Numbers usually tail off towards the end of Lent. It's as if people are saving themselves for a sacramental binge during Holy Week and Easter. But today, the church is almost full. Even the children are there. Dorcas has brought them in from the school, and they are lined up in the front rows. As he walks in, they gather on the altar steps and turn to face the congregation. The school music group begins to play. They never have music at the ordinary weekday Mass.

> *You shall cross the barren desert, but you shall not die of thirst.*
> *You shall wander far in safety though you do not know the way.*

He takes his place on the altar and tries to swallow. His eyes mist up. The familiar faces arrayed before him have never looked so lovely.

Be not afraid.
I go before you always.
Come follow me, and
I will give you rest.

He is gazing out at a sea of saints, the divine spark disguised in the fleshy flux of mortal life. Dorcas is standing erect in the front row, sombre as always, and yet full of quiet pride as she watches the children. The teachers are there, smiling encouragingly at the children arrayed on the altar steps. Holly is there, and Steve is sitting beside her. Steve hasn't been to Mass since Sarah's funeral. Lucy is there too, without her family. She is sitting on the end of a row, and as he catches her eye she gives him a small smile.

If you pass through raging waters in the sea, you
shall not drown.
If you walk amid the burning flames, you shall not
be harmed.
If you stand before the pow'r of hell and death is at
your side, know that
I am with you through it all.

He raises his hands. He has put a fresh plaster on the cut on his palm.

The grace …

The words won't come. He swallows and clears his throat.

The grace of our Lord Jesus Christ,
and the love of God,
and the communion of the Holy Spirit
be with you all.

'And with your spirit,' they reply.

The readings for today are difficult – the people of Israel grumbling, and Moses lifting up the fiery serpent in the desert. John's Gospel with Jesus speaking in riddles.

He rests his hands on the edge of the lectern to steady himself. He hasn't prepared a homily, and the readings don't inspire him, but he feels he ought to say something. He takes a deep breath and gazes out at them.

'Thank you,' he says. He licks his lips and swallows. 'Thank you,' he says again. He lets the silence spread. His legs are unsteady, but he suddenly feels out of place. He never stands in the lectern during a children's Mass. Painfully, he makes his way down the steps of the lectern and down the altar steps, to stand on their level. 'You've probably noticed I'm limping,' he says. 'I've also cut my hand.' He holds his hand up.

'What did you do, Father?' asks Elizabeth, the little girl who all those centuries ago on Ash Wednesday spoke of Jesus raising Lazarus from the dead when he asked the children to think of a miracle.

'I went for a walk along the beach yesterday – near Charmouth,' he says. 'Some of you know Charmouth, where all the fossils are. Remember we went on a parish outing there last year?' James's hand goes up. 'Yes, James, do you remember?'

'I found a fossil. I've still got it. Look, I keep it in my pocket all the time. It's my good luck charm.' He digs in his pocket and holds up a small piece of grey rock. John reaches over the heads of the children to take it. He looks at the exquisite sculpting of an ancient fern, so delicate, permanently etched in the rock. He thinks of James taking Danny's chocolate, and of his torment in the confessional. He hands the fossil back to James.

'That's beautiful James. Think of how, millions of years ago, that plant was alive because it had God's life in it. Isn't that amazing? It's nature's art, there to remind us how wonderful God's creation is.

'Anyway, when I was walking on the beach yesterday it began to rain, and I slipped and fell on the rocks. I banged my knee and I cut my hand.' He stands there and his legs begin to shake again. 'I – umm – what I really wanted to say was thank you, that's all. Thank you for being here for me. You've no idea what it means to me. Thank you. I – I love you. You are my family. You're all I have.' He lets the tears run down his face. It no longer matters.

Suddenly, there's a quick little movement in the row just to the left of where he is standing. Amy is squeezing her way along the pew. She comes to stand next to him and takes his hand in both of hers. She turns it over and plants a kiss on his palm.

'I want to kiss it better, Father John,' she says. 'Don't cry. It will be alright.'

He bends down and lifts her up in his arms. He thinks of Phoebe and Stephen, of the murdered women and the stranger, of the vast, vast swell of the ocean and the blackness of the rocks and the wildness of the storm all around. He hides his face in her hair and whispers 'Thank you Amy,' in her ear. Then he remembers the email from Amy's mother. 'I'm withdrawing Amy from the First Communion Class.' He puts her down and dreads the repercussions when she tells her mother that he picked her up and cuddled her during Mass. He stumbles back up the steps to take his place at the side of the altar, as Deacon Jack prompts them to begin the creed.

Back in the presbytery, Edith sniffs the air like a terrier as they walk through the cloisters to the lounge. 'Father, have you had one of those tramps in here again? This place stinks.'

John catches a faint whiff of dog and Eric's unwashed body wafting from the clothes on the floor as they pass the spare room. He closes the door before Edith can see the rumpled bed and dirty clothes. 'Eric and his dog arrived on the doorstep last night. I let him stay over.'

245

She tsssks and shakes her head. 'I suppose it's what our Lord would have done,' she says, 'but it was different in those days. Everybody probably stank before they invented bathrooms.' She pauses. 'Except our Lord of course. He never stank. He was pure. Like Our Lady.'

He can't be bothered arguing, so he just laughs and ushers them into the large soulless lounge.

Edith sits primly upright in the armchair, her body managing to communicate simultaneously her disapproval of John's inappropriate hospitality and her girlish desire for Jack. Jack sits awkwardly in one of the other chairs, radiating a happiness that he cannot conceal as he tells John that they have fallen in love and want to get married soon after Easter.

John's joy breaks through all the pain and confusion. 'Congratulations,' he says. 'This is the best news I could possibly have to brighten one of the worst days of my life.' He tries to steady his voice. 'I want to thank you both,' he says.

'What for?' asks Jack.

'For being here. For whatever you did to make this morning's Mass so supportive and loving and ...' His voice dries up. Jack looks embarrassed.

'We were shocked when we saw the news,' says Edith. 'Even if there is some mad priest out there – and I still think it's an imposter Father, really I do – but even if it's not, we know you. We love you. Jack got on the phone and asked people to ring round so that as many of them as possible would come to Mass. Then Dorcas phoned and said she wanted to bring the children in.'

'Thank you,' John says, looking at Jack.

Jack blushes. John finds Jack's blushes endearing. He seems so large and gruff and tough, but he's a gentle soul and Edith will lavish him with care and attention.

He watches them leave, Edith thin and quick in her movements, Jack lumbering beside her with that solid gait that always makes John feel secure.

He goes upstairs and tries to focus on the day's chores. There's an email explaining arrangements for the Chrism Mass next Thursday morning. There's another email saying that the bishop wants to meet them all this evening at six o'clock for an emergency meeting 'to discuss the situation in Westonville'. And then there's a heavy black deluge of abuse, row upon row, words leaping out at him: 'Paedophile.' 'Whoremonger.' 'Pervert.' 'Murderer.' 'Son of Satan.' Curses and condemnations and expletives.

His stomach knots with disgust and fear, as he selects them all and deletes them, then he goes into the delete folder and deletes them permanently, lest he ever be tempted to read them.

He feels the thing rising up inside him, that forgiven and forgotten thing that is not forgotten and might not be forgiven. A sin, once forgiven, should not be confessed again, but did he really confess properly that first time in Rome? Was he really shriven and cleansed and made new again? Is there still some lingering shadow on his soul, some secret desire to keep it all to himself, lest God take away the desire as well as the darkness? He goes to the phone and calls Father Martin.

Yes, the old priest is there all day and of course John can come to confession. 'Come any time. I'll see you later,' he says.

John fumbles in his pocket for his rosary and goes through to the church. All the candle stands are aglow, so that the air seems to be breathing and alive. People must have lit them when they came to Mass this morning. Warm light shimmers around the feet of Saint Joseph and the Pietà and the statue of Mary and the infant Christ in the Lady Chapel. He goes to the kneeler in front of that statue and, grimacing with the pain in his knee, eases himself down onto his knees.

Mary's jewelled crown sparkles in the candlelight. 'Our Lady of Bling,' Holly calls her. He lets the rosary beads trickle through his fingertips, and he wonders if she sways slightly towards him and her smile widens a fraction.

Then he senses it. The cold. The smell of death. He squeezes his eyes shut, too terrified to move. He waits.

The cardinal is making his way up the aisle in a swishing explosion of silk and lace. He is smiling, mouldering yellow flesh fraying around his teeth in their casing of bone. Behind him are altar boys carrying his train, boys he has raped and abused, boys who are also skeletons clothed in the remnants of flesh and liturgical garments. They're coming closer and closer. The smell is overwhelming. He can feel the cold breath on his skin. He waits for the skeletal hand to reach out and seize him. He hopes it will be quick.

'Oh sweet Jesus, Father, you gave me the fright of my life!' It's Brigid, solid sensible Brigid who works as a cleaner and never complains. 'I just popped in to say hello to Our Lady on my way back from the shops. Isn't it awful, all these girls! Bejesus, you can't believe a priest would be doing that, sure you can't? And here's me interrupting you at your prayers.'

'That's alright. I'm just leaving,' John says, and struggles to his feet.

She puts her plastic shopping bags down with the same kind of rustling sound that a silk *Cappa Magna* might make. 'Sure then Father, I'll say my prayers for you too. God bless us, can you believe it?' She shakes her head.

'Please pray for me Brigid. I need your prayers,' he says. 'These are difficult times. And pray for the women, and pray for the murderer too.'

'Sure be to God, Father, there's a long list, when I've got to pray for my Maria whose pregnant there in Cork with twins, and that useless character she's married to out there betting on the horses 'n all. I'll tell you what, Father, I'll pray for you and those girls – I'm a mammy myself, and I can't imagine what their mammies are going through – and I'll leave you to pray for him that's doing it.'

'Thank you Brigid.'

She wrinkles her nose. 'These flowers are turning a bit ripe. It stinks in here. Maybe I'll just have a clean-up while I'm here. I suppose with all that's going on, Siobhan won't be minding me sorting things out with the flowers.'

'Thank you Brigid. I'd appreciate that,' he says, and again he has that sense that this is what keeps the wheels on the universe, when everything is falling apart. It's people like Brigid, and Adnan, and Jack, and Edith, and even Eric. People who offer small words of kindness and gestures of help in dark, dark times. What do they say? It's better to light a candle than to curse the darkness. Who said that? One way or the other, he must be attentive to these small signs of grace, for they may be the whisper of God in the silence of the void.

He hobbles back into the presbytery and picks up his car keys. He drives through the city to the retreat centre on its hilly perch overlooking the gorge and the forests beyond. Father Martin comes to the door and leads John through to the room with its Ikea chairs and scented candles and aura of incense. They sit down and the old priest puts his stole over his shoulders. 'Now then John, you don't look well, I must say.'

'I'm not well Father. I had a fall and hurt my knee and cut my hand. There's something wrong with me – with my mind. I – I haven't prepared myself properly for this confession. I can't. I don't know how. I've confessed it all before. I don't even know if I should be here.'

'John, you're here to have a conversation with the Lord. When we have a problem or we're struggling with something, we often have to discuss it with people we trust over and over again. Your desire to confess is a desire for the Lord's mercy and compassion and love. Remember that, and just unburden yourself. He's listening.' He leans back and folds his hands on his stomach and waits.

John takes a deep breath and closes his eyes. He begins with a croak, clears his throat and begins again. 'When I was at the seminary in Rome – it was the end of term. We went out to celebrate. Six of us. We were all gay.' He opens his eyes. Father Martin nods and says nothing.

John lowers his eyes and focuses on a small silver speck clinging to his trouser leg. It's confetti from Siobhan's wedding. It must have been on the kneeler in the church.

'We went drinking. We drank too much. Three of us were celibate, but the other three were – well, …' What were they? He doesn't know what word to use. 'They – they weren't celibate. They had a reputation. You know. The kind of thing they say about the seminaries in Rome.' He glances up. Another nod. He looks down again and tries to lick the dryness from his lips. 'One of them – Robert – he and I, we held hands. I – I wanted him. I would have – you know – I would have broken my vow of celibacy if – if I'd had the chance that night. We – one of the other three – suggested we go on somewhere. I didn't recognise the name of the place – *La Dolce Vita* – I thought they were suggesting a trip to the cinema.' He tries to laugh but fails. It sounds like a sob. He glances up. Father Martin's expression hasn't changed. 'It was a club. A gay club. I shouldn't – I should have left – but, but I wanted to go in there because of Robert. I was drunk. I just – I wanted him so much Father. It felt impossible to resist. Everything in me – I can't describe how I felt. It wasn't just lust Father. It wasn't lust. I loved him. We'd studied together for two years. He was my best friend. I – it was love.' His voice wobbles and he pauses.

'It's alright John. Take your time.' The old priest's wrinkles are set in a permanent expression of kindness, as if his habitual expression has carved itself into his face. His blue eyes shine with tenderness, giving John the courage to continue.

'We went in. There were lights, and music, and – and men and – and, I lost Robert. I couldn't see him among all those bodies, and – and the dancing – and – and the darkness. But Damian – Damian was there. Somehow, I was with Damian, in – in a kind of changing room. We were taking our clothes off. He – umm, he –' He clears his throat and squeezes his eyes shut. 'He touched me – you know, I – I had an erection. Then he – he tied a small white towel round me and – and did a kind of knot. I was looking for Robert, but I couldn't see him anywhere.' He rubs his face with his hands and forces himself to continue. 'Then – then – it gets confused. I – we went to a bar and – I had another drink. Damian – he gave me some kind of powder to sniff. I think it was cocaine. Then we had our towels off and – and we were in a sauna. Everybody was naked. There were hands and – and – um – men's bodies – private parts. Lots of them. Touching. Emmm – fondling.' He shakes his head. He can't go on. He wants to run away. He can't look at Father Martin. 'Sorry. I can't – I can't,' he says.

'John, dear John, it's alright. Take your time. I have all day. Let's just sit here until you feel stronger. Let's ask the Lord to hold you close and comfort you. This isn't easy. I know that. An honest confession is one of the most difficult things any of us has to do.'

In the corner of the room there's a simple wooden tabernacle with a small electric fountain beneath it. Water burbles over the artificial stones, and the candle glows red above the tabernacle. Everything in this room is designed to console and to soothe.

John tries to take deep breaths, but they snag in his throat. His hands begin to shake. He looks desperately at the old priest and shakes his head. 'I don't know – I can't go on.'

'John, you don't need to say everything. Our Lord knows. Surrender your guilt and your pain to him without words. He understands.'

John shakes his head. 'No. I need to say it. I need to confess. Otherwise, I won't be sure. How will I know I'm forgiven, if I don't know what I've really confessed to?'

Father Martin smiles. 'Let's wait till the words come then.'

John takes a deep breath. 'Somebody put my penis in his mouth, and I had – I ejaculated. I had an orgasm. I was holding somebody else's penis – I don't think it was the same person – and he came too. There were others – mouths, hands, voices – then suddenly – I panicked. I got up and left. It was dark. I was sweating. I found the door. I went out and grabbed a towel and wrapped it round my waist. I wanted to get out. But Damian was there – I don't know where he came from. Maybe he followed me out, or maybe he was waiting for me. He – he redid my towel the way it was before. I felt dizzy. I told him I wanted to leave. He didn't listen. He took my arm, and then – then he was there. Cardinal Michael Bradley. Damian took me to him.

'He – he told me to suck his cock. That's what he said. "Suck my cock". He had a lisp, so he spoke with a kind of hiss. I did. I did what he told me to. Then he – he took me to some kind of lounger – and – and Damian and he – I had to lie on my stomach and – and bend my knees – I think they both – they both – umm, you know – umm, they had sex with me.'

He puts his hands over his face, only dimly aware of the old priest's presence as he sobs. He gasps and swallows and rubs his eyes. Father Martin pushes a box of tissues towards him, and John blows his nose and wipes his face. Father Martin goes over to a small sink in the corner and fills a glass of water. He gives it to John and John gulps it down. He is so thirsty.

Father Martin sits down again. After a while he asks, 'Is that all John?'

John shakes his head. Now the words tumble out of him in a babble of disgust. He wants to say it all and get it over with. 'Damian took me back to the seminary. He took me to his room. I slept in his bed and we did more things. He warned me never to tell anybody. I swore I wouldn't. I went to confession the next morning. I mean, that's different, isn't it Father? It's secret. It's not telling anybody other than Christ, is it?'

Father Martin nods. 'The seal of the confessional is absolute, John. You know that. You did the right thing.'

'I left Rome a couple of days later,' says John. 'I was due to come back anyway. I'd finished my training. I – it was soon after that that Cardinal Bradley left. There were rumours, but – he left the priesthood and went to work in New York.'

Father Martin nods. 'And he was killed on 9/11,' he says. 'I know the story John.'

'The thing is Father – I – he's not dead. I – he's here, in Westonville. I'm sure of it.'

For the first time, the old priest's expression darkens. 'What do you mean John?'

'I think I saw him. In the confessional. I can't – I can't say any more, but I don't think he died.' Father Martin is looking at him intently. 'You don't believe me, do you?' says John.

'I have no reason to doubt you John, though it seems unlikely. But John, this is first and foremost a time for your confession, and I see little if any guilt in what you've said.' Father Martin pauses. 'Let me change that. I see enormous guilt. I see a mortal soul in danger of everlasting damnation, but it's not your soul. You were raped John. You were the victim of shocking abuse. I wish you had gone to the police, but I understand why you didn't. I don't know this Damian you speak of, but I know a fair bit about Cardinal Bradley. I hope for all our sakes he died as they say he did. I can't quite take in what you're saying about him being here in Westonville. If he is, then maybe you should still go to the police.' He takes a deep breath. 'These murders John, is that what you're afraid of? That these murders have something to do with this – this thing you saw, whether it's real or whether it's an apparition?' John nods. Father Martin sighs. 'John, it's not that I disbelieve that you saw the cardinal, but memory and imagination are very powerful. We're all disturbed by the murder of these poor women, and by the idea that a priest might be doing these terrible things. I believe that you are still deeply traumatised by what happened to you that night in Rome, and maybe these wounds are bleeding into each other.

Perhaps your memories of Rome and your imagination about what's happening to these women and who's responsible are becoming mixed up and leading you to experience terrifying flashbacks rooted in those unhealed memories. And you're not well. I think you need to see a doctor. Maybe you should ask the bishop to send somebody to stand in for you so that you can rest and get better.'

'I can't do that Father. I can't leave my parish over Holy Week.'

Father Martin nods. 'Well, be gentle with yourself lad. There's no point in us preaching God's love and mercy if we don't experience that reality for ourselves. Sometimes, it's the hardest thing, to forgive ourselves. It's not God who punishes us John. It's we who punish ourselves, because we don't simply trust God's promise, we can't accept God's unconditional forgiveness.'

John tries to reflect on Father Martin's words as he drives back to the presbytery, but he feels exhausted and feverish and unable to concentrate. The skin around the plaster on his hand is red and tender. He switches on the radio because he thinks he no longer cares. He thinks he is beyond shock and fear and agitation. But he is wrong. There is life in him yet.

'We are going immediately to Ruth Jackson who is reporting from Westonville on the latest dramatic events to unfold in that city. Ruth, over to you.'

'It's a beautiful day here in Westonville, with the sun shining and a blue sky. Yet there's a sense of shock and disbelief hanging over the city today, as its residents come to terms with what has happened here this morning. Westonville will join that small list of cities which will forever be remembered first and foremost for the serial killings that happened in its quiet suburban streets.

'I'm here outside the Parish Church of Saints Felicity and Perpetua, which is cordoned off with police tape as forensic teams do their work. After yesterday's gruesome discovery of the charred and mutilated body of a woman outside the church, police this morning found a second woman's body in a building skip behind the church. The parish priest, Father James Forrester, has been arrested and is being held in custody for questioning.

'Parishioners are refusing to comment, but Kirsty Smith lives next door to the church, and she spoke to me earlier this morning about her impressions of Father Forrester.' There's a pause and a rustle. 'Kirsty, this is quite a shock for all of you, I'm sure.'

'Yeah, we can't believe it. I mean, we all fancied him a bit – Father Jim. He were a bit of a looker, if you know what I mean.' Kirsty burrs her r's and twangs her vowels through her nose. 'Can't believe it, can you? Us in here with our kiddies, and them poor women being done that to just next door. It's hard to take it in.'

'Did you know the priest?' asks Ruth.

'I used to say hello to him. He were always polite, always stopped to chat. We girls used to joke that he were a bit of a ladies' man. We was joking, him being a priest and all, but we didn't know the half of it, did we?'

John switches the radio off in shame and disgust. He parks outside the chemist on the main road near the presbytery. He needs painkillers and something to take away his fever. His thoughts are veering and swerving and leaping through lurid landscapes of lust and loathing and violence and dread. He wants to die. He wants to die.

He locks his car and stumbles into the chemist, vaguely aware of huddles of people on the pavements gossiping. Are they watching him? Are they talking about him and pointing at him? He thinks they are, but he can't concentrate or focus enough to know.

He weaves past the perfumed aisles of cosmetics and the feminine hygiene section, past the teeth and dental hygiene section, past the male toiletries section, and the signs leap out at him, ridiculous and mocking in their dissected body parts.

May Johnson, another of his parishioners, is on the counter

behind the pharmacy section. She frowns as he approaches her. 'Father, whatever has happened to you? You look ghastly. Are you not well?'

'I think I'm getting flu,' he says. 'I just need something to bring my temperature down.'

'I think you need to see a doctor Father.'

'No, I'll be fine. I'm going home to bed. I'll just take some paracetamol or something.'

She disappears behind the counter at the back of the shop and he can see her speaking to the pharmacist. She comes back a few minutes later with a packet of pills. 'Mr Gupta says you should take these, but if you're not better tomorrow you should see a doctor.'

She hands him the packet and he takes his wallet out. She looks at him and what he sees is not condemnation but kindness and relief. 'So Father, however terrible the news, at least life can go on now. They've arrested Father Forrester, and we can all stop worrying and wondering.'

Through the fog of fever and fear, he feels a stab of conscience, a need to defend the innocent. 'He hasn't been charged May. It might not be him.'

A little cloud of something that frightens him flits across her face and disappears, then she says, 'Here's hoping for all our sakes that they've got the right man Father.'

As he leaves the shop, he reminds himself that the full force of suspicion has been on every priest in town, including him. He thinks of all the people in the church this morning – fewer than half the people in the parish – and it dawns on him that those who stayed away were communicating a different message. Were they the ones who secretly believed it might be him?

Back at the presbytery, he takes two pills and lies down on the bed. He thinks he will sleep off the fever and get up in time for the meeting with the bishop. He sets the alarm clock and closes his eyes.

The sleep has refreshed him and the tablets have taken away the worst of his fever, but he feels weak and his head aches. He considers not going to the meeting. There is something in him though, a mix of curiosity and disbelief and shock, that makes him want to be there with his fellow priests and the bishop, to share this sense of disorientation and collective shame. His own guilt might have been assuaged, but he wakes to the greater realisation of some horror that will not be erased or calmed just by the arrest of James Forrester. The murders might have stopped, but now begins the long slow process of the community and the Church coming to terms with what they have harboured in their midst, and the endless unanswerable questions about why and how and what for.

He puts on his black clerical shirt and dog collar – the bishop has made clear that he expects them to dress like priests when they come to meetings – and he drives through the wooded hillside suburb where the bishop lives in a rambling Victorian house. The housekeeper lets him in and ushers him into the wood-panelled dining room that doubles as a formal meeting room. Generations of bishops look down from the walls, some in cardinals' garb, dating back to the mid-nineteenth century when the Catholic Church was allowed to emerge from banishment and re-establish its presence in England.

Several priests are already there, also dressed in black, sitting in silence around the table. He greets them and sees the various expressions of fretfulness and shame on their faces. There's a contagion in their midst, and the arrest of the culprit has not been enough to cleanse their consciences or to still their fears. Years of scandal over the sex abuse crisis have left them all raw and reeling, and this new crisis has scraped away the fragile aura of trust that they have been working so hard to cultivate. Hovering over them all is a question mark, like an Ash Wednesday smear on their foreheads – what if the police have arrested the wrong man? What if it's one of them?

Bishop Donald is a tall, balding man who walks with a stoop. He comes in and nods a grim-faced greeting. He is wearing a heavy gold cross over his black shirt. He used to be known as a liberal and a good pastor to his people, but in recent years the stresses of his calling have taken their toll and he has become apathetic and indifferent towards the priests in his care. His reputation has been tarnished by rumours that he could have acted sooner to report Ignatius Brandon, that he was complicit in a cover up that allowed the priest to move from parish to parish, abusing children wherever he went.

He sits in the high-backed chair at the head of the table. 'You know why I've asked you to come here today,' he says. He has a high-pitched, reedy voice, so that his words lack the gravitas of his office. 'We cannot assume that Father James is guilty, but we must pray that he is indeed the culprit and that his arrest will put an end to the murders.'

John thinks there's something odd about that – priests praying that a fellow priest is a serial murderer – but he tries to focus on what the bishop is saying.

'I would ask you all to avoid any contact with the media. I don't want any of you making statements or giving interviews. Is that clear?' They all nod and murmur their assent. 'The diocesan press office will handle all enquiries. We have to minimise the scandal this will create for the Church. We have to be seen to do the right thing.'

'Perhaps we should be praying for the victims and not just worrying about our own reputations.' It's Christopher Lynch, a wiry-haired Justice and Peace activist with a ginger beard and freckles.

The bishop makes an impatient gesture with his hand. 'Of course we pray for the victims,' he says, 'that should go without saying.' Christopher raises an eyebrow and gives a sardonic smirk – 'as if,' his expression says – but he doesn't say anything.

'Do you have any more information, bishop? Other than what the news is telling us?' It's Father Patrick O'Leary, middle-aged and jovial, one of those ordinary priests whose understated goodness goes unnoticed and unremarked by all except those who fall within his orbit of care. He has a warm voice and a plump gentle face. John thinks how improbable it would be that he would be the murderer, and he finds himself looking around at all of them and thinking the same. But then, James doesn't look like a serial killer either. What would a serial killer look like?

'I understand that they are holding Father James in custody during their investigations. The second body was found in a skip buried beneath rubble where they're digging up the old car park behind the church. Of course, the diocese is ensuring that Father James has access to the best lawyers, but justice must take its course. The bodies haven't yet been identified. There have been no reports of missing women, so police are assuming that they were prostitutes and possibly illegal immigrants.'

'Bishop, I believe the words you should be using are sex workers and asylum seekers,' says Christopher, and there's a white ring of anger around his lips. 'Before we spend quite so much energy on worrying about one of our own, may I suggest we pray now for these murdered women and their families?'

The bishop nods irritably. 'Yes, alright. Fine. Maybe you could say a prayer, Father Christopher.'

Christopher crosses himself and they all do the same. 'Lord Jesus Christ, you were the friend of women who sold their bodies in harsh and unjust societies, because they had nothing else to sell.' He sounds as if he himself has something to sell. Justice. Righteousness. The Kingdom of God is at hand. Roll up, roll up. Buy your tickets here. These are uncharitable thoughts, but John feels irritable and short-tempered. He just wants to get this over with and go home to bed.

Christopher preaches on, instructing Christ on what He presumably already knows. 'You saw their woundedness and their vulnerability. You saw then as now how women are used and abused by men, silenced and beaten by the powers of patriarchy. You came to show us a different way. You reached out to those women in friendship and love. You gave them back their dignity and their humanity.' There's a restless fidgeting around the table now. Christopher is well-known for his florid intercessions and long dramatic homilies. John thinks he's a Marmite priest. People love him or loathe him, but few are indifferent to him. Jennifer in the Justice and Peace Group loves him. His voice is shaking now. He is moving himself to tears. 'Help us, Jesus Christ, to learn from your example and to reach out to our sisters on the streets in compassion and love. Help us to see you in their bodies beaten and crucified for love, in their sorrow and suffering. Help us to stand alongside them.' There's a long silence, then he solemnly says, 'Amen.'

There's a reverential pause and a fluttering of relief that he has finished, but then, eyes still closed, he says, 'and now my brothers, maybe you too would like to pray for our murdered sisters and all women who walk the city streets tonight.'

Father Thomas Chukwu is a visiting priest from Nigeria. He begins to pray in a deep voice that rumbles through the room like an ancient chant. 'Dear God, Almighty Father, protect your priests from the temptations and seductions of women. Help us to resist the forbidden fruit that they hold out to us with such cunning smiles and wicked ways. Help us to resist them not with violence and murder, but with the power and conviction of Jesus Christ, our Lord and God, in your holy name. Forgive those women their sins, redeem their bodies and souls from the everlasting fires of hell, and save them through the suffering and death of your Son who died for them. Amen.'

Eyes flicker open and exchange glances. There's a nervous clearing of throats around the table.

Father Joseph Agambire from Ghana begins to pray. 'Dear Jesus, forgive my brother for his lack of charity. You know that women in Africa suffer a double burden of poverty and patriarchy, and that we priests are often guilty of blame and persecution of our sisters. Help us to love one another, and to remember that in Christ there is neither male nor female, slave nor free, black nor white, but we are all one in you. We pray for the souls of our sisters murdered in this city, and for their families. Amen.'

The bishop intervenes before anybody else can add their voice. 'We bring all our prayers before you, Lord, as we say, "Our Father ..."'

They pray the Our Father and the bishop tries to pick up the threads of the meeting, though John senses they have all lost their way.

He looks at the faces of the priests around the table. The tablets are wearing off and his vision is beginning to blur. He feels dizzy and sick. He is glad when the bishop draws the meeting to a close.

He tries to make his escape, but Patrick O'Leary stops him in the doorway. 'Are you alright John? You look sick.'

'I have a bit of a fever. I'm alright. I'll go to bed when I get home and try to sleep it off.' John can barely form the words.

'Are you okay to drive? Do you want me to give you a lift?' How has Patrick managed to resist the mood of conflict and gloom? John remembers a thought he had earlier, about kindness and candles and darkness, but all he can think of are the everlasting fires of hell.

He says he's fine, but the drive home through the evening gloom is an ordeal of shifting, melting landscapes and moving shadows. He is glad when he can lock the presbytery door behind him and fall into bed.

TWENTY THREE

FIFTH WEDNESDAY OF LENT

The darkness seethes and swarms and screeches and howls through the long feverish night. He wakes drenched in sweat, body on fire, heart pounding, hand pulsating with pain. When sleep comes again, it arrives in a lurid carnival of images. The cardinal prances and prowls through his dreams, hissing and snarling and seducing. His erect phallus protrudes from his red silk vestments, glistening and throbbing to the rhythm of John's pounding pulse. A woman with a mangled body and blood pouring from her mouth bends down and takes the phallus in her mouth. The cardinal laughs and looms over John. Creatures crawl out from under his wide-brimmed hat – red-eyed bats flitting around the room and tiny, web-footed demons crawling over John's bed, into his mouth and eyes and nose. One of them begins clawing at John's chest, squealing and scratching, trying to get inside him, weighing down his body so that he can't breathe.

He wakes and opens his eyes. Shula is pummelling his chest, meowing, wanting to be fed. Morning light is streaming through the window, slicing into his brain so that his head pounds. Somebody is coming upstairs. He hears the creak of their movements, the heavy weight of their body. Please let it be quick. Please let it all finish now, let this torment be over. Let me die.

There's a knock on the door and Deacon Jack comes in, his face pale and his brow furrowed with anxiety. 'John, what's happening? It's quarter to nine. Are you not well? Aren't you coming to say Mass?'

'I'm sick,' says John, and his voice is ragged. He is aware that he probably stinks, his breath rancid with fever and stale sweat oozing around him.

Jack lays a cool hand on his forehead. 'You're burning up John. You have a fever. I'll call the doctor.'

'No. I'll be fine. Can you tell the people I'm sick? I got wet in the rain the other day. I've just got a touch of flu. Can you do a Eucharistic service instead of Mass? Tell them I'm sorry. I'll be fine by tomorrow.'

Jack looks dubious. 'I think you need a doctor, John.'

'No. I'm fine. I just need to spend the day in bed.'

'I'll send Edith in,' says Jack.

'Maybe if you would just feed Shula on the way out, let Edith come in after the service. I want to go back to sleep for a bit.' He closes his eyes. He cannot bear the thought of Edith fussing around him.

Jack leaves the room and comes back with a glass of water and two paracetamol. 'Here, take these. I'll feed Shula and I'll ask Edith to come in later and see how you are.'

'Thanks Jack.' John rolls over to face the wall and pulls the duvet around his ears. His body is on fire but he is shivering with cold. He drifts in and out of sleep and wakes with somebody putting something cold and wet on his forehead. He is on his back and his mouth is open. His tongue feels swollen and dry. He forces himself to open his eyes.

Holly is there, sitting on the edge of the bed, wiping his face. 'Hey you,' she says.

He tries to smile, and he feels a crack in his lip open and begin to bleed. She rummages in her handbag and smears something moist and soothing over his lips. Her face is full of tenderness and love. He has never seen her looking like this before.

'Has the cardinal gone?' he hears himself say.

'The cardinal?' She smiles. 'What cardinal?'

'He was here,' says John. 'He was here last night.'

'There's no cardinal John. It's just me. Edith wanted to come in and look after you, but I thought you'd probably rather she didn't. I said I'd come in and sit with you.' She is saying something else but he can't hear. He feels himself floating, drifting, and now there are no demons. He is on the beach, and the sun is shining. Holly and Sarah are walking beside him. Sarah is holding his hand. Phoebe and Stephen have run on ahead, gathering fossils. Their laughter drifts back, bright and burbling in the sunlight. Kate is there too, and she and Holly are chatting about something. He can't make out what they're saying, but that doesn't matter. He holds Sarah's hand in his own, and he feels a great sense of relief that whatever was happening before, it's over. He walks on towards Phoebe and Stephen, and then Sarah lets go of his hand and skips away from him. She turns and smiles. She is carrying Shula, and behind her that dark landscape of rocks juts out into the sea. He wants to call out to her to be careful, the rocks are dangerous, but his voice won't come.

He opens his eyes. Kate and Holly are both there. Holly is standing by the door, holding her car keys in her hand. Kate has taken Holly's place on the edge of the bed. She smiles at him.

'Well, what have you been doing to yourself?' she says.

'Kate? Are the children here? Where are the children?' He thinks he shouldn't be asking that, but he can't remember why.

A shadow crosses her face. 'They're at school John. I – I'll bring them to see you when you're better. For now you need to rest.'

'Don't let the cardinal near them,' he says.

'What?' She frowns. 'What cardinal?'

'The cardinal. He's a monster. Tell them to look out. He's wearing his *cappa magna.*'

Kate and Holly exchange glances, then Kate takes his hand in hers and speaks in the voice he imagines she might use when treating a sick child. 'John, the cut in your hand is infected.

I've written a prescription for antibiotics. Holly is going to the chemist, and I'm going to take you over to the convent so that the sisters can look after you. You might have to go to hospital if the antibiotics don't clear things up, but let's see how you get on today.'

He hears her through a fog, her words drifting and coming apart so that he has to struggle to understand what she's saying. He lets her help him through to the bathroom and undress him. She is his sister. He wonders if this is alright, but she's a doctor too, and her arms are strong and supportive and reassuring. He rests against her as she helps him into a cool, shallow bath. He manages to wash himself, and then she helps him out and pats him dry. He knows, because he has done this for Ben, that his nakedness is safe with her. She dresses him in clean pyjamas and ties his dressing gown around him.

At the convent, Sister Martha guides him to the spare room with its white cotton bedding and yellow curtains. There's a bowl of flowers on the dressing table, and the room smells of fresh laundry and summer flowers. Holly arrives with the antibiotics and the three women move quietly around him, bringing him tea, giving him medicine, tucking him into bed.

He feels himself sinking into sleep, and he lets it come. This is not the demon-infested sleep of the night but the quiet, healing sleep of a body being nursed back to health. Mary comes to stand by his bed, with the infant Jesus in her arms. The jewels in her crown send rainbows arcing over his body, as she bends down and places a hand on his cheek. Sarah is there too, standing next to her. She has Shula in her arms. John murmurs to them. 'Please don't go. Stay with me. Don't leave me.'

'I won't leave you John. You know I won't. We've come for you. We want to take you home.' Mary is speaking with Holly's voice. He floats towards them as the room dissolves into mist and his body turns to some luminous substance, lighter than the motes of dust that drift in the sunbeams streaming through the window. They want him to go with them, out through the window and up, up, up into the clear blue sky. They want him to let go of the solidity of the world and melt into all the cracks in time and space, the invisible join where the moments don't quite meet, where matter and spirit reach out to one another but don't quite touch across the gap. That's where he needs to go, to be with them. If he can just shrug off this weight that holds him, the solid confines of his flesh that pin him down. If only he can wriggle free of the world.

And then the cardinal swoops down upon them in a silken swirl of wrath. His billowing red cape sweeps away those fragile beings that are lighter than light. He laughs, and the things swarm out of his mouth like some devouring plague, black winged creatures small enough to crawl up John's nostrils and into his mouth and ears and eyes. He tries to claw them away but there are too many of them. They burrow under his skin and wriggle through his body, eating him from the inside like maggots. He is infested with them. The cardinal is leering, a cadaver from hell come to claim the living for his own, his face dreadful in its rotting death mask.

Someone is shouting. It's John's own voice. Who is shouting with his voice? 'Go away! Go away! Please leave me alone. I don't want to die. Jesus, save me. Mary, Mary come to me. Go away! Jesus help me!' He tries to get out of bed. He needs to escape. Hands hold him down. Voices are speaking to him, but he can't hear them. He tries to tell them, 'The cardinal! The cardinal has come for me. Look. The cardinal has risen from the dead. He has come to take me to hell.' The cardinal laughs, and his laughter is a stinking ooze of some thick black substance that spills over John and blocks out all light and air and sound.

He opens his eyes and a strange room tilts and steadies itself around him. He is on a high bed, and a tube is snaking up from his hand to a metal contraption beside him. Holly is there, sitting on a chair by the bed.

'Where am I?' he says.

She smiles her broad, ironic smile. 'You're in hospital. We thought you were dying. Jesus Christ John, don't ever do that to me again. Don't you dare die and leave me alone in this world. You were delirious and burning up with fever, so Kate called an ambulance and they brought you in. You're on intravenous antibiotics. That's why there's a tube in your hand.'

'What day is it?'

'It's Wednesday night. You came in just before lunchtime. They said the antiobiotics would work quickly, and they obviously have.' She shakes her head. 'Jesus John, you scared the life out of us. You crazy man.'

He smiles and reaches his hand out towards her. She takes it in both her own. Then he remembers Shula. 'What about Shula?' he says. 'Somebody needs to feed her and look after her.'

'Jack and Edith are taking care of her.' Holly grins. 'Apparently they're getting married,' she says.

'Yes. It's wonderful news. Jack has been so lonely since Penny died, and Edith – she's a good soul, despite her funny ways.'

'She's a sour old shrew,' says Holly, but there's affection in her voice. 'I think a few nights of passion with lusty Jack will do her the world of good.'

He laughs weakly and tries not to picture it. 'What about the parish?' he asks. 'Who will say Mass?'

'Father Thomas Chukwu has offered to step in.'

'Thomas?'

'Yes.' Holly grimaces and rolls her eyes. 'It will all be hellfire and brimstone. You'd better make a speedy recovery and come and rescue us. The other visiting priest, Father Joseph something, is covering for James up at Saints Felicity and Perpetua. Dear God, what a bloody drama.'

'Is James still in prison?' John struggles to piece the memories together.

'He's in custody. Apparently they have permission to hold him for further questioning.'

John closes his eyes. He wants to stay in this small space of healing and tenderness, purged of the demons that are waiting, waiting, waiting to return.

TWENTY FOUR

FIFTH THURSDAY OF LENT

He wakes in the morning to the clatter and rattle of the hospital staff preparing for the day. He is in a small private room similar to the one Gertrude was in, with a window looking out over the hills beyond the city. The dawn sky is lustrous, a mother of pearl veil lifting over the horizon. He feels a deep sense of peace and well-being, as the nurses flit in and out taking his blood pressure, checking his drip and exchanging pleasantries with him. He surrenders himself to their care, thankful only to be alive and lucid and free from pain. The murders and the nightmares have faded to a faint watermark on the edges of consciousness. They belong in a different world, beyond this cocooned bubble of sickness and healing, of the living and the dying.

There's a steady stream of visitors during the afternoon visiting hours. Edith and Jack arrive and John is touched to see that they're holding hands as they walk into the room. Edith's tight, sparse body fits neatly into the plastic chair. Jack stands beside her, wisely choosing not even to try to sit in the other chair. They assure him that Shula is fine, and all the people in the parish send him their love and prayers.

'Father Chukwu came to say Mass this morning,' Edith tells him. 'I must say, I was a bit worried. You know, it's not because he's black or anything. I'm not racial, Father. You know me. I'm full of admiration for Dorcas, and she and I get on so well together, and she's as black as the Ace of Spades and it doesn't bother me at all. But all these cultural things and the accent and things. I wondered how he'd get on.' Her eyes are bright with holy zeal. 'But oh Father, he is such a good priest. They don't make them like that anymore. So full of Catholic conviction and so strong in his faith. I think Our Lord sent him to us to keep us strong while you're away from us.' Jack is half-nodding, though John can see he doesn't entirely agree with Edith's verdict.

'I'd better not be away too long Edith,' John says, 'or Father Chukwu and you will be introducing the Latin Mass next.'

'There would be nothing wrong with that, Father,' she says primly, and then she pats his hand. 'But it's not the same. You're our priest, and we want you back soon.' He knows it's as close as he is ever likely to get to being praised by Edith.

Bonnie comes to visit with a bunch of spring flowers, but the nurse says they don't allow flowers in the wards in case of infection. Bonnie laughs in that good natured way of hers and says she'll take them home and enjoy them herself.

Dorcas comes to visit too. He loves the aura that she brings with her – the gracious serenity that seems to emanate from somewhere deep within. She is carrying a large manila envelope, and she's smiling that rare and glorious smile that illuminates the room.

'The children have done some drawings for you,' she says, and puts the envelope on the bed. Navigating carefully around the drip attached to his hand, he opens the envelope and pulls out an array of cards and paintings and drawings. He reads the messages and he feels as if the whole universe is sparkling and singing with love. 'Get well soon Fatter.' 'Cum bak. We miss you.' 'Amy loves Farther John'. There's a small blonde stick figure holding a heart.

'Thank you,' he says. He swallows. 'Tell them I said thank you,' he says. 'Tell them I love them. Sorry.' He rubs his eyes with the back of his hand.

'They love you too, Father,' she says.

He closes his eyes and lets the tears slide beneath his lashes and trickle down his face. Her silence soothes him. When she leaves, he feels abandoned. He closes his eyes and prays for Jesus and Mary to stay with him.

'We've come to visit you.' It's Kate's voice. He opens his eyes and there she is, with Stephen and Phoebe beside her.

The children come hesitantly over to the bed. He wants to hold out his arms and hug them, but the bed is too high and the drip restricts his movements.

Kate bends and kisses his forehead. 'Hi little brother,' she says. 'I thought you might like to see the children.'

'Hello you two,' he says, trying to sound natural. He doesn't want to alarm them with the intensity of the love and delight he feels.

'Hello Uncle John.' Phoebe leans over and kisses his cheek. On the other side of the bed, Stephen comes close enough for John to wrap his free arm around him. Kate sits in the plastic chair and Phoebe and Stephen explore the room.

'You look better,' Kate says. 'You gave us all quite a fright.'

'What happened?' he says. 'I don't remember coming to the hospital.'

'You were delirious – screeching and ranting about some cardinal.' She grimaces. 'Not that you'd have to be crazy to be frightened of those weirdos,' she says. 'Cardinals terrify me too.'

A shiver of apprehension goes through his body. 'What was I saying?' Does he sound casual enough?

'Oh, nonsense mostly. Things were coming to get you. Bugs were crawling up your nose.' He senses she's glossing the details. The children are listening now, wide-eyed in fascination. She shrugs and laughs. 'Don't worry. It's perfectly common when people have a high fever or an infection for them to go a bit bonkers.'

'What kind of bugs?' asks Stephen.

'I don't know. Better ask Uncle John,' says Kate.

'Beetles and snails and things with funny feet,' he says, his imagination recoiling from the horror of what it was like.

'How big were they?' Stephen is gazing at him in wide-eyed fascination.

'Tiny,' says John. 'Small enough to fit up my nose.' He tries to sound amused. He thinks Kate could be a bit more sensitive and spare him this interrogation. He isn't sure that she should be quite so candid with the children.

'What's a cardinal?' asks Phoebe.

'He's a senior bishop,' says John. 'You've probably seen them on TV. They wear red dresses and silly hats.'

'Are they ladies?' she asks.

'No sweetheart, they're men in drag,' says Kate.

'What's drag?' asks Stephen.

'It's when a man wears women's clothes,' Kate tells him.

Stephen looks earnestly at John. 'Mummy says we mustn't tell daddy we came to visit you,' he says.

John looks at Kate. She flushes but she meets his gaze and doesn't look away. That's Kate. Whatever it is you're dealing with, look it full in the face. 'Give him time John. These murders have shocked everybody. You know what Chris is like. He'll come round.'

John nods, but he feels betrayed by her. She should stand up for him. She should tell Chris that he can't stop the children from seeing him. He's their uncle, and he has nothing to do with the murders. He is innocent. He says it again to himself, I have nothing to do with the murders.

As if reading his mind, Phoebe asks, 'Do you know Father James, Uncle John?'

'Yes, I do,' says John. 'We priests all know each other. There aren't many of us.'

'He killed some ladies,' says Stephen. 'They were whores.'

'Stephen, what a terrible thing to say! Who taught you to speak like that?' Kate flares up, eyes blazing at her son.

Stephen shrugs nonchalantly. 'That's what Brian at school told me. He told me that the dead ladies were whores. What's a whore, mummy?'

'It's a horrible word for a poor woman who sells her body for sex to men, because she has no job and no money and no food for her children,' Kate says. 'And besides, Father James might not be the murderer. He hasn't been accused of anything yet,' she reminds them.

John feels uneasy again. Stephen is only seven. Surely, Kate should be a bit more discreet? John had no idea what sex was at that age.

Phoebe gives John that serious adult look of hers. 'Uncle John, do you think Father James is the murderer?'

'I don't know Phoebe. I find it hard to believe that anybody could do those things, let alone a priest I know.' He tries to match Kate's honesty.

'But if it's not him, do you think it's one of the other priests?' she persists.

'That's what the newspapers are saying, but the newspapers don't always get the facts right,' he says. The thought that Father James might turn out not to be the killer is more than he can bear to contemplate.

'Come on, you two little ghouls. I'm sure Uncle John doesn't want to spend his time with you talking about murders. Why don't you tell him about the camping trip we're planning after Easter?' says Kate.

'We're going to France,' Stephen says, though John can tell he thinks that talking about the murders was much more exciting. 'Mummy and daddy are buying a camper van.'

And so the time passes in a burble of children's chatter and easy conversation with Kate. When the time comes to leave, he watches them go with an aching heart, wondering when he will see them again, and feeling a terrible darkness descending upon him. He is tired from all the visitors, welcome though they were. He doesn't want to brood and fret. He takes his rosary from the bedside cabinet and lets it trickle through his fingers as he drifts off to sleep.

TWENTY FIVE

FIFTH FRIDAY OF LENT

He wakes to a clean, fresh world. Two nights of sleeping soundly have rested and restored him, so he feels better than he has for several weeks. He has avoided the news while he's been in hospital. He has no desire to buy a newspaper from the hospital trolley or to watch the television attached to the wall next to the window.

The nurses and doctors treat him with respect, their manner free from the taint of suspicion that has clung to him and presumably to every other priest in the city because of the murders and the rumours. He wonders if it's their professionalism that allows the people caring for him to be so gentle and friendly towards him, or if it's simply that everybody wants to believe that the murderer has been caught and the nightmare is over. He is not so sure, but he refuses to think about it.

A young Scottish nurse comes to wash him and to take his blood pressure and his temperature. Her name is Elsa. She chatters good-naturedly as she moves around the bed, her movements calm and confident, intended to minimise any awkwardness or embarrassment as she sponges down his body and helps him to change into clean pyjamas.

'You seem much better today, Father John,' she says. 'Your blood pressure and your temperature are both back to normal. I imagine they'll let you go home later, once the doctor has done her rounds. They try to avoid keeping people in over the weekend if they can avoid it.'

He thinks about going home and it's an uneasy thought. He realizes how safe he feels here in the hospital. The thought of the presbytery with its echoing cloisters and gloomy rooms depresses him.

'Is there any more news about the murders?' he asks Elsa, because somehow that seems connected with the thought of going home.

She shakes her head. 'They still haven't identified the two latest victims. That priest is being held for further questioning.' She smooths the sheet over his legs and tucks in the corners. 'I suppose everybody is waiting to see what happens tonight. If it was him, then the murders will stop, but what if there's another one tonight?'

It's an unthinkable thought. 'Let's pray that doesn't happen,' he says.

'Would you like me to raise your bed a bit so that you can sit up?' she asks.

'Yes please.'

She pushes a lever so that the top of the bed lifts, then she helps him to sit up and plumps up the pillows behind him. She is wearing a light floral perfume that makes him think of summer days.

'I could stay here forever,' he says. 'I feel so safe and cared for.'

After she goes, he lies on the bed and gazes out of the window at birds drifting in the blue morning air. Somewhere along the corridor, a man cries out in pain or fear. There's the distant clatter of the food trolley bringing breakfast, and outside John's door a young man dressed in white is deep in discussion with a nurse in a blue uniform, both of them bent over a clipboard.

A porter pushes an old woman in a wheelchair down the corridor, and he hears the crackle of her voice complaining as they pass. From down the corridor the cry comes again, a wail of distress that he hopes is answered soon.

His missal is on top of the bedside cabinet. Somebody must have brought it in. Edith probably, ever mindful of his priestly duties. He opens it and attempts to do the reading for the day. It's from the Book of Hebrews.

You are a priest of the order of Melchizedek, and for ever.

He tries to imagine being a priest forever, but he can't. He thinks of Luke, and of a different life that might have been. Surely, there will be an end to this solitude, to this yearning for all the ordinary consolations of love and intimacy? God is the source and end of our deepest desires. He tries to remind himself of that, but it isn't God he wants right now. It's Luke, and he cannot be a priest forever and also long for Luke as his heart's greatest desire.

He is glad when the trolley arrives, and he can immerse himself in the distracting business of breakfast. The toast is cold and smeared with something greasy that doesn't even attempt to pass itself off as butter, and the scrambled eggs are leaking a watery white substance onto the plate.

He has almost finished when Elsa comes in. 'Father, apparently one of your parishioners was admitted during the night and her husband is asking to see you. Her name is Jane Sanderson and his name is Pete. She went into labour and they had to do an emergency caesarean. Is it alright if I let him come and talk to you? He seems quite distressed. I thought you might want to see him.'

'Yes, of course,' says John. 'Where is he?'

'He's outside, at the desk. Shall I bring him in?'

Pete looks dreadful. His cheeks are sunken and his skin is ashen. There are deep shadows under his eyes, and he walks with an exhausted stoop.

'Hello Father,' he mumbles, as if the effort of talking is too much. 'I'm sorry you've been so ill. I hope I'm not disturbing you.'

'Of course not Pete. I'm fine now. But come and sit down and tell me what's happened. Shut the door.'

Pete creaks into the plastic chair and clasps his hands between his knees. 'It's Jane,' he says. 'she began bleeding last night – well, early this morning. I think it was about half past four. It was terrible Father.' He closes his eyes and shudders at the memory. 'There was blood everywhere, all over the bed. I had to call an ambulance. Jane's mum came to stay with the children. They tried to stop the bleeding. It's too early Father. The baby's not due yet. In the end, they had to do an emergency caesarean. They said they were doing it to save Jane. They couldn't make any promises about the baby.' He coughs and sniffs and rubs his face with his hands, then he folds his arms across his body and squeezes them, as if to stop himself from falling apart.

'How are they? How's Jane? What about the baby?' John asks.

'Jane hasn't come round properly yet. They're giving her a blood transfusion. She looks terrible Father. The baby is in intensive care. It's a little boy – just a scrap Father. He looks so tiny and vulnerable, lying there with tubes coming out of his body. They're worried about him. Apparently he had the cord around his neck, and he's not as developed as he should be.' His voice drops to a whisper. 'I'm so scared Father. I'm so frightened.'

'He's in good hands, Pete. They're both in good hands. We must trust the Lord and pray for them both.'

'The thing is Father – if Jane died, I couldn't bear it, if anything happened to Jane. She's my life Father. She's my whole life. And I'm frightened that God is punishing me, you know, because of what I did, with those women.' He loses his struggle not to cry.

Mindful of the drip, John reaches out carefully and rests his hand on Pete's arm. 'Pete, God isn't like that. You've confessed your sins and God has forgiven you. You must believe that. In the eyes of God, it's as if those things never happened. God loves you and God loves Jane, and your new baby. Your lives are in God's hands Pete, and nothing can ever change that.'

'I wish I could believe that Father, but bad things do happen. People die. People like Jane, and the baby. And – and I don't feel forgiven.' He gulps and snorts back the mucus gathering in his nose and throat. 'I don't feel as if God has forgiven me. I betrayed Jane. I'm so ashamed Father. I'm so ashamed. Bad things happen to good people, but I'm not a good person. I've done something terrible. Why shouldn't I be punished?'

'God has forgiven you, but you haven't forgiven yourself, Pete. That's the hardest part of all – when you confess your sins, believing that you are truly forgiven.' When John is lost for something to say, he always asks himself what Father Martin would say in this situation.

'What if Jane finds out? What if somebody tells her?' Pete is staring at him now, wide-eyed with terror.

'Jane loves you Pete. She would still love you, even if she knew.' John hopes he is right. He believes he is.

'Maybe I should tell her,' says Pete.

'That's your decision, but sometimes it's more loving to carry these burdens ourselves. Wait until she's better and then see how things go.' He smiles. 'What are you going to call the baby?'

Pete looks embarrassed. He glances up, his eyes red and watery, then he looks away again. 'We thought we'd call him John,' he says, 'after you.' He rubs his eyes. 'You've been good to us, Father. I know I'm not much of a Catholic. I mean, I don't go to confession and I don't pray and go to Mass often the way Jane does. But we know you're there for us Father, and the children all love you. It was their idea, to call the little one after you.'

John tries to find his voice. 'I don't know what to say Pete. It's – it's the best thing anybody's done for me. Thank you.' He laughs. 'See, I'm crying too now.'

After Pete leaves, John's mobile phone rings. He hadn't noticed it there, on the cabinet beside his missal. It's Sister

Martha. He assures her that he is much better and will be going home later.

'Do you need anything?' she asks. 'I'm going into town. I can stop off if you want me to bring you anything.'

'Would you bring me my anointing oil and my stole, Martha? They're in the sacristy.'

Later, when Elsa has taken the drip out of his hand, he puts on his dressing gown and slippers and follows the signs to the maternity ward through a labyrinth of corridors and up two floors in the lift. Attempts have been made to brighten the institutional ugliness of the building with its vinyl floors and glossy cream paintwork. There are photos of landscapes and sunsets on the walls, and through the windows he can see an enclosed garden with a fountain and a wooden table and chairs amidst a profusion of plants.

A trolley goes past with a mummified figure lying inert upon it, surrounded by tubes and wires. The porters pushing it are solemn-faced. Death is so close here, you can reach out and touch it at every turn. And yet it's also natural, benign even, altogether different from the savage annihilating force that seizes people unawares as they go about their daily business – driving to work, climbing ladders to paint their homes, standing on street corners soliciting strangers who might be murderers. He closes his mind. Don't think about that, he tells himself.

The ward sister shows him to a ward with six beds. Most of the women look healthy and happy. Some have their babies in cots beside them. Jane is lying inert against the pillow. Her face is grey and her breathing is shallow. A bag of blood stands suspended beside her bed, trickling down the tube into her arm. Pete is sitting beside her, looking lost.

John pulls the curtains closed around the bed and puts his stole over his dressing gown. Jane drifts in and out of consciousness, opening her eyes and murmuring occasionally, but without recognition or meaning. He anoints her forehead and her hands. Her skin feels clammy. When he's finished, he asks Pete to take him to the baby.

The tiny body is naked except for an enormous nappy and a knitted blue bonnet fringed with silken hair. John looks at the shrivelled face, the matchstick limbs and miniature hands and feet. He tries to ignore the machines and the tubes and the monitors, to focus all his thoughts and prayers on this fragile little creature clinging to the edges of life, so precariously claiming his place in the world. John. His newborn namesake.

He reaches in and touches the baby's hand, and the tiny fingers curl instinctively around his own huge index finger. The skin is so soft he can barely feel it.

He anoints the child and goes back to his ward, fingering his rosary in his pocket as he goes, trying to focus on Jane and Pete and all their children as he says Hail Marys.

Elsa comes to tell him that the doctor has been delayed. She won't be doing her rounds until late afternoon. Elsa seems apprehensive and apologetic. 'Sorry. I know you must be wanting to get home, but we're short of staff and she's covering for two sick colleagues.'

He doesn't want to go home. He would like just to stay here forever, free from all responsibilities and care, here among the sick and the recovering and the dying. He could anoint them and pray for them, and at night he could sleep in the knowledge that he was surrounded by living, breathing human beings and not by echoes and memories and ghosts.

Pete comes back just after lunch. Jane is awake and wants to see him. Pete looks less stressed than he did, but his clothes are crumpled and he looks weak with exhaustion.

John makes his way along the corridors again, this time with Pete for company. People are arriving for the afternoon visiting hours. Their faces wear expressions of anxiety and care, of optimism and relief, of tedium and weariness. A young couple squeezes into the lift beside them. The girl has dark purple hair with silver rings through her nose and ears, and a bright tattoo on her arm. She's wearing torn jeans and heavy boots. Her man has long fair hair and a bedraggled t-shirt. She looks too bright and bold for him.

'… told her I'll look after the kids. She's scared stiff that he'll get to keep them. I told her, I said, "You're my big sister, you are." Y'know what I mean? I said, "There's no way that fucking bastard is getting anywhere near my nephew and niece."' The girl has a local accent. A grey-haired woman in a pink cardigan shuffles her feet and makes a little tutting sound, just like Edith would. 'Wot you tutting at my lover?' says the girl. 'If you could see that fucking twat my sister married, you'd 'ave somethin' to tut about, believe me. And now she's dying an' all, what the fuck am I meant to do?'

'It's your language,' says the woman. 'It's not appropriate.'

'Yeh? I'll tell you wot for nuffink my lover. It's my sister dying that's not appropriate. That's what the fuck is not appropriate. Put that in your pipe and smoke it, why don'cha?'

The lift stops and John follows Pete to the maternity ward. Jane is flopped back against the pillows.

She opens her eyes when they walk in and attempts a smile. 'Hello Father John,' she says. 'I'm sorry to hear you haven't been well.'

He goes through the usual assurances and explanations, but she's not listening.

'I'll leave you two alone,' says Pete. 'I'll go and see how the little fellow is doing.'

John sits in the chair beside Jane's bed. She has her head turned to one side and she is gazing into nowhere. Her hair is matted and clinging to her forehead. The air around her bed has a pungent hormonal smell of blood and sweat and musk.

'I didn't want this baby, Father,' she says, mumbling so that he has to bend closer to hear what she's saying. Her breath is sour. 'And now, I think God must be punishing me for being so ungrateful.'

John feels suddenly weary. Dear God, how often must I explain? Why all this guilt and fear, and why is it always the wrong people who feel guilty and afraid, while those who should be afraid seem oblivious to their guilt?

'God loves you Jane, and your baby, and Pete,' he says, and hopes he sounds convincing.

'I don't deserve them,' she says. 'I'm a terrible wife and mother.' She closes her eyes. 'The thing is Father, I can't ever say this to Pete, but if there's something wrong with the baby – I don't think I can cope – if he's disabled or something – I'd rather – I'd rather he died.' She closes her eyes and tears squeeze out onto the pillow. 'I hate myself for saying that, but it's true, Father John. I'd rather we'd both died, than have to cope with all that.'

'We're here for you Jane. The parish is here for you. We'll support you. Just concentrate on getting well, and trust God to look after the future.' His assurances seem banal in the face of her fear. 'I've brought my missal. Shall I read to you from today's psalms?'

She nods. 'Yes. Yes please. I'd like that.'

He skims through the readings and psalms. They are all about affliction and persecution, guiding people to identify with Christ's suffering in preparation for Holy Week – as if life didn't do that to them anyway. Jane needs consolation and hope, not abandonment and crucifixion.

It's nearly seven o'clock when the doctor eventually arrives, harassed and apologetic. 'I think you're fine to go home Father,' she says. 'Do you want us to call you a taxi, or will somebody come to collect you?'

Outside the window, the sky has faded to blue and gold, with a warm glow enticing him into the city streets. He suddenly craves fresh air and exercise. 'It's such a beautiful evening. I think I'll walk. It's not very far.'

'I'm not sure that's such a good idea Father,' she says, with a furrow of concern puckering her forehead. 'You're probably still quite weak from the infection. I think you should go home to bed and tomorrow you can go for a walk if you're feeling up to it.'

'Let me see how I go,' he says. 'If I'm not feeling well I'll call a taxi.'

'Promise?' she asks.

'Promise,' he says.

Somebody has brought his backpack in, and there are clean socks and pants and a clean shirt for him to put on. He marvels again at the thoughtfulness of people, as he packs his dressing gown and pyjamas and toiletries. There's a gift-wrapped box of chocolates too, with a sticky note attached to it: 'Give it to the hospital staff to say thank you.' It's Sister Martha's writing on the note. He goes to the desk and thanks the nurses sitting there and gives them the box of chocolates. They are effusive in their wishes of good health and he marvels again at their capacity for cheerfulness amidst so many demands and crises. He goes down in the lift to the ground floor and stops in the shop in the foyer to buy a bottle of water.

The evening papers are there, with a photo of James Forrester emblazoned across the front page. They have chosen a photograph that makes him look like a murderer. His eyes are sunk in shadows and his mouth is set in a tight, grim line. He has the dark and sinister good looks of a Heathcliff. John doesn't remember ever seeing him looking like that, and he wonders when and where the photograph was taken. 'KILLER PERVERT PRIEST?' bellows the headline. He pauses to read the first few lines.

'As another Friday night arrives, residents of Westonville are praying that the police have caught the serial killer who has prowled the city streets for the past five weeks. James Forrester, a Catholic priest, is still being held in custody for questioning, but what if there is another murder tonight?'

John turns away, refusing to contemplate that unanswerable question. He pays for his water and pushes through the revolving doors into the city streets.

He strolls slowly, feeling light-headed and weak. It's a pleasant feeling. His body feels ephemeral, drifting through the streets as if invisible. He thinks of the presbytery waiting for him, empty and cold, and he wants to prolong the walk home as long as possible. He goes into a café and buys a coffee and a sandwich. He sits at a table in the window and watches the passers-by, and ecstasy floods through him.

He steps out into the night as the last golden glow dissolves into darkness and the starlight thickens in a blue velvet sky. He puts his hand into the pocket of his anorak and trickles his rosary through his fingertips as he walks.

He reaches the main road and knows that he should walk straight on towards home. Instead, he crosses the road and turns right into the narrow cobbled streets of Saint Peter's. He tells himself that he is simply enjoying the evening and prolonging the walk. He tells himself that he has no intention of going past the Queen's Arms or stopping to talk to the women on the streets.

The atmosphere of the city changes as he weaves through the lanes, away from the rush of the traffic and the bustle of the pavements. He pulls up the hood of his anorak, suddenly wanting to hide his face. The night seems dense with threats and promises. An anarchic spirit of defiance emanates from the bright graffiti and the strange juxtapositions of age-old poverty and newly acquired wealth. Narrow houses that used to be the city slums have been transformed into bijoux residences with glossy front doors. It's easy to differentiate between the habitual residents and the upwardly mobile newcomers. Well-dressed couples strolling arm in arm towards the fashionable restaurants and bars avert their eyes from the ragged blankets and sleeping bags of homeless people huddled in doorways, and from the blank-eyed gaze of drunk or drug-addled youths clustered on corners. A few women are there too, lounging against lamp posts, sauntering along the pavements, defiant and determined to ply their trade or maybe just too despairing to care. John wonders how long it will be before the process of gentrification squeezes them out, and where they will go when that happens.

He avoids turning into the lane where the Queen's Arms makes a bright splash of colour and light, with its rainbow flags, pink walls and beckoning windows. He turns into the road where he met Babbs, a lifetime ago.

He thrusts both his hands into his anorak pockets and takes hold of his rosary in his right hand. The fingers of his left hand curl around some folded bank notes. How did they get there? He tries to remember. He takes them out and counts them. Five ten pound notes. He folds them and puts them back, puzzling over where they came from. Perhaps it was whoever brought his clothes and backpack into the hospital, wanting to make sure he had money if he needed it.

Then he sees her.

Babbs is standing in the shadows, half-hidden behind a wheelie bin. He sees a flicker of fear cross her face as he approaches, but she calls out to him all the same, her mantra of the night: 'Thirty quid for a blow job, lover.'

'Babbs. You shouldn't be out here.'

'Oh Jesus, it's you Father. It's you who shouldn't be out here, lurking around with that hood over your face. You'll get yourself arrested if you're not careful.'

'I'll give you fifty pounds, if you go indoors,' he says, desperate to save her from this annihilating trade with its murderous men. He is close enough to see the stains on her teeth, to smell the sourness of her body beneath the cloying sweetness of her perfume.

She grins. 'Do you know how long a blow job takes, my lover? I suppose you don't, being a priest and all that. I'll tell you. I can do three or more in an hour. There aren't many other girls out here tonight. I can make a killing on a night like this. The punters like the younger ones, but I still have my regulars and some of the others will be so desperate they'll pay for what they can get.'

'It's Friday Babbs. It's the night when that – that killer might be out here. I beg you. Please go indoors.' He takes the fifty pounds from his pocket and holds it out to her.

She ignores the gesture. 'They've arrested him,' she says, and gives him a look that he can't decipher.

'They haven't charged him. What if it's not him? What if the murderer is still out here?' He has to speak the unspeakable words.

She shrugs. 'You're a sweet man, Father John. But do you know how much I need to buy enough skag to keep me going? Give me three hundred pounds and I might stay off the streets for a couple of nights, but I'll have to come back out sooner or later, and I'm not sure what people would say if they knew a priest had given a hooker three hundred pounds to spend on skag. I think you blokes are already in enough trouble with all that kiddy stuff, and now this priest being arrested.'

'What's skag?' he asks, because he can't think of anything else to say.

'Heroin to you, Father,' she says, putting on a mock posh accent.

He looks away, feeling helpless and frustrated. There's a MacDonalds sign with its brash red and yellow logo on the other side of the dual carriageway that divides Saint Peter's from the city centre.

'I'll buy you a coffee and a Big Mac,' he says, thinking he will keep her talking and that way at least she'll be safe for a couple of hours. 'And here, please, take the money. Just stay off the streets tonight. I beg you. I know it's not enough. I'd give you more if I could, but it's all I have.'

She looks down at his outstretched hand, then she takes the money, rolls it up and tucks it into her cleavage. 'Why are you bothering, Father? I'm just an old slag. I'm going to die soon one way or the other. Why should you care?'

'Because – because you're a human being. Because you're in danger. Because I don't want you to die.' Why does he care? He really doesn't have an answer. 'I like you Babbs. You've helped me these last few weeks. You've helped me to understand things I never understood before.'

She smiles, and in that smile he sees kindness and humility. 'Jesus,' she says. 'You're a bleeding odd ball, you know that? Here's you, a Catholic priest, thanking a slut like me. C'mon then, I'm fucking ravenous. Let's go and you can buy me a burger.'

He is already regretting the offer as they begin to walk towards the brightly lit shops. What if somebody sees him? What if somebody suspects him of being the killer? He feels as if his body is floating beside her. He should have gone straight home to bed. He is not thinking clearly.

She says she wants a strawberry milkshake and a Big Mac and chips. He orders a mug of tea for himself. They sit opposite one another at a table for two in the bright glare and bustle of the place. He feels ashamed of himself because he is terrified that somebody will recognise him.

She eats with gusto, chewing noisily on the burger as if she hasn't eaten for a long time. Maybe she hasn't.

'When did you last have a meal?' he asks her.

She shrugs. 'I had a bag of sweets this morning I think. I don't remember.'

'You ought to eat regular meals, you know.'

'Yeah. I ought to stop using crack and smack, I ought to stop fucking strangers for money. So many things I ought to do, Father.'

He looks at her, slurping her milkshake with a look of childlike satisfaction on her face. He wonders if that look comes from drugs, or if it might be the genuine delight of a woman who has few real pleasures in life.

'Tell me about yourself Babbs. How did you come to be living like this?' he asks.

'I was born at the wrong time, in the wrong place, to the wrong woman, I suppose,' she says.

'Tell me your story.'

'It's horrid. And boring.'

'I'd like to hear it.'

'Okay, but you won't like it.' She tosses her head and pushes her hair away from her face. 'My mother came from Ireland. She ran away from home and ended up on the streets in London. She had me when she was sixteen, and she'd had five more kids by the time I was ten, with three different fathers.' It's a litany of sorrow that she has recited too often before, even if only inside her own head. 'My two stepbrothers started raping me when I was ten. When I was fourteen I met someone – same old story. Always the same old story.' She shakes her head and gazes into the distance, then she burrows in her mouth and digs a piece of meat out from between her teeth and looks at it before putting it back in her mouth and swallowing it. 'He said he loved me and he wanted to marry me. He was thirty. He got me started on drugs, then he said I had to sleep with his friends to pay for my drugs. I put up with that for a while, but it was getting worse. The violence. The number of friends I had to fuck to get a fix. I decided if I was going to sell my body for a living, I might as well cut out the middle man.' She gives him a bright, defiant grin. 'So here I am. Self-employed. Self-sufficient too. There are worse ways to live, Father, really there are.'

He tries to imagine what they might be. He can't. He wants to weep, because he has seen the wounds behind the mask of that rotten-toothed grin and those vacant, hopeless eyes.

'Don't look so miserable,' she says. 'Honestly. There are nice things about it.'

'Such as?'

'Such as meeting you.' She smiles. 'When you think about it, there's not such a difference between you and me anyway.'

'What do you mean?'

'We're both in the business of loving. You do God, I do sex. What's the difference? It's all about people wanting more love than they can get in their ordinary lives, isn't it? That's what they're all looking for – the perfect fuck, the perfect life, the perfect God. They think we can give it to them, if they just keep coming back, if they ask in the right way. But we can't, can we Father? They're not ours to give, are they?'

He wonders how it's possible that she has just taught him all he ever needs to know about theology, and in that process she has rendered worthless all he ever thought he knew and all he was ever taught. She is on a roll now, and he wants her to keep talking.

'And another thing,' she says. 'People trust us both with their secrets. We both know things about other people that nobody else knows. My mother was Catholic, you know. Well, she would be, being Irish. Every Sunday morning, she made me haul my poor fucked little body out of bed and go to Mass. I used to go to confession too. I used to tell the priest that my stepbrothers were fucking me. You know what he told me? Don't dress so provocatively. That's what he told me. Jesus. I was ten.'

John's mouth feels dry. 'Didn't he tell you to tell your mother?'

'Nah. There'd have been no point. My mother was off her head most of the time. She couldn't cope with us lot. I think she knew anyway. It would just have been too much trouble to stop them.' She slurps at her milkshake again. 'You'd be amazed what some blokes tell us working girls,' she says. 'Some of the punters are monsters, like that bastard who's out there killing girls, but most of them are just sad and lonely. Guys whose wives don't want sex any more. Guys who have funny tastes, things they want us to do that they're too shy to ask their wives or girlfriends to do. Like, you know, there's this one punter – Jesus, Father John – like I say, we whores never ever tell people's secrets – but I trust you, because you're a priest, and – and you're kind. You've got eyes that make me trust you.' She snorts. 'You're probably the fucking serial murderer!'

'Babbs – no, please –'

'Calm down. Joke. D'you think I'd say that if I thought you were? So, there's this punter, and he comes to me and gives me a lot of money. He's a consultant in the hospital. He's really rich. Every week, he gives me two hundred pounds to sit in his car and hold him in my arms while he wanks off, and all I have to do is keep saying "Mummy's here, Mummy loves you." That's all. He never wants sex or any funny stuff. He always says thank you afterwards. He's a real gentleman. You know, most of the punters are like that. I mean, usually they want some kind of sex, but they're not bad men, they're just – kind of – well, kind of hurt by life. We girls understand that. We're hurt by life too. No bloke would pay for sex from a smelly old hooker like me, if he could get it at home from a woman who loves him, would he?' He thinks of Pete, and wonders if Pete ever had sex with Babbs. She guzzles up the dregs of her milkshake and crams the remains of her burger into her mouth. 'I need a cigarette,' she says through the mouthful. 'Can we get out of here?'

He follows her out. Her back looks heartbreakingly vulnerable in its thin purple top, with her shoulders thrust back in defiance against the world. They cross the dual carriageway to Saint Peter's. She perches on a low garden wall and lights a cigarette.

'It's not him, you know,' she says, gazing through the smoke and not looking at him.

His heart jumps. 'What do you mean?' he asks, though he knows what she means.

'The murderer. They've got the wrong guy.'

'Good God, Babbs. How do you know?'

'There's been this weirdo around. One of the other girls saw him talking to Sissy the night she was murdered. He's older than that priest they've arrested.'

John's blood is surging through his body, making his temples throb. 'You've got to tell the police, Babbs. Why don't you go to the police?'

She shrugs. 'We just don't. We don't trust them.'

'I know one of them. I know the detective in charge of the case. He's a good man, Babbs. Won't you talk to him? Please?'

She drags on her cigarette and turns to look at him. 'It was Ana. Ana saw Sissy talking to a bloke, and Ana was the next one to be killed. She didn't describe him. She just said he had grey hair and he was on foot. He wasn't driving like most of the punters.'

The night feels cold and dark and John feels suddenly alone. He sees how defenceless Babbs is, how alone against the world. 'What about the other two?' he asks. 'They were found at Father James's church.'

She shrugs again. 'The murderer might have wanted to frame him. Maybe he wants them to blame it on a priest.'

'Do you know who those women were?'

'No.' She pulls on her cigarette again and he watches it flare up and dim. 'They were probably trafficked, or under age, or both. Those ones don't come out on the streets. They keep them locked up. There are basements, terrible places. We girls on the street, we're the lucky ones. I tell you Father, there are places of torture down there beneath our feet.'

'I don't believe you.'

She turns and looks him full in the face. 'Ana knew,' she says. 'They kept Ana in a basement with no windows. She was fifteen when they brought her here, in the back of a lorry. They told her mother they were going to send her to college to learn English and get a good job. They promised she would send money back to her family. Her mother paid all her savings for them to bring Ana here and look after her. When they got here, they took her to this place where she was locked up with ten other girls. She was the eldest. The youngest was nine. We girls on the street, Father, our punters are usually the good ones. The paedos and sadists know where to go. They don't come to us. Ana told me that the men who took her made films. You know, porn, snuff movies, things like that.'

'What's a snuff movie?'

'It's when you kill someone for real, and film it.' Her face looks ghostly in the streetlights – pale and sallow, wreathed in the smoke from her cigarette.

'But Babbs, I don't understand. The police. How can those men get away with it? Why don't the police find them?'

'They're clever Father,' she says. 'Jesus, this place is full of basements and cellars. It's like looking for a needle in a haystack. If those two girls that they found outside that church were from somewhere like that, nobody will ever identify them.'

'I don't understand why you don't tell the police,' he says helplessly. He can make no sense of this anarchic world she is describing.

She gives a derisory snort. 'Tell them what? That there are trafficked girls locked up somewhere in Westonville, but we have no idea where? They already know that Father. Besides, rumours are that some of the police are in on the act. They're just blokes, after all. Last time a pig stopped me, he came and asked my name and tried to charge me for soliciting. I told him to fuck off, so he goes and parks his car and comes back. I gave him a blow job and he went back to work. That's how we live Father. That's what happens, when you live like we do. The laws can't touch us, because we know things about them. We know the lawyers and the policemen and the judges, and they know we know. We know better than to trust them. Out here on the streets, a punter is a punter. There's no difference between a judge and a doctor and some poor bugger just wanting to get his end away, spending his dole on buying cunt and then going to the sisters up the road for food the next day, because he's broke. Sorry about my language, Father. I forget I'm talking to a priest.'

His head is reeling. He remembers his promise to the doctor, that he would take a taxi home if he felt unwell. But his own fears and concerns, his own health and well-being, all the suffering he has ever known, amount to nothing in the face of what Babbs is telling him.

She grinds out her cigarette beneath her heel. 'Look John, that was really good. Really. But I need to go now. Don't worry about me. I can look after myself.'

'Babbs, let me give you my phone number. If ever you're afraid, if ever you want to talk, you can phone me any time. Any time at all.'

'You're not real, are you? Fucking hell, John, you're fucking Jesus Christ, that's who you are.'

'No. No. Babbs, don't say that. I'm just – I'm like the rest of them – I'm like you – I'm also wounded by life. I know what it feels like.'

'D'you think he fucked Mary Magdalene?'

'Who?'

'Jesus.'

'No, of course not.'

'Why not?'

He shakes his head. 'I don't know. I just don't think he did.' He realizes he has no answer that would satisfy himself, let alone her.

She nibbles at her finger nail. 'Why d'you think God made us the way we are, needing sex and all that, if He thinks it's so bad?'

'It's not bad. It's just – There are other important things in life, and sex is – sex can get in the way of those things.'

She narrows her eyes and peers at him. 'Did you read *The Da Vinci Code*?' she says.

'Yes, but it was fiction. It wasn't real. It wasn't true.'

'What's real? What's true?' she says.

'We're real. You're real. I'm real. This is true.'

'I tell you what else is real. My fucking habit is real. So I'm outa here. I need some punters.' She leans over and plants a kiss on his cheek. 'G'night, my lover,' she says.

'Be careful, Babbs. Be careful.'

Terror surges out of the night as he watches her totter away on her ridiculous high heels and spindly legs. He wants to call her back. She didn't take his phone number. He wonders if she was trying to protect him.

He feels faint and light-headed and disorientated. He knows he should find a taxi and go home. He walks to the end of the road and turns left and then right, and there ahead of him the Queen's Arms spills its light onto the pavement. A sign outside announces 'Tonite – Live Music – Golden Oldies'. He lets himself be lured inside.

The warmth and the music and the laughter engulf him. The place swirls giddily around him. The live band is on a raised platform to the left, and people sway and twist and jive on a small dance floor. There are men and a few women. Some dance in pairs – men with men, women with women, men with women – others dance alone or in groups. Luke is standing near the bar talking to some friends.

John shrugs off his anorak and straightens his shirt. As he begins to walk towards the bar, Luke sees him. His eyes are aglow as he crosses the small space and takes hold of John's arm.

'John! I've been so worried about you. I heard you were in hospital. I wanted to come and see you, but – well – I wasn't sure you'd want that. Let me buy you a drink. What will you have?'

'I'll have a beer, thanks.' He knows he shouldn't. It's Lent. He is on strong antibiotics. But Babbs has stripped away the rules and shown him the futility of should and shouldn't, right and wrong. She has taken him to a place where love and longing and a rage for life must prevail, for the encircling darkness is everywhere, trying to get in.

'Why don't you go and sit in that alcove?' says Luke. 'I'll join you when I've bought the drinks.' He gestures towards a secret nook with a plush red velvet settee and a candle flickering on an elaborate gilt table in front of it.

'What about your friends?' asks John, though the sight of that dark space just for two draws him irresistibly.

'They'll understand,' says Luke, and his expression tells John all he needs to know about Luke's hopes and desires – and why not?

Luke comes back with a bottle of champagne in an ice bucket. John thrills at the sight of it.

Luke sits next to him, not quite close enough for their thighs to be touching. 'I thought champagne might be better for you than beer,' he says. 'It's therapeutic.' He raises his glass. 'Cheers,' he says.

'Cheers,' John replies. He feels shy and lost for words. He looks away, unable to meet Luke's open, hungry gaze.

'Are you better?' Luke asks. 'I thought you were still in hospital. Or at least, that you'd be resting at home.' Luke sounds nervous too. Perhaps he is less confident than John thinks. He feels better knowing that they're both experiencing something new and strange and unsettling.

He lets his glance flicker up to meet Luke's and then quickly looks away again. 'They said I could go home this evening. I decided to walk. They didn't want me to, but it was such a lovely evening and I felt like being outside.'

'Yes. The weather has been glorious,' says Luke.

'And warm for the time of year,' says John. 'Easter is so early this year. Lent isn't usually so cold. I mean, when Easter is later.' He is losing his way. He gulps at his champagne to fortify himself, feeling it fizz through his head. Once again he has that sense of being disembodied, of floating through some different dimension. He looks at the people around him, at the bodies on the dance floor in the swirling lights, and his senses prickle with the thrill of being here.

Luke tops up his glass and gives a little laugh. 'I can't believe we're talking about the weather,' he says.

John meets his eyes, and he dares to ask, 'What do you think we should be talking about?'

Luke gives him a lop-sided grin and clinks his glass lightly against John's. 'To us,' he says.

John hesitates, then he raises his glass. 'To us,' he says.

The band begins to play a jaunty hit from the 1960s.

'Do you remember dancing together at the wedding?' Luke asks.

'The Gay Gordons. How could I forget?' says John. They laugh, and their laughter is a release of tension and a shared anticipation of something nameless moving delicately towards them through the bodies and lights and sounds of the night.

John remembers, in the confessional, gazing at Luke's hair curling around his ear, and how he longed to reach out and hook his finger through that solitary curl. He turns slightly, so that he can see Luke properly. Yes, that curl is just the way he remembers it. Luke moves closer, so that their knees are touching. John reaches out. He slips his finger behind Luke's ear and twists the curl around it, all the while not looking away, holding Luke's gaze. Luke has grey eyes, and his pupils are wide in the candlelight. John allows his fingertip to linger on the soft skin behind Luke's ear, then he withdraws his hand.

'I've so often wanted to do that,' he says.

'I love you,' Luke says.

John says nothing, but the words thrill him. He wants to let it happen, whatever it is that's happening between them. Is it love? He no longer wants to look away. He takes Luke's hand in his and, with the other hand, he traces the veins threading across his knuckles. He strokes the pucker of skin between his thumb and forefinger. He reaches across and runs his palm down the side of Luke's face and around the curve of his jaw, then he trails his fingertips down his neck and lets them linger in the hollow at the base of his throat. He strokes beneath his collar to feel the delicate curve of his shoulder. Luke keeps his eyes on John's face, his mouth slightly parted, his breathing steady and deep and smooth. It all feels natural and unhurried. They drink in easy silence, feeling the night ahead of them, letting its wonder settle over them.

Yes. The word floods through John. Yes, yes, yes to this.

The door pushes open and three men walk in. John barely notices them, but something makes him look again. It's Christopher Lynch and Joseph Agambire, with a third man he doesn't recognise. What are two priests doing in a place like this?

And suddenly he is not in paradise but in the circles of hell. The beast snarls and seizes him by the throat. Sssuck my cock. Is the cardinal here too? Is it happening all over again?

He puts down his glass and stands up. 'I have to go,' he says.

Luke looks stunned. 'You're joking. Why?'

'Because it's late, and I have to say Mass in the morning.' He pauses and lets his eyes caress Luke's face. 'Thank you Luke. Thank you for tonight.'

He turns abruptly and pushes his way to the door before he can weaken, keeping his head averted from the three men who just walked in. He steps out into the night and he hears Luke behind him.

'John, wait. Please. Don't just walk away like this. What happened? I don't understand.'

John moves away from the pub so that he can't be seen, then he turns around. 'I must Luke. Please, don't make it difficult for me.'

'Don't make it difficult for you? What about me, John? This isn't all about you. It's about my feelings too.' Luke's voice is hoarse with anger and frustration.

John is conscious of people passing by. He has to get away before somebody recognises him. There's a dark alley next to the pub, where they keep the dustbins. He steps into the alley and Luke follows him. He is right there behind him, pressing up against him.

John leans back and lets Luke bear his weight, feeling the welcoming strength of his arms wrapping around him. He is slightly shorter than Luke, so that he can rest his head back against Luke's shoulder. He stands there, feeling the other man hard and erect in the small of his back, then he twists around and lifts his face.

He nuzzles his nose against the cushion of Luke's earlobe. He licks the rim of his ear, tracing its delicate whorls with the tip of his tongue. He buries his face in the curve of his neck and breathes in the warmth of his skin and the smell of his aftershave. He licks the skin and tastes its salt, mingled with the tang of the aftershave. He moves his face up, and finds Luke's lips. The taste of him. The feel of him. The smell of him. He pushes his tongue deeper into the tunnel of Luke's mouth, licking and probing its warm, moist recesses. He presses his body against Luke's, wishing that he could melt and dissolve into his beloved flesh.

'I love you, John. I love you. Not here. Not in a lane by stinking dustbins. Please. Let's not do it this way. Come home with me.' Luke's voice is urgent.

'I can't Luke. You know I can't.'

'Do you love me John?' He's whispering now, his mouth up against John's ear. 'Tell me you love me. Tell me you love me John.'

'You know I do. I love you more than I can say. But I can't.' John's voice sounds strange in his own ears, also hoarse and keen with desire.

'I want to marry you John. For five years, ever since I came to live here, I've wanted you. I've waited, and I've felt something so real and deep and forever growing in me. Every other man I've fucked, every naked body I've been with, has been you. Every one of them has just been a way of expressing what I feel for you. Marry me, John. Leave the priesthood and marry me.'

'I'm sorry Luke. I'm sorry.' John pushes against his chest and steps back. 'I have to go. I'm sorry. I can't. I love you, but I have to go. I'm sorry.'

'Just one night then. What harm would it do? Nobody will ever know. Please John. Just this one time, and I promise I'll never ask you again.'

What harm would it do? What harm could such love possibly do? He hesitates. Luke reaches out, cups his hand in the small of John's back, and pulls him in. As John allows himself to be drawn again towards the body he wants more than anything else in all creation, he sees a shadow – a swift blur against the wall of the alley, and then nothing.

'There's somebody there,' he says, terrified now. Luke releases him and looks around.

'Where?'

'There. At the back of the alley.' Luke steps away and looks behind the dustbins. A cat slinks past and streaks away into the darkness. John notices a single gold sandal with a high stiletto heel discarded beside one of the bins. The sight of it fills him with dread. The spell is broken. He hurries out of the alley and down the narrow lane. He hears Luke calling but he doesn't turn back. On the main road, feeling sick and dizzy and faint, he hails a taxi and lets the darkness swallow him.

TWENTY SIX

PALM SUNDAY

Palm Sunday dawns in a flood of light, with sunbeams trickling through a gap in the curtains. John pushes aside the duvet and gets out of bed.

He spent Saturday sleeping, too exhausted and afraid to think, using his illness as an excuse to escape from the clamour of his feelings and the busy preparations for Palm Sunday and Holy Week. Father Chukwu said Mass and heard confessions. John felt too defeated even to care.

But now he feels ready to face whatever the day brings. The Palm Sunday liturgy is too long to include a homily (he knows his parishioners' limitations), so there's no need to spend time reflecting and writing. He decides to hold on to this sense of calm for as long as he can. He picks up Shula and holds her close. He tries not to brood over what happened on Friday night with Luke.

He resists switching on the radio, and instead opens the back door to listen to the birdsong as he feeds Shula and waits for the kettle to boil. He takes his coffee and his missal out to the bench beneath the cherry tree, enjoying the cold lick of the dew against his ankles. He dries the bench with the sleeve of his dressing gown and sits down.

> *Bless the Lord, my soul!*
> *Lord God, how great you are,*

Clothed in majesty and glory,
Wrapped in light as in a robe!

He prays the psalm slowly, letting the words soak into him. He feels a deep sense of gratitude for this inexplicable peace, however transient, that holds thought at bay. The light lifts over the garden, turning everything to liquid patterns of gold on green. Bless the Lord, my soul! I am alive. I survived. It's enough. This being alive is enough for me.

Shula comes padding across the grass, delicately lifting her paws to avoid getting wet. She jumps up onto the bench beside him and crawls onto his knee, nudging his face with her nose and purring. He strokes her and closes his eyes. He lets himself imagine, just for a moment, Luke's skin beneath his fingertips. He banishes the memory before it slides into darkness, and lifts Shula up to his face. He snuggles her into the crook of his neck and feels the sensuous miracle of her presence, warm and soft and comforting. Then she wriggles away and jumps off the bench, looking back at him disdainfully as if to remind him of his lowliness in the hierarchy of being where surely, cats reign supreme.

The Palm Sunday Mass always begins in the graveyard with the blessing of the palm leaves, re-enacting Christ's entry into Jerusalem, marking the beginning of a journey through death to life. He waits in the sacristy with Deacon Jack and the altar boys and girls as the people collect their palm leaves from the back of the church and twist and tie them into crosses, some more expertly than others, before making their way through the small wooden gate to stand near Sarah's grave.

'I hope you don't mind, Father, but I rang a few people to let them know you would be saying Mass today,' says Jack. 'I was worried that they might not come if it was Father Chukwu. I mean, Edith thinks he's wonderful and Sadie Blake and Mary Carpenter like him too. So do Jonathan and Mary Mellors. I'm not being uncharitable or anything, and I don't want you to think that they all took against him. He has his way, and he's a man of God. But lots of them weren't happy, and I thought they might go somewhere else today if they thought he'd be saying Mass, so I wanted to put the word around so that they'd know that you would be here.'

'Thank you Jack. I really appreciate that.' John hesitates, then he says, 'I wonder if some of them are still a bit suspicious – you know, with the murders, and nobody being charged yet. I can't help but feel that all we priests share in the guilt until they find who did it.' He has just articulated something he has hardly been able to admit, even to himself.

Jack nods knowingly, but his expression is full of trust and reassurance. 'Father, I don't think anybody would suspect you for a minute. And besides, there hasn't been another murder, and Father James is still being held in custody, so everybody is hoping that the case has been solved.' He shuffles his feet and looks embarrassed. 'Thing is Father, we all – we care deeply for you. We thought you were going to die. The sisters told us how sick you were. We all want to thank God for giving you back to us.'

John feels something too deep and lovely for words as he steps out from the church porch into the sunshine and looks over towards the cemetery.

He has never seen so many of the congregation gathered together. Even the Christmas vigils never had this kind of attendance, back in the days when the church was full. They stretch out among the yew trees around the graves, and through the gate onto the presbytery lawn. As they catch sight of him, they begin to clap.

'Welcome back, Father,' somebody calls, and a great cry goes up from all of them. 'Welcome back, Father!' 'Praise be to God!'

Tears of joy flood his face. It's over, he thinks. Whatever it was, it's over. However great his longing for Luke, however deep and faithful his love for Luke, he will never betray his vocation nor the trust of these people.

He has lunch with Edith and Jack, enjoying the awkward domesticity of their relationship, the blushing newness of their affection. As he watches them, he tried not to imagine what it would be like to grow old with Luke, to be absorbed in the small details of preparing Sunday lunch together and planning an afternoon of gardening. But the ache of such imaginings is soothed by the memory of the morning Mass, which has left him with an enduring sense of being loved and trusted and protected.

Later that afternoon, he sits in the garden with Shula on his lap, wanting to enjoy the last warmth of the day. He tries to read a much-praised book on the spirituality of Holy Week, but his thoughts drift inconsequentially, sleepily, through pastures of quiet reflection.

His phone interrupts his thoughts with its irritating rumble and tinkle. He doesn't normally carry it around with him, but he took it when he went for lunch and it's still in the pocket of his trousers.

'Father John, it's Frank.' Something in Frank's voice makes his heart lurch.

'Hello Frank, what can I do for you?'

'There's been another murder, John. A woman's body was found just after lunch today. We've released Father James without charge. We had the wrong man. So we're back to square one I'm afraid. – Hello? Are you there John?'

'Yes. Yes I'm here.'

'It had all the hallmarks of the previous murders. She had been crammed into one of the bins outside the Queen's Arms pub down in Saint Peter's.'

Something cold and vicious rises up in John's gut. It's an ice cold hatred beyond all fear, such as he did not know was possible. It's the cardinal. The cardinal is framing him. Sssuck my cock. It's the cardinal.

'John, are you still there?' Frank's voice is cold too, dangerously cold.

'Yes, I'm still here. Why are you ringing me, Frank?'

'I'm ringing to warn you, John.'

'Why? Why would you want to warn me? What are you warning me about?' Please. Please no. Not this. Not now.

'Because they're likely to start questioning all the priests in the area. I know you haven't been well. I just thought you should be prepared, in case they come to the door. I don't want you to be frightened.' Frank allows the merest hint of warmth to take the edge off the harsh implications of what he is saying. 'Also,' he continues, 'I need help John. I need all the help you can give me to find the bastard who's doing this. I hope he burns in the deepest fires of hell, but before that I want to get him and to let the world know who he is and what he has done. We've had forensic tests back from the bodies at Saints Felicity and Perpetua. One of them was thirteen years old and the other one was fifteen. The thirteen year old was three months pregnant. The devil can have the evil bastard when I've finished with him. Help me John. Every priest in town is now guilty until proven innocent. Even you, which is why I'm begging you to help us.'

Frank's fury is like larva, hot and molten and pouring across the distance between them, directed not at John but at some nameless malevolent presence beyond them both.

'I – I don't know what to say Frank. Sorry. I just – this is too overwhelming to take in.' The words sound insincere. He feels as if he is accusing himself with every word he says.

'I'll come and see you tomorrow,' says Frank, 'and I'll try to keep the investigating team away from you for as long as I can. God knows, they have enough to do tracking down the ones who might be guilty.'

John is frozen with something beyond feeling or thought, something inhuman that could murder, something that could annihilate. If the cardinal were here now, he would be capable of

305

inflicting upon him any torture, any punishment cruel enough to fit the crime, a vengeance worthy of the evil that has been done.

Oh yes, he will help Frank. He will find the cardinal and he will bring him personally to justice. If it's the last thing he does, he will do it. Even if it kills him, he will do it. Even if he consigns himself to eternal damnation along with the cardinal, he will ensure that justice is done.

Until this moment he has never realized how pure and absolute hatred is, how cleansing and purging. This is god-like. This is the perfect oneness of being, the perfect intensification of desire and feeling and thought, the annihilation of self and the surrender to the absolute. The words from a psalm shine like a polished blade in his soul.

If only you, God, would slay the wicked! Do I not hate those who hate you?

Aquinas was wrong. If hatred is evil, if rage is evil, then pure evil is possible, because John has never felt so pure in heart, so absolute in his commitment.

He sits with this cold, determined fury as the sun slides down the sky and the shadows whisper across the lawn. His face and hands feel cold, and doubt and confusion begin to creep into his mind. What seemed so clear a moment ago becomes turbulent and murky as he tries to order his thoughts.

He tells himself he should go inside. He has been ill. He mustn't sit here shivering. He picks Shula up and wraps his arms around her for warmth, but in his agitation he grips her too tightly and she squirms and leaps out of his arms.

He hears footsteps coming towards him along the path. He looks up, expecting to see the cardinal, preparing himself to confront him. It's Holly.

'Hello John. What are you doing, sitting out here in the cold? You've been sick. You ought to be resting indoors.'

'Holly! Why are you here?'

'I've come to sit with Sarah for a while. I thought I'd sit by her grave and prepare myself for Holy Week. Are you alright John? You look ghastly.'

'There's been another murder. It wasn't James Forrester.'

She is standing in front of him. She puts her right hand to her throat. In her left hand, she's holding a spray of freesias to put on Sarah's grave. 'Dear God,' she says. 'How do you know?'

'Frank rang me. They're going to start questioning all the priests in town.'

'You've nothing to be afraid of John. You mustn't let this distress you. You've been ill. You need to look after yourself.' Her voice is calm, but she has turned pale, and her eyes are wide with the kind of shock and dread that he knows will soon infect every person in Westonville. Except the killer. Except the cardinal.

'Holly, would you mind if we go for a walk? I'll go and get my jacket while you take your flowers to Sarah.'

'Of course. It's a lovely evening. Let's do that.'

They make their way through the quiet suburban streets to the nearby park. People are walking their dogs, and a few children bundled into brightly coloured anoraks are still in the playground, watched over by their parents. He suspects that the news of the murder hasn't been announced yet. Surely, if it had, there would be a palpable sense of dread and not this ordinary delight of people trying to eke out the last pleasures of the day?

Arm in arm, Holly and he stroll past the neatly tended flowerbeds towards the wooded area at the far end of the park, where bluebells are blooming among the trees and the last of the daffodils dip their withered heads towards the ground.

They walk in silence, both lost in thought, until John asks one of the questions he has been longing to ask. 'Holly, did Thomas Aquinas believe in ghosts?'

She gives a surprised little laugh. 'Ghosts?' Then she pauses. 'John, is this about Sarah?'

He regrets his insensitivity. He was thinking of the cardinal. He hadn't made the connection with Sarah, with telling Holly about Sarah's appearances. 'No. No, it's not about Sarah.' He isn't sure how much he should tell Holly. Is he afraid of burdening her, or is he afraid of something else – of her finding out about that night in Rome perhaps? 'It's a theological question I'm struggling with.' That's true. The supernatural. The nature of evil. Those are the issues he's struggling with.

'Aquinas was a man of his time John. Their world was alive with spirits, seen and unseen. Nature was saturated in grace but also in magic – good and evil spirits – in ways that are hard for us to understand.' Holly is at home in the world of ideas. Her voice warms to her theme. He thinks she must be a wonderful lecturer, and he hopes her students appreciate her. 'Aquinas might have become the defining theologian in the Catholic tradition, but his ideas are interpreted very much through a modern lens. Most people who think he's the greatest authority on everything to do with God would be shocked if they knew some of the things he wrote.'

'Such as?'

She laughs. 'He thought menstruating women could tarnish mirrors just by looking in them. He thought the sex of a foetus was determined by the prevailing wind conditions when it was conceived.'

He tries to laugh with her. He wants her to think that this is a casual conversation. 'I suppose we were all taught to read him selectively in the seminary,' he says. 'But tell me more about magic and the supernatural.'

'Aquinas believed he inhabited a cosmos where all of nature participated in God, but where evil spirits were constantly trying to find a way in. He would have perceived nature as teeming with angels and demons, and the human soul was their ultimate playground. The Reformation did away with all that, but it lingered on. The soul is still full of hidden hauntings and mysteries, but today we turn to Freud rather than theology to explain that.' She makes the esoteric sound vivid and real and relevant. Her pleasure in her subject would normally be infectious, but nothing can distract him today.

'So what powers did the demons have?' he asks.

'Where's this going John?'

'The murders. I just – I suppose we all have such a sense of evil, don't we? It's as if some evil force has been unleashed among us, and – I don't know – well, of course it's a human being doing these things, but that doesn't seem to offer enough of an explanation.' Careful. He feels himself skirting towards the edges of what he can say without exposing too much.

She nods thoughtfully. After a while she says, 'I know what you mean. I felt that when Sarah died – as if some cosmic power of evil had engulfed me. I couldn't see a glimmer of good anywhere. God only knows what the mothers of these murdered girls feel.' She bends down and picks a bluebell, holding it to her nose. 'I love the smell of bluebells,' she says.

He wonders if she is trying to change the subject, but after a while she goes on. 'You know, after we lost Sarah, I wanted to murder Betty. I couldn't forgive her. I didn't know it was possible to feel such hatred and darkness and violence. I used to lie awake in bed at night, thinking up tortures and punishments. I wanted her to suffer. I wanted her to know what she had done. I wanted her to know what I was feeling, how I imagined my Sarah might have felt in those last few moments of her life.' She chokes up and swallows. 'I would imagine getting up and going to her house with knives and hammers and god knows what. I dreamed of locking her in a basement and leaving her to starve. There was nothing too horrific for me not to want to do it to her. I never knew what stopped me, whether those were impossible fantasies – a kind of catharsis almost – or whether I really was capable of doing those things to another human being.' She snorts. 'And I used to sum all that up in the confessional by saying I felt murderously angry, and you used to give me some soothing penance, when really I wanted to turn all that rage and hatred and grief in on myself. It was me I wanted to torture. It was me I wanted to punish. Because I was alive and my baby was dead. Because I wasn't a good enough mother to her. Because I had squandered all those thousands of seconds and minutes when I could simply have been there with her and now she was lost forever, and what had I ever been doing that was more important than being with Sarah with all my heart and mind and soul? And I hated myself for not having the courage to end it all. "Suicidal thoughts". That's what I called them in the confessional. Dear God, John, how would you survive if you saw what darkness we bring into that little box? Sometimes I think you're too naïve, you're too good for this job.'

The shadows are lengthening around them and the wooded path is sliding into darkness, heavy with unseen presences. He wants to speak, but he is afraid. He wants to tell her about the cardinal. He wants to confess to the terror and the growing conviction that the man in the confessional is the dead cardinal come back to life, and he is the murderer. He wants to tell Holly what darkness he has heard, and how it has robbed him of his innocence. But he says nothing for fear of saying everything.

When she speaks again her voice seems to seep out of those shadowy absences all around, where the dead await their moment of revelation. 'Sometimes I wonder – can any of us know what we'd really be capable of, given enough provocation?' she says. 'They say there's a rapist inside every man, but maybe there's a murderer inside every human, if only the outrage is intense enough. Maybe that's why we pray to God to deliver us from evil. None of us knows the evil we might do, until we're confronted by the darkness in our own souls.' Another pause. Another long, drawn out silence when the shadows whisper and hiss and threaten to yield up their secrets. Then she speaks again. 'And then, when Betty had that stroke, I knew I had to go and visit her. I think it's the hardest thing I ever did John. The hardest, hardest thing. Harder even than holding Sarah that morning when she died in my arms, harder than Sarah's funeral, and I didn't believe anything could ever be harder than those two things.

'I went to the hospital, and I stood by her bed. She was all slack-faced and twisted, and her breathing sounded awful. She was so small, and shrivelled, and I had a sudden terrible insight into what she must have been through in the months since Sarah died. She had written to me saying how sorry she was, but I tore her letter up. She never tried to contact me again. I don't know if she still went to church, because I'd stopped going. But I stood there by her bed, and I saw that nothing I could have done to Betty would have punished her as much as she had punished herself over those months of guilt and regret. And John, when I suddenly understood what she had been through, it became easy.' She takes a deep breath and shivers. 'I took her hand, and I bent down and whispered in her ear. I told her who I was. I told her I knew it was an accident. I told her I forgave her. I asked her to give Sarah my love when she got to heaven.' She sniffs and wipes her nose on the cuff of her jacket. 'I had such a feeling of freedom, John. That night, it was like the night you told me about seeing Sarah, I felt so liberated from fear and loss and pain. Of course it all comes flooding back – there's no real escaping it – but every experience like that is a kind of metamorphosis. That's what's so mysterious about grief. It doesn't ever go away, but it does change. I'd still rather be dead than alive sometimes, but at least now most of the time I feel I'm alive again.'

Silence too can metamorphosise. The ghosts shrink back into the shadows, and the evening light becomes benign and soothing. She links her arm through his again, and they hold one another up as they swish through the cowslips and bluebells clustering around the path.

Eventually, she picks up the thread of their earlier conversation. 'Now, what were we talking about,' she says. 'Oh yes, angels and demons, and Thomas Aquinas. In the early church, they believed that there really was a cosmic battle between God and Satan, and human beings were in some ways the innocent bystanders who got caught up and wounded in the struggle – a bit like Job. But by the time Aquinas came along, philosophy was beginning to exert an influence. The rational human intellect was becoming a more significant concept – but of course John, you know all this. You studied theology in Rome. You probably know more about Aquinas than I do.'

'I was never very good at theology. A lot of it seemed irrelevant and boring at best, and dark and draconian at worst.' He pauses, then decides to risk a question. 'Do you remember Cardinal Michael Bradley?'

'He was the one who mysteriously disappeared and then it turned out he'd gone to New York and set himself up as a hedge fund manager. He was killed in the 9/11 attacks. I remember the stories well. People thought he'd be the next pope, until there were rumours of some sex scandal. I suppose it was yet another cover-up.' Her voice curdles. 'And still they're covering up and dodging the issues. If there's a hell, it was made for the likes of them.'

His heart is pounding, but he says casually, 'Cardinal Bradley taught me moral theology.'

'Jesus, no wonder it was dark and draconian. He was the worst of the lot. Whatever made him pack his bags and give up on his papal aspirations, it was a happy day for the Catholic Church,' she says.

He realizes he mustn't talk about the cardinal or he will say too much. 'Anyway, back to what we were talking about. Good and evil, and rationality. Tell me more,' he says.

She plucks another bluebell, scrutinising its tiny, bell-shaped flowers and frowning in concentration. 'Aquinas believed that the demons play havoc with our desire, but they can't make us do something that really is against our will. The will was a more complex concept then than it is today. It wasn't about will power or determination but about how we choose to align our freedom with our desire. That's why he thought it was so important to discipline our desire, to purge ourselves of evil desires, because the demons are always prodding away at us, trying to find that weakness where they can get in and make us do something that we know is wrong, but deep down we still desire it.

'Of course, Aquinas thought it was impossible to desire evil in itself, because evil is lack and one can't desire something that doesn't actually exist, but one can be deeply confused as to the nature of the good. So we would always convince ourselves that what we want is good and not bad. We're very skilled at justifying things to ourselves. You know, if you ever read about the things the Nazis said, they never said they were doing evil, they said they were doing good. He was a man of his time, but Aquinas was a brilliant psychologist despite his medieval superstitions. He would have recognised that the desire to do evil was a sign of mental illness and therefore not culpable, because no person in their right mind would actually desire evil, but a rational person can convince themselves that something evil is actually something good, and that makes it rational to desire it.

'When I had those thoughts about Betty, I really believed it was about justice and righteous vengeance. But deep down, something in me knew I was wrong.' She gives a small laugh of resignation. 'Maybe I did get a little benefit from those Catholic school days after all. Maybe they formed my conscience. That's the only difference between me and a murderer. In the end, the demons couldn't get in because in my heart of hearts I had learned the difference between self-deception and disciplined desire.' She pauses. 'So our murderer out there, whoever he is, has left a little window of opportunity for the demons of deluded desire to get in, because believe me John, this man thinks he is on a crusade. You have to be absolutely convinced of the rightness of your cause to murder the way he does.' A shudder of recognition runs through John. How on earth does she know that? She continues before he can say anything. 'It's so pathetic John. There's something seductive about the word "evil", but really, as Hannah Arendt recognised, evil is utterly banal.'

There is so much he wants to tell her, so much he wants to ask her, but he tries to steer clear of the swamp. 'So give me an example,' he says. 'What would be an example of an evil act that's actually motivated by a desire for good?'

She contemplates for a while, then she says, 'Suicide. Aquinas thought suicide was an unforgivable sin, but it was motivated by the desire to bring an end to unbearable suffering, and that's a desire for something good, even though one can't justify doing evil in order to bring about something good.'

The mention of suicide brings back memories of Robert McDonald, of that night in Rome and the subsequent false accusations of abuse, of Robert's body hanging forlorn and forsaken from the banister in an empty, lonely presbytery. The memory twists in John's gut, but he pushes it aside. A question is taking shape, a question that might have been there all along but lacking any recognisable form that might enable him to pin down its meaning, to articulate the unthinkable possibility – a possibility that he only now acknowledges has haunted him maybe since the first murder, but certainly since Frank told him about the nature of the killings. He approaches it obliquely. 'Holly, would Aquinas have believed that a ghost could murder somebody?'

'Jesus John, this is a bloody weird conversation, if you don't mind my saying so. But I suppose we're all feeling a bit weird tonight.' She tosses the bluebell aside. 'No. A ghost couldn't directly murder somebody, but it could arouse the desire to murder that might be latent in some human, and so it could drive that person to murder by feeding the desire. That's why he thought it was so important to master our desires, to avoid those demonic temptations.'

'Go on,' he says. 'I'm listening.'

'Augustine had no problem with the idea that angels and demons had immaterial bodies that could act directly on the material world, but Aquinas rejected that idea. He believed that demons could assume the appearance of bodies so that they could be understood by humans, but those weren't real bodies. They couldn't directly do the things that bodies can do. So, for example, for a demon to impregnate a woman, it would first have to take the form of a female body in order to seduce a man and steal his sperm, and then it would have to take the form of a male body in order to use that sperm to impregnate the woman. It couldn't make the sperm itself.' She laughs. 'Bloody Catholic Church and its preoccupation with fucking,' she says.

Now the question rushes at him. It swoops down from the darkening sky and seizes him with a sickening realization that he doesn't even try to hide from Holly. 'Holly, is it possible that –' He swallows. This is too hard, but he has to ask her. He has to share this terror with somebody, and Holly is the only person he can talk to. Holly, and Father Martin. But Holly is here and Father Martin is not, and the question won't wait. 'Is it possible that some demon is taking possession of me?'

She stops dead in her tracks and turns to face him. Her eyes are wide in the gloom, and her face is pale. 'What do you mean, John?' There's a catch of fear in her voice.

'Could I be the murderer, and not know I'm doing it?' There. He has said it. The words are out there, solidifying, acquiring confessional power by the saying of them. That's the fear that has been growing in him. The cardinal's ghost has taken possession of him, and is driving him to murder. The cardinal's ghost is punishing him.

He feels her fear. She glances around, as if suddenly aware of how isolated they are. He realizes how easy it would be, here in this place of shadows and secrets, to reach out and murder Holly. He could do it in an instant, and she would be helpless to stop him. Could he do it? Would he do it?

She turns away from him and bends her head. Her hair is tied up in a purple scarf, so that he can see the white skin on the nape of her neck beneath her hairline. It looks vulnerable – an enticement to violence perhaps. How little it would take, to murder her. How easy it would be.

Slowly, she raises her arms and lifts her face to the sky. He gazes at her cruciform shape silhouetted against the twilight glow. 'Do it John,' she says. 'Put me out of my misery.'

Her henna hair is the colour of dried blood. Her velvet patchwork jacket makes jewels of colour along her arms and down her back. Her fingers quiver, and the jewelled jacket ripples with the shivering of her limbs.

Somewhere nearby, starlings are settling in the treetops, with a cacophony of birdsong rising around them. In the far distance, he hears the wail of a child.

He reaches out. He puts his hands on Holly's neck and moves his fingers round to her throat until his fingertips are touching. He feels her stiffen, and the cartilage in her throat shifts beneath his touch as she swallows.

So this is how it happens. A touch. A squeeze. A gasp. That's how you murder somebody.

He slides his hands up the side of her face to cup her cheeks in his palms. He lets his fingertips rest against her temples and feels the flutter of her pulse. He leans forward and puts his lips to the back of her head, breathing in that warm familiar smell of cigarettes and perfume, and a deeper undertone of some dark musk which must be the smell of fear and sorrow and longing. He moves so that his face is resting against the side of her head, and he trails his hands slowly along the length of her arms. He slides his hands under hers, so that he is supporting her on his outstretched arms. She leans back into him, the way he leaned into Luke on Friday night. And there they stand.

Eventually she murmurs, 'Jesus Christ. I'd kill for a glass of wine.'

The consoling companionship of sharing a bottle of wine in a pub with Holly deserts him as soon as he steps into the presbytery afterwards and feels the gloomy chill of the cloisters wrapping around him. Without bothering to switch on the lights, he goes upstairs to his study. There's a tide rising and rising inside him – of rage and loathing and determination. He must find the cardinal. He must find him and stop him, whatever it costs, whatever it takes.

He sits down at the desk and opens up his laptop. He goes to Google and types in "Cardinal Michael Bradley".

The Wikipedia entry comes up first, but he skips past that. There's an old entry from a diocesan directory, and various church notices and comments that don't seem to offer any insights. He skims through them, occasionally opening a page and scanning it for clues. Eventually, he goes back to the search box and types in "Cardinal Michael Bradley" followed by Twin Towers. Several news reports come up. He clicks on a report in a Catholic weekly. There are two photographs – one showing the cardinal in his red robes, and another showing the same man in a suit. He reads the news report.

The Vatican has confirmed that former Cardinal Michael Bradley is missing presumed dead in last week's attack on the Twin Towers in New York. Bradley was one of the most senior cardinals in the Vatican and was widely believed to be a future candidate for the papacy. He was highly respected as a moral theologian who belonged on the conservative wing of the Church, having taken a robust stand against homosexuality, contraception and abortion.

It caused shock and disbelief when Cardinal Bradley announced he was leaving the priesthood in the year 1999, owing to a crisis of faith. There were unconfirmed rumours that his departure had been precipitated by a sex abuse scandal and a cover-up by senior figures in the Vatican, but no evidence ever came to light to substantiate these claims.

Following his departure from Rome, the cardinal is believed to have used his connections in the United States to secure a high-ranking job as a hedge fund manager in RGF Investments, based on the 92nd floor of the World Trade Center's North Tower. He has not been seen since last Tuesday morning. CCTV shows him leaving the elegant Manhattan apartment block where he lived at 7.30 am, which means he would have been in the office at the time of the attack.

Father Damian Thomas is a priest in the Diocese of Brooklyn. He studied under Cardinal Bradley when he was a seminarian in Rome. He told our reporter that he is devastated by the cardinal's death.

'I knew him during my time in Rome,' Father Damian said. 'He was a wonderful teacher and we all looked up to him. His faith was strong and he was a man of great conviction and integrity. We couldn't believe it when he left the priesthood. I'll always be grateful to have studied under him.'

Father Damian dismissed any suggestion of a sex scandal. 'He was a pure and good man,' said Father Damian, 'and such men have enemies. Some people were jealous of him. Some of the liberals hated him because he was uncompromising in his morals and his doctrinal rigour.'

John feels nauseous. Damian Thomas. That night in Rome, it was Damian who took him to the cardinal, Damian who buggered him, Damian he spent the night with in a drug-addled haze. His heart is pounding.

He keeps searching until he finds an email address for Damian Thomas. He discovers that Damian is now an archbishop in Washington. He feels a surge of energy running from his gut to his fingertips, almost as he feels when he is inspired to write a good homily.

> *Dear Damian,*
>
> *You probably don't remember me, but we studied together at the seminary in Rome from 1997 to 1999. I have many happy memories of those years!*
>
> *I was deeply distressed to read of the death of Cardinal Bradley in the Twin Towers. I know that he had a crisis of faith and left the priesthood, but for me he was one of the finest and most inspiring priests of his generation – a role model for so many of us in our priesthood.*
>
> *I recently heard from somebody that, although he was reported missing presumed dead on 9/11, he did in fact miraculously survive the attack and is now living somewhere in the UK. I've tried to contact him without success. I wonder if you keep in touch with him and if you know how I might contact him. He was far more than a teacher to me. He was a mentor and an intimate friend. If he is indeed still alive I should love to renew my relationship with him.*
>
> *Yours in the Lord,*
> *John Patterson*

Will Damian believe it, or will he know that John would never, ever countenance a renewed relationship with either Damian or the cardinal?

John tries to recall what happened after that night in Rome. He forces himself to remember Damian's room in the seminary, a room that was very different from John's small room, with its narrow single bed and bare desk, the cream walls adorned only with a crucifix and an icon of the Madonna and Child. Damian's room was larger, with a double bed and a comfortable seating area complete with drinks cabinet and television, and framed prints of famous paintings on the walls.

He remembers waking up naked in a lather of shame and humiliation. Damian was nowhere to be seen. John hurriedly gathered up his clothes from the floor, got dressed and scuttled back to his room, praying that nobody would see him. He showered and changed his clothes, then he made his way down to the dark wood confessional in the chapel, where every morning one of the priests waited to hear confessions before Mass. He went and knelt behind the grille, because he felt unable to bear the face to face scrutiny of his confessor.

He tries to remember the words of his confession, the attempt to make a good confession without naming what he had no words for anyway. They had been told that one could confess to breaking the sixth commandment and that would cover all serious sexual sins. He tried that.

'Bless me Father, I have sinned. I have broken the sixth commandment.'

He remembers the movement on the other side of the grille, the priest leaning closer. He recognized him. It was Jonas Schmidt, an elderly German cardinal who was reputed to be one of the Pope's trusted advisors. Sometimes, senior churchmen like Cardinal Schmidt heard the seminarians' confessions. John's misery was multiplied by having to make such a confession to a senior member of the hierarchy.

'You are saying you have violated your chastity with another seminarian?' probed Cardinal Schmidt.

'Worse than that.' John felt compelled to expose the extent of his sin.

'What do you mean, worse than that?' The voice was heavily accented but free from any hint of shock or condemnation. It made John feel a little less afraid.

'I went to a club. There were men there,' he said.

'What kind of men?'

'Seminarians. And a cardinal.'

'A cardinal? That is a very serious charge,' said the voice on the other side. The accent was guttural, but it was an observation rather than an accusation. 'Who was this cardinal?'

'It was Cardinal Michael Bradley,' John said, but he felt uneasy. Should Cardinal Schmidt have asked him that question? Should he have responded?

'And what does this cardinal have to do with your confession?' came the voice from the other side.

'He had sex with me. Oral sex. And – and anal sex.' The words tumbled out. 'I think I was drugged. I – I didn't try to stop him.'

He remembers that the confession drew quickly to a close after that. Cardinal Schmidt had seemed eager to end it. Too eager? He had pronounced absolution and John had left the confessional feeling worse than when he had entered it.

He pushes himself away from the desk and goes to look out of the window. The garden broods in darkness. A solitary bird twitters into the night, confused by the streetlights into thinking it's dawn. He wonders if Sarah is out there somewhere. And the cardinal. Spirits of the night. They're all out there, demons and angels, lurking just beneath modernity's blinkered consciousness.

He goes back to the desk and reads the email again. He marvels at his own duplicity. Will Damian really fall for it? Before he can give way to his doubts, he clicks 'send'.

He spends the rest of the night sitting at his computer, trapped in a dark obsessive spiral of internet searches. The cardinal, ghosts, serial murders, 9/11, gay clubs, sexual sins and confessions, the Westonville murders, paedophile priests and reports of abuse. He reads things he had never imagined, ramblings and rantings and outpourings of anger and lust and fantasy and grief and shame and torture and violence and self-loathing, until his soul feels saturated in the all-pervasive toxic ooze of original sin.

TWENTY SEVEN

MONDAY OF HOLY WEEK

He goes downstairs, eyes gritty with sleeplessness, feeling overwhelmed by the emptiness and the futility of the week stretching ahead. Holy Week.

He wonders where Shula is. He opens the back door and calls, waiting for her to appear from among the shrubs. She is nowhere to be seen. He tells himself that she must be out hunting mice, but the anxiety and dread of the night congeal around her absence. Where is she?

He turns on the radio as he waits for the kettle to boil. It speaks into the nothingness. It tells of the nothingness. Murder. Fear. Suspicion. Rage.

Another mother sobs her grief into the abyss. 'She was my little girl. She was so good and kind. She wasn't a prostitute. She had just started at university. She lived at home. Why would anybody do this to her?'

The experts offer up their useless theories. The newsreader injects just the right note of solemnity and tension into her voice. She sounds lascivious. A woman interviewed on the streets of Westonville declares a curse on the murderer. A man with a thick west country accent blames the Catholic Church and says every priest in the city should be thrown in a dungeon. Frank is interviewed again.

'This marks a worrying shift in the pattern of the murderers, Detective Lambert,' says the interviewer. She sounds combative, as if Frank were to blame.

'What do you mean?' He sounds irritable, impatient with this time-wasting exercise when he could be tracking down the killer.

'Well, it seems this latest victim was just an ordinary middle class girl. She wasn't a prostitute. That means no family in Westonville is safe now. Everybody is terrified for what might happen to their daughters,' says the journalist primly.

'The other victims were also ordinary girls, somebody's daughters. Just because they were sex workers doesn't mean their murders were any less terrible.' Frank's tone is contemptuous.

'No, of course not. Of course nobody is suggesting that.' She sounds flustered, and eager to cover over her blunder. 'But even so, it's a worrying development and so far the police seem to be no closer to catching the killer. How many more young women must die, Detective Lambert, before you admit that you need to call in experts from outside?' She is on the defensive. She sounds petulant. John switches the radio off. He doesn't like to hear Frank being humiliated.

Nobody comes to confession. John sits in the small enclosed space, too listless even to anticipate or dread the cardinal's arrival. He says the morning Mass and then goes back into the presbytery to wait. What is he waiting for? He is waiting for Shula to come back. He is waiting for anything that might kick start him back into some semblance of a functioning human being.

He goes to look for Shula. He stands at the back door and calls, longing for her familiar shape to come slinking out from wherever she's hiding. A rook squawks ominously in a nearby tree and a blackbird alights on the lawn and begins tugging urgently at a worm. He makes his way across the lawn to the cemetery and calls again. He pushes open the gate and wanders through the cool shadows, with a growing sense of panic. Something has happened to Shula. Even when she goes wandering at night, she always comes back in the morning to be fed.

He goes back to the presbytery. Shula. Where's Shula?

There's a large brown envelope on the table. It wasn't there before, was it? No, surely not. He would have seen it. He gets closer and he sees what is written in black letters across the front of the envelope:

CURIOSITY KILLED THE CAT.

His hands shake violently as he opens the envelope and pulls out four sheets of paper. The first is a photograph of two men kissing. It's blurry and dark, but he recognizes his anorak. It is Luke and he, in the alley beside the pub.

The second one is vivid, and at first he cannot make out what it is. Then he remembers what Frank told him. The killer rapes his victims with a crucifix.

He knows what he's looking at, and he knows that all eternity will not be long enough to purge that image from his memory. This is the knowledge that kills. This is the knowledge of evil. This image of a woman's naked, raped torso will impose itself on every image of beauty and goodness and tenderness for as long as he lives.

He sits down and cradles his head in his hands. There is no longer any doubt. He must go to the police. He must phone Frank and tell him everything.

He dreads what he might see if he looks at the other two pages, but he knows he must look. He keeps his eyes averted as he shuffles aside the photograph and turns it over so that he never again has to see what he will never again not have seen. Scarcely daring to look, he pulls the pages towards himself.

The top page is a photocopy from an Italian newspaper. The date has been written across the top in the same black felt tip pen.

8th July, 2000.

His Italian is rusty but good enough to understand the gist of the article. It's about a police raid on *La Dolce Vita* club, following a tip-off that young Afghan boys were being trafficked as sex slaves and sold to the nightclub. Some were believed to be as young as twelve. There were reports that the club was a favourite haunt of some senior members of the Catholic hierarchy, as well as seminarians. Some said the scandal would go to the highest levels of the Church. The Vatican had denied all allegations. Cardinal Severino Agnelli, head of the Vatican press office, said that the press reports were lies. He said that, like Jesus Christ, the Church was being attacked and condemned by the agents of the devil.

John slides out the last piece of paper. That too is a photograph – grainy and indistinct, but he knows exactly what it is as soon as he sees it. Somebody had a camera that night. Among the naked bodies, he recognizes himself, and the cardinal.

He has been delivered into evil. He is defeated. The monstrous genius of the cardinal has lured him into a trap, and there is no escape. He was there, in a gay club, being buggered by the cardinal in the presence of twelve year old trafficked children. There is a photograph and a news report to prove it. The cardinal has won.

He wasn't a child. He went there of his own accord. He was drunk. He could have chosen to stay away, as David Williamson did, as Robert did too, for he did not see Robert anywhere in that cauldron. He could have gone home, with just the warm memory of that evening to comfort him for the rest of his life.

He must phone Frank. He doesn't need to tell Frank about the press cutting and the photographs of him. He can just tell him about the cardinal and give him that one photo, that photo which shows what Frank must deal with every time a murder happens.

How does a person see such things and live? Is it possible to become hardened, to get used to such images, to see and touch and smell such mutilated bodies and stay sane? To look into the face of the murderer who did it, and not become a murderer too?

And that terrible message on the front of the envelope. Curiosity killed the cat. The cardinal has killed Shula. No. No. Please, please no. He throws back his head and bellows his rage at the ceiling. 'NO!!!'

John remembers what Holly said about wanting to kill Betty. If the cardinal walked in now, he would kill him. He would take a carving knife from the knife rack and he would drive it in between his ribs and twist it and turn it and relish the sight of the cardinal dying. Or maybe he would torment the cardinal as he had tormented those women. Maybe he would do to him what he had done to that body in the photograph. Violate and torture him. Castrate him. Make him suffer.

He holds those thoughts because they give him energy. He goes to the back door and pushes it open. The cardinal will have buried Shula in the garden. He is sure of it. He is meant to find Shula's tortured body. Shula will look like that girl in the photo. It's all part of the plan.

Over by the shed, Jack has left a spade leaning against the fence. John walks across and picks up the spade. He carries it over to the cherry tree. That's where the cardinal will have buried Shula. He has been watching John. He knows how special that place is. Maybe he has seen Sarah standing there.

And then the cardinal is there, watching him from the lane at the far side of the garden. He is wearing a suit and an open necked shirt. He is standing with his hands by his side, watching. He is smiling.

John picks up the spade and runs towards him with a ferocious energy, his fury and hatred propelling him forward. He will batter his brains out with the spade. He can feel the rush of adrenalin, and the raw desire to kill surging through him. He will avenge himself and all those murdered women, all those young boys sold into slavery to whet the insatiable appetites of the princes of the Church, Shula tortured and killed and buried God knows where. But the cardinal ducks behind the hedge and is gone.

'Wait! Come back here!' His voice is shockingly loud. All the neighbours must have heard. He swallows back the threats and curses that are surging up and wanting to be screamed into the morning air.

The lane is deserted. He runs to the car park, but that too is deserted. All along the lane, there are garden walls with closed doors and gates. Some have garages backing onto the lane, but they too are closed.

He knows that he will not find the cardinal. He knows that the cardinal will have planned his escape, and that he will be gone.

He lifts the spade up and slams it down on the ground with all the force of his anger, and he is glad of the pain that jolts through his arm because it's real. He remembers his illness, and he longs for this dark storm in his soul to become physical, to become bodily suffering and pain, because that is something he could cope with. The body is after all limited to its own space, along with its pains and torments. But the soul billows out like a winding sheet into the air and it visits in memory and imagination that which the body can only visit within the limited confines of its own place.

He goes back to the presbytery. He picks up the envelope and climbs the stairs to his bedroom. He reaches up and pushes the envelope onto the top of the wardrobe. There's slight resistance, and the clunk of something heavy being pushed aside. What is it? He will look later. He doesn't care what it is.

He goes into the study and sits in a chair and does nothing. How long does he sit there for, before his phone pings into life? He looks at the message on the screen. He doesn't recognise the number. 'I'm in the confessional. I want you to hear my confession.'

So this is it. He remembers the feel of the spade in his hand. He remembers slamming it down on the ground and the brief satisfaction of imagining it was the cardinal's head. He thinks of the tools in the presbytery basement. He could take a hammer, or a kitchen knife. He thinks of folding his hands around Holly's neck, and of feeling the delicacy of her pulse and the softness of her skin, and of being overwhelmed with love for her.

But if it were the cardinal's neck – what then? He imagines the gristle beneath his fingers. He imagines squeezing and squeezing until the cardinal's eyes bulge and his face turns purple and his life chokes away. The thought gives him a feeling of satisfaction as intense and dark and bitter as the finest chocolate.

But the cardinal is always one step ahead of him. If the cardinal is in the confessional, he is prepared for that eventuality. And what if the cardinal has a hammer or a knife or a gun? What if the cardinal is waiting to strangle him? The cardinal is taller and stronger than John. He was always fit, known for his visits to the gym and his mountain climbing and his winter skiing. John would be no match for him, no match at all.

Suddenly it doesn't matter, because he knew all along that this day would come, this final test. The cardinal has been planning this, and his plan has been unfolding ever since that Ash Wednesday morning. This is the ultimate liturgy, and the cardinal is a theological genius.

Do not be afraid.

He sees with startling clarity that this is the answer to everything. It will prove his innocence to the world. Even if the cardinal tells everybody about *La Dolce Vita*, even if he shows them the photograph and the news report, people will know that John was murdered by the man who raped him, by the serial killer who has brought such fear and horror to the town. John will become like those murdered women, his own wrongs forgiven and forgotten in the greater wrong he has suffered.

He crosses himself and sinks to his knees. 'Dear God, if I am to die now, help me to die in your love. Forgive me my sins, forgive me my doubts, and gather me to yourself. Father, into your hands I commend my spirit.' He crosses himself again, and he imagines Shula and Sarah and all the murdered women waiting to welcome him into heaven. He goes downstairs, and as he approaches the door that leads into the sacristy his knees feel weak and his hands begin to shake.

Is the cardinal waiting on the other side of the door? Will he torture him as he tortured those women? Will he rape him?

The church has thick walls. It's Monday. It could be hours before anybody comes by – mothers stopping off to pray on their way to collect the children from school, people coming in on their way home from work, parishioners gathering to pray the Stations of the Cross and say the rosary, as they do every evening during Holy Week. He imagines them finding his body, bloodied and dead or dying on the altar steps.

The children. He doesn't want any of the children to be the first to find him. Please, let the cardinal put his body out of sight. Please let somebody find him who can cope with the discovery. But who could cope with such a thing?

He doesn't want to die. A sudden passion for life surges up and lays claim to him. He fights the urge to run away and forces his body to go through the door.

He drapes a stole across his shoulders, and on impulse he takes a collar and tucks it around his neck. He wants to look and feel like a priest. He can't help but look over his shoulder to make sure nobody is standing behind him. He opens the door that leads into the church.

How empty and cold and dark it is. The statues are all draped in purple and there are no flowers. On Saturday there will be flowers in abundance and the candles will make merry in their stands and the bells will ring and the people will sing their hallelujahs, but this is the week of sorrow. This is the week of walking to Calvary step by step in darkness.

The tabernacle light glows red in the gloom. He genuflects. His feet feel like lumps of lead dragging him down. He takes his place on the chair in the confessional and the shadow on the other side of the grille shifts. The confessional is lit only by the bleak grey light of an energy-saving bulb.

'Bless me Father for I have sssinned.' John sits in silence. 'I'm sorry about your cat,' the voice says. The silence stirs and thickens. John can't speak. 'I said I'm sorry. This is the confessional Father. Aren't you supposed to say something?'

'What have you done to Shula? You've killed Shula! Why did you kill Shula?'

'The cat was innocent. I had to teach you a lesson, but I wish I could have done it without torturing an innocent creature.'

'You've murdered six women. How can you feel sorry for killing a cat?'

'You're getting ahead of yourself, Father John. We'll speak about the women later in the week. It's Holy Week. We mustn't rush things. I intend to confess everything, but I shall do it in my own time, day by day, and on Good Friday you will thank me from the bottom of your heart because you will know that I was sent to guide you to the cross. You will walk every step of the way to Calvary with Our Lord, and like the Good Thief you will be with him in paradise while I – I shall be in the everlasting fires of hell.'

'Please. Kill me now. I'm ready to die.' John doesn't care. He just wants everything to end now.

'Oh John, what a naïve little thing you are. I'm not going to kill you. That would be far too easy. I want you to suffer John. I want you to suffer as I have suffered. I want you to be put to the test and see if your Jesus will save you.'

'I don't know what you're talking about.'

'There's unfinished business between us John. You haven't paid for what you did.'

'I did nothing wrong. You seduced me and raped me. And even if it had been my fault, I went to confession. God has forgiven me. I've done nothing wrong.'

'Oh yes, I know you went to confession. You went to confession, and you told the priest everything. You even told him my name, you fucking traitor.'

It's the first time John has heard any emotion in that voice. 'How do you know?' The words come out as a whisper.

'It was a witch hunt John. They couldn't risk a scandal. Why do you think I had to leave?'

'But it was the confessional. I don't understand. What about the seal of the confessional?' The rom is lurching around him. Everything is out of place.

The cardinal laughs his terrible laugh. 'The seal of the confessional! Sweet Jesus and all the angels and saints, you don't really believe that nonsense, do you?'

'I don't understand.' John's collar is beginning to choke him. He can't swallow.

'You went to confession, and you told that stinking old cardinal Jonas Schmidt what you had done and who you had done it with. Of course he told them, those men at the top who wield absolute power. They were running scared. What if the media got hold of the story? The sex abuse scandal was becoming news. I was one of the most senior cardinals in the Church. They offered me a choice. They would make a public example of me, show the world that the Church would not be lenient with abusers, or I could say publicly that I'd decided to leave the priesthood and they would wash their hands of me. So I left. They gave me a lot of money.'

John shakes his head and tries to swallow again. His mouth feels full of saliva. 'I don't understand,' he says again. 'The confessional.' He manages to swallow. 'It was a confession. The seal of the confessional. How could Cardinal Jonas – I don't understand.'

'You're probably the most naïve person I've ever met, John. But I know you respect the seal of the confessional. In fact, six women have died because you respect the seal of the confessional. Another will die on Friday. Good Friday. Seven. The perfect number. But you can save her if you want to John. I have a plan.'

The silence crushes in around him. It would be absolute were it not for the breathing of the thing on the other side of the grille.

'Who are you?' he finally manages to say.

'You know who I am.'

'You're dead.'

'I've been raised from the dead. Like Lazarus. Like Jesus.'

'You know the confessional isn't sound-proofed. Somebody might be listening. I must warn you.' He doesn't want to hear any more. He wants the cardinal to disappear into that vast silence out of which he emerged and never to speak again.

'We're all alone, John. I locked the church doors when I came in.'

'You can't do that. The church doors are never locked.'

'They are now. It's just us, John. We're all alone, unless you count the Blessed Sacrament, but I don't think he'll do much to help you now.' He laughs, and John imagines that's what hell might sound like. 'So back to your cat. That's my confession for today, Father John. I am sorry it was necessary to do what I did to your cat. I'm sorry you left me no choice.'

'You always have a choice. You didn't have to kill Shula. You chose to kill Shula.'

'You were getting curious John. I had to warn you. You shouldn't have sent that email to Damian Thomas.'

John's heart lurches again. 'How do you know I sent it?'

'You really are such an innocent, dear John. You could have become my closest friend, my lover. I would have protected you. You too would have been a cardinal one day. Look at them, John. They all have their beautiful young men whom they're grooming to follow them. You might have become Pope one day. If only you hadn't betrayed me. What a mistake that was. One mistake and look how many lives you've ruined.'

'How do you know I sent that email?'

'Damian isn't like you, John. Damian is a faithful and loyal friend. He told me you were trying to find me. We've kept in touch all these years. But even if Damian hadn't told me, I have your passwords John. How stupid you are, having them all there on your desk. I can access your emails, your internet searches, even your bank account, though what's in there would hardly keep me in wine for an evening.'

'How did you get in? How do you know what's on my desk?' John already knows the answer.

'I have a key. You know I have a key. Remember the plumber?'

'Please. Please go. Please leave me alone.'

'Aren't you going to pronounce absolution, Father John? I said I'm sorry about your cat. Do you think your loving God is incapable of forgiving me for that? Dear oh dear. He's not quite as good as you say, is he, this God of yours?'

'I – I – I can't. May God forgive you. God forgive you.'

'One more thing, Father John. I think by the end of this week you will realize how anybody can become a murderer given the right provocation, given the right justification. I'm going to play a little game with you. How far will you go, how much are you willing to do to protect the seal of the confessional and to save a girl's life? You can do it. I've provided you with the means. Look on top of the wardrobe in your bedroom but be careful. The safety catch is off.' John remembers the object that he felt when he pushed the envelope on top of the wardrobe. He feels sick. The cardinal laughs again, that snigger of contempt that turns the air to ice. 'I've devised a plan, John. You can kill me and save a woman's life, and everybody will praise you. But that's for another day.' He pauses as if waiting for his words to register, then he says, 'I'll be back for the second instalment of my confession, tomorrow at the same time.'

The shadow rises and is gone. John hears the distant thud of the door as the cardinal leaves the church.

He feels too numb to move. The silence roars around him. He is shivering. The church is so cold. The effort of thought is too much. The effort of standing up is too much. The effort of breathing is too much. He would like it all to stop.

Eventually, he forces himself to his feet and leaves the confessional. He stands in the aisle and stares at the altar with its shrouded statues and glowing tabernacle light. He goes and kneels in front of the tabernacle and the emptiness and silence ooze into him. The dull ache in his knee reminds him of his fall and the illness that followed, but that was a lifetime ago. He should have died then. Why didn't he die then? God could have spared him this torment. But there is no God. There is no God.

The presbytery is deathly quiet. John goes upstairs and carries the chair from his desk into the bedroom. He climbs up and peers on top of the wardrobe. The envelope is there, and behind it is a gun. Its muzzle is pointing towards him.

With shaking legs and trembling hands, he climbs down and steadies himself against the wardrobe door. He thinks of what's inside the envelope. The photographs. That unthinkable, impossible image, and the other one, the one that has been lodged in some part of his memory for the past eighteen years. He thinks of the news report. He tries not to remember the thin limbs and fragile penis clasped in his hand in the steam room. A child. Why didn't he realize it was the body of a child?

He picks up his phone from where he left it on the bedside table and checks for messages.

There are fifty missed calls. His voicemail is full. What's going on? He starts to listen to the messages. They're all journalists, wanting to interview him about the murders. He deletes them all, until only the named callers are left. Pete. Holly. No Kate. Please Kate, please phone me. Please tell me the children want to see me. Please invite me over for dinner. I need you Kate. I need you. You're all I have.

He listens to Pete's message, then to Holly's.

'Hello Father. It's Pete here. Em, I'm not calling about anything really. Just to tell you there's no change. Baby John is still in the incubator. I hope Jane might get home today or tomorrow.'

'Hello darling. It's me, Holly. Just checking up to see you're okay. No need to call back. Ring me any time if you need to chat.' He listens to that message again, because the sound of Holly's voice is a small, warm glow in the wasteland. He wants to phone her and tell her about Shula, but he doesn't know where to begin and where to end, how to disentangle the horror of Shula's death from the horror of what awaits him on top of the wardrobe.

He phones Pete and hopes his voice sounds normal. 'Hello Pete. It's Father John here. Thank you for ringing me.'

'That's alright. I mean, I wanted to. I get frightened. You know. On my own. I'm not on my own really. Jane's mother is here to help look after the kids. But I can't talk to her. You know. About what's on my mind. Anyway, it's nothing. Just to tell you about Jane and the baby. I'm going up to the hospital in a minute.'

'Why don't I meet you for a coffee Pete, and we can go to the hospital together afterwards? There's quite a nice place just down the road from the hospital. I often have coffee and cake in there when I do my visits.' Does Pete hear the desperation in his voice, the panicked urge to escape the loneliness and the terror, to be away from this place of horrors?

'Would you Father? Oh, that would be good. I'd like that,' says Pete.

It has clouded over and it's drizzling outside. As he stands in the hall putting on his anorak, he becomes aware of voices outside the door, above the swish and rustle of the plastic fabric. He pulls open the door to see a group of about a dozen men and women clustered around the porch. A large furry microphone is thrust towards him, and several cameras click into life. What's going on?

'Father John, would you tell us about the murders?'

'We want to ask you about the murders, Father John.'

'They say it's a priest killing these women, Father John. What do you think?'

He pulls the hood of his anorak up to shield his face and pushes his way past them. He wants to run, but some instinct tells him to look calm and behave normally. He forces himself to walk steadily down the path to the gate, saying nothing, not looking around, as they crowd around him. Somebody punches his arm. He staggers, but walks on. He goes to the carport beside the lane and unlocks his car. One of them tries to push past him to block his way, but he manages to climb inside and lock the doors. He starts the engine and drives slowly away, afraid of hitting one of them. On the road, he grips the steering wheel and tries to concentrate. The fear is everywhere. The fear and the violence and the suspicion. Dear Jesus. Mary, Mother of God. Please help me. Our Father, who art in heaven, hallowed be, hallowed be ...

The words trail away inside his head. What's the point?

Pete is waiting for him in the café. They order coffees and croissants and sit opposite one another at a table in the corner, each with his own terrors.

'Thanks for coming, Father.'

'That's alright Pete. You know I'm here for you. You said Jane might be coming home today?'

'Yes, or tomorrow. They say it's too soon to know about the baby. He might have some kind of brain damage. They won't know for a few weeks.'

'I'm sorry Pete. It's hard for you.'

'I'm alright Father. The baby and Jane are alive. That's all that matters. I just – I wish I didn't feel so guilty. As if this is my punishment, you know, for what I was doing.' He shakes his head and fidgets with his teaspoon. 'I'm still so frightened Father. What if Jane finds out? What if the police come knocking at the door? I was so relieved when they arrested that priest, and now it has started all over again.'

John looks at him across the table and sees the hollows in his face, the shadows under his eyes, the lines of exhaustion around his mouth. He wants to say something comforting, but he can't find the words. He can't tell Pete that the police won't come knocking at the door, because they might. He can't tell Pete than Jane won't find out, because she might. Why doesn't he just tell Pete, there's no point in anything? There is no God. You might as well surrender to the darkness.

Jane is sitting in a chair beside her bed, with a blue shawl draped over her shoulders. The colour has returned to her face, and she has brushed her hair. She smiles when they walk into the ward and holds her cheek up to be kissed. John kisses her lightly and watches as Pete bends over and strokes the side of her face, resting his cheek on top of her head with his eyes closed. She catches John's eye and smiles enigmatically. What is she thinking?

There's an empty chair beside her. She gestures to a pile of plastic chairs heaped on top of one another against the wall. 'Bring over another chair,' she says.

'I think I'll go and see the little one first,' says Pete. 'I'll leave you and Father John to catch up.'

They watch him go, and then John turns to face Jane. She reaches out her hand to him and he takes it in both of his. She has long, slender fingers.

'How are you Father John? I've been thinking of you. This must be a dreadful time for you, with all these murders and all these rumours.'

He is moved by her concern. 'It's not easy Jane, but I just hope they catch whoever is doing this.' She nods. A shadow flits across her face and she bites her lip. She's about to say something but thinks better of it. 'What about you?' he asks. 'How are you feeling?'

'Physically I feel much better, but I'm frightened Father. The baby – he's so fragile. I'm so afraid that I won't be able to cope.

I – I feel so confused sometimes. I wanted him to die, you know. I prayed he would die. I really meant it. I thought it would be easier, to mourn a dead baby than to cope with whatever lies ahead.'

'You will cope, Jane. You'll be given strength.'

She holds his eyes in a long, steady gaze. Jane has lovely eyes, grey flecked with blue, with long curling lashes. She half-smiles. 'Do you think I should tell Pete I know?'

'Know what Jane?'

'Come on Father. Don't pretend he hasn't told you.'

John swallows. 'Told me what?' He feels as if he's walking on ice that might shatter at any moment and plunge him into the freezing darkness below.

'That he's having an affair. He thinks I don't know, but I've been thinking about things here in the hospital, and I've put all sorts of clues together. The times he would suddenly disappear, and I wouldn't know where he'd gone, and he would come back looking flustered and guilty. I was always too busy to think about it. Maybe I didn't want to know. But things have to change between us, I know that.'

John makes himself hold that limpid, honest gaze. He wonders how much Pete will tell her, and how she will cope if she knows the full story. He suddenly recognizes the strength in Jane, as if the difficulties of the last week have unleashed some power in her that even she doesn't realize is there – and he knows it will be alright.

He drives back to the presbytery, resisting the urge to turn towards the distant hills and drive and drive until he loses himself in some other place, some other time, some other world. But this is the only world there is, and it is no longer a world he recognizes as the graced expression of the love of God. All those ancient heretics were right. This world is the work of an evil demiurge, and one must escape the anguish and corruption of the body into some realm of pure light in order to be free.

He has no appetite. By evening he feels weak with hunger, but he can't eat. He goes to look for Shula again in the drizzle of the night, even though he knows it's a hopeless task. Shula is dead.

Compared to so many murders, the death of a cat should count for nothing at all, but Shula is everything to him. His companion. His soulmate. The only constant, living presence in his life. A cat. Not a hair falls from your head that isn't counted by God. Not a sparrow falls from the sky that God doesn't see and care about. Then how much more does a beloved cat matter in the enormity of things?

Clouds billow across the sky. He goes into the cemetery and calls futilely into the darkness, clicking his tongue against his teeth, whistling and calling her name. 'Shula!' The light of the rising moon seeps through the branches of the yew trees, casting a bleak glow over the graves. The trees sway and moan in the wind, so that it sounds as if the dead are crawling out of their graves and beginning their nightly prowl about the earth. He remembers something his grandmother used to say, about the poor souls in purgatory wandering the earth at night, unable to rest in peace. The thought makes him dizzy. He stops by Sarah's grave and the angel gazes down at him, cold and indifferent to his misery. 'Sarah?' he says. 'Sarah, are you there?' The small grave mocks him with its silence.

He tilts his head back. 'Please!' he moans. 'Please!' He sinks to his knees on the muddy path and crouches over with his head on the ground, and he sobs.

Eventually, cold and stiff and barely able to move with exhaustion and grief, he hobbles back to the presbytery. He locks the door behind him but wonders why he bothers. What would it matter if the cardinal murdered him in his sleep? It would be a blessing, a reprieve from the torment of living without Shula. He discards his muddy clothes on the kitchen floor and climbs upstairs in his socks and underpants.

TWENTY EIGHT

TUESDAY OF HOLY WEEK

For the second time in two weeks, he awakes to find Deacon Jack beside his bed, shaking him awake. 'Come on lad, you've over-slept again. You've missed hearing confessions and Mass starts soon.'

John struggles to consciousness, trying to gather his thoughts. Then he remembers. 'Shula,' he says. 'Shula is dead.'

Jack shakes his head in sympathy and sorrow. 'I'm so sorry to hear that John. What happened?'

'She's disappeared.'

'That doesn't mean she's dead. Cats do that – disappear for days on end and then come back as if nothing has happened.'

'No. Somebody killed her. She's dead, Jack. I know she's dead.'

Jack pats John awkwardly on the shoulder. 'Maybe you should just stay in bed today, Father. Perhaps you're still not well. I can do a Eucharistic service again.'

'No. No. There's no need for that. I'll get up now. Give the people my apologies and say that Mass will be a few minutes late.'

He has a quick shower and gets dressed. He hurries down to the sacristy feeling unprepared and agitated, but also glad of the distraction. At least for now he can avoid thinking about the unbearable days and weeks of living without Shula, and the lure of the internet telling him that it holds the answer to all his questions, if only he knew where to look.

Jack is even more clumsy and awkward than usual as he moves about the sacristy preparing for Mass, and Edith's quick, nervous gestures communicate her anxiety. For once, John doesn't want silence. Tying the girdle around his waist, he says, 'Shula's dead. Somebody's killed her.'

'Oh sweet Jesus!' Edith claps her hands to the side of her face and widens her eyes.

Jack looks him in the eye for the first time that morning. 'John, I don't think you should assume she's dead just because she hasn't come home for a day or two. I told you, that's what cats do.'

John doesn't bother to argue. It's too complicated. He can't begin to explain to Jack the reasons for his certainty that Shula is dead.

Jack shuffles his feet and lowers his eyes. 'Edith says there have been comments on the website. There's so much hatred and violence out there Father. I wonder where God is in all this.'

'You wouldn't want to see them Father, those comments,' says Edith, with a thrill of horror in her voice. 'They hate us you know. They hate Catholics, especially priests.'

'Maybe people have good reason to hate priests right now Edith,' he says.

'I refuse to believe it's a priest doing these things,' she says. 'Look at poor Father James. They arrested him and he was completely innocent. It's a plot Father. It's probably an atheist, or one of those Moslem terrorists.'

He wonders what planet Edith lives on, to retain such blind faith through all the scandals and horrors of the last few years. 'What about the comments?' he says. 'Are they on the website?'

'Holy Mother of God Father, no. I moderate the comments. Nothing goes on the website unless I approve it.'

'And what happens to the comments you don't approve?'

'I could delete them, but I leave them there just in case. You know, it's like these terrorists with their emails and Facebook conversations. The police might want to use them as evidence if they track down the murderer. Nobody sees them but me.'

'Could I see them?' John knows what they will be – an endless stream of poison like the ones sent to his personal email address, but somewhere in that torrent of hatred there might be a clue, some sign as to the cardinal's identity and whereabouts.

'You could read them if you logged on,' says Edith. 'I can give you the password. But seriously Father, why would you want to poison your mind with that stuff? It would make you ill, seeing what they say.'

'You read it, and you seem to cope,' he reminds her.

'It's my duty,' she says, 'and every time I log on I sprinkle my head with holy water – you remember, I brought that big bottle back from Lourdes last time we went – I booked my bag into the hold so that I could do it. I don't know why these security people can't tell the difference between a good Catholic woman bringing a bottle of holy water back from Lourdes and a Moslem terrorist with a bomb, but that's the kind of mad world we live in with all this political correctness these days.' She tuts and shakes her head. Edith is in her element, thinks John. 'Anyway, before I read those comments I sprinkle myself with holy water, I put a crucifix on the desk, and I pray to Our Lady to protect me.' She sighs and shudders. 'It's satanic Father. That's what it is. You have to be careful not to let the devil in.' She gives a coy little smile. 'It might sound ridiculous Father, but I think of myself as a bit like Saint Michael with a sword, protecting the parish from evil. And the cross I have to bear is that I have to read all that stuff. I don't see why you should have to read it too Father.'

'Maybe it's my duty too Edith – as parish priest,' he says.

She sniffs. 'If you insist, I suppose. I'll come with you and show you how to log on after Mass.'

Contend, O Lord, with my contenders;
Fight those who fight me.

Take up your buckler and shield;
Arise in my defence, Lord, my mighty help.

As they say the entrance antiphon, he looks out at the smattering of
people in the pews, and he thinks how few they are. He tells himself
that it's only Tuesday, and even though it's Holy Week people have
busy lives – jobs to go to, homes to clean, children to look after.
Even so, he would have expected there to be more people.

The antiphon makes him think of Edith, and for a brief
moment he feels thankful for the loyalty and friendship of Edith
and Jack. He lifts his hands to say the opening prayer, and he
tries not to think of Shula or the cardinal or the murders.

After Mass, Edith follows him into the presbytery. The
kitchen door is open.

'Sweet Mother of God, Father, what are your clothes doing
thrown all over the kitchen floor like that?' She's walking
purposefully towards the muddy pile of clothes on the floor.

He puts a restraining hand on her arm. 'It's fine Edith. I went
for a little jog last night, to try to calm myself down. You know,
I was so worried about Shula, and I thought if I had a run I
might sleep. I'll wash my clothes later.' She eyes him dubiously
but he steers her towards the stairs and she complies, reluctantly.
'Would you like a cup of tea or coffee?' he asks.

She shakes her head. 'No thank you Father. Jack and I have a
busy day today, getting things ready for Easter. I'll just come up
and show you what to do, and then I'll be on my way.'

They go upstairs, and Shula's absence stabs through him
with such anguish that he has to pause on the landing and lean
against the wall to catch his breath.

'Are you alright Father?'

'Yes, I'm fine Edith. I'm just a bit weak still. I haven't got my
strength back yet.'

They go into the study and he turns on his laptop. She makes
a small impatient gesture, but her voice is indulgent when she

says, 'Honestly Father, it's time the parish bought you a new laptop. That old one of yours takes an age to boot up.'

Every time Edith uses a technical term she gives a little smirk of self-satisfaction. 'Boot up.' Smirk.

He looks out of the window as he waits, and he imagines Shula padding across the dewy lawn, jumping up onto the bench to do her morning grooming session.

Edith rummages in her handbag and takes out a plastic bottle from Lourdes – shaped like the Madonna with a blue, screw top crown. 'I brought some holy water,' she says. 'We need to make sure we don't expose ourselves to evil. Luckily, I have some prayer cards in my bag. I always carry them with me. You never know when you might need them.' She delves in her handbag again and takes out two cards with a picture of the Immaculate Heart on the front. She hands him one and keeps the other for herself. 'Now then Father, we'll say it together.'

August Queen of Heaven, sovereign Mistress of the Angels, who didst receive from the beginning the mission and the power to crush the serpent's head, we beseech thee to send thy holy angels, that under thy command and by thy power, they may pursue the evil spirits, encounter them on every side, resist their bold attacks, and drive them hence into the abyss of woe.

Most holy Mother, send thy angels to defend us and to drive the cruel enemy from us. All ye holy angels and archangels, help and defend us. O good and tender Mother! Thou shalt ever be our Love and our Hope. Holy Angels and Archangels, keep and defend us. Amen.

'There then,' she says briskly. 'That will keep us safe.' She picks up the bottle of holy water and unscrews the crown. She pours a little of the water into her left palm and sprinkles it over them both with the fingertips of her right hand, then she crosses herself and he does the same.

He is consoled by the ritual, and by Edith's unshakable faith. He feels as if no evil would dare to approach after all that, so long as she's here.

'Now then Father, you ought to be able to log on. You have the password written there with all the rest.' She indicates the sheet of paper taped to the desk. He remembers what the cardinal said about having his passwords, and a moment of panic grips him. He tries to concentrate on what Edith is telling him.

She shows him how to get into the website and go to the comments. She explains to him the difference between those that have been published and those that are awaiting moderation. 'It's the ones awaiting moderation that I don't put on the website, but I leave them there – I don't delete them. As I say, they might be evidence one day.'

She stands up and offers the chair to him, then she stands behind him making little bird-like tutting noises as he settles himself down and begins to read. 'Look at that Father!' she says. 'They're still coming in. There's a whole lot of new ones since I checked last time.'

There's the same dark torrent of abuse and vitriol that dry his mouth and make his pulse quicken. He feels ashamed reading the curses and expletives with Edith standing there. They seem to come mostly from ultra-conservative Catholics and angry atheists, hurling abuse at each other. Much of it is either anonymous or clearly pseudonymous. *AngelsatmySide. PopesProtector. HatingHeretics. HolyKnight. SavingGod. DawkinsISGod. SuperstitionKills. PervPriestProsecutor.* Some just have first names. He skims down the list, and there, third from the top, something leaps out at him.

Ask Father John about La Dolce Vita. Ask him about the little boys in the sauna. Ask him about his male lover. Ask him about the cardinal.

Surely, Edith must hear his heart pounding? It's one of the most recent ones. He pushes down the top of his laptop, hoping she hasn't had a chance to read it. 'I can't read this filth,' he says.

'I did warn you Father. Satan is attacking the Church. I have to be on my guard all the time with this website.' She sounds pleased. 'Anyway, now you know how to log on, you can keep an eye on the website if you want to, but don't worry. I'm not going to let any of that disgusting stuff get out into the public. I'm sure you don't need to be reading it as well.'

She clears her throat and makes a little gesture with her hand, as if she's about to stroke his arm and then thinks better of it. 'I'm sorry about your cat, Father,' she says, 'but remember what Jack said. She'll probably come back. Maybe I should print out some posters? I once had a friend whose cat climbed into a visitor's car as he was leaving and the cat ended up back at the visitor's house. And you'd never believe it Father. I read in the paper last week about a cat that climbed into somebody's suitcase when he was packing to go on holiday and he didn't notice, and then when he got to Spain out popped his cat! Can you believe it?'

She is trying to cheer him up, and he draws some comfort from what she's saying. Maybe she's right. There is a perfectly reasonable explanation for all this, and Shula is probably fine.

'Actually Edith, I know you're busy, but I'd be so grateful if you would help me to find Shula. I think it's a good idea to do some posters. We could put them up on lampposts round about. I'm sure Adnan would put something in the shop window.'

'Leave it with me Father. Do you have a photo of Shula?'

He tries to remember. There was a photo that Kate took in the presbytery garden last year. He goes over to the shoebox where he keeps his photos, and rummages until he finds it. He is standing in the garden holding Shula up to his face. It's a close-up. He's wearing his dog collar for some reason, and Shula is snuggled against his neck, peering out at the camera with her wide hazel eyes.

'Here, this is the only one I have,' he says.

She looks at it. 'Hmm. Maybe I'll crop it so that you're not in the picture. You know, with all that's happening, it's probably better not to put your photo up. It just invites more abuse, doesn't it?' She tucks the photo into her handbag, along with the bottle of holy water and one of the prayer cards. 'I'll leave the other prayer card with you Father,' she says. 'It's a very powerful prayer for warding off evil. You should say it every time you feel afraid.'

'Thank you Edith.' He wonders if he should indulge such superstition, but he has no energy to resist her. 'Edith, I'd really like to have that photo back. I'd like to keep it, if you don't mind.'

'Of course Father. I'll scan it and give it back to you tomorrow. I'll save it as a JPEG file.' Smirk. 'I can print copies off,' she says.

He goes downstairs with her and watches as she marches purposefully down the path, ready to fight the good fight for another day. He goes straight back up to the study, unable to resist the addictive lure of the website. Several more comments have come in during the short time it took to see Edith to the door. He scrolls down to the comment about *La Dolce Vita*:

> *Ask Father John about La Dolce Vita. Ask him about the little boys in the sauna. Ask him about his male lover. Ask him about the cardinal.*

He looks at the email address: LaDolceVita@gmail.com. He reads the message again and again, then his eyes drift up and a word leaps out at him: Shula. The email is from the same address: LaDolceVita@gmail.com. The subject is 'Where's Shula?'

> *Ask Father John what's happened to his cat. When did he last see Shula?*

Despair settles over him, like death. He goes to the window and looks out. Two young mothers push their babies in buggies along the lane. The window is open a crack. Their voices drift up, light as the morning air. The garden is quiet and still, the dewy lawn untrodden, the cherry tree garlanded in green.

He remembers his clothes on the kitchen floor and drags himself downstairs. He bundles up the clothes and puts them in the washing machine. He imagines Shula coming through the cat flap, wrapping herself around his legs. The day yawns ahead of him. Will the cardinal come back for another confession? Of course he will. John's heart pounds with terror.

He knows he must speak to Frank. He must tell him the whole story before Friday, without betraying the seal of the confessional. But before he tells Frank, he must hear the cardinal's story. This week, the cardinal will tell him everything. He will listen. He will discover all there is to know. On Friday, he will know what to do. On Friday, he will tell Frank in time to do whatever needs to be done to prevent a seventh murder. If he tells Frank now, the cardinal will go into hiding. John knows he will. And a seventh woman will die.

The thought of that overwhelms him. He goes upstairs to his bedroom and climbs under the duvet. He curls up into a tight ball. He yearns for Shula. He yearns for Luke. He yearns for death.

The bells are ringing, and the church spire looms out of the mist. An empty grave awaits its new inhabitant. Whose funeral is this? He struggles to see, but he can't move. It's dark. He is trapped. It's his funeral. He is in his coffin. He's not dead. The bells are ringing, ringing. He wants to call out. I'm alive. He wants to hammer on the roof and beg them to release him, but he can't move. His limbs are paralysed, his mouth is frozen. Help. Help. The words won't come. There's something on his face. It's wet. What is it? It's Shula. Shula's body. Shula is bleeding. The bells are ringing.

He is suddenly awake. The doorbell is ringing. The duvet is tangled around his body, and he's sweating. He sits up. His shirt is stuck to his chest and he has pins and needles in his arm. What time is it? It's three o'clock. He has been asleep all morning.

He flings back the duvet and wriggles out of his shirt. He pulls a clean shirt out of the wardrobe and the memory of what's on top of the wardrobe surges back. He forces himself into the bathroom to splash water on his face and comb his hair. He is still wearing his shoes and socks. He hurries downstairs and opens the door, not fully thinking about what he's doing. Only as it begins to open does he realize he should have asked who is there. It could be the journalists again. It could be the cardinal.

It's Frank. 'Jesus, John. I've been ringing and ringing. What's going on?'

'Sorry. I fell asleep. Come in.'

'I've been trying to get you on your mobile all morning.'

'I left it in the kitchen. The journalists. They keep calling me. I hadn't planned on going to sleep. I just lay down for a rest. I don't think I'm over that infection yet. I'm still taking antibiotics. They make me sleepy.'

Frank eyes him suspiciously but doesn't say anything. John considers taking him upstairs because it's more relaxed up there, but he thinks of the envelope and the gun and some instinct makes him want to keep Frank as far away as possible from that incriminating evidence. He doesn't want Frank prowling around up there while he's making tea. He takes him into the living room.

'Would you like a cup of tea?'

'No thanks. I just want to have a chat with you.' Without being asked, Frank pulls out one of the dining chairs and sits down at the table. John sits opposite him and tries to remember how he might sit if he were innocent. But surely, every priest is on edge right now? Wouldn't it be more suspicious if he looked completely nonchalant? He opts for resting his elbows on the table and assuming a look of concerned bewilderment.

Frank pushes his chair back and crosses his left ankle over his right knee. 'I need your help John. This case is driving me crazy.' His tone is friendly and confiding. Half-formed possibilities and questions are skittering around John's brain, jumbled and random, too quick to lay hold of. 'You know you're all under suspicion,' Frank says.

John nods. 'I know that.'

Frank shrugs. 'I was so sure we had our man, and now we're back to square one.'

'Surely you have some clues, some idea of who it might be?' says John.

'Well, it's either a priest or somebody with inside knowledge of Catholicism. They could even be some kind of Satanic ritual killings, Black Masses even. We're not ruling anything out.' He looks at John, and his gaze seems almost sympathetic. 'The bodies are all mutilated in particular ways. I told you about the crucifixes, and the rosaries around their necks. It seems they were anointed too, as if they'd had the last rites. We couldn't tell with the burned one, of course, but there were traces of oil on the others, and there were empty pyxes too. I've already told you they'd been given communion. There were undigested communion wafers in their stomachs.'

John doesn't try to hide the fact that his hands are shaking. Why wouldn't his hands shake? He runs his hands over his face. 'Dear God,' he says. 'Dear God.'

Frank shifts his position, putting both feet on the ground and resting his hands on his knees. He purses his lips and looks around the room, as if searching for clues, then his eyes settle on John's face.

'So have you noticed anything strange, John? Hosts going missing? Anybody prowling around the church? Anything at all that you want to tell me?'

John shakes his head. 'No,' he says. 'But people are always coming in and out of the church. It's only locked for a few hours every night. You know that.' He swallows, and frowns. He is moving into uncharted waters. He tries to look as if he has suddenly remembered something, which in a way he has. 'There is one thing,' he says. 'It seemed a bit strange at the time, but I didn't really think about it afterwards.'

Frank leans forward. The movement is almost imperceptible, but John has a feeling that every move Frank makes is calculated and choreographed. He, on the other hand, is groping blindly, fumbling in darkness, trying to find a path through this and out to the other side. He tries to control his voice.

'There was a plumber who told Edith I'd reported a fault with the church heating. Edith hid a key for him, and he put it back under the mat when he'd finished. The thing is, I hadn't reported a fault with the heating.' He pauses. 'I mean, I'd noticed the heating seemed to be playing up. The church felt cold sometimes. But I hadn't reported it. Or at least, I don't remember reporting it.'

'You would surely remember something like that?'

'Yes. Yes, I'm sure I would. It's just – I've been quite stressed lately Frank. Obviously the murders have added to that, but even before. I – um – I need a break. I've been overdoing things. Sometimes I doubt my own grip on things. And then, being ill, it all feels a bit too much, to be honest.'

Frank narrows his eyes. 'What was the plumber's name?'

Robert McDonald. What if the name gives him away? What if Frank tracks down the connection all the way back before the suicide to *La Dolce Vita*?

'I can't remember,' he says.

'Surely Edith told you.' Frank sounds impatient now. John thinks of the emails. He thinks of taking Frank upstairs and switching on his laptop. He tries to remember what emails are on there. The email to Damian is there. Frank will see it. Frank will find out about the cardinal. What if he decides to search the place? What if he finds the envelope, and the gun?

He lowers his eyes. 'There's something else,' he says.

'What else?' Frank says, and there's an energy emanating from him now which seems to crackle and spark in the space between them.

'I didn't say anything because – because I'm still not sure that I'm not imagining things. There's a cardinal – he was in Rome when I was studying there – Cardinal Michael Bradley – I don't know if that name means anything to you.'

'Why should it?' Frank sounds impatient.

'He left the priesthood quite suddenly in 1999,' says John. 'There were unconfirmed rumours of a sex scandal. He went to New York and became a hedge fund manager. He worked in one of the twin towers. He was killed on 9/11.'

'I'm a convert, remember. I never had much interest in the Catholic Church before I married Mary. So no, I don't remember that story. But then, lots of people died on 9/11. There's no reason why I should remember one name out of so many.'

'No. No, I suppose not. It's just that – I can't be sure – but I thought I saw him in the back of the church one day. But he's supposed to be dead, which is why I decided I was imagining things.'

'And why are you telling me this?' Frank's voice is spiked with adrenaline.

'What if he's not dead? What if – what if he has something to do with the murders?'

There is no ground beneath John's feet. He is walking through emptiness, plucking words out of a vacuum. Some instinct is driving him. What is it? Survival? Is this how Shula felt when she went slinking across the lawn, so silent that she seemed to be melting into the air around her, so focused on her own survival and her own need that nothing else existed for her except those measured movements of her paws, that sleek body stretched out in space, that small bird or mouse just ahead of where she was? Her universe had shrunk to that one single task, that one single aim rooted in the ancient law of the jungle from which she had once emerged – to outmanoeuvre her prey and survive to live another day. Maybe somewhere, Shula's spirit is driving him, telling him what to do, lending him her primal feline consciousness which in the end will serve him so much better than his rational human mind. And so, cat-like, he faces down Frank's unflinching gaze and finds that he can do this after all.

'Hold on a minute, John. You're asking me to believe that some cardinal who is supposed to be dead is walking around Westonville murdering prostitutes? Jesus. I've heard some tall tales in my time.' Frank's tone betrays his attempt at incredulity. He believes John.

'I'm only telling you what I think I saw,' says John.

'Cardinal Michael Bradley, you say?'

'Yes.'

Frank looks at his watch. 'Alright, we'll do a check on that name and see what we can find. In the meantime, find out the name of that plumber. And get some rest John. You look fucking awful.' He pushes back his chair and stands up.

'Is that it?' asks John.

'What do you mean, is that it?'

'Don't you want to ask me any more questions?'

'There's plenty of time for that John. You've been sick. Quite frankly, I wonder about your mental state. You're all over the place. But John, I don't think you're our man. I can't protect you – correction, I won't protect you – but I think we're wasting our time with you. I've been in this job a long time John. I've learned to trust my instincts. There's something about you that doesn't add up, but whatever it is, I don't think you're a murderer. But don't leave town. I'll be back. Where's your cat, by the way?'

A spasm of terror grips John. How much does Frank really know? Why on earth is Frank asking about his cat? He answers honestly.

354

'Shula has disappeared. I'm sure she's dead. I'm sure somebody has killed her.'

'And you didn't think that was relevant information?' Frank's voice is sharp and accusing.

'I thought – people hate priests right now. There were journalists on my doorstep this morning. I don't suppose I'm the only priest to be targeted for some kind of punishment.'

How easy it is, once you begin to lie. How effortlessly the words slide into place. How little practice it takes. Is killing like that too? Only the first time is difficult, and then, once you start, it's easy to keep going. Is that what it's like for soldiers? For executioners? For torturers? For murderers? He has become a liar. He has joined their ranks.

'I have to go because I have another appointment John, but we need to talk again. I'll be back. Like I said, don't leave town, will you?'

'Of course I won't Frank.'

He sees Frank to the door and hurries inside before any snooping journalists can pounce on him from their hiding places. He stands in the hall and feels Shula's absence gaping around him. Eventually, he forces himself into the kitchen and checks his phone. There are two messages. The first one arrived at noon from a number he doesn't recognise. It must have arrived just after he fell asleep. 'I'm in the confessional.'

The second arrived at 12.30. 'Where were you? I was in the confessional and you weren't there. I'll be there tomorrow at 12.00. Remember, a woman's life depends on this.' It's from the same number. He calls it back but is not surprised to find that the number is unavailable.

John has a strange feeling of relief as well as dread. The fact that he was not there at the cardinal's beck and call feels like a small gesture of resistance, even though it shrinks to nothing in the face of his overwhelming fear of what might happen next.

He switches on his laptop. There's a dark deluge of emails in his inbox. He ignores them, afraid of their contents, as he scrolls down to find the emails about the plumber. He reads them again, and they seem innocent enough. He tries to see them through Frank's eyes, looking for hidden signs or slips that might give away the identity of the sender. Frank knew nothing of the scandal surrounding Cardinal Bradley. Would he ever even have heard of Robert McDonald, just another priest caught up in a sex abuse scandal? And it's a common enough name anyway.

He gets up and goes to look out of the window. A figure is walking up the road towards the presbytery gate. His heart lurches, but it's only Paul Mellors, one of Jonathan and Mary's sons, doing his paper round.

He watches as Paul approaches the gate and sees him pause and look up. He steps back from the window to avoid being seen, because he doesn't want to have to go down and say hello. Paul turns to look back down the road and then he looks up at the window again. He seems nervous. Eventually, he hurries up the path and John hears the rattle of the letter box as he delivers the *Westonville Evening Gazette*. Paul half-runs back down the path and disappears along the lane.

John goes downstairs and picks up the newspaper. His photo is on the front page – a photo of him leaving the presbytery yesterday morning when the journalists took him by surprise. It's a terrible photograph. His eyes are wide and his mouth is set in a rictus. There's another smaller photo, of him pulling his hood up to hide his face.

'WHAT ARE YOU HIDING FROM, FATHER JOHN?' shrieks the monstrous headline.

John carries the newspaper into the bleak downstairs living room and spreads it on the table. There is very little about him in the article that goes with the photos. It's all about the latest murder, and the release of James Forrester, with speculation about who the murderer might be. He is only one of many possibilities. There are more than a hundred priests in the diocese, fifty of them living in local deaneries in and around Westonville. The newspaper implies that they are all under suspicion, until the murderer is caught.

The latest murder victim has been named as Aggie Watson. The detective leading the case, Chief Superintendent Frank Lambert, says that her body bears similar signs of torture and mutilation to those of the other murder victims. She was found in a dustbin outside the Queen's Arms in the early hours of Saturday morning. Aggie was a student at Westonville University and was not involved in the sex trade.

There's a photograph of a studious looking young woman with soft brown hair and spectacles. John gazes down at the photograph until it swims and blurs before him. Overcome by exhaustion, he rests his forehead on that image and closes his eyes. He wakes with the doorbell clanging through the cloisters.

He no longer cares who it is. The cardinal. Frank. Journalists. It doesn't matter. Whoever it is, he will hand himself over and let them do what they want. He has nothing left to lose. They can't make him speak. They can't make him break the seal of the confessional. Let them search the place and find the envelopes and the gun and the emails. He doesn't care. He won't speak. Let them kill him. Let him be a martyr for the faith, the way he sometimes dreamed of as an ardent young priest.

He drags himself to the front door, barely able to move his legs. He turns the key and pulls the door open.

Kate is standing on the doorstep. She looks pale and distressed. Her eyes are swollen and red with crying.

'Hey, my little brother. What are they doing to you?' she says. 'I saw the newspaper and came straight here. Fucking bastards.'

'Kate!' He begins to cry too.

She steps inside and puts her arms around him. She rocks him against her body and whispers, 'Shhh, shhhh, it's alright,' burying her lips in his hair.

357

'Shula,' he says, 'they killed Shula.'

'Shhh, shhh, it's alright.'

'Shula. Shula. Shula.'

'Shhh, shhhh, shhhhh, it's alright now.'

As she holds him, he begins to feel something loosening inside him, and with the loosening comes a memory.

He is twelve years old, and he has just been to confession. He has ridden home afterwards, choking and spluttering, the wind wiping the tears from his face as he rode. He is terrified that they will take one look at him and know – his parents, his sister Kate, his brother Paul. As soon as he walks in the door, they will see his filth and his shame and his guilt. They will see his thing in the priest's hand, and they will see his pleasure in the touch, even as he was drowning in shame and confusion.

He tries to look normal as he pushes his bike through the gate and leans it against the shed. He opens the hall door and Kate is there, ready to go out, in jeans with a bright blue top and red lipstick and her hair piled on top of her head and big gold hoop earrings and her perfume filling the air.

She looks at him, and whatever she sees, she understands. She says those same words – Kate's signature greeting in all the hard times of his life. 'Hey little brother.' She holds out her arms, and he buries his face in that blue top and breathes in her perfume and cries.

Now, the memory comes back and it gives a shape to his grief, something for it to attach itself to in the tumult.

'Do you remember that day, Kate, when you were dressed to go out and you held me just like this?' he says, drawing back enough so that the words can come out. 'When I got home on my bike, and I was upset, and you knew?'

'Yes. I remember. You never told me what was wrong.'

'A priest had just – had just abused me. In the confessional.'

'Oh no, John. Oh my sweet brother. If I had known – why didn't you tell me? Why didn't you report him?'

'I just didn't. I was scared. I thought it was my fault.'

He can feel the heat of her outrage in the way she strengthens her grip on him and her voice grows tight in his ear, but he also senses her trying to restrain herself as she keeps murmuring and soothing him.

'I wish you'd get out,' she says eventually. 'I wish you'd get out of this evil church with its poisonous priests and its toxic ideology. I wish you'd find a lover – ten lovers – a hundred lovers – and let yourself become the beautiful erotic gifted wonderful man you are.' She makes it sound possible. She makes it sound easy. She doesn't know about the cardinal and the envelope hidden upstairs. She doesn't know about Luke.

'I went to a gay club,' he says.

She gives a soft, delighted laugh. 'Oh little brother, I hope you got fucked to your heart's delight.'

'I was twenty. I was raped. By a cardinal.'

She freezes. She drops her arms and steps back, and he sees the tight, white ring of anger around her mouth. 'You must report it John.'

'I can't.'

'You must. Otherwise you're colluding. If you don't report it, you're doing what they all do – lying and hiding and protecting them.'

'I went to confession. My confessor told somebody. The cardinal was sent away. He went to New York and started to work for some big money company. He was killed on 9/11.'

'You still have to tell somebody, John. The more of you who tell the truth, the harder it is for them to keep getting away with it.' She's staring at him, and her open, honest gaze makes him squirm with embarrassment and fear.

'Let's go and sit down,' he says.

They go into the kitchen and he puts the kettle on. 'Tea or coffee?' he asks.

'Don't you have anything stronger? Wine?'

'It's Lent.' He hears how ridiculous it sounds even before she snorts with laughter.

'Oh Jesus,' she says. 'Your lot are swanning around the world raping children and murdering whores, but you can't have a fucking glass of wine because it's Lent? Give me a break, little brother.'

'It's actually Holy Week,' he says, regretting the edge of defensiveness in his voice.

'Yeah. And I'm sure Aggie Watson remembered that when she was being tortured and raped with a crucifix and having a host shoved down her throat before she was throttled.'

'How do you know how she died?' He is dumbfounded by her knowledge.

'I'm a doctor John. I know the pathologist. These women had communion wafers in their stomachs. They had rosaries around their necks. They had crucifixes up their vaginas.' Her eyes fill and her voice breaks. 'One of them was only thirteen. She was pregnant. That's one of the girls they found at the church. The other one was sixteen.' She swallows back her rage and her tears and goes to the fridge. She yanks it open and looks inside. 'Good God, John, this fridge is like Old Mother Hubbard's cupboard.'

'I know. I haven't been shopping for a while. There's a cake in the tin, and some biscuits.'

She turns to face him, hands on hips. 'Go upstairs and get ready. We're going out for dinner.'

'I can't Kate. I'm not hungry.'

'Well, I am, so you can sit and watch me eat.'

She picks up her phone and he hears the thin distant sound of Phoebe's voice. 'Hello Mum. Dad's driving so he can't answer his phone. He's just picked me up from swimming. Where are you?'

'I've been held up with somebody I'm looking after. I'm going to be late home. I'll grab something to eat in town. Don't wait for me. Tell Dad to get you all some dinner,' says Kate.

John realizes she has told the truth without telling the facts.

It's what he has been trying to do, until this afternoon. Now he has crossed to the other side of some invisible dividing line which separates people like him from people like Kate. 'Outside are the dogs, those who practice magic arts, the sexually immoral, the murderers, the idolaters and everyone who loves and practices falsehood.' The Book of Revelation. He is on the outside, with the murderers.

Kate drives them to a small Italian restaurant on the high street. They could have walked, but he doesn't want to be seen. He is glad of the low lighting, the warmth of candle glow, the discreet positioning of the tables and the muffled conversations which blur into indecipherability. He realizes that he is hungry after all. Kate orders a bottle of wine.

'You're driving,' he reminds her.

'So you'd better help me to drink it,' she says.

As they wait for their meal to arrive, he sips his wine and dares to broach the question that churns inside him and won't give him peace.

'How are the children, Kate?'

'They're fine,' she says briskly, then she puts her glass down and clasps her hands on the table. She lifts her chin and closes her eyes, takes a deep breath and opens them again. 'Actually, they're not fine. These murders are affecting everybody. Phoebe in particular is very withdrawn and preoccupied. I'm quite worried about her, to be honest.'

He swallows. 'Do they – do they suspect me? Do they think I might be the murderer?'

'Of course not, John. No, absolutely not. They love you. They miss you.' She reaches out and rests her hand on top of his, then she lowers her eyes. 'It's just – well, it's Chris.'

'Does he suspect me?'

She shakes her head. 'I don't think so, but it's an excuse for him to take it out on you. You know what he's like. You're a Catholic priest. You're guilty by association. It's a collective thing in his eyes. He doesn't see you, the man, the person, my little brother. He just sees a priest, and he associates priests with – well, with the kind of behaviour you've been telling me about tonight.' She removes her hand from his and swallows a mouthful of wine. 'I don't blame him either, John. I don't begin to understand why you want to be part of it.'

He thinks of Holly and Bonnie and Pete and Sister Gertrude. He thinks of Amy and Lucy and Danny. He thinks of Dorcas and Carol and Edith and Jack. He wishes he could find some way to explain, but there are no words for what he wants to say.

'Because I love Jesus,' he says.

He waits for a blast of sarcasm, but her face softens. 'You know, John, I love Jesus too, but I find it easier to do that in the hospital and the doctor's surgery than in a Mass with paedophiles in red robes prancing around the altar telling me what to do with my sex life.'

It strikes him that maybe his vocation isn't so different from Kate's. The wine is warming him and relaxing him.

'I think maybe I feel about my parishioners the way you feel about your patients,' he says.

They let something delicate rest between them in silence, and then she begins to chat about work and the children as the waiter brings their meal.

Driving home, she says, 'John, you have to report what happened to you. Not just for your sake, but for the sake of all those victims who are afraid to speak out, or who speak out and get accused of lying. You have to find the courage to say what happened to you.'

He wants to change the subject. 'I went to the Queen's Arms,' he says. 'I'm in love with a man who goes there every night.' He realizes that he wants Kate to think he has another life, a secret love life that brings him into the ambit of what she considers normal. He glances at her profile but can't read her expression. She says nothing.

She comes into the presbytery and drinks a cup of strong

coffee to sustain her on the drive home, though in fact he ended up drinking most of the wine. He suspects it was a ruse on her part to get him to relax.

'Are you going to be okay?' she asks. 'Do you want me to stay over?'

'No, I'm fine,' he says. It would be comforting to know that Kate was there, sleeping in the spare room downstairs, protecting him through the long dark night, but she has a family and work and he needs to find some way to cope with this on his own.

He lies awake in the darkness and thinks of her words. 'I hope you got fucked to your heart's delight.' What would that be like? Is that what Kate experiences, when Chris and she make love? He can't imagine it. Holly once told him that, through it all, Steve and she consoled each other with sex. He thinks maybe Holly would know what it feels like to be fucked to her heart's delight. Then he thinks of Carol and Pete, and of Lucy in the confessional, and sex seems as mysterious and elusive as God, and his capacity for both has been destroyed by the cardinal – or maybe even before that, by the priest in the confessional whose breath smelled like the sulphurous fires of hell.

TWENTY NINE

WEDNESDAY OF HOLY WEEK

In the morning he ignores the Missal on the bedside table. He takes his coffee into the study and does something he never does – he switches on the television to watch the morning news.

The newsreader's name is Catherine Redfern. She has sleek black hair and a heart-shaped face. Her good looks and robust interviewing technique have made her a national celebrity. He wonders why they never choose overweight middle-aged women to read the news.

Police in Westonville are continuing to search for a serial murderer, after the discovery of yet another woman's body in the city in the early hours of Saturday morning. All those killed so far are believed to have been working in the sex trade, but this latest victim, Aggie Watson, was a first year psychology student at Westonville University. Her friends say she was a devout Catholic who rarely went out, though it's understood she had been to a bar popular with students in the city's Red Light district of Saint Peter's on Saturday night. The bar next to where her body was found is popular with Westonville's gay community, though police have not said whether or not she had been into the Queen's Arms that evening. Police believe she was walking home alone when she

was attacked, and her killer may have mistaken her
for a sex worker. Earlier today, Aggie's parents made
an emotional appeal at a press conference.

The screen changes to a table with a couple who are perhaps in their forties, sitting beside Frank Lambert. The woman is leaning her head on the man's shoulder, eyes averted from the cameras. She has a small gold crucifix around her neck.

The man's eyes are glazed with shock, and his voice is low and hoarse with the effort of speaking. 'Aggie was the most beautiful daughter any parent could hope for,' he says. 'We were so proud of her when she got a place at Westonville University. She was so full of life. She was so kind and gentle.' He shakes his head and crams his fist against his mouth. 'Sorry,' he mumbles.

His wife raises her head and looks straight into the camera. 'No other family must ever suffer what we're suffering,' she says, her voice thick with tears but fierce and determined. 'If you are watching this and you know anything, anything at all, which might help the police, I beg you, help us to find the man who killed our little girl before he strikes again. If Aggie's death helps to find her killer, if her death saves even one other life, then she won't have died in vain. Please, please help us.' She too chokes into silence.

The camera switches to Frank. 'Somebody out there knows who is doing this,' he says. 'There must be a partner, a friend, a flatmate, somebody, who knows. If you suspect anything at all, however irrelevant it seems, please come forward.' He seems to be looking directly at John. 'And if the killer is watching this, then please give yourself up. We will find you, and we will bring you to justice.'

The newsreader comes back on.

Police say that the murderer is somebody with a
deep understanding of the Roman Catholic Church,

though they are not ruling out the possibility of Satanic rituals of the kind that imitate the Catholic Mass. All the killings have taken place on Fridays during Lent. The first victim, Nan McDonald, was killed two days after Ash Wednesday. The second victim, Sissy Jackson, was killed the following Friday. Both women had been tortured in ways that involved Catholic symbols and rituals, though police are not releasing any further details. Ana Milkovic's badly burned body was found a few days after her murder, but she too was killed on a Friday night, the second Friday of Lent. The two still unidentified females whose bodies were found outside Saints Felicity and Perpetua Church in Westonville are believed to have been killed a week apart, both on Friday nights. The parish priest, Father James Forrester, was arrested, but he was released when Aggie's body was found. She was murdered while he was in prison, so he could not have been the killer. That is one murdered woman on every Friday of Lent. This is Holy Week, when Catholics around the world prepare for the holiest time in their faith. But there is only one question in the minds of us all this week, whatever our religious beliefs. Will the killer strike again this Friday, Good Friday, the day when Christians celebrate the crucifixion of Jesus Christ?

The word 'celebrate' seems bizarre to John. Is that what the Church is doing – celebrating torture and killing? He tries to concentrate on the television.

'With me in the studio to discuss the killings is Detective Chief Superintendent Frank Lambert. Good morning, DCS Lambert,' says the glamorous Catherine.

'Good morning Catherine,' says Frank.

'DCS Lambert, people are asking why the police haven't tracked down this killer yet. It's now Tuesday. If this is a pattern, then another woman will die on Friday unless you find him. Why is it taking so long?'

Frank clears his throat. 'We are investigating every possible lead, but whoever is doing this is very, very clever at covering his tracks. That's why we are appealing to the public to come forward with any clues or suspicions. In the meantime, we're also appealing to women not to go out alone after dark, and to make sure they are vigilant with regard to their personal safety.'

'Some would ask why you're putting all the onus on women? If this is the work of a Catholic priest, as people seem to think, wouldn't it be easier just to keep track of all the priests in the area? There can't be that many, surely.'

'We have no evidence that it's the work of a priest, but obviously the Catholic Church is cooperating with us fully in our enquiries. We're in daily contact with the bishop, and we're also interviewing all priests in the area.'

'You are a Roman Catholic, aren't you detective?'

'I don't see what that's got to do with it.' It's one of the rare occasions when John has heard Frank sounding defensive in an interview.

'Some are saying that it might cloud your judgement, that you might be reluctant to probe too deeply,' says Catherine.

'Let me tell you this. Yes, I'm a Catholic, but I'm first and foremost a member of the police force with a duty to protect the public. I'm using all the inside knowledge I have of the Catholic faith to help our enquiries, and there is nothing that would deter me from going as far as I have to go to catch whoever is doing this.'

Catherine raises her eyebrows and gives him a smile that turns her pretty face into a mask of contempt. 'That's all very well, but we only have your word for it, and the public have good reason to mistrust the Catholic Church.'

Frank straightens in his chair and outstares her. 'Do you know why I'm in the police force, Catherine?'

'No, but time is limited so please keep it short,' she says.

'My little brother disappeared when I was fourteen and he was ten. The police never found him. It destroyed my parents. My mother started drinking, and my father withdrew completely into his shell.'

John turns up the volume. He vaguely remembers Frank making some reference to his family.

'When I left school,' says Frank, 'I joined the police because I wanted to do something. If I couldn't find my own brother, I would find other missing children, I would hunt down the murderers and rapists and kidnappers and paedophiles. I would protect the innocent, whatever it took.' Frank's voice is cold, and suddenly John realizes that his apparent coldness might be a defence against unbearable mental anguish. 'I persuaded them to reopen the case of my brother's disappearance. I went over every clue. I investigated every lead. Eventually I found the person who killed my brother.'

There's a long pause. Catherine seems to have forgotten the need to keep to her schedule. The camera closes in on Frank's face, unmasking a moment of grief that should never be broadcast to the nation.

Frank's voice trembles only for a moment, and then that cold composure returns. 'It was my mother,' he says flatly. 'It had been a terrible accident. My father had helped her to dispose of the body. She had been drinking – I discovered that her drink problem had started long before my brother died, though she had been good at hiding it.' He shifts in his seat, and his shoulders hunch up, his body language betraying his distress despite the mask of officialdom that has once more settled over his features. 'She was reversing the car out of the driveway one night. She'd had a row with my father. My brother was walking home from a football game with his friends. He had just turned into the driveway.

368

She didn't see him. She hit him with the car, and he died. It's a long story, but my father helped her to get rid of the evidence and to bury my brother's body. She was drunk. They were totally dependent on each other, and neither of them could bear the thought of her going to prison. It would have been a double loss for my father. Their grief was real, but the guilt destroyed them.' Another pause, then he fixes Catherine with his gaze. 'They were both arrested and sent to prison as a result of my investigations.' There's a long pause, then Frank leans back and sinks into his chair. 'I think the public can trust my dedication to my job, which comes before every other loyalty and responsibility,' he says.

His voice is harsh, his face chiselled out of stone. John can see from her moist-lipped, muffled excitement that Catherine knows this interview will go viral. She has a major scoop. Perhaps her loyalty to her job comes before anything else too.

He switches off the television and the silence hums around him. He thought his capacity for shock had been exhausted, but he is stunned by Frank's revelation. He wonders why Frank has never said anything before, but why would he?

From her frame on the wall, the Madonna gazes down with pity in her eyes, and the infant in her arms looks fearfully behind him at an angel holding a cross.

'What would you do?' he asks. Her sad smile seems sadder still.

He picks up the crucifix that stands on his desk and fingers the small carved body. He thinks of Luke, and the wood feels silky as skin beneath his fingertips. 'Forgive me,' he whispers. 'Forgive me.'

He goes to hear confessions before the morning Mass, no longer afraid in case the cardinal is there because now he knows that the cardinal will come after Mass, when the church is deserted and they can be alone with their sins and their guilt.

Jack is waiting in the small queue. Jane and Pete are there, and so is Lucy. He is warmed and strengthened by their presences. He thinks it's a sign of trust.

Jack's confession is brief and fraught with embarrassment. He no longer masturbates, but when Edith and he make love he closes his eyes and pretends she's Mary. Didn't our Lord say that to look at another woman with lust was to commit adultery? Isn't this something like that, to be making love to one woman and thinking of his dead wife? He loves Edith, but Mary was the love of his life. He thanks God for Edith and all that she has brought to him, but he can't let go of his love for Mary.

John aches for the purity and innocence of this man, for his plain human goodness. He tells him to say the Lord's prayer, and to thank God for giving him such an abundance of love.

Jane comes in next. She's wearing make-up and she has had her hair cut. She's wearing a dark blue dress that looks new. There is something about her – a determination, an intensity of resolve that John has never seen before. Pete has told her everything, she says. John wonders if everything really is everything, but he doesn't ask. They're going to make a new beginning, starting with confession.

For the first time that he can remember, Jane doesn't cry as she confesses her anxiety about the baby, the times she wished the baby would die, the knowledge that she might wish that again many times, but the fervent hope that the baby will live and that she will be given the strength to cope with whatever the future brings. For her penance, John asks her to pray the *Salve Regina*.

Pete is next in, light and full of that joy which comes with the unburdening of secrets and shame. He has indeed told Jane everything. She knows about his visits to prostitutes. They will get through this, he says, he knows they will. He knows there will be difficult times ahead, but they love each other and that's all that matters. He wants God to know and forgive everything – the visits to prostitutes, the misery and frustration, his lack of trust in God.

'You see Father John, I never really believed that things could or would get better. I thought – when I lost my job, and then started going to prostitutes, and Jane was always tired and irritated with me and the children, I just thought my life had ended.' There's a spark of excitement about him, like a little child. 'And Father, I was wrong. I should have trusted God. I got a phone call this morning, offering me a job. I had the interview last week, but with all the worry about the baby I wasn't really thinking much about it. It's a good job, as a manager in a photocopy shop on the high street. It will bring in more money, which I think we'll need to care for baby John. God is good, John. God has been good to us. Why did I ever doubt Him?'

He is expecting Lucy next, but he was wrong. It's Luke. He feels his face flushing and warmth floods through his body. Luke reaches out his hand. John hesitates, then he takes Luke's hand and squeezes it.

Luke sits down and caresses John's face with his eyes. 'I'm in love with you John. I can't stop thinking about you. I can't think of anybody else. I haven't been with anybody else. All through Lent, since I came to confession on Ash Wednesday, I've been faithful to you, to my love for you John.'

John is a priest. He must think and speak and react as a priest. This is the confessional. 'These are not sins, Luke. In fact, they are graces and virtues.'

Luke gives him an odd look, and then continues. 'I fuck you day and night John. I do it when I'm standing in the queue in Starbucks waiting for a coffee, when I'm sitting at my desk, when I'm walking down the street. In bed at night I masturbate and I undress you and I know every orifice of your body. I know what you feel like and smell like and look like when you come. I've imagined you a million times like that.' He swallows and licks his lips, in a gesture that hovers between anxiety and eroticism. 'I know the tightness of your arse and the softness inside your mouth and the feel of your prick in my mouth and the weight of your balls in the palm of my hand.'

John feels the quickening of his own breath and the deep flush of desire spreading through him. His priesthood is receding into the distance. In the small space of the confessional there's nothing but yearning and a tumbling towards that beloved in the void of an impossible love.

And then Luke suddenly backs off. 'That's my confession, John. I am fucking my parish priest with my imagination every minute of every day. And I'm sorry, not because I'm offending God, but because in some way I think I might be offending you. I think I'm violating you, because this is not what you have chosen or consented to – but I can't help myself.'

No, Luke, this is not violation. I know what violation feels like. I have been violated, and it's not like this. This is love, Luke. This is of God. Don't apologise. Please don't apologise. This is the gift I long for. Please keep going. Tell me again. Say it all again. Tell me you love me. Tell me Luke, tell me. Better still, do it. Let's do it. Please Luke. Seduce me. Make it happen. You can if you want to.

John swallows back the unspoken words and closes his eyes. When he trusts himself to speak, he pronounces absolution in the standard formula.

'For your penance, I want – I want you to read the Song of Songs,' he says. He cannot bring himself to meet Luke's eyes, cannot bring himself to wonder at the nature of the penance and his own collusion in the dynamics of arousal and lust.

Lucy is last in. She has that hollow-eyed, sad look about her, a look which makes her seem like a small child, and yet with that deep wisdom that gazes out of the eyes of children.

She sits down and flicks her hair back. She briefly meets his eyes and looks away. 'Me again,' she says.

'You again,' he says, and smiles.

She smiles back, and there's a brief moment of eye contact before she looks away again. 'It's not really about me this time,' she says. 'I mean, I'm not doing anything I can confess about. I'm not having sex or doing drugs or anything,' she says.

He wonders if she knows that her mother and father no longer come to Mass. He suddenly wonders what they would say if they knew she was in here on her own with a man they suspect of being a serial murderer. The thought freezes out the lingering warmth of Luke's presence.

'So what brings you here?' he asks, trying to sound normal.

'That girl who was murdered – Aggie,' she says. 'I knew her.' She chews her lip and looks down at her feet. 'When I went to have the abortion, she was there. I – I didn't speak to her, but I recognised her in the photograph in the paper this morning. I don't know if she told anybody, but she also had an abortion. I just – I thought I should tell somebody.'

John feels a dark sense of foreboding. 'You should tell Frank Lambert, Lucy. He's in the parish. You can trust him. It might not mean anything, but it means there was a boyfriend or at least a man she'd had sex with out there. They need to find out who the father was and interview him.'

She shakes her head vehemently. 'I can't. I mean, first of all, I'd have to tell him why I was there, in the abortion clinic. But also ...' She pauses and nibbles at the corner of her fingernail, then she folds her hands in her lap and he senses the effort it takes to look him full in the face. 'I don't want to betray her. I don't want to upset her parents. The news is saying she was a good Catholic girl, and her parents, they're Catholics too.'

'So why tell me Lucy? This isn't really a confession you know. What you're telling me isn't about anything you've done wrong.'

'I know that. I just – I know I can trust you. I know that if I tell you something in the confessional, you won't tell anybody else. I know that whatever I say in here is secret. I wanted to tell somebody, and you were the only person I could think of.' She looks him full in the face, her expression stripped of all guile and evasiveness. It is the pure, open-eyed gaze of a person with nothing to hide.

He feels helpless in the face of Lucy's trust and the burden it puts upon him. Enough, dear God, enough. I'm only a man. How much more of this can I carry before I break?

'Lucy, I swear to you that I would never break the seal of the confessional, not for anything, but if you give me permission, I can mention this without having to reveal who told me.'

She shakes her head again, more vigorously still. 'No. You mustn't Father. You mustn't tell anybody. She wanted everybody to think she was a good Catholic girl. Please, let her parents keep believing that.'

'Lucy, good Catholic girls sometimes have abortions. It doesn't make you any less good or any less Catholic. After all, you're a good Catholic girl,' he says.

'No I'm not!' He is surprised by the passion in her voice.

'You're one of the best, Lucy. One of the very best.'

She looks stunned. Tears slide down her cheeks. He lets himself reach out and stroke the hair from the side of her face. Her skin is soft beneath his touch. It makes him think of the wooden crucifix on his desk. He hands her a tissue.

She blows her nose and sniffs, then she gives a small, sweet laugh. 'How's your love life?' she asks.

'Non-existent,' he says. 'A bit like yours.' He wonders how much she heard of what Luke was saying. The confessional isn't sound-proof. Parishioners simply rely on the discretion of others not to sit too close to the door.

'Life is simpler that way,' she says with resignation. He wishes that were true.

He says Mass for the diminished congregation, and then he goes back to the presbytery to sit and watch the hands of the kitchen clock creep towards midday. He is expecting the message, but it still startles him when his phone pings. 'I'm in the confessional.'

He puts the stole around his shoulders and, as he approaches the confessional, he thinks he could yank open the door on the other side and confront the man. He wonders why he didn't just contact Frank and tell him to be here. Frank could be hiding inside the confessional, waiting to arrest him. Or would the cardinal evaporate into sulphur and smoke as Frank reached out to touch him?

John pauses. He stands outside the penitent's door and tries to summon up the courage to open it. Then some inescapable sense of duty makes him take his place on his own side. He too has an overriding responsibility to the job he has chosen. Like Frank Lambert. Like Catherine Redfern. But did he choose it, or was he chosen?

There's a sigh from the other side, and the lace curtain over the grille shivers in the man's breath. 'Where were you yesterday, Father John? Why did you ignore my message?'

'I fell asleep. I didn't hear the phone.'

'We have a lot to talk about this week if we're going to keep to schedule. I advise you not to miss another confession, Father John. A woman's life depends upon your cooperation.' He pauses to let his words sink in. John says nothing. Eventually he says, 'So, where were we? I hope you're ready for the next gripping instalment, Father John.'

John decides to take refuge in the rite and not deviate from it for a single moment, whatever the cardinal says. 'In the name of the Father, and of the Son, and of the Holy Spirit. May the Lord be in your heart and help you to confess your sins with true sorrow.'

'Sorrow? Maybe. Let's see if the Lord comes to help me and make me sorry, shall we?'

John ignores him and perseveres with the words of the rite. 'In your own time, you may unburden your heart, knowing that the Lord is rich in mercy and slow to anger.'

The cardinal's voice oozes through the grille. 'What keeps you from going to the police, Father John? The seal of the confessional, or the shame of being found out?'

John feels his confidence draining away, but he tries to sound firm. 'This is the confessional. It's not about me. It's about you.'

'Oh yes, of course. Thank you for reminding me. I'm sorry that my confessions are so complicated Father. It must be much easier when it's a pretty little blonde like Lucy. Though you're not into girls, are you?'

'How do you know Lucy?' The sound of her name on this man's lips fills John with dread. The words are out before he can stop them.

'You need to soundproof the confessional, Father John. You really don't want everybody to know about these good Catholic girls and their abortions. There's so much shamefulness in the world, when you think about it.'

John closes his eyes. The small space around him is beginning to spin out of control. How could the cardinal be listening? Somebody would have seen him. Somebody would have mentioned it, surely? He wasn't in the queue for the confessional, so where was he? How much did he hear? Did he hear what Luke said?

'Anyway, where was I?' comes the voice. The shadow shifts, as if getting into position. 'After you had made it impossible for me to stay in Rome – after you had destroyed my life, John – I went to New York. A cardinal in the American church found me a job with a hedge fund company run by a wealthy Catholic Republican who made generous donations to the Church. I decided that I'd given my all to God and he had rejected me, so why not try Mammon instead? We had a suite of offices high up in the North Tower, overlooking New York.' There's a brief silence. He sighs. 'It was a beautiful morning, John. There's nowhere quite like New York when it wakes up beneath a blue sky and the skyscrapers seem brushed by angels' wings. Oh, it was a miracle. It was truly written in my destiny, that morning.' Again, there's a silence. John resists the urge to scream or to take flight.

'You see, it was the first time John,' says the voice, smooth as satin. 'The first time I ever knew what it was like to kill another human being. Of course, it wasn't about sex. I've never wanted a woman's body in that way. All those folds of flesh. The slime and the smell. The formless ugliness of it. I can think of nothing more repulsive.' Silence. Nausea. Horror. John waits. He has no choice. He can't move. Eventually, the voice comes again.

'For me it was always about justice. It was always about retribution. It was always about salvation. I bring women to Jesus, John. I send them to their graves absolved, their sinful lives forgiven. I hear their confessions. I give them communion. They go to their deaths crying out to Jesus to help them. How can He resist such anguished cries? How can He ignore the crucified? It's beautiful, John. That's what I discovered that morning. The beauty of sacrifice.'

John's flesh is crawling, as if maggots are burrowing under his skin. He waits in silence. He waits, and he waits, and his dread of hearing more is not quite as excruciating as his desire to hear everything.

'That morning, I passed a whore lurking near the World Trade Centre, soliciting men on their way to work. It was a moment of inspiration, John. It was a miracle. Later, I would realize it was the moment when I began to truly believe in God, and everything until that moment had been play-acting.

'Before then, I had paid women to let me abuse them. I needed to vent my anger, and they needed the money. I needed to have a woman in front of me, to see the expression on her face, and to hurt her until I felt better. Some of them enjoyed it. They liked being hurt. But then there was no pleasure in it for me. I needed them to be terrified. I needed them to beg me to stop.' He sighs again, a sigh of deep satisfaction. There's a long pause, as if he is savouring the memory. Eventually be speaks, and his voice slithers and coils around John.

'I was hurrying to get to the office for a meeting,' he says. 'There wasn't time to take that hooker to a hotel, to negotiate, to persuade her to pretend to be my mother and to let me hurt her and to keep telling me she was sorry. I'll tell you about my mother tomorrow, by the way. Then you'll understand.

'We walked a couple of blocks and went into an alley. I put my hands around her neck and began to squeeze, and I spat in her face and said all the things I wanted to say to my mother.' His tone darkens, but when he speaks again he has composed himself. 'She thought I was going to kill her. She was choking. She began to ask Jesus to help her. She was babbling. "Sorry Jesus. Jesus help me. Holy Mary." She was a Catholic, just like my mother had been. She had a gold crucifix around her neck.'

John sees the shadowy movement behind the grille, and he thinks a smile might have spread across the featureless shape of the face. He hears that smile in the man's voice when he begins to speak again. 'Normally, I would have stopped then. She had given me what I needed to get on with the day. But suddenly, the heavens came crashing down. The noise. The panic. The confusion. The screams and the explosions and the terror of it all. It was the apocalypse. But all I could see was that face turning red, and that little gold Jesus on his cross, and I squeezed and squeezed in the thunder and the fire and the smoke, and I was in hell and I was in ecstasy. To see the face of God and live. John, I wish every priest could have that moment of pure and perfect union with God.'

Silence. What now? There are no words left for John to use. All language has been incinerated. Only the cardinal retains the mastery of words.

'That whore was dying as the most penitent of sinners and the greatest of saints,' he says. 'She was like Mary Magdalene and all those women martyrs, though she was no virgin. I was sending her to glory, John, even as I was consigning myself to hell. And that makes me greater than Christ, because I will not rise again on the third day, I will not take my place at the right hand of the Father. I have sacrificed my eternal soul to bring sinners to God. I am the Messiah, the true Messiah. I have become sin, John. I give not just my mortal life but my eternal life for the life of the world.'

'You're mad. You're mad,' says John. But this is not madness speaking. This is the most ruthless and rational sanity, isn't it? This is theology at its most pure and its most terrifying, unflinching in the face of its darkest claims. John buries his face in his hands. 'Go away. Please go away.'

'If I go away now, Father, you will not have heard my confession. Another woman will die, and all because you refused to look your faith in the face and see it for what it is – a faith that sees torture and murder as a price worth paying for eternal life. Now, shall I continue?'

John rides out the silence because he has no choice. He has read that sometimes, when anaesthetics fail, people remain conscious throughout but their muscles no longer function. They can't cry out or tell anybody that they are in agony. That is how he feels.

'Good. I shall take your silence as a yes,' says the voice eventually. 'When I knew she was dead, I walked away and left her there in the chaos, and I stopped to marvel at what I saw. They all did, you know John. Who wouldn't stop to watch the greatest plane crash in history? People queue up to see such things. They pay to watch such disasters in the cinema, but now Hollywood had entered the real world, and deep down they had all hoped for this. This was the real thing. Beyond all the boring artifice they had manufactured to cocoon themselves from reality, the real had come crashing in and made life interesting again, and it was all for free, and life would never be boring again. Oh, how they stopped and stared and filmed and gawped.' Again, John hears a smile filtering through the words, as if the cardinal is enjoying the reminiscences. Which of course he is. John raises his hands to his face, because he suddenly feels as if his spine might collapse and his head might topple off his neck if he doesn't hold it secure.

'I walked away,' says the voice. 'I was one of those declared missing, presumed dead. I had discovered my vocation. It was easy in those days of madness to buy a new identity.'

John drops his hands and forces himself to look at the shape behind the grille. He thinks he sees a glint in the man's eyes, but he is no longer sure what he sees, or what separates the real from the imagined, the living from the dead.

'What's your name?' he asks and is astonished by how calm he sounds.

'Ah John, do you really think I'd tell you that? You can look for me, but you will never find me. I am the One who has no name – like the God of the Old Testament whose name is too holy to utter.'

'You're not holy. You're evil. You're satanic. You – you're the devil incarnate!' The words erupt from John, loud and echoing in the abysmal emptiness.

'Mmm. It's interesting, isn't it John? If Christ came to reconcile all things to God, then he too must be the devil incarnate. Surely, if he assumed within himself the whole human condition, if he redeemed creation from its captivity to sin, he assumed the evil as well as the good, wouldn't you agree?'

'No! No! Go away! Leave me alone.'

'You never were very good at theological debate, John. You always wanted everything to be nice. Gentle Jesus, meek and mild. But think about it John, you and I are the Janus-faced truth of the incarnation. The good priest and the evil priest, united now in an unbreakable bond of sin and redemption, love and death, torment and liberation. This is beautiful in its symmetry and its logic, beyond what even I had planned, now that I think about it.'

John thinks he might vomit. He stands up and reaches out to prop his body against the wall. A cold sweat bathes his face. 'Go. Please go.'

'Really John? Don't you want to hear the rest of my confession?' John can't speak. 'I came prepared John. I prepared myself to confess. You're a priest. You must hear my confession.' John slumps back into the plastic chair and it groans beneath him.

'Good,' says the cardinal. 'I must say John, you look quite beautiful through the grille and this foolish lace curtain. You look like an angel dissolving into mist. I can see why I wanted you. Think of all that might have been if only you had become my lover. What a waste, John. What a waste. So many women would be alive today. I might have been Pope, and you John, you would have been my trusted confidante, the cardinal ever at my side, maybe even the next Pope.' He pauses. Does he really think John is going to say anything? What could he possibly say? He could say, 'I've never had any of those ambitions. I've never wanted anything more than to be a good parish priest. This is all I want in life.' That would be true, but his mouth won't fit the shape of the words. He wishes he could pray, but still the impossibility of language engulfs him, so he waits until the cardinal speaks again.

'Yet it was meant to be, John. You were an instrument of God after all, for God had other plans for me. So here's my confession. I confess that I never really believed in God until that day when thunder and lightning came crashing out of the sky, and I knew that God was real. So I'm confessing my lack of faith. That is the sin for which I seek absolution, Father John. I want God to forgive me for not believing in Him and trusting Him to bring me to this moment of revelation, this awe and thunder of the Almighty crashing in upon us both.'

'No. That's not your sin. Your sin is murder. Your sin is blasphemy. Your sins are legion. You must confess your sins to be granted absolution.' He speaks mechanically, the words drifting from him in meaningless syllables.

'But I've already explained. That is my vocation, even if it means I am damned.' The cardinal is speaking with the same calm reason that he might use in a theology seminar. 'What would have happened, John, if Judas had repented on his way to Gethsemane? If he had failed to finish what he started? One must be led by the Spirit, even into evil. The Spirit led Christ into the wilderness, after all, to an encounter with Satan. God must have led Satan into the wilderness too, don't you think? This was Job all over again. God and Satan, making bets, trying to outdo each other.' His tone changes, from serious debate to casual *bonhomie*. 'So here we are John. The four of us living out the old, old story. You are just a plaything, tossed backwards and forwards between Satan and God. Like Job. Like Jesus. Like me.'

'Why me? Why did you choose me?'

'I thought that would be obvious, Father John. You are a good priest. You have absolute faith in the seal of the confessional. You thought you could name me to your confessor and there would be no repercussions. I marvelled at your naïvety and your trust John, but I hated you for all you had destroyed and taken away from me. Then at last I realized that you were my saviour. You had opened the path to my true vocation. And now I have been called back to put you to the test.'

'No! I ...'

The cardinal interrupts him. 'God must love you very much, John. God must trust your faith to put you through this, to call me to this, to invite me to torment you as Satan tormented Job. One day, you will be a saint in glory, and I will be the eternally damned angel of darkness presiding over an empty hell. That is the sacrifice I am called to make, because I love Jesus Christ and give him my all – even my eternal life. I make up the one thing lacking in his suffering – the one thing human beings fear above all else, that he never shared. Eternal damnation.'

'He descended into hell.'

'Yes, of course. On Holy Saturday. And then, on Easter Sunday, he rose again. A day or two, Father John. That's all. A person can endure anything for a couple of days if they know they're about to become King of the Universe.'

'There's no time in hell. It was an eternal day.' What does that mean? John has no idea. There is no theology, no spirituality, no prayer, in this cold, dark room. There is no meaning and no time. There is no God. Is this what hell is like?

'So, Father John, will you pronounce absolution?'

'No.'

The man's laughter curdles the space between them. 'If I die unshriven, you will have that on your conscience, Father John.'

'Yes. I know.'

'This is perfect. If I go out now and kill myself, you will have helped me to achieve my vocation. I have watched sinners die in torment, Father John, and every one of them has cried out for God's mercy. But my sin, my sin is the absolute freedom of total despair, and despair is not what you think it is. Despair is an invincible pride in oneself and one's power. Even God has no power to force me back. Even God will abandon me and leave me to my fate. I shall live forever in hell, and in so doing I shall have conquered God. There will be one sinner whom Christ did not redeem, and that will be the undoing of all His work.'

'Hell isn't like that. Hell is separation from God,' whispers John, knowing that he himself is in hell. He knows what hell is like. It is this separation from all that ever gave meaning and hope to the world.

The cardinal laughs again, that terrible laugh. 'And heaven will never be heaven, as long as there is one single soul in hell to trouble the conscience of God, to make Christ's work a failure. One single soul eternally separated from God, and all Christ's work is undone,' he says.

'Please, go now.' John is too desperate to care if the man hears the pleading in his voice.

'Don't you want to forgive me before I go, Father John? Do you really want me to leave here in the triumph of knowing that my sin is greater than God's mercy?'

'I don't believe this is a sincere confession. I don't believe you're sorry.'

'I am sorry, John, I am truly sorry for the wasted years, when I misunderstood my vocation. I am sorry for the gay saunas and the sex and the little boys – you know all about those. You were there. But God has delivered me from those sins and temptations. Now I am pure and righteous. I am at last able to honour my vow of celibacy.'

'I – I can absolve you of those sins, if you repent,' John says, clutching at any faint glimmer of escape.

'No need. I confessed them long ago. I was truly sorry. I was washed whiter than snow, as you were when you made your confession all those years ago.'

Dear Jesus, help me. Give me the words. John raises his right hand towards the figure on the other side of the grille.

'For all that is truly penitent and unconfessed in your heart and soul, I absolve you in the name of the Father, and of the Son, and of the Holy Spirit. I pray that you will have the grace to return to the God of all mercy and love, and to seek redemption through the cross and suffering of his Son, Jesus Christ. Amen.'

The shadow looms through the curtained grille as the cardinal stands up. 'By the way, John, I hope you read that newspaper article I left for you. Your Italian is probably a bit rusty by now, but I'm sure you got the gist of it. Some of the boys in that sauna were trafficked. Those young Iraqis and Afghans, twelve and thirteen years old, they have the most perfect bodies. I must admit I miss them sometimes. I wonder what your parishioners would say, if they knew.'

John can take no more. 'Please,' he sobs, 'please, leave me alone. I didn't know.'

'John, you were there. That's enough to condemn you. But please, don't worry. So long as you honour the secret of the confessional, I too shall honour your secrets. I won't tell if you don't tell.'

'I didn't know. You can't be condemned if you were in a state of ignorance.'

But the cardinal has gone. Out into the cold and the empty church. John hears the heavy wooden door clunking shut, and the silence is as dense and choking as the grave. He pulls open the door and blunders out of the confessional and into the presbytery, locking the door behind him. He tugs the stole from his shoulders and drops it on the floor.

He will do the penance he knows he must do. Father Martin says he did no wrong. He was the victim, not the perpetrator, but John knows it's not that simple. The cardinal was right. He confessed to salve his own conscience, to spare himself the shame of facing up to what he had done. He was too quick to forget, too quick to forgive himself. Now he must pay the price. Now he must do what he should have done all those years ago. He must face the shame and humiliation of his sin.

He phones Holly. 'Are you free? Can I come and see you?'

'I have to see a student, then I'll be heading home. Come for tea. I should be back about five-ish.'

'It's private Holly. We need to be alone.'

'Steve and the boys are out until later. We won't be interrupted.'

The hours blur and melt into one another. Eventually, it's time. He walks from the presbytery to Holly's house. She holds him close and ushers him into her warm living room with its rich colours and lingering smells of incense and perfume and the vapes she uses instead of cigarettes when she smokes indoors. He feels as if he is about to destroy one of his life's most precious gifts, the only one that remains after the loss of Kate's children. They will never, ever be allowed to see him again when the story gets out. Then he thinks of Luke, and he knows that there will still be one last sacrifice, one last confession that will leave him forever alone.

'Tea, or wine?' she asks.

'Just a glass of water,' he says.

'Bloody hell John. I know it's holy week, but what is this?'

He tries to smile. She leaves the room and comes back carrying a large glass of red wine for herself and a glass of water for him.

'So,' she says, settling herself down in the plump armchair opposite him, 'what's this about?' Her voice is full of warmth and friendly curiosity.

He clears his throat. 'There's – um – there's something you should know about me Holly.' She doesn't say anything, but she looks open and ready to listen. 'When I was in Rome. When I was training to be a priest. I went to a gay club.'

She smiles. 'Is that all?' she says.

'No. That's not all. It was also a male brothel.'

She nods, no longer smiling but still with that look of understanding on her face. 'A brothel's a brothel John, and thousands of men go to brothels.'

'There were young boys there. They were trafficked. I – umm – I abused one of them.'

Her eyes widen, and he sees the colour drain from her face. She winces as if he had struck her. She puts her hand to her throat. 'How old was he?'

'I don't know. It was dark. It was in a sauna.'

'So how did you know it was a child?'

'His body. His body was young.'

'How young?'

'I told you Holly. I don't know. Maybe fourteen or fifteen. Maybe younger.'

There's an abysmal darkness in her eyes, and a rictus of horror has made the tendons in her neck bulge. With great care, she puts her wine glass down on the table beside her.

'Please go, John,' she says, not looking at him. He waits, hoping she will say something to soften the blow, but her voice is harsh and hoarse with shock. 'Go now. I need – I need time to think.' She covers her face with her hands. 'Go,' she says again.

He gets up and walks out of that room where he has experienced the loveliest friendship of his life, and he feels that at last he is paying the price for what he did. He can never give back to those trafficked children what was stolen from them, but if there's some eternal reckoning, some scales of justice in which the guilt and sorrow of the world are being weighed, then he can at least help to balance the two. His sorrow must become as great as his guilt.

He leaves, and he walks the streets of the city until it's time for the next act of penance. As night falls and the milk of the full moon spills over the city, he weaves through the backstreets to Saint Peter's, to where he thinks Babbs might be. There's nobody there.

He goes to where homeless people gather on the steps of a derelict building. Ben is there as he had hoped he would be, huddled over a bottle of cider with his companions of the streets. John is wearing his anorak over an open-necked shirt, with no dog collar. Ben's friends eye him warily. Maybe they think he's a plain clothes policeman.

'Father John!' Ben tries and fails to get to his feet. 'Bless my soul. Look everybody. This is my priest. This is my guardian angel. This man is a saint, I tell you, a saint.'

A stout woman peers at him from beneath a tangle of yellow hair streaked with brown. 'Is he one of those paedo priests?' she says. 'How do you know he's not the fuckin' murderer? Jeez, Ben, what the fuck are you bringing these pervs here for?'

'He's not a perv, you stupid cow. He's Father John. I told you. He's a saint,' says Ben, slurring.

'Ben, I'm actually looking for Babbs,' says John. 'Do you know where he is?'

'Fuck!' screeches the blonde. 'You lay a finger on Babbs and she'll cut your fucking dick off and feed it to you for dinner with your balls for pudding, you pervy bastard,' she says.

'Hush, Cathy, don't you dare speak to Father John like that. I'm sorry Father. She doesn't mean it. She doesn't know you.

We're all a bit on edge, that's the problem.' Ben has managed to get to his feet, and he sways unsteadily as he turns to the woman. 'Father is Babbs's friend. He's been watching out for her. She knows he's a saint.' He turns back to John. 'She should be in her usual place,' he says, 'on the corner of Willow Lane.'

'She's not there, I've already looked,' says John.

'How come your saint priest is out here looking for his favourite whore?' says the blonde. 'Is he one of her regulars?'

'I'm gay,' John says. 'And I'm celibate.'

'You're wot?' she says.

'Celibate. It means I don't have sex.'

'You don't even wank?' He's glad that before he can reply, she rattles on. 'But I wasn't talking about that, darling. I know what celibate is. I'm celibate too now, though I used to be like Babbs, and I still like the occasional shag but it doesn't count because most of the time I'm like you. It was a rhetorical question though. You said you're gay. I said, "You're wot?" cos I was a bit surprised. Not by you being queer – I mean, excuse me for my honesty Father, but I could tell that a mile off. It's just priests don't usually say things like that. They usually say queers'll burn in hell, even though some of them hang out down the Queen's Arms. We all know that. But they would never meet you in the street and say, "I'm gay" like you did. So I was surprised. That's why I said, "You're wot?" Like I say, it was a rhetorical question.' She drags on her cigarette and swigs from the bottle of red wine she's holding.

Ben shrugs. 'Sorry about that, Father.' He looks embarrassed.

'That's alright Ben. I just – I wanted to see Babbs, and I wondered where she might be.'

'As far as I know, she's in her usual place. She doesn't move around, because her regulars know where to find her. She's probably with a punter. She'll be back soon.'

John thanks him and heads back through the lanes to Babbs's corner. There's hardly anybody around. The place has a desolate feel to it. The murders have cast a dark shadow over the city. He decides to wait, hoping she will turn up, praying for her to be alright.

Eventually, a car slows down and is about to stop, when it revs away and disappears around the next corner. A few minutes later, Babbs comes teetering up in her short skirt with her ridiculous platform shoes. 'Jesus, John, what the fuck are you doing?' she says.

'Nice to see you too, Babbs,' he says, smiling because he is so relieved to see her.

'You terrified the life out of my punter. Jesus. He thought you were a policeman. I told him you were just one of my regulars, but you mustn't do that, you bloody idiot. Hanging around my pitch for all the world to see. Are you crazy? There are journalists and pigs everywhere. You'll have that stupid mug of yours all over the papers again if you're not careful.' Her tone has gradually changed from anger to affection. She pulls down her skirt and wrinkles her nose. 'Sorry if I stink. He was a smelly bastard, that one. The condom helps a bit, but I can still smell him on me.'

'You're fine Babbs. You're beautiful. I'm so glad to see you.'

She gives him her red, gap-toothed smile. 'You're an idiot, Father John.'

'I need to talk to you. Shall we go to MacDonalds again?'

'You know, I really do think you are the craziest man I've ever met. You want to go and sit in a place like that with an old slag, when every policeman and journalist in the city is crawling the streets, looking for bait? Imagine what the papers will say. You're lucky you got away with it last time, Father. I tell you, my lover, you have to be more careful.'

'I'm not the murderer Babbs. So what if they see me? Why should I hide away like a criminal?'

'Because people talk, Father. Because you're a priest and I'm a hooker. Because they've already put your picture in their

389

rotten papers once. Anyway, I've got work to do. Nice to see you Father, but you need to go now.'

'Please go home Babbs.'

'Are you kidding?'

'How much do you need? How much would you need to stay off the streets for the rest of the week, until the weekend?'

She rummages in her bag and takes out a packet of wipes. 'Sorry about this Father, but the smell is driving me mad.' She fumbles under her skirt and wipes herself, then she takes more wipes and rubs them over her hands and face. She tosses them over the low garden wall next to where they're standing, into a garden full of weeds and rubble. She lights a cigarette and he sees that her hand is shaking. He waits. Eventually she looks him up and down as if calculating what he's worth.

'Ben and me, we think you're a saint Father. If every priest was like you, we'd all be fucking Catholics, I tell you that. I might come to Mass in your church some time, for old times' sake. Would you mind?'

'I'd love it Babbs. Please come. Why don't you come tomorrow night? It's Holy Thursday. The priest washes the people's feet on Holy Thursday. Would you let me wash your feet? It would be such an honour Babbs.'

'Are you serious? Father, I've probably fucked half the men in your parish. I'd love to see their faces!' John thinks of Pete, and the pavement tilts beneath his feet. 'But no, of course I'm not gonna let you wash my bleedin' feet,' says Babbs. 'For fuck's sake, Father. There are limits to all this Mary Magdalene stuff.'

John feels inordinately disappointed. He nods and says, 'Back to the question. How much would you need to – to take a few days off. To have some leave. Go and visit somebody. Family? Children? Do you have children Babbs?'

Her face darkens and she blinks. 'I have three,' she says. 'Bradley was taken away from me ten years ago, when he was five. My little girls were taken away when they were born.

Jacintha will be nine now, and Hayley will be seven. I don't know where they are. Fucking social workers!' Her voice cracks and she grinds her fist against her eyes, smearing mascara over her face. 'I had abortions with the other pregnancies. I wasn't gonna carry my precious babies for nine months to give them to the state. That's what they want, you know. They want women like me to have abortions. It's cheaper and easier. That's why they've put that new clinic here. It's called eugenics Father. I'm not as stupid as I look. They want to kill our babies to keep the world safe for their nice middle class brats.'

John thinks of Lucy in the confessional. 'I don't think it's like that Babbs. I think it's because men still regard women as commodities. They don't take responsibility. They want sex without consequences. Isn't that why they come to women like you?'

She drags on her cigarette and peers at him through smudges of black. 'I'd have loved to get married Father. I did once. I was married to Bradley's dad. He used to beat me up. By then, I was already on the drugs. I told you, that started way back, when my uncle groomed me.' She grinds her cigarette out under her heel. 'Three hundred quid, in answer to your question,' she says.

'Three hundred pounds? And you would go away somewhere until the end of the week?'

'I could stay off the streets for a few days, if I had that much money. That's how much I need to keep me going – you know, to buy the stuff I need to make life bearable.'

John doesn't have three hundred pounds. He never has more than he needs for a week at a time in his bank account. It's a personal discipline he decided upon – to have only what he needs and give the rest away. But he has already planned what to do.

'Babbs, if I bring you three hundred pounds, will you promise me that you'll go away somewhere for a few days?'

She shrugs. 'Yeah, if that's what you want, though I think you're totally mad, Father John.'

'It is what I want, Babbs.' He looks around, feeling helpless. 'I need to go somewhere. I won't be long, but I don't want to leave you out here. Can I bring the money to your house? Where do you live?'

She snorts. 'My house? They call it a studio flat – social housing, they call it. It's up there,' she says, pointing back along Willow Lane. 'It's flat 6, 25 Burnley Road.'

He takes out his mobile phone and taps in the address. 'Go there now Babbs. Wait for me. I'll come with the money.'

She throws her arms around his neck and plants a kiss on his cheek. 'Father John, you are the craziest fucking priest I ever met.' She drops her arms. 'Okay. I need a shower anyway. I'll go home and have a shower. You come with the money when you're ready. I would offer you something in return, but you don't do women. I suppose you don't do men either, being a priest. Jesus, I thought they'd stopped making men like you.'

He watches her totter away, then he turns and heads towards the Queen's Arms, praying that Luke will be there.

His prayers are answered. Luke is sitting on his own in a booth with padded red velvet seats and ornate gold mouldings around it. He looks troubled – eyes downcast, face solemn, fiddling with the stem of his wineglass. There's a bottle of wine on the table.

John allows himself a moment of gazing at that face, knowing that again he is about to destroy something that he will never be able to repair. 'Hello Luke.'

Luke looks up, and the radiance of his smile makes John want to weep. Who could doubt that Luke loves him? He slides into the booth to sit opposite Luke.

'John! I was just thinking about you. I'm so sorry – about the picture in the paper, and all the gossip. It must be awful for you.'

'I'm okay, Luke. It's good to see you.' Luke offers his hand across the table and John gives it a brief squeeze.

'Let me get you a glass and pour you a drink,' says Luke.

'No. I'm not stopping. At least, I need to go somewhere and come back.' Now comes the hard part, the very hardest part. He wonders if he can do it. 'Luke, I need you to give me some money.'

'How much?'

'Three hundred pounds.'

'Can I ask what it's for?'

'No, but – but I've been thinking. In exchange, I'll – I'll come and spend the night with you.' The words tumble out.

Luke looks as if John has hit him. He stares in silence, then he says, 'My God, John.' He shakes his head. 'I don't know what to say.' His mouth twists into a cynical smile, bitter and cruel. 'Three hundred pounds to shag a priest. Well I never.'

The words go through John like a knife. 'That's not what I meant,' he says. 'I just – I don't know when I'll be able to pay you back, and I'd be so grateful. I want to show you how grateful I am.'

Luke is looking at him as if he is seeing him for the first time. 'What's wrong with you John? What's come over you?'

'Nothing. I can't tell you Luke. Please trust me.'

Luke stares at him for a long, long time, and John wants to squirm. He tries to hold Luke's gaze, but he has to look away. Eventually, Luke snorts a contemptuous laugh.

'You humiliate us both, John. You revolt me for doing this, and I revolt myself because I'm so desperate to have you at any price that I'm going to say yes. I've no idea what you're playing at, but do you know what you're destroying in me? My faith John. My faith in you, and you were my everything. My Jesus. My saviour. My hope.' He stares into the distance, his lips curled in disgust. Eventually he shuffles out of the booth. 'Wait there. I'll go to the cash machine.'

John watches him go – the neat, lithe shape of him, the men who turn and watch him as he leaves, and he wonders how he can still be living and breathing when the pain is so acute.

Luke comes back a few minutes later, holding a wad of bank notes in his fist. He slides back into his seat and takes more notes out of his wallet. He pushes them across the table. As John reaches out to take them, Luke closes his hand over John's. He squeezes, in a vicious, violent grip that speaks of lust and betrayal and contempt. 'Fuck you John. I hate you for this,' he says.

'I'll be back in half an hour,' John says. 'Thank you Luke. I'm really grateful, and I'm sorry. I'm sorry to humiliate you. I hadn't thought. I wasn't thinking clearly. I was only thinking about myself. I'm sorry.'

Luke waves his hand in the air. 'Just go, John. Don't come back here. Come to my flat. It's not far. I'll text you the address if you tell me your phone number.'

How strange, John thinks. This is the love of his life, and they don't know one another's phone numbers and he has never been to Luke's home. He tells Luke his number and Luke taps the digits into his phone. As John is leaving, he hears the ping of a message. He looks at the address and turns and waves to Luke. His heart is pounding with fear and desire and shame.

He rings Babbs's doorbell and she presses the buzzer to let him in. 'Come on up, lover boy. I'm on the second floor.'

There's a reek of chips and cigarettes in the entrance hall, and a pile of unopened mail. The stair carpet might once have been green. It's littered with dog ends and discarded burger wrappers and paper cups.

He climbs up to the second floor and Babbs opens the door. She is wearing warm blue pyjamas and her hair is wet. Her face is scrubbed clean of make-up. She smells of soap and shampoo. There's something childlike about her. She reminds him of Phoebe.

'Come in, Father. Sorry about the mess. See – I'm not going out again. I've put my pyjamas on.'

In fact, there's very little mess. There are a few dishes piled in the sink in a small kitchen area to one side, and some magazines strewn on the floor by the bed. The room is dominated by the bed, majestic with a black satin cover and an array of purple velvet cushions. There's a heavy smell of perfume, masking the smell of cigarettes and a ripe hormonal smell that for a brief, disconcerting moment reminds John of *La Dolce Vita*. He pushes the thought away. He can't think about that now.

There's an armchair pushed up against the wall, and a small table with two chairs. The carpet is shaggy purple pile. On the wall there are old film posters – Ingrid Bergman and Humphrey Bogart in *Casablanca*, Audrey Hepburn in *Breakfast at Tiffanys*, with a slinky black dress and a long cigarette holder, and Vivien Leigh and Clark Gable in *Gone with the Wind*. The posters move him, with their longing for love and romance in a room where there has perhaps been very little of either.

Then he sees an array of photographs on the wall beside a kitchen cabinet. He goes over and looks at them. 'Is this your son Babbs?'

She saunters over to stand beside him. 'Yeah, that's me and Bradley when he was two and I took him to the seaside. And that's him on his first day at school. They took him away from me the week after. I was trying, Father, I was really trying to stay clean. I didn't want to lose my baby, but that bastard I was living with was beating me up, and one day he hit Bradley, and the school reported him.' She points to two empty frames. 'See those? Those are my other babies. I'm not allowed to have photos of them. I don't know what they look like. Those empty frames are all I have.'

'I'm so sorry Babbs.'

'Yeah. Life's a bitch Father. But I'm okay. At least I have somewhere to live, and I can still draw the punters, even though I'm a smelly old slag.'

'You're beautiful Babbs. You're a precious child of God, and God loves you. Don't ever forget that.'

She nods. 'Yeah, yeah,' she says, then she looks pensive. 'You know, Father John, I often think, Jesus was also a whore, wasn't he? Is it blasphemy to think that?' John shakes his head, wondering what she means. She sighs. 'We working women know what it feels like, to give your body for others. "This is my body, given for you." Jesus, I could say that fifty times a week. I remember the words Father. I never go to Mass, but I remember the words. Sometimes I pray to Mary, because she's still my Mum. My real Mum died. I only heard about that afterwards. She'd been dead for two years when I found out.'

'Babbs, I need to go, but I promise I'll pray for you every day.' He takes the money from the inside pocket of his anorak. 'Here, here's three hundred pounds. Will you promise me you won't go out for the rest of the week? If you'd like to go away somewhere, I can arrange it. Why don't you have an Easter holiday? I know some nuns who live near the seaside in Cornwall. Why don't you go and stay with them? Or even here, in Westonville, I know some nuns you could stay with.'

'Nah. I can't go that long without skank Father. But this will keep me going for a few days. I'll be okay.' She shuffles her feet and looks embarrassed. 'I'm really grateful Father. I wish I could repay you.'

'Look after yourself, Babbs. Stay safe. Try to find a better way to live. That would be all the repayment I'd ever want.'

'Father, will you bless me? I mean, will you ask Jesus and Mary to help me?'

He rests his hand on her head and says a blessing, and he has never felt the power of God as strongly as he does in that moment. Babbs makes the sign of the cross with the easy familiarity of a cradle Catholic. He hugs her and turns to the door, then he goes out into the night.

He looks at the address on his phone. Luke's flat is a few streets away, in one of the old lanes that has recently been renovated. John wants to pull up his anorak hood to hide his face, but he resists. Let the world see his shame. The cardinal was right. He hasn't suffered enough. He hasn't experienced the humiliation of his sin and his guilt. If the journalists are out there watching him, he will give them their story. He is not a murderer, but he has abused a child, visited the house of a prostitute, and is about to spend the night with his lover. He wants the world to know what kind of person he really is.

He rings the bell and Luke presses the buzzer to let him in, just as Babbs did, but there the similarity ends. Even though there are only a few lanes between them, even though they are both in Georgian terraces, Luke's flat belongs in a different universe.

Two houses have been knocked together, and the flat is on the top floor. It's a bright, clean expanse of space, with a large open plan living area and a balcony overlooking the city. Everything is tasteful and coordinated, mellow and discreet. It's a show house, a place which lacks something essential that would make it a home. Babbs's bordello felt more like a home than this. John follows Luke into the room.

'Sit down,' Luke says, gesturing towards a black leather sofa. His voice is cold. The sofa sighs beneath John's weight. Luke goes to the gleaming kitchen area and pours two large glasses of white wine. John doesn't protest, as Luke hands him the frosted glass and sits a little distance away from him on the sofa. He raises his glass to John. 'Cheers,' he says.

'Cheers.'

What now? John's mouth is dry and his hands are clammy. He wonders if he should make the first move. What should he do? Kiss Luke? Undress? What do people do in this kind of situation? He does nothing, glad of the distraction of the wine.

'John, I want you to drink your wine and go home,' Luke says, and his voice is icy cold. 'I wish you had never said what you said. I wish you hadn't reduced what we have to a transaction. I want you more than words can ever begin to say. I want to spend a night with you more than I want anything in the world, but I'm not going to fuck you like some male whore. So I want you to go, and I never want to see you again.'

John wonders if he knew all along that this would be Luke's reaction. Did he make the offer safe in the knowledge that Luke would reject him?

He thinks of walking out of this clean space and through the city streets. He thinks of the presbytery, dark and lonely and cold, with its empty echoing spaces. He thinks of the forbidden, secret imaginings that have swirled through him during the last few hours. He puts down his wine glass and twists to face Luke.

'I want to spend the night with you Luke,' he says. 'That's all I can give you, all I can ever give you. I'll never leave the priesthood. I can't offer you anything other than my promise of lifelong fidelity to this one night with you, but I can offer you that. Please Luke, don't send me away. It's not about money. It's about you. It's about loving you. Those things you told me in the confessional, they weren't violations. I know what violation is, Luke. You made me feel loved and desired. It was a beautiful feeling Luke. I want all that and more for just one night.'

Luke gazes at him for a long time, and it's like watching the clouds dissolve after a thunder storm, and seeing the watery sun breaking through to light up the earth. Luke puts his wine glass down and reaches out to touch John's face with his fingertips. John takes his hand and sucks his fingers. He closes his eyes. This. Just this. It's all he will ever ask, and it's enough.

THIRTY

HOLY THURSDAY

John walks home in the quiet light of dawn. He should go to the Chrism Mass in the cathedral. All the priests in the diocese will be there, and so will Frank and half the police force and hordes of journalists. They will be trying to spot the killer on the altar.

He realizes he cannot face that this morning. His body is still too fresh from the night with Luke. He cannot stand there amidst all his fellow priests and act as if nothing has happened, nothing has changed.

Besides, today might be the cardinal's final confession, and he must be ready to hear it. He is like a moth fluttering around the candle flame, unable to escape the deadly heat of the cardinal's sin.

He phones the bishop's secretary and explains that he is unwell. The secretary is a young conservative priest called Anthony. He sounds disapproving but says he'll pass the message on.

The text comes, as John knew it would, and he makes his way to the confessional. His body still tingles and glows with Luke's caresses, but the anticipation of the cardinal's confession is crowding out every other thought. Already, the magic and mystery of the night are dissolving into unreality. Later, there will be time to remember and reflect, to savour and escape again and again into that sacred space, but first he must get through today and tomorrow.

He mutters a plea for help to a God he does not trust. He glances at the door to the cleaning cupboard next to the confessional, and he has a sudden urge to crawl inside and hide. Then he wonders if that's where the cardinal has been, hiding in that large dark cupboard, listening to people's confessions. It occurs to him how ludicrous it is, to place so much emphasis on the seal of the confessional when any passing stranger can lurk nearby and hear everything that people say. 'Vanity of vanities, says the preacher. All is vanity.' Meaninglessness and vanity. That's all there is. That's all there has ever been. The vanity of the priest who mutters empty words and thinks he can call down the presence of God.

He pushes open the door on his side of the confessional. He sits down and waits for the cardinal to speak. He will not go through the charade of a meaningless rite. The words are empty. They have always been empty. Vanity of vanities.

The silence goes on and on. The shape on the other side of the grille is perfectly still. John's nerves begin to scream, but he will not speak. He will not play the cardinal's game. The shape moves and leans in towards the grille. The confessional is cold. There's that smell, that terrible smell. Pure evil. Waiting. Waiting. He will not speak.

'Blessss me Father. I have ssssinned.'

John resists making the sign of the cross. He will not sanctify this place of desolation. 'Confess your sins,' he says.

The dark thing slithers into position, waiting. Its body is uncoiling, filling John's being. What is its name? It has no name. It is the purity of evil, the void. The silence stretches out, but John is in no hurry. He can wait forever. If this is a genuine confession, then he knows that the cardinal's need to speak is greater than his need to know. That is the nature of a true confession – the patience of the priest, and the irresistible desire of the penitent to tell the truth and seek forgiveness.

Eventually, the voice comes curling through the grille. 'I hated my mother, and that was wrong of me. It took me too long to discover that God was calling me to redeem her. That is a sincere confession of guilt, Father. A confession I have never made before. A sin that has never been forgiven.'

Yes, John knows it is sincere. There's a change in tone, almost tenderness in the cardinal's voice, and genuine regret.

'Carry on,' says John, afraid that if he says the wrong thing he might immediately seal up that first ever opening there has been in their encounters – an opening into something that brings with it the faintest glimmer of hope.

'My mother was a whore, John, and I am redeeming her through the suffering of others.' He stops. John waits, rigid with anxiety because the balance of this moment is so delicate. It could tilt into desolation or redemption, and the future of the universe seems to depend upon which way it goes. If there is a single soul in hell, Christ has failed. He cannot be the redeemer of the cosmos, if there is even one solitary individual outside the universality of that redeeming love. This is what John has feared most. Not his own shame, not even the horrors of the murders, but the possibility that it has all been in vain after all.

The cardinal continues. 'When I was a year old, she put me to sleep in my cot and went out. She thought she'd be back before I woke up. That's what the other whores told the police. She just "popped out" to earn enough for the rent and the groceries.' He stops. The shadow is moving. The cardinal is shaking his head, slowly, with his chin dropped down on his chest. Is he crying? That's not possible. Pure evil doesn't weep. What would it weep for?

Eventually the voice comes again, thick with something that cannot be expressed, crawling through the grille. 'They found her body in a storage unit a week later. A week, John. My mother left me in that cot for a week, crying with hunger and fear, though presumably at some point I would have been too exhausted to cry. I was almost dead when the police broke the door down.' He is whispering.

'She was murdered?' The question is out before John can stop himself.

'Raped and tortured and left to die.'

'It wasn't her fault. She was your mother. She loved you. She would never have knowingly left you.' The words are tumbling out, desperate to reach the man on the other side of the grille, desperate to find some meaning in this.

'She was a whore. She left her baby alone to go out whoring. It was her fault. Or maybe it was God's fault. Suffer the little children.' There's another silence. John's head is reeling. He wants to howl. No, no, no. This cannot be true. A baby. A baby alone for a week, screaming with hunger and thirst and fear. No. No. A woman slowly dying and knowing that her baby is locked in a house alone. No. Please no. These things don't happen. These things can't happen. Dear God.

The cardinal is speaking again. 'I was adopted by a wealthy couple who couldn't have children. They were from an English recusant family, and they brought me up as a devout Catholic. But a baby alone in a cot for a week learns the hatred of the world before it learns anything else. I grew up knowing nothing about my mother's death and the way she abandoned me. I was sixteen when they told me. Some boys would have gone to pieces, but I did the opposite. I decided my vocation was to wage war on sin and impurity and lust. I decided to become a priest. I would avenge myself on women like my mother. I would tell the world about the flames of hell that consume women like her.'

'But you were there, in that club,' says John.

'I was the greatest sinner of them all John. I was driven by lust. No matter what mortifications I imposed on my own flesh, they simply fed the heat of my unquenchable desire. I tried self-flagellation, I fasted, I wore a cilice round my thigh, and the more I hurt my body, the more my body demanded from me. It was as if it had learned the lesson of pain in that week, and that was the only thing it trusted.' He laughs, and that laugh makes

John want to cry out in anguish. 'That's the therapist talking,' says the cardinal. 'I went to a therapist. Nobody can say I didn't try to be healed. Nobody can say I didn't beg God to make me pure. And now, I am pure John. Now I am chaste. I have put to death that abandoned baby inside me that had to keep hurting itself to know it was alive. God has answered my prayers.'

He stops talking. John sits in silence in the rigid plastic chair with the box of tissues beside him and the empty chair in front of him, and the dark malevolent thing inside him fades to nothingness. There is only mourning now. There is only desolation. The sin of the world is not evil but an unquenchable sorrow and yearning.

The shadow grows restless, shuffling on the other side of the grille and eventually continuing with its story. 'When my purification came, it came as a lightning bolt out of a clear blue sky – an apt metaphor, don't you think?' John says nothing. 'That morning in New York was my salvation John. When I left Rome, I began to turn my hatred from myself to my mother. Maybe I had always hated her, but this was different. Now, I wanted to show her how much I hated her. I paid women to indulge me. I made whores pretend to be my mother, to let me hurt them. I never raped them. Dear God, John, that would have been incest. I punished my mother by hurting them, and they went along with it because I paid them well. I was a rich man, John. I still am. It was all controlled, all within boundaries, until that morning in New York when I went all the way, as they say.

'As I watched that woman die, I realized God was showing me what I had to do. She was calling out to Jesus. She was begging for mercy. I wondered if my mother might have done that too, but what if she didn't? Her sin was monstrous, John. She had gone out on the streets filled with lust, and she had left her baby to starve in his cot.'

'She had gone out to get money for food. She was doing it because she loved you. She was poor. She cared about you.' The images in his mind are unbearable. A dying woman crying out to God for the baby she knows is starving in his cot. 'She did it for you,' he says again. 'She loved you.'

'No one may do evil that good might result. It's the first lesson of moral theology, John. I'm surprised you've forgotten.'

'She didn't do evil. Her intention was good. She did what she did because she loved you. She sacrificed herself for you, Michael. She's in heaven praying for you right now.' He wants this man to believe that he was loved. It's more important to him right now than anything else, to convince the cardinal that his mother loved him. John sees, with earth-shattering clarity, that all the evil in the world is the work of wounded souls crying out for healing and love. He sits out the silence and feels the change in mood.

Eventually, the cardinal speaks, and for the first time John hears uncertainty and doubt in his voice. 'Even so, I want to be sure that my mother is in heaven John.' It's the voice of a child, begging John for something but John is not sure what.

'You can be sure of that,' says John. 'Your mother died praying for you, Michael. You know she did.'

There's another silence, as if the cardinal is carefully choosing his words. Is he afraid of betraying himself, afraid of revealing his sudden lack of confidence? When he does speak, some of the self-assurance is back, but it sounds hollow now.

'When the skies fell down that morning in New York, that was my epiphany. At first, I thought it was enough to have killed one woman. A life for a life. I felt sorry for her too, because when she was dying I began to see what my mother might have suffered, and that was what turned my hatred to pity and love. I discovered that I loved my mother after all. I did not want my mother to burn in hell. Maybe that love and pity would have been enough to send me to purgatory rather than hell, a glimmer of goodness that would save me from damnation, but gradually I realized that God was calling me to something greater still.' His voice grows in confidence, as he reminds himself of what he has convinced himself for all these years to be true.

'After that, when I was missing presumed dead, I began travelling under an assumed name, visiting different countries, living for the moment. I had money. I knew which cardinals to approach. I knew which cardinals would protect the Church from scandal at any price. I made them buy my silence, because imagine if I had told the world the real reason why I left the priesthood. Of course, those cardinals who bribed me to keep quiet didn't know about the murder. Nobody noticed a murdered whore among all those murdered thousands that week in New York. But the cardinals knew about the orgies and the trafficked children, and they knew that they must do everything in their power to protect Christ's Church from such a scandal. Their intentions were good, John. They put the eternal truth of the Church before any temporal human sinfulness. I'm sure you understand that. After all, you would rather protect the seal of the confessional than report a murderer, wouldn't you?'

John doesn't know what to say. The pity he feels is beyond comprehension and justification, but it will not let him go. He lets the voice from the other side wash over him.

'At first I was enjoying my new life, John, but my purgation was not complete. I had saved my mother and learned to love her, but I still hated you for what you had done to me.'

'I had to,' John whispers. 'Can't you understand, Michael? I had to confess my sin. It was my sin, not yours, that I was confessing to. I trusted the confessional. I trusted the priest.'

'Well then you were betrayed John. Betrayal is like that. You betrayed me, and you yourself were betrayed.'

'I didn't betray you. I didn't know.' But John realizes that, even if he had known, he would still have confessed. He could not have endured a single hour of a single day with that night on his conscience, unconfessed, unforgiven, unredeemed. And yet ...

405

'I'm sorry I named you,' he says. 'I can see how that felt like a betrayal. I didn't have to name you. Forgive me.' Dear God, what's happening? Who now is the priest, and who is the penitent?

'I gave you that reading, John. Don't you remember? That first week, after I killed Agnes McDonald, I gave you a reading. "If your brother does something wrong, rebuke him and, if he is sorry, forgive him. And if he wrongs you seven times a day and seven times comes back to you and says, 'I am sorry,' you must forgive him." But you didn't give me a chance, John. You didn't come to me and give me a chance to say sorry. You didn't offer to forgive me seven times a day. You went straight to confession to save your soul, without a thought for my soul. And then you ran away to save your own skin, with never a thought for what you had done to me, your brother in Christ.

'So John, I knew that I had to do something to put things right with God, and then God showed me the way. I told you that you had been chosen John. I was sent to test you. I was sent to put your priesthood to the test. I was sent to show you the extent of your sin, and to call you to judgement. You sacrificed my earthly hopes in order to save yourself, but now I'm offering you more. Repent, John, repent. Remember the first part of that reading I sent you? "It would be better for such a person to be thrown into the sea with a millstone round the neck than to be the downfall of a single one of these little ones." Oh, there were little ones in that club John, and you haven't really repented of your sin of that night. You haven't let the world see your shame. You haven't paid the price for your sin. All you've done is to prop up your own complacent sense of self-righteousness before God and the world. You make forgiveness too easy John. You offer cheap forgiveness from a cheap and sentimental God. You're too easy on yourself and too easy on the people you absolve with such casual disregard for the wrath and the judgement of Almighty God. I intend to die in the pride of my own sin, and you're going to help me John, because you have been called. This is your penance. I'm showing you the cost of true repentance and forgiveness.'

All the menace has gone. The voice sounds pathetic, almost pleading. The cardinal wants John to believe in the power of evil. He wants John to submit to his plan. The last thing he wants is John's pity and love. John waits in silence. The shadow shifts. The cardinal has yet to play his trump card.

'Tomorrow, there will be another murder, the seventh and final murder, the completion of my Lenten penance and my mission to bring you to full awareness of your sin, your terrible sin and depravity,' he says.

'My sins are forgiven,' says John. 'This is your confession. This is about your sins.'

Again, he senses that anxiety on the other side of the grille. The body is stiff, the sense of satisfaction from tormenting another is not there. 'My sin is greater than God's mercy. That is my only sin, Father John, my unforgivable sin, the sin for which I am going to hell. That's what Catherine of Siena says is the only unforgivable sin. The sin of pride in one's own sin. The sin of believing that my sin is greater than God's mercy.'

'You are not going to hell, Michael. Your sin can never be greater than God's love.'

'I'm going to give you three options,' says the cardinal, ignoring John. 'You must decide what to do. Tomorrow, after the Good Friday liturgy, I'm going to be in the graveyard next to that old nun's grave among the trees at the back.'

'Sister Gertrude's grave, you mean?'

'Yes. It's well-hidden. Nobody can see it from the car park or the presbytery garden. Your liturgy ends at half past four. At half past four, I want you to come to Sister Gertrude's grave – alone. Listen carefully John, because it's complicated, and a girl's life depends upon you. You must make sure you're alone, and you must bring the gun that I left in the presbytery.'

John closes his eyes. 'Go on, I'm listening,' he says. He is surprised to hear the calm in his voice. He hopes that it unsettles the cardinal. Wherever this leads, he must follow.

'You must shoot me. Put me out of my misery. Send me to my destiny. Send me to hell. I deserve it, don't you agree?' says the cardinal. John's pulse quickens, but he says nothing. 'In my hand, you'll find a host – a consecrated host – and written on the host will be the place where I've hidden a girl. If you act quickly, you'll be able to rescue her before she dies.' The cardinal has regained his bravado, and John feels his own confidence draining away. He should have realized that there was worse to come. The cardinal would not let him off so lightly.

'I won't! I can't!' His voice betrays his agitation.

'You can have your vengeance, John, and nobody will ever know – except you, and God, and Satan, and me. My fingerprints are all over that gun. You can say that you shot me in self-defence. You can eat the host, and you can tell the police that as I was dying I told you where the girl was.'

'Please. Please don't do this. Don't make me do this. I can't. I won't.'

'There are two other options, but I don't recommend them because the girl will die. She will be in a place with very little air, and no food or water. She will suffocate long before the thirst and hunger kill her, but there will be enough air for you to get to her and save her after you know where she is, after you shoot me. But if you refuse to go along with my plan, then here are your other options. Option two. You can tell the police and they can arrest me, but I won't tell them where she is. I shall eat the host as soon as I realize that you've betrayed me. She will die, because you refused to suffer to save her.'

'You're sick. You need help,' says John.

'I love this modern psychobabble. Nobody is evil these days. Everybody is sick. Every murderer is somebody's victim.'

'You are a victim,' says John. 'You're a victim of the man who murdered your mother. You're continuing his work.'

There's a silence on the other side, and then that shifting again. The curtain over the grille trembles. When he speaks, his voice is angry. 'Stop interrupting me and let me finish telling you my plan. It has taken me months to plan this. You're not going to stop me now.'

'Alright, carry on. I'm listening.' John feels suspended in limbo, but he also feels the calm coming back. The cardinal is anxious. That gives John the smallest advantage.

'If I suspect you're not alone, if I have even a hint that you've told the police, I'll eat the host and the girl will die, so don't try any clever business,' says the voice.

John makes himself keep quiet. Eventually, the cardinal speaks again.

'Third option. You can shoot yourself, John, but somehow I suspect that's not an option. That will get you out of the predicament, but it won't save the girl and it won't help the police to find me. Even if you tell them everything before you die, they have no name, no clues, nothing to go on. They will never find me, and you will have committed a mortal sin rather than live with the consequences of that night in Rome. All these murders, all this killing, John, is because you betrayed me. I can understand that you might find it difficult to live with that knowledge. It would be so much easier to shoot yourself.'

John wonders which of those three options the cardinal hopes he will choose. Murder? Betraying the seal of the confessional by going to the police, even though he knows that another woman will die as a result? Suicide?

'There is a fourth option,' he says.

'What?' He hears fear in the cardinal's voice.

'You hand yourself in to the police,' says John. 'Tell them everything. Ask God to forgive you and put yourself under the law.'

'You haven't listened to me John. All these weeks, all this theology, all this preparation, and still you don't understand. I'm going to hell in my mother's place. I want to go to hell. I'm greater than Christ, because he was rewarded with eternal power and glory. There's no reward for me. I'm paying the ultimate sacrifice. I am the sin of the world. I am pure evil. I am the Messiah.'

'No, Cardinal Bradley. You are not the Messiah. You're a human being whose soul has been mortally wounded by the evil that was done to you, but you're also a child of the living God and it's never too late. The worse the sin, the greater the act of forgiveness and redemption. You taught me all those years ago that, if Judas had repented, he would have become the greatest of the apostles. Peter betrayed our Lord. Saul persecuted and killed Christians. Saints Peter and Paul are the greatest of saints. You too have that option.'

There is a long, long silence. The cardinal is breathing heavily. The curtain ripples. John continues. 'Do you ever think that you're imitating the man who murdered your mother? Do you ever wonder about his motives, his twisted desires? Do you ever think that the women you murder might have children waiting for them at home?'

'Stop it! I forbid you from speaking!'

'No, Michael – you're going to hear me out. Your mother cannot be in heaven if her son is in hell, Michael. How can a mother enjoy eternal bliss with God, if she knows that her son, her only son, is in hell? Your mother loved you Michael. She is waiting for you in heaven. Repent. Confess. Hand yourself in. Give your mother a chance to show you how much she loves you, how much she sorrows and mourns over what happened to you, how ashamed and guilty she feels.'

'I told you to stop it! I told you to keep quiet!'

'I can't kill you Michael, any more than I could have killed that baby in his cot, crying for his mother.'

'You hate me! I raped you! I'm going to make you kill me!'

'No, you can't make me do anything Michael. I have no desire to kill you or to kill myself, and you can't make me act against my deepest desire. I have the greatest possible desire to save that woman's life, and to bring you to repentance, but these things are beyond my power. I can only pray and trust God that there will be a way through this. I don't hate you Michael. I pity you. I pray for you. I shall pray for you every day for the rest of my life. If you hand yourself in, I promise I'll visit you in prison and I'll never abandon you. Together, we'll find a way through this. But I won't do what you're asking, and if another woman dies, that's on your conscience.'

'I have no conscience!'

John stands up. He goes out of the door and opens the door on the other side. The man is there, kneeling, trembling with frustration and rage. John squeezes into the small space and closes the door behind him. He puts his hand on the man's head and feels the thinning hair and the skin and the skull beneath. A real body. A living man. This is no ghost.

The man knocks his hand away. 'Don't you dare touch me. Stay away from me.'

John holds his hand above his head.

> God, the Father of mercies, through the death and resurrection of his Son has reconciled the world to himself and sent the Holy Spirit among us for the forgiveness of sins; through the ministry of the Church may God give you pardon and peace, and I absolve you from your sins in the name of the Father, and of the Son, and of the Holy Spirit, Amen.

He makes the sign of the cross and then he takes the stole from his shoulders and drapes it over the cardinal's shoulders.

'You're still a priest,' he says. 'I shall pray for you. You know what your penance is.'

411

The cardinal rips the stole away. John turns and leaves the confessional.

In the afternoon, he visits the men's prison and says Mass, then he takes communion to the sick in hospital. Back at the presbytery, he sits in the garden and gazes over at the graveyard. He goes over what the cardinal said, trying to find a response or a solution, but his thoughts unravel on the impossibility of what is being asked of him.

Eventually, he allows himself the solace of remembering his night with Luke. He closes his eyes and lets the images and whispers and caresses flow through him until his body feels saturated with love and longing and loss.

He tries to hold on to that feeling as he goes back into the presbytery to prepare himself for the Mass of the Lord's Supper this evening. He sits at his desk and thinks about what to say. He won't do a homily – the service is already long enough – but he wants to offer a few words for them to reflect on as they prepare for Good Friday and Easter.

The doorbell clangs. Surely it can't be the cardinal? He thinks of what happened in the confessional and the cardinal's growing anger and distress. What does he want? He goes downstairs and opens the door, resisting the desire to ignore it.

It's Dorcas from the school. She is standing on the doorstep with that immense serenity, but her face is ashen. It's as if the flesh has drained away from beneath the dark sheen of her skin, so that she looks gaunt and chiselled in stone.

'Dorcas. Come in.' She steps inside. He wonders if she has seen the newspapers.

'Father, I know you said I should come to confession on Saturday, before I'm received into the Church at the Easter vigil, but I can't wait that long. Will you hear my confession now? I want to do it before tomorrow. I want to do it before Good Friday.'

'Of course Dorcas. We can go into the confessional, or if you prefer we can sit in my study upstairs. Just say what would make you more comfortable.'

'I'd like to sit in your study Father. I'm still not really used to all the ritual.'

He guides her upstairs and invites her to sit in one of the armchairs. He sits in the other and twists to face her. He tries to offer her words of reassurance and encouragement.

She takes a deep breath and lowers her eyes. Her hands are folded in her lap and her body is rigid. She speaks quietly so that he has to lean forward to hear her.

'When I was living in the Congo, before I came here, the rebels came to our village one night. They killed all the men and raped the women and girls. They killed some of them too, but some of us managed to escape into the forest and hide. They burned our huts and stole our goats and chickens. We could hear the dying people screaming and crying, but we couldn't go to them. We ran away.

'There were seven of us – an old woman, two mothers with babies, an eight year old girl, and me. I was fourteen. We lived in the forest. We picked berries and drank water from streams. After a few weeks, the old woman and the girl were both dead. The old woman was too weak to survive, and the girl had been hurt when they raped her. She had an infection. She died.' Her voice has no emotion. Her body doesn't move. Her face is expressionless.

'The women with the babies decided to go and find shelter in another village. I was alone. I was pregnant because of the rape. When the time came, I gave birth. It was a girl. I left her there under a tree. I ran away. I heard her crying, but I didn't turn back. I came here six months after.' Her eyes flicker up to his face. He returns her gaze.

'I'm so sorry Dorcas,' he says. 'I'm so sorry.' The words are inadequate, but what can he say? His own problems, vast though they are, shrink in the face of what he's hearing.

'There is more Father. I have HIV from that time, from that rape. My husband knows about the HIV, but he doesn't know about my baby girl. He is not infected, and neither are our children. I worry that if the parents in the school know, I'll lose my job. I'm very careful, but there's still stigma.'

'Dorcas, there is no reason why anybody should know, and if by some chance they ever found out, I promise you that I'll stand by you. You will not lose your job.'

She nods, and now she meets his gaze with a deep, deep darkness in her eyes. 'Thank you Father.'

They pray together. John guides her to the door and watches her walk down the path with her head held high and her shoulders back. Weep for yourselves, mothers of Jerusalem. He thinks of the cardinal's mother, frantic for her baby as she lay dying. He thinks of Babbs, parted from her children, with nothing to put in the empty photo frames. He thinks of Holly, and that terrible day when Sarah died.

He was new to the parish. He had only been here for a few weeks. He had said the family Mass at ten o'clock and he was chatting to one of the parishioners afterwards when a terrible wailing went up from the car park. They all rushed over to see what was happening. Holly was sitting with Sarah's head in her lap. There was blood everywhere. It was Holly who was wailing.

Betty Barker, eighty five years old, arthritic and losing her eyesight, had decided she would keep driving to Mass, even though she no longer had a licence, because it was just up the road from her house. What harm could it do – such a short distance – and she had never missed Mass in her life? She was reversing out of the car park and hit the accelerator rather than the brake, just as Sarah was skipping past. Sarah died before the ambulance arrived.

John wipes his hands over his face. He goes into the desolate church and kneels in front of the tabernacle. There are no words.

There are very few people at Mass, and yet John's heart lifts when he sees those who are there. Holly is there, and so is Jennifer. Dorcas is there with her husband and children. Jane and Pete are there, and Luke, and Bonnie and Steve. His sister Kate is there too. Ben and Babbs are there, sitting together in the back row, and Adnan from the corner shop. Patrick and Mary are with Siobhan and Anthony. There are a few other regulars and a few he doesn't recognise. He wonders if any of them are journalists. There's no sign of the cardinal, but John knows that he won't see him again until that time of reckoning tomorrow.

When the time for the washing of feet arrives, the people come up to take their places on the twelve chairs that Jack has arranged in front of the altar. Kate and Holly. Dorcas. Ben and Babbs. Adnan. Edith. Jane and Pete. Jennifer. Luke. Patrick.

John takes the bowl of water that Jack has left beside the altar. Jack drapes a towel over his arm, and they begin to make their way along the line.

Each foot seems to John to encompass the whole life and personality of the person it belongs to. He lets the tears flow, because whoever chose these people, they are the most perfect representation of all that he cares about and all that his priesthood means to him. He suspects it was Jack, but there must also have been some mysterious power at work for how could Jack know exactly who to ask? Or did they volunteer, knowing that the church would be empty, knowing that there might not be twelve willing parishioners on this dark night of suspicion and dread?

His sister's foot is first, slender and white. He trickles the water over it and remembers running barefoot in the garden when they were children. He thinks of her own children's feet, and wonders when or if he will ever see those children again. He bends over and kisses her foot, and she rubs the arch of her foot tenderly against his cheek.

Edith has a bunion, and her toenails are painted bright red. It moves him to think of this secret adornment intended for Jack's pleasure. Her foot stiffens in his hand as he kisses it. He senses Edith would rather not participate in this tactile ritual, and he is moved that she agreed to do it because she cares for him.

Patrick's bones show through the thin, translucent flesh, as if his skeleton is slowly seeping through to the outside. His healing was a short-lived miracle, lasting only long enough for him to celebrate at Siobhan's wedding. Even Lazarus would one day die again. Patrick is no longer in remission. He came to confession earlier in the week and confessed his lack of courage, the terror of telling his beloved family that death was coming fast to claim him.

Holly is also wearing red nail polish. She has stencilled letters on her toenails, LOVE U, facing so that he can read them. Her foot is strong in his hand, with a high, firm arch. He thumbs the side of her foot with all the gratitude that it's possible for touch to communicate. She curls her toes around his fingers and he feels her strength flowing through him.

He holds Dorcas's foot and feels how calloused it is – the foot of a woman who has trampled barefoot through a jungle to survive. Again, he tries to communicate through the touch of his hand on her skin, hoping that she feels all the compassion and love and respect he is capable of giving.

Then it's Luke's turn. He resists the temptation to look up. He cups Luke's hand in his palm and rests a moment in the ache of longing. He sees the delicate hairs that sprout from the top of Luke's big toe, and the clean, chiselled shape of his toenails. He traces his thumb along from the heel to the toe, and with his fingers he discreetly massages the soft flesh underneath. He remembers that foot in his mouth, sucking the toes, licking the folds of flesh between each one. He trickles the water and draws out the drying because he longs to stay here, like this, forever. He bends over and puts his lips against Luke's skin, and he allows the kiss to linger before he moves on to Jane and Peter and Jennifer, praying for each of them, feeling his intimate knowledge of each of them in the touching and the kissing, but with the feel of Luke's skin still on his lips, ineradicable and forever.

Finally, he comes to Babbs and Ben, with the waft of ripe cheese growing stronger the closer he gets to Ben. Babbs's dark purple nail polish is chipped, and her toenails are ragged. There's a bruise on the side of her foot. John takes his time, letting his hands tell of his love for her. At first she wriggles in his grip, as if embarrassed, but then she relaxes and lets him caress her and wash her and dry her.

He wonders if Jack deliberately put Ben at the end of the line, in case the others were put off by the smell of his feet. Ben has thick stubby toes with horned yellow toenails sunk in cushions of flesh. His feet are calloused like Dorcas's. John wonders if they are painful to walk on, as Ben trudges around the city every day. He resolves to find comfortable new shoes for Ben after Easter, and it suddenly hits him that he has no idea what 'after Easter' means. There may be nothing at all beyond whatever tomorrow brings.

The people file out of the church in silence. Some go to kneel in front of the monstrance that stands on the altar in the side chapel, surrounded by candles and lilies that spread their scent over the heads of those kneeling in front of them.

John kneels among them, sinking into the silence and stillness that surrounds them, a silence that emanates from the depths of their fears and longings for something beyond what words can say. A few of them remain there until midnight, when John removes the consecrated hosts from the monstrance and the tabernacle. He puts them in a ciborium and closes the lid, then he carries them to the altar of repose that Edith has set up at the back of the church, in a small room leading off the porch. They will remain there through the drama of Good Friday and the limbo of Easter Saturday. The people leave and he stands in that forsaken silence, then he closes the church and makes his way into the presbytery garden.

417

The full moon casts a pale light among the shadows. The cherry tree holds aloft its branches swathed in fresh green growth. The flowers so carefully tended by Jack are budding and blooming in the late spring warmth, and the jasmine that sprawls up the wall by the lane lends its sweetness to the moonlit air.

He pushes his way through the gate into the cemetery, where the angel keeps watch over Sarah's grave. He goes and kneels on the grass in front of it and breathes in the scent of the freesias and lilies that Holly has left there. The angel seems to shimmer and move in the moonlight.

John closes his eyes and he prays to the Mother of God for the mothers of the world. He prays for the cardinal's murdered mother, for Babbs and Dorcas and Holly, for the young pregnant prostitute and all the other women murdered by the cardinal. *Salve, Regina, Mater misericordiae.* He prays for the cardinal, and for all the world's children who suffer abandonment, violence and neglect. He weeps. *Ad te clamamus exsules filii Hevae.* He prays for himself, for whatever tomorrow will bring. *Ad te suspiramus, gementes et flentes in hac lacrimarum valle.* He prays for Luke. Thank you sweet Jesus for Luke. Thank you for our love. Thank you for loving us. *O Clemens, O pia, O dulcis Virgo Maria.*

He kneels in silence as the dew seeps through his trouser legs. He senses the play of moonlight and shadows on his eyelids, and then he senses something else. Car engines. Voices. He opens his eyes. Blue lights are flashing in the car park. He stands up. Armed police are making their way up the path to the presbytery door. He hears them banging on the door and shouting.

'Come out with your arms up, or we'll break the door down.'

The air in front of the angel thickens and a small shape forms. 'Don't be afraid,' whispers Sarah.

418

THIRTY ONE

GOOD FRIDAY

They twist his arms behind his back and handcuff him. They take the presbytery key out of his pocket and ask him where his computer is. He tells them. They rummage in his pockets again and ask him where his mobile phone is. He tells them it's on the kitchen table. A camera flashes, momentarily blinding him.

'Fucking journalist,' says one of the policemen.

He wonders why they drive to the police station at high speed with the blue light flashing and the siren wailing. What do they think he might do? He closes his eyes.

Inside, they search him. He has nothing in his pockets except for a handful of loose change. They take that and put it in a plastic bag, along with his watch. They ask him to take off his shoes, and they put those in a bag too. They swab the inside of his mouth for a DNA sample. There's suppressed excitement in the way they handle him – not quite violent but charged with energy. They believe him to be a serial killer. He is probably the most interesting criminal they have ever arrested, and it shows in their movements and on their faces.

They take him to a small cell with a blue plastic mattress on a narrow bunk and a toilet in the corner. It smells of excrement, and there's graffiti on the walls. Somewhere a man is shouting and swearing. They take off the handcuffs and lock the door. He waits. He feels no need to think, to calculate, to make sense of things. Whatever this is, it's far, far beyond his control.

Eventually, a sallow-faced young policeman unlocks the door and handcuffs him again. 'Sorry to do this Father,' he says. His touch is different. Does he think John is innocent?

'Don't worry. It's your job,' says John. 'I understand.'

'I'm a Catholic,' says the young policeman. 'I don't go to Mass, but my Mum would be upset if she knew I was handcuffing a priest.'

'That's alright,' John says, then on impulse he adds, 'I didn't do it, you know. I just want you to know that. I'm not the murderer.'

The young policeman blushes. His skin bears traces of acne. He nods. 'I believe you,' he says.

He leads John down the corridor to an interrogation room. The walls are painted grey, and the room is empty apart from a white formica table stained with coffee rings, and three hard black plastic chairs – two on one side of the table and one on the other. There is a camera mounted on the wall, pointing towards the table.

John sits and waits. He has no idea how long he waits for. Ten minutes? Two hours? The room is brightly lit with a harsh fluorescent light. For all he knows, it could be daylight outside.

Eventually, two people come in. There's a tall woman who looks to be in her mid thirties, with dark hair pulled back and soft brown eyes. Behind her is a slightly shorter man who looks older, with a bristle of greying hair and stubble on his chin. They're both wearing dark trousers and white shirts. She has a laptop and a bundle of papers under her arm. They sit opposite him and she does the introductions.

'My name is Superintendent Elizabeth Jefferson,' she says, 'and this is Inspector Colin McBane.' She sounds brisk but respectful, with a neutral accent. She pushes several pieces of paper stapled together across the desk and asks him to read his rights. He says he doesn't want a lawyer. She asks him if he wants to tell someone where he is.

'Does Frank know I'm here?' he asks. He sees an unguarded moment of something enigmatic cross her face, but it's gone too quickly to interpret.

'You mean Detective Chief Superintendent Frank Lambert?' asks the Inspector. He has a Scottish accent.

'Yes,' says John. 'I thought he was handling the case.'

'He is,' says the woman, taking control again. 'He's gone home to get some sleep, in preparation for whatever might happen later today. It's Friday. We're expecting another murder. But you know that.'

'Does he know I've been arrested?' John asks again.

He senses something uneasy about the woman. He suddenly remembers Frank telling him he was sleeping with a colleague. He wonders if it's her.

'We haven't told him yet,' she says. 'New evidence has come to light, but we said we wouldn't disturb him unless there were any major new developments. We just want to ask you a few questions.'

John takes some reassurance from that. It suggests that his arrest is not yet tantamount to a murder charge.

She takes some papers out of a file and spreads them on the table in front of him. 'These were sent to the press anonymously – we don't know who by. The press have agreed to withhold publication for the time being, but obviously sooner or later they're going to be published.' Her voice is calm and almost sympathetic, like a stern but loving mother confronting a recalcitrant child.

John looks at the photos. They were taken at night without a flash, but even so, he recognizes himself. There's one of him leaving Babbs's flat, and another of him going into the Queen's Arms. A third one shows him on the street corner with Babbs, and the last one is the stomach-lurching image of Luke and him kissing each other. There's the same photocopy of a page from the Italian newspaper with the story of *La Dolce Vita* that was left in the presbytery, and the grainy photo of the cardinal on top of John, raping him in *La Dolce Vita*.

'Is this you?' the woman asks, jabbing her finger towards the photos.

'Yes, it's me.'

'Do you have an explanation?' she asks, briskly but not aggressively.

'It's all true,' he says.

'What do you mean, it's all true?' This time it's the man, gruff and challenging. He spits the question at John. Good cop, bad cop, John thinks, but he no longer cares.

'When I was young, I went to a gay club in Rome. I didn't know there were trafficked children there until I read that report. I've befriended one of the prostitutes in Saint Peter's. I started going there after the murders.'

'Why?' barks the man.

John meets the man's pale blue gaze. 'Because I'm a priest. I felt – I felt a sense of responsibility.' He knows it sounds pathetic. He continues. 'I'm also gay. I meet somebody, somebody I love, from time to time, in the Queen's Arms.' He swallows. 'It's us, in that photo,' he says, indicating the one of them kissing.

'Jesus Christ!' says the policeman. The woman gives him a warning glare.

'Father John, we're not here to pry into your private life. We're investigating a series of murders, and that's all we're interested in. Do you understand that?'

John feels grateful for the compassion in her voice. He nods, not trusting his voice. Eventually he manages to say, 'It's not me. I'm not the murderer.'

'You just happened to be snogging your boyfriend in an alley where a woman's body was found a few hours later,' says the policeman. 'And you hang out with whores because you feel sorry for them, is that it?' There's contempt in the policeman's voice. The woman, Elizabeth, is watching, but she doesn't say anything. John nods again. 'But you want us to believe that it's not you, it just happens to be another priest murdering them?' says Colin.

'We don't know that it's a priest,' interjects Elizabeth.

John thinks of trying to explain, but his thoughts are so tangled that he doesn't know where to begin. He feels lethargic, his thoughts and emotions deadened with the impossibility of what's happening to him. Any minute now, he will wake up. It will all have been a dream, a terrible nightmare. It will be Ash Wednesday, and the parishioners will be queuing up for confession, and the season of Lent will begin its slow, prayerful unfolding – uneventful, laced with boredom and that vague sense of frustration that he is not getting it right, that there must be more to it than this. That's the way it always is, before the high point of Holy Week and Easter.

Elizabeth pushes open her laptop, and the screen lights up. 'Father John, I want to show you some clips we've taken from CCTV cameras around the city,' she says. As he watches, he sees Babbs and he making their way across the road and going into MacDonalds. He is wearing his scruffy old anorak and she is tottering beside him on her skinny legs and high heeled shoes. 'Is that you?' she asks.

'Yes, with a woman called Babbs,' he says.

'We know Babbs,' says Colin. 'She's well-known to the police.'

He remembers what Babbs told him, about a policeman parking his car and letting her off a charge of soliciting in exchange for oral sex. Pigs, she calls them. He looks at the cold-eyed man opposite, with his bristle of hair and his low-set brow. 'Pig,' he hears Babbs saying, and the sound of her voice comforts him.

'Babbs is a friend of mine,' he says. 'I respect her.' He wants to warn them not to call her a whore, not to say anything disrespectful about her. 'She's had a difficult life,' he says.

Elizabeth nods. She strikes John as more professional, more practised at this business of interrogation than her colleague. Or maybe this is just how they do their double act.

'I'm afraid that's not all,' she says. 'We also have this. One of your parishioners reported seeing you near Saints Felicity and Perpetua Church on the same night that a woman is believed to have been murdered in the grounds. We checked the CCTV cameras.' She moves the mouse and taps a key. He sees himself, walking down the dark lane and onto the railway bridge, pausing and looking down at the tracks. Again, the image is blurred but his anorak makes him clearly identifiable. It's a nondescript anorak like thousands of others, but they know it's him so why bother to deny it?

'Yes, that's me,' he says.

'So you admit that you were at the murder scene on two different occasions, that you spend time with sex workers in Saint Peter's, but you're still denying that you have anything to do with the murders?' she says, and her voice has hardened slightly.

'Yes,' he says. 'I'm not the murderer. I had nothing to do with the murders. I wouldn't – I wouldn't hurt another human being for anything.' He remembers fantasising about killing the cardinal, so he corrects himself. 'What I mean is – I can't imagine harming an innocent person.'

'But in the eyes of a Catholic priest, those women were not innocent,' says Colin, and he sounds lascivious now. 'They were whores. They were sinners, weren't they Father?'

'Some of Jesus's closest friends were prostitutes,' says John. 'They're not sinners. They're women who have been wounded by life. That's why Jesus had a special love for women like them.'

The man laughs. 'So you think you're Jesus Christ, do you?'

John returns Colin's stare. He holds his gaze until the man looks away.

'You say you didn't know there were trafficked children in that club until you read the newspaper report,' says Elizabeth. The warmth has gone from her voice. John remembers the way Frank switched between warm camaraderie and that ruthless determination to get to the truth, whatever it cost, even if it meant imprisoning his own parents. Why did Frank never tell him that story? Elizabeth is waiting for an answer. He nods.

'Father John, we're not investigating that story, but I'd like to know when you saw the report.'

Too late, John sees the tripwire. He wonders if his panic shows on his face. It must. It has seized his whole body. He feels frozen. Tell the truth, the whole truth and nothing but the truth, so help me God. The news cutting. The photographs. The one photograph that wasn't sent to the press. Is Elizabeth holding that back, the final incriminating image that will find him guilty as charged? The image that is imprinted indelibly forever on his memory and will forever haunt his imagination.

She is waiting, her eyes fixed on his face, and he knows that he will never be able to stare this woman down. He lowers his eyes, and he struggles to anticipate what might happen next, and how to respond to her question

And suddenly, in a blinding epiphany, he sees. If he is arrested and charged with the murders, the cardinal will stop. There won't be any point in murdering another girl, if John is in prison accused of the murders. Will that be the cardinal's downfall, his final defeat? John will steal his glory. It will be John, not Cardinal Michael Bradley, who will be evil incarnate in the eyes of the world, who will go to his grave knowing he was innocent, but silent before his accusers. Silent before his accusers. The words fill his being with a new sense of purpose, glowing with the radiance of a truth he has never understood until now.

'Father John, when did you see that news report?' she asks again.

He raises his eyes and now he can hold her gaze. 'Where's Frank?' he says.

She looks impatient. 'I told you. He asked not to be disturbed unless there were any major developments.'

'This is a major development. I want you to phone him.'

He can see her struggling not to let her excitement show. He hears the edge of it in her voice when she speaks again. 'John Andrew Patterson, we have all the evidence we need to charge you with the murders of Cecilia Jackson, Anastasia Milkovic, Agnes McDonald, Agatha Watson, and two unidentified women found at Saints Felicity and Perpetua Church. Are you saying that you want to make a confession?'

There is a moment of *déjà vu*. Agnes McDonald. That's what the cardinal called her. The media call her Nan. But it's more than that. There is something he ought to know, something that he cannot quite grasp, but it is of the utmost importance. What is it? His mind is whirring but he holds her gaze. She does not look away. Eventually he says, 'I refuse to speak to anybody except DCS Frank Lambert.'

Years in the confessional have taught John to read people's faces, to see buried emotions revealed in the slightest twitch of a muscle or shift in the shape of a person's lips or brow or eyes. He has touched a raw nerve in Elizabeth, and he thinks he understands what it is. He averts his eyes, because his scrutiny feels intrusive. He knows what's upsetting her. His confession is a prize that she wants for herself. Whether or not Frank is her lover, she doesn't want him to have this trophy.

Abruptly, she closes her laptop and stands up. 'You know what, I need a cup of tea. How about you Colin?'

Colin looks like a fisherman whose catch has just swum away. 'Tea? Now? I don't think this is the right time for a tea break.'

He bears the full brunt of Elizabeth's frustration, so that John feels sorry for him. 'Detective McBane, may I remind you that I'm in charge of this investigation, not you.'

'DCS Frank Lambert is really in charge,' he mutters.

'When Chief Superintendent Lambert is off duty, this is my case,' she barks. 'Now, please do as I say and leave the suspect to decide what he's going to do.' She turns to John, and switches immediately from stern superior to trusted confidante. 'Now

Father John, you must be quite exhausted. Shall I bring you a cup of tea and a sandwich?'

He cannot face the thought of eating or drinking, but he doesn't want her to vanish into the night and leave him alone, so he says yes please, he'd appreciate that.

As they leave, Colin can't resist having the last word. 'We have all the evidence we need to charge you,' he says, and his tone makes clear it's a threat. 'We're going to give you some time to think about what to do next. If you'd just confess, life would be a whole lot easier for everyone – and you could go back to your cell and get some rest.'

He follows Elizabeth out of the door, slamming the door behind him in a way that makes John feel suddenly abandoned and afraid, alone with his dark imaginings.

Sitting alone, he tries to follow that elusive feeling he had when he heard the names of the murdered women. What is it? What is it he ought to be seeing?

The door opens. It's not Elizabeth. It's the young policeman who led him from his cell. He looks uncomfortable as he walks over and puts a cup of tea and a sandwich on the table in front of John. 'There you are Father,' he says.

'Thank you,' says John. The young man stands there awkwardly, as if waiting to be dismissed. 'What's your name?' John asks.

'Simon, sir. I mean, Father,' he says.

'Simon, will you do something for me?'

Simon blushes, bringing a bloom to his acne scars. 'Um, depends,' he says. 'Depends what it is, I mean.'

'Will you pray for me?' says John.

Simon shuffles his feet. 'I don't know how, Father,' he says. 'I mean, I went to a Catholic school, but I don't do those things any more.'

'You know Simon, even if you just think a small kind thought about me, that will be all the prayer I need. In fact, just bringing me tea and a sandwich is a prayer.'

'Really?'

'Yes. You've no idea what this means. Not the tea and the sandwich, but your kindness to me. I'll pray for you Simon. You're a good man. Tell your Mum I said that. You showed me kindness when I needed it most.'

Simon's smile is broad and grateful. 'Thank you Father. Thank you,' he says, and then he turns and hurries away, as if suddenly overwhelmed by shyness.

John wishes he had a pen and paper. He would like to write the names down, to see if that helped him to see the missing link. He closes his eyes and imagines them written in the air. Agatha. Agnes. Perpetua. He says the names aloud, quietly. Anastasia. Felicity. Agnes. Perpetua.

And suddenly it's there, fully formed, sliding into shape, familiar from years of repetition, the litany of names from the first Eucharistic prayer:

> *For ourselves, too, we ask some share in the fellowship*
> *of your apostles and martyrs, with John the Baptist,*
> *Stephen, Matthias, Barnabas, Ignatius, Alexander,*
> *Marcellinus, Peter, Felicity, Perpetua, Agatha, Lucy,*
> *Agnes, Cecilia, Anastasia and all the saints.*

The cardinal has been killing women according to the names of the women saints and martyrs in the prayer, and there is one woman who must still die to complete the number seven. Lucy. LUCY! NO! LUCY! NO, NO, NO!

He rushes over to the door and begins banging on it with his fists, shouting at the top of his voice. 'Colin! Simon! Elizabeth! Somebody – please, please, somebody!'

The door is solid, and his fists make nothing more than a dull thud against the wood. Surely though, somebody must hear him shouting? Somebody will come. He bangs and shouts until his throat hurts and his fists throb.

At last, the door opens. It's Simon. 'Father? Are you alright?'

'Simon! Oh thank God. Simon, you need to help me.'

The young man looks frightened. He has gone pale. 'I'll call Superintendent Jefferson,' he says.

Through the terror, John glimpses a possibility. 'No,' he says. 'No – don't do that. Please Simon, come in and close the door. I need to ask you to do something for me. I know it's breaking the rules, but I need you to trust me.'

Simon hesitates. He looks anxiously over his shoulder. 'I'm not supposed to –'

'Please Simon. A young woman's life depends on it. I'll take the blame. I'll say I forced you. I'll say I threatened you. I'll say anything, but please, please help me.' Simon eases his body inside and closes the door. He looks as if he is ready to make a quick getaway. 'Simon, I need you to phone Frank Lambert. I need you to get hold of his mobile number and phone him. Tell him that I need him. Tell him he must come at once. I know he will, if somebody just gets that message through to him.'

'I don't know his number,' says Simon.

'They've got my phone. Do you know where they put my belongings? Frank's number is there, on my phone. If you can get my phone, you can use that. He will answer if he thinks it's me calling.'

Simon looks up at the camera on the wall and back at John. John sees in that moment that Simon is going to help him, but he must play along. The young man's eyes widen, and he glances at the camera again. John gives an imperceptible nod and waits for Simon to give him a cue.

'I'm sorry Father. I'd lose my job. I'm sure Chief Superintendent Lambert will be here soon. I'll go and fetch Superintendent Jefferson. You can talk to her. Sorry, but I can't break the rules.'

John nods in resignation. 'Okay. Yes, I understand. I'm sorry. But please ask Superintendent Jefferson to come and talk to me. It's very urgent.'

'I'll do my best,' says Simon, and he leaves.

John sits at the table and waits, trying not to think the unthinkable. He wishes he could get hold of Lucy's parents and tell them to keep her safe indoors. He wishes Frank would come. He marvels at the diabolical genius of the cardinal. Surely, human powers alone could not plan everything so perfectly, so infallibly? Like some grand master, the cardinal has anticipated every possible move, every possible threat, and he has outmanoeuvred John every single time. Why would he fail now? Lucy! Oh no! Lucy!

Eventually, the door opens. It's not Elizabeth or Colin. It's Simon again. He is attempting to look sheepish, but beneath that John sees something else. Simon is nervous, but he is also excited. He has broken the rules, and in so doing he has lifted his mundane job into something brave and dangerous.

'I'm sorry Father, but Superintendent Jefferson has told me to take you back to the cell. She says they will continue the interview later.'

He handcuffs John, but this time he allows him to have his hands in front of his body rather than behind, which is more comfortable. As he fastens the cuffs, he presses gently with his thumb on John's wrist and gives the smallest of nods. John meets his eyes, and he sees affirmation there. He is choked up with admiration and gratitude.

He sits in the cell and tries to ignore the smell of shit and the demented howls coming from another cell. The words of the Eucharistic prayer go round and round and round in his mind. He has one single mission, one single purpose which is driving him to stay alive and alert and free. Once he has saved Lucy, he doesn't care what happens to him.

He hears the scrape of the lock and the cell door opens. 'Frank! Oh dear God, thank God, Frank, thank God you're here.'

Frank is unshaven and he looks furious. His hair is unbrushed and his clothes are crumpled, as if he has been sleeping in them.

Maybe he has. He throws John's shoes onto the floor. 'I don't know what the fuck you're up to, but his had better be worth my time. Put your shoes on.'

John does as he's told, and he follows Frank in silence out of the building and into the car park behind the police station.

Frank eases himself behind the wheel and starts the engine. 'You have one hell of a lot of explaining to do, John. That young man is likely to lose his job because of you. You know a hell of a lot more than you're telling me, and quite frankly I don't give a damn about your secrets and vows. There's a serial murderer out there and unless I find him he's going to kill another woman tonight. So you'd better make your mind up to tell me everything you know.'

'Frank, we have to go straight to Lucy's house – Lucy Pierce – Carol and Jim's daughter. She's next. She's today's victim.'

'What the fuck are you talking about?'

'I'll explain, but please, just drive, Frank.' He tells Frank the address.

As Frank drives, John tries to explain. 'It's the women saints and martyrs in the Eucharistic prayer. He's killing women with the same names. Cecilia, Anastasia, Agnes, Agatha. The two who haven't been identified were at Saints Felicity and Perpetua Church. There's only one more name in that list. Lucy. Lucy's the last name. Frank, Lucy knew Aggie. I can't tell you more than that, but there's a connection between them. I think that's why Aggie was murdered. I think that's why Lucy is next on the list.' He swallows. He feels dizzy and sick with the horror of it. 'So yes, it's a priest or bishop or cardinal or somebody who knows the Catholic liturgy inside out, and this is all planned,' he says.

'And you want me to believe it's not you, despite the fact you seem to know so fucking much about it,' says Frank. His lips are set into a tight, thin line as he grinds the gears and slams to a stop for a traffic light that turns red as he approaches at high speed. 'Bloody roads are empty,' he says, 'and here we are sitting at a fucking red light.'

'What's the time?' asks John. There's a sliver of light on the horizon, pushing back the darkness.

'It's half past six,' says Frank. 'You want me to believe you're not the murderer. You were seen on CCTV at two of the murder scenes. You've been canoodling with your boyfriend in public places and chatting up prostitutes, you seem to know more than any of us about the victims, but you really want us to believe you're not the murderer.'

'Frank, please, Lucy is all that matters now. I'll confess to the murders. I don't care. All I know is that if we don't get to Lucy she'll be next.'

The lights change. Frank accelerates so hard that his tyres screech on the tarmac. John thinks his speed is driven by fury rather than urgency.

'I'm almost a hundred percent sure you're not the murderer John. Almost. Not entirely, but almost. That bloody woman should never have arrested you. She went way over her authority. She wants revenge. Mary wants us to give our marriage another go. Elizabeth was a bloody good fuck, but Mary's the love of my life. Elizabeth wants to get your confession. She wants to be the one to solve this case. You know, when you've been on this job as long as I have, you learn that when evidence mounts up, it's not always one plus one plus one plus one adds up to proof. Sometimes, it's one times one times one times zero. That's all we have on you. You're a fucking idiot but you're not a murderer. Jesus Christ, what the fuck were you thinking of, hanging around with hookers on street corners?' He grinds the gears again.

'I'm sorry about your parents,' says John. 'You never told me that story.'

'No. I don't talk about it. But when that bloody journalist questioned my integrity. I won't let anybody question my willingness to see justice done, whatever it takes.'

'Will he really lose his job? Simon, I mean,' John asks.

For the first time, Frank permits himself a smile. 'If I have my way, he'll be fast-tracked to promotion. Being a good detective is knowing which rules to break. An unjust law is not a law. One of your lot said that, I think.'

'Saint Augustine.'

'Right. Simon did the right thing.' Frank rummages in his jacket pocket. 'Here's your phone, by the way. I forgot to give it back to you. And your keys.'

'Where are we going, Frank? This isn't the way to the Pierces' house. You should have turned left at the junction.'

'I'm taking you home first.'

'No, please Frank, let me come with you. I want to see Lucy. I want to see for myself that she's safe.'

'Listen, lover boy, I hate to tell you this but Carol Pierce is one of those loyal parishioners who has been informing on you. Nothing specific, but she made her mind up that Lucy had developed an unhealthy relationship with you, and she got the wind up. So she rang me and told me that she couldn't put a name to it, but she was worried that something was going on. She got some anonymous email apparently, warning her to keep an eye on you.'

'Did you investigate who sent the email? Who was it from? Did you follow it up?' He sees the look on Frank's face. Frank knows he has missed something.

'No. Malicious emails about priests are all over the place,' he says. 'We can't follow them all up.' He sounds defensive.

'It's important Frank. You must follow it up. They've taken my laptop. You need to check if it's the same person. I've been getting strange emails too.'

'Why didn't you tell me?'

'Because as you say, it's happening all over the place to lots of priests, but I think this might be different.'

Frank pulls up outside the presbytery. 'We can discuss that later. Please John, stay here today. I know you want to do the Good Friday liturgy, but I'm trusting you not to leave the premises. Don't go anywhere other than the church and the presbytery. I need your absolute word that you won't go wandering about the red light district chatting up your hooker friends or meeting your boyfriend or getting yourself in the way of any CCTV cameras in places where you shouldn't be. If it turns out you're our man and this is all some wild goose chase you're sending me on, I might as well put a bullet through my brain. Do you understand that?'

'You can trust me, Frank.'

'Yes, I believe I can. That's why I'm doing this.'

Inside the presbytery, John tries to concentrate. He feels consumed by dread, and keeps telling himself that any minute now, Frank will ring to say that Lucy is safe at home and the police will protect her. But some deep intuition tells him that that's not going to happen. The cardinal is not going to be outwitted at this late stage. He has everything under control, and everybody is unknowingly doing exactly what he wants them to do.

He tries to think clearly about his options. What will he do when he knows that Lucy is safe and protected from harm? He will tell Frank everything, provide him with all the evidence, except the confessional. There's a carapace of evidence now to lay over the dense dark secret of the confessional. There's a gun, the news clippings, the photographs, the emails, the names of the women – the whole story can be told, except that. And if Frank asks why John didn't reveal everything before, he can answer truthfully that he was afraid of the scandal, afraid of what would happen to him when the media got hold of the story of *La Dolce Vita*.

For a few moments, a deep peace alights upon him. If only Lucy is safe, everything else will fall into place. Fortified, he goes upstairs and takes the gun from the top of the wardrobe, along with the envelope. He carries them downstairs and puts them on the table in the living room, ready to hand over when Frank returns.

Will they believe him? Will they begin searching for the cardinal? Or will they simply think this is an elaborate alibi that hasn't worked, and he, John, is the murderer after all? Is that what the cardinal wants? Is that what he is planning?

It doesn't matter. Let them arrest him. Let them lock him up for the rest of his life. Whatever happens next, only one thing matters – that Lucy should be safe.

He goes back into the kitchen and sits at the table to wait. Surely, Frank will come back soon? He must be at the Pierce's house by now. He must know by now that Lucy is safe. Or?

And then another thought strikes him, slicing through his fragile peace of mind so that all his nerve ends are exposed. What if it's not Lucy Pierce? What if one of the women on the streets is also called Lucy? What if another young woman suffocates slowly to death, because John did not carry out the cardinal's instructions?

He is trapped. There's no way out. The cardinal has thought of everything.

John slumps forward with his head on his arms. He must do what he was told. He must kill the cardinal or sacrifice a woman to salve his conscience. He is too exhausted to panic, to weep, to think. He longs for Shula with all his being. He imagines picking her up and enfolding her in his arms, nuzzling his face against her fur and finding solace in that velvety dark presence.

His phone rings. It's Frank. 'John, Lucy is missing. She went out last night and she hasn't come back. They were all still asleep when I arrived. They assumed that she had stayed out late, but her bed hasn't been slept in.'

John thought there was no more energy left in him, but now the terror overwhelms him, and everything else is dwarfed by its magnitude. He can't speak.

'We've checked with her friends in case she stayed over, but nobody has seen her since she left the pub last night,' says Frank, and his tone is bleak.

'Oh no. Oh Frank. Please Frank. You must find her. Please. You must find her.'

'I'm going into the police station now. We'll pull out all the stops John. We'll do everything we can.'

'I'll help. Let me help.'

'Jesus John, don't you think we have enough to do without you turning amateur sleuth?' He pauses, and then John hears the pity in his voice. 'John, you've done everything you possibly could. Stay there today and I'll update you with any developments, but I need to know you're out of the way.' Another pause. 'Besides, Lucy trusts you. Maybe there's an explanation. Maybe she's worried about something. She might turn up at the presbytery looking for you, so you need to be there.'

'You'll tell me if there's any news?' he says.

'I give you my word,' says Frank, and the phone clicks off.

John thinks of Lucy's distress about the abortion, and for a brief moment he persuades himself that she's alright, she will turn up on the doorstep and ring the bell any minute now, needing to talk, needing to confess, needing to confide in somebody.

He gathers up the evidence from the dining table and drags himself upstairs. He puts the gun and the envelope back on top of the wardrobe, because even if Lucy is found safe and well, he can't be sure that another Lucy isn't the cardinal's intended victim. Only tonight when it's all over will he be able to hand everything over to Frank. He goes into his study and switches on the television in time to catch the eight o'clock news. Lucy's disappearance is headlines.

> *Police in Westonville are searching for teenager Lucy Pierce, as the city awakes to another Friday and the dread of another possible murder. Lucy left her home yesterday evening at half past eight, and she was last seen leaving a pub nearby at quarter to eleven to walk the short distance back to her house.*

436

It seems that she never arrived. Police are appealing for anybody who lives in the area who might have seen anything to come forward.

The camera switches to Superintendent Jefferson. She looks pale and tense. 'If anybody saw anything at all in the region of the Grapevine Pub last night, we are appealing for them to come forward. Any information, however insignificant it might seem, can help us in our enquiries.' A number flashes up on the screen. John can't bear to watch. He goes downstairs and unlocks the door to the church.

He sits in front of the empty tabernacle in the cold, dense silence. He is conscious of the altar of repose in the small room at the back of the church, wrapped in a glow of candlelight. He wonders if anybody is in there in silent adoration. Maybe people will avoid this church altogether today. Do they know about his arrest? Surely, somebody would have seen and heard? Holly? Jack? Kate? Where are they all? Does nobody care?

He pushes away the loneliness and sense of abandonment. He must gather his thoughts. He must concentrate and find a way through this.

He gazes up at the tabernacle with its open door and extinguished candle. The sense of absence is absolute.

He tries to think about his options. The first is to follow the cardinal's instructions. He imagines taking the gun and going alone into the graveyard, to Sister Gertrude's quiet grave in the far corner beneath the yew trees, hidden from sight. He images the cardinal standing there, taunting him. He imagines taking the gun, pointing it at the cardinal's head and shooting him, as the cardinal told him to do. He imagines the host falling from the cardinal's hand, picking it up and reading what's written on it. Then what? Phone Frank? Go to the place himself? The cardinal did not tell him what to do next. Maybe he doesn't care. He will after all be dead. John will have murdered him.

437

And what if there is no address written on the host, or no host at all? What if he shoots the cardinal, and Lucy still dies? What if even now Lucy is bleeding to death, terrified and wounded, alone in some place of infinite darkness? Oh no. It can't be possible. Please not that.

What if it's all some monumental mistake, some murderous fantasy spun out of the deep dark recesses of John's unconscious where perhaps the cardinal remains a figure of hatred? Is this what hatred has done to his mind? Is he mad? What if this is all some terrible desire for vengeance which is allowing demonic forces to wreak havoc with his sanity?

What if he, John, is the murderer, and all the rest is fantasy?

He remembers what Holly said. Even Satan cannot make you do something unless you harbour a secret desire to do it. He has never wanted to murder a woman. He did not murder those women. But the cardinal? Yes, it's possible that beyond his powers of admission and confession and penitence, he has felt murderous towards the cardinal. Somebody has murdered the women, and John has imagined the rest.

He tries to pull his thoughts back to the alternatives, to tell himself that this is really happening. He is not going to wake up from this nightmare. He is not going to be sectioned and sent for psychiatric care. This is real.

What if he simply tells Frank everything? A police marksman can hide among the trees. John can go with the gun and the marksman can shoot the cardinal. John will be innocent, and the cardinal will be dead. But what if in that split second of realization the cardinal swallows the host? And even if he doesn't, John will have betrayed the seal of the confessional in order to save his own soul, and he will have trapped another person into bearing the guilt of killing the cardinal.

What if he calls the cardinal's bluff? What if he goes to the graveyard without the gun and begs the cardinal to speak to him, to confess, to repent? He remembers the cardinal's agitation in the confessional yesterday. Was he beginning to crack? Was there a chink in the armour, a moment of grace that might yet make him change his mind?

And what if at the end of it the cardinal kills Lucy anyway? What if the cardinal doesn't show up?

Oh Jesus, help me. The tabernacle gapes. Jesus has other things on his mind today.

He makes his way back into the presbytery and upstairs to the study. He is thankful that his laptop has gone, removing the temptation to read emails and search Google for clues. He slumps in front of the television, and he watches as the news of nothingness unfolds. There are interviews with Lucy's friends and strings of experts. There are repeated updates with images of the four murdered women playing across the screen, and blank heads representing the unidentified women found at Saints Felicity and Perpetua church. Photos of Lucy appear again and again – a recent one where she's smiling into the camera, with a wisp of hair blowing across her face. It's her Facebook profile picture apparently. There's another one of her in the pub with her friends last night, holding up a glass of Prosecco and laughing into the camera, with her arm around the girl beside her.

With every image, John's desperation intensifies. He cannot drag himself away, and yet it's torture watching as the hours roll by and Lucy remains missing. At lunchtime there's a news conference. Frank and Lucy's parents sit behind a table. Jim stares into the camera like a rabbit captured in the glare of the headlights. Carol confronts the world with an expression of fury and despair so intense that John wonders why the television screen doesn't shatter with its power. Usually it's the father who speaks in these situations while the mother weeps and hides her face. This time, it's Carol who speaks, and her voice quivers with an odd mix of determination and terror.

'Whoever you are, we are going to find our daughter and get her back. We will search every inch of this city until we find her.

Give yourself up. Whatever you've done, it's not too late. Please!'
The last word sounds like more of a command than an appeal.
'Lucy darling, be strong. Be brave. We're going to find you. We're
not going to let this man win. Hang on in there, my beautiful,
beautiful daughter. Be strong. We love you. I love you. I love you
Lucy. I'm going to rescue you. I swear on my life I'm going to
find you.' Only then does her voice crack.

At three o'clock, John walks into the church behind Jack
and the altar servers. The aisle seems very long. The church is
almost empty. Just a few of the most faithful parishioners are
there – Holly, Jane and Pete, Patrick and Mary, Siobhan and
Anthony, Dorcas, Edith and a few others. Jack explained that
there are search parties all over the city and in the surrounding
countryside, and most of the parishioners are helping to look for
Lucy. The explanation reassures John. He wants to believe that
they haven't stayed away because of him.

They pause and Jack and the altar servers make their way up
the steps to stand behind the altar. John prostrates himself. The
floor is hard against his body. He would like to stay there, not to
move, not ever to get up, to leave others to deal with whatever
the rest of the day might bring.

'Why have you forsaken me?' he says to the void.

The people leave the church in silence. He is alone. The time
has come.

He goes back into the presbytery. He will do what the cardinal
said, and he will live with the consequences for all eternity.

He forced himself to leave his phone on the lounge table
during Mass, resisting the almost irresistible temptation to set it
to vibrate and keep it in his pocket just in case there was news.
But what would he do? Halt the liturgy to answer the phone?
Sweat it out knowing that something had happened, somebody
had tried to contact him?

He picks up his phone. There's a voicemail message. He dials
1571. 'New message received today at fifteen forty five'.

'John, it's Frank. We have our man. He walked into the police station and gave himself up just after three o'clock. He is Cardinal Michael Bradley, aka Robert McDonald, aka Christ knows how many fucking false identities. I wanted to let you know. He says Lucy is in the old deep freeze in the presbytery basement. An emergency team is on its way there now. I know you'll be in church, but I wanted to tell you. He insists I remind you of your promise to stand by him and to visit him in prison. Jesus John, if that God of yours exists, you'd better pray that we find her alive.' The phone goes dead.

John stares at it, frozen to the spot and stunned with disbelief. Then he puts it in his pocket and goes into the kitchen to look out towards the car park. Over the hedge, he sees the flashing blue lights of ambulances and police cars.

He goes out of the back door and walks across the garden to the cemetery. He goes through the gate and then out of the other gate that leads into the car park. A straggle of people who had been at the service are huddled there, wide eyed and silent. Carol and Jim are there, with Elizabeth Jefferson standing beside them. Elizabeth is holding Carol's arm, possibly to restrain her or possibly to support her. Carol is so still, so rigid with dread, that she seems barely alive.

The basement door is open, with two police women standing guard to prevent anybody from going in. John goes across to where Holly and the other parishioners are standing. Holly comes to stand beside him and wraps her arm around his waist. 'Oh John,' she says.

The wait seems interminable. At last – at long, long last, a shadow forms in the open doorway, and Lucy comes blinking into the light, with Frank holding her on one side and a policewoman on the other. She is wrapped in a blanket. Her hair is tousled and her face is blanched of all colour and expression. Carol rushes forward but Lucy ducks away from her mother's outstretched arms. She is carrying something beneath the blanket. She's looking around. Frank points to John, and Lucy comes towards him. She stands in front of John and holds out her arms. The blanket falls away.

Shula is panting and her fur is matted and dull. The outline of her ribs and spine show through the thin coating of flesh that remains on her body. But she is alive. Shula is alive.

John holds out his arms and takes the cat from Lucy. Shula raises dull eyes to his face, and he feels her wasted body vibrate with the feeblest of purrs.

'She was in there,' Lucy says. 'He had put her in there and left her to die, but I found her when he put me in there too.' Only then does she turn and let her mother embrace her.

Holly has moved a little distance away. She is standing on the spot where Sarah died. Beside her stands a small child. As John watches, Sarah turns and skips across the carpark and through the cemetery gate to vanish amidst the yew trees.